THE LOVECRAFT SQUAD

SQUAD

ALL HALLOWS HORROR

THE LOVECRAFT SQUAD

ALL HALLOWS HORROR

JOHN LLEWELLYN PROBERT
CREATED BY STEPHEN JONES

PEGASUS BOOKS
NEW YORK LONDON

THE LOVECRAFT SQUAD: ALL HALLOWS HORROR

Pegasus Books Ltd
148 West 37th Street, 13th Floor
New York, NY 10018

First Pegasus Books hardcover edition March 2017

Interior design by Sabrina Plomitallo-González, Pegasus Books

ISBN: 978-1-68177-333-9

10 9 8 7 6 5 4 3 2 1

Printed in the United States of America
Distributed by W. W. Norton & Company, Inc.

He told me of things that slumber beneath the earth,
that gather wisdom and strength in darkness but must not be troubled
in their midnight vegetations. But, said he, there will come a time when their
master shall summon them, and the dead will arise and walk the earth.

—*The Life of Samuel Johnson LL.D* (1791)
by James Boswell
[Omitted from the final published version.]

Lasciate ogni speranza, voi ch'entrate.
(Abandon all hope, you who enter here.)

—*Divine Comedy* (1308–20)
by Dante Alighieri

And you will face the Sea of Darkness,
and all therein that may be explored.

—*Book of Eibon*

ONE

THEY HAD BEEN DIGGING.

The machines had stopped now of course, now that the billowing curtain of night had been drawn, the thickness of its fabric rendering too dark for safety the land of mud and treacherous trenches over which it held sway. The workmen had gone home, leaving excavators and earthmovers to lie silent. Sleeping beasts of metal and glass, they had been transformed by the darkness into the mechanical monsters of a fever dream, resplendent in their brightly painted colors in the daytime, now altered by the nearby neon street lamps into the shades of nightmare. The bright yellow of the diggers was now a burned, infected ochre, the dark green of the power compressors the ugly black of wet gangrene. Even the deep crimson bulldozers looked jaundiced and ill.

The barriers the men had erected before leaving had served to keep out all but the most persistent of trespassers, and now, at just after eight o'clock on a chilly October evening, the building site became a silent wonderland, a snapshot of frozen industry awaiting the sunlight to reawaken its activity with the first blush of an autumn dawn.

Heaps of reddish earth peppered with small stones, piled higher than the nearby machinery, glistened with the same freezing moisture that had collected on the angular metal of the vehicles that had dug the soil out. In the distance, sealed sacks of cement and neatly stacked piles of bricks waited patiently, their role in the proceedings to come a little later, when the foundations of the supermarket had been dug, the concrete poured, and the real work of building could begin.

The evening sky, neon-drenched and smothered with cloud, was the texture of bloodstained cotton wool as two small figures pushed their way between the DO NOT ENTER signs. Once within the building site's perimeter, they ran to a nearby excavator and crouched beside its mud-clotted caterpillar tracks. Their attempt to conceal themselves was unnecessary. Aside from the fact that there was no one around to see them, even at their full height they were hardly taller than the racks of metal teeth by which the machine moved itself.

Their breath steamed in the chill air, the nervous vapor merging with the mist that was now beginning to rise from the chilled mud of the ground.

"Told you we'd get in." Jason was the taller of the two by an inch, and older by a month.

"It's fucking freezing," his companion Mark moaned. "What did you want to come tonight for?"

"Because, you twonk," Jason said, rolling his eyes, "by tomorrow they'll have filled it all in with concrete, won't they? We won't have a chance of finding anything then."

Mark gave a sulky sigh. "I don't even know what we're supposed to be looking for."

Jason slapped his friend across the head. "Don't you listen to anything in school?" he said.

"You don't," came the reply. "You're too busy waiting for a flash of Miss Goldstrop's thong."

"Only if it's a day when she's wearing one," Jason sniggered. "Besides, I'm not talking about Maths. I meant History."

"With old Carstairs?" The more elderly and unattractive contingent of the female teaching staff did not merit an honorific. "Why the fuck would I be listening to her old shit?"

"Because if you did you'd know this place is where H. G. Wells's house used to be." Jason stamped the ground for effect. The earth beneath his feet gave more than he was expecting, and he almost slipped.

"Who's he?"

A large plume of vapor came from Jason's mouth as it was his turn to sigh.

"Remember that film she showed us last week?"

"What, the one about how building sites can kill you?"

"No, that was the week before, you dingbat. How can you have got the two mixed up? The one I'm talking about was in the History classroom, not the assembly hall."

There was a moment's silence while Mark pondered. "Oh yeah," he said eventually. "I remember. That old bitch said she couldn't believe we'd all got to the age of thirteen and hadn't seen it. It was the one about the bloke who could travel places even though he never really moved?"

Jason's silhouetted head nodded encouragingly. "Because he was moving in time instead. And it had those monsters in it at the end."

"Fucking hated them," said Mark. "Fucking hate things that come out of the ground to get you. What the fuck are we doing here again?"

"Being a fucking Sweary Mary is what it sounds like." Jason snickered again, and when it became obvious his friend didn't find what he had said at all funny, his amusement became a forced, full-throated laugh.

"Fuck off," was all Mark could manage in the way of a verbal riposte, and so instead he took a swing at his friend, missed, and ended up whacking his fist against the caterpillar track.

That just made Jason laugh all the more. "Fucking clumsy spazz as well. Your mum's going to wonder how you did that."

Mark rubbed his scraped and bleeding knuckles. "My mum isn't going to be home 'til late, and I'll be in bed by then. She's never going to know I was here. Anyway, at least I have a mum."

That was below the belt, which was where Jason tried to punch Mark for coming out with it. The other boy dodged and tried to return the blow but his friend was too quick, stepping aside in the darkness and getting Mark's neck in a headlock.

"Do you submit?" Jason squeezed tighter as his friend managed to emit a sound that was little more than a gurgle.

"Do you submit?"

An anguished howl from the other side of the building site caused them both to look up. Jason released his friend, who immediately stumbled back three paces. Once he had recovered himself, Mark turned to leave.

"Hey! Where are you going?"

Mark shook his head. "You said it would be safe." He pointed past Jason's shoulder. "What the fuck was that?"

His friend snickered. "Just a cat. Or a dog who's found a cat. Don't be such a wuss."

Mark took a step back toward the fence, still unsure. "I've never heard a cat that sounds like that."

Jason chuckled. "You live in a high-rise, mate. The only pussy hanging around there are the crack whores."

"Like your mum you mean?"

The cry came again, but it seemed farther away this time, muffled, as if something didn't want it to be heard.

"See?" Jason was ignoring Mark's jibe. "It's going away, whatever it is."

"Or being dragged away." Mark returned to his friend's side, the implication of his wussiness sufficient to persuade him to brave whatever might be lying out there for them among the mud and bricks. "You still haven't told me why we're here."

"I've been trying to." Despite his previous assurances that there was no one around, Jason dropped his voice to a whisper. "Carstairs told us that H. G. Wells wrote loads of books in Victorian times, right?"

"Right." From the sounds of it Mark obviously didn't have a clue, but for now he was happy to go along with his friend.

"And this is where his house was, right?"

"Right."

"So there might be stuff here that's valuable, yeah?"

Mark pondered this for a moment. "Like what?"

Jason hadn't thought that far. "I dunno." He shrugged. "Bits of the time machine?"

"I thought that was all made up."

"Doesn't mean he didn't try building one himself does it, piss stick?"

Mark shivered. "That is the single most stupid reason for coming out on a Monday night I can think of." He took another step back. "I'm going down to the arcade."

"All right," Jason called after his retreating form. "Just means when I find something I get to keep it. And all the money I'll get for it."

Mark halted and turned around.

"Money? You sure?"

Jason pointed to the narrow trenches and heaped earth. "Only one way to find out."

Mark was retracing his steps. "How are we going to see?"

Jason switched on the flashlight he'd been concealing in his pocket.

"Okay," said Mark, holding his watch up to the beam to see what time it was. "I'll stay for half an hour. Then I'm going."

The mist had thickened considerably while they had been talking. Now it covered the damp earth like a nebulous shroud, drifting gently with the breeze that had sprung up, but it was still willing to part for the feet of the two boys as the worn soles of their filthy sneakers disturbed its gossamer-like serenity.

As they walked, the building site seemed to transform. The deep trenches that had been dug for the foundations became open graves, the towers of bricks monolithic tombstones. The machines were in the background now, silent witnesses to what was about to unfold. The flickering beam of Jason's flashlight only added to the sense of altered reality, especially as it kept flickering on and off.

"This place is like a bloody graveyard," Mark whispered.

"Glad it's not just me." Jason suppressed a shiver. "It's just a building site."

"It's fucking creepy is what it is." Mark stopped and reached down.

"What's the matter?"

"My foot's stuck. It's sinking in. Just a minute." Mark grimaced as he scooped away the sticky, cloying earth from around his foot. "I might have found something."

"Something good?" Jason shone the flashlight as Mark brought his hand up into the beam.

"I dunno. Feels like maybe necklaces?"

It was only when his mud-caked outstretched palm was in the harsh glow of the light that they both saw what it was.

The worms were all different sizes. Some were as thick as Mark's fingers and moved slowly, curling themselves away from the brightness with almost lazy indifference. Others were much smaller and writhed with a frenzied intensity that pushed the paler, stubbier grubs into the spaces between the boy's fingers, from where they fell to the ground.

Mark flicked his hand to rid himself of them while Jason made noises of disgust. Once the worms had vanished back into the dark patch of earth, Mark rubbed his palm against his fleece jacket and held it up once more.

"Shine the flashlight again," he said.

Jason shook his head. "That was gross," he said. "I don't want to see what else you want to make me sick with."

The other boy grabbed his hand. "I wasn't trying to make you sick you wanker, my foot really was stuck. Now let . . . me . . . see."

The worms had gone, but their passing had left behind a sticky residue. A layer of dark green slime coated Mark's palm. Tiny pools of what looked like clotted blood were floating in it.

Jason's eyes widened. "Shit! Did they bite you?"

Mark choked down a terrified sob that his friend wasn't meant to hear. "I'm all right," he said, rubbing his palm against the soft material as vigorously as he could. "I couldn't feel them bite me, so they can't have, right?"

"I don't know." Jason was playing the dutiful unhelpful friend. "Aren't there some worms that can burrow inside you and you don't feel a thing until it's too late? I saw a documentary on it once—they eat away at your insides until there's hardly anything left. Then they burst—"

"Fuck off." Mark looked around. It was impossible to tell which way they had come. "I'm going home. Now." He picked a direction and started walking.

"Well I'm not helping you." Jason shone the flashlight in the opposite direction. "I'm staying until I've found something."

Mark, his face tear-streaked and his hand beginning to throb—if only in his imagination—began to pick his way between the graves.

Not graves not graves not graves, he told himself over and over. Just trenches. Dug by those machines we saw on the way in.

Behind him, Jason flashed the beam of light in a number of unhelpful directions, with likely little intention of helping him find his way, but it did allow Mark flashes of a path he was able to follow that would lead him to the perimeter fence.

There was something up ahead. Between him and the wooden boards that hopefully led to freedom.

Something crouched close to the ground.

Something with a lot of thick, jointed legs radiating from a body so bulbous and black that it even absorbed Jason's light.

"Jason!" The two syllables were barely comprehensible because of the mixture of snot and fear in the terrified boy's throat.

The beam flashed Mark's way once more.

The thing had moved closer.

He could see the legs moving now, clawing and bending as the blackness crawled toward him, edging closer on its multiple silent feet.

"Oh fuck help *meeeeeee!*"

The last word became a drawn out cry as Mark took a step back, his heel met with nothing but air, and he slid backward into a trench. Warm urine coursed down his leg as he felt more wriggling things try to work their way out from beneath his body. The memory of the public information film they'd been shown after assembly the other week came rushing back to him. At the time he and Jason had giggled about the out-of-date fashions and the ridiculous acting. Now all he could think about was the bit where the kid got buried alive in a hole just like this one.

Just like this one.

"Jason! Help!" He dug the heels of his palms into the rotting earth either side of him, trying desperately to lever himself up. But the trench was easily ten feet deep and the ground wasn't about to help. Instead a myriad tiny fragments of gravel dug into his flesh, puncturing his skin and burning the raw tissue beneath. Was it his imagination or could he feel things trying to burrow into him? Wriggling between the joints of his fingers to get to the bone so they could gnaw at it?

Mark raised his arms and dug desperate fingers into the sides of the trench. A splatter of sodden, fleshy mud hit him in the face. He tried to wipe it away but only succeeded in smearing the stinking stuff over his mouth and nose. A fleck of something disgusting lodged itself in his left nostril. It stank the way his guinea pig had when it escaped and got itself stuck behind the radiator when Mark was five. There'd been no one in the house and by the time his mum had gotten home, his pet was dead and already rotting in the damp atmosphere of the flat.

That was how Mark felt now—trapped and already starting to decompose. It was difficult to tell where his scrabbling hands ended and the watery slime began. He opened his mouth to scream but before he could make a sound a clod of something wet lodged itself in his throat. He coughed and spluttered, showering his chin with a mixture of spit and solids. Were there wriggling things in it too? Nausea overwhelmed the boy and he vomited, the partially digested remains of the burger and fries he'd eaten before coming to the building site cascading in a semi-solid mass down the front of his fleece. He coughed. The stink was almost as bad as the fetid earth. Almost, but not quite. He wiped his mouth once again, resisting the urge to clean his hand by wiping it on his diseased surroundings. Instead, his fleece ended up even filthier than it already was.

"Jason!" Where was his friend? Mark tried to stand, but the earth beneath him, with its mixture of slime, mud, and creatures desperate for his flesh was much too slippery. As he fell down once more he called again, his cries becoming increasingly desperate. He kept shouting until his voice became so hoarse all he could emit was a croak, the kind he imagined the creatures hiding in the darkness around him might make if they were big enough. He tried to climb again but every attempt to claw his way out led to another cascade of crumbling, wet fleshy mud. If he kept doing that he was going to end up buried by the stuff.

Mark tried to swallow, but the stink of whatever was in his throat was so bad it threatened to cause him to vomit again. He was surprised he wasn't crying, but he guessed that was because tears would be useless. He was about to give up hope when the flashlight beam caught him between the eyes.

"There you are!"

Mark's overwhelming relief at the appearance of his friend was expressed the only way a teenaged boy knows how. "Fucking hell, where the fuck have you been?"

The outline peering into the trench gave a dull laugh. "Looking for you, you twat. What did you have to go and fall in there for?"

Even though it was too dark for anyone to see, Mark could feel the embarrassment of his face reddening. "I slipped."

"You slipped? You fucking slipped? And how am I supposed to get you out?"

It was a good point. Even with Jason's outstretched arm there was a gap of at least four feet between him and his friend.

Mark shouted up. "Isn't there a ladder around somewhere?"

There was silence as Jason was hopefully scanning the site. "I can't see one," he said. Then there was another pause as he shone the flashlight around the site once more. "Hang on."

It felt like an eternity for Jason to reappear. When he did he was holding something in his other hand. "I've found a rope."

"Hurry up and throw it down, then!" Now that there was a real chance of escape, desperation had turned to impatience.

"Just a minute! If you pull me in we're both fucked. I'm going to go and find something to tie it to."

And Jason was gone again. Mark resisted the urge to call out for his friend not to take too long, because he wouldn't, would he? He wouldn't leave Mark down here any longer than was necessary. Even though Mark had put dog shit in Jason's bag that time for a laugh? Or that he'd made that snide remark about Jason not having a mum when he knew she'd died when Jason was born? He wouldn't leave Mark there because of any of that, would he?

Would he?

The mist that coated the site was creeping down the sides of the trench now. Its steady progress was probably because Mark had stopped moving, but he was exhausted and couldn't bring himself to sweep it away. All he could do was sit and shiver, the involuntary spasms of his tired and aching muscles doing their best to keep his body above freezing as white tendrils of ice-cold moisture poured over the sides of the trench and snaked their way toward him.

Mark hugged his knees. He could feel his freezing fingers through the mud-smeared denim. *Oh God Jason, hurry the fuck up!*

A snake hit him in the face.

No, not a snake.

A rope.

"Jason?" The outline of a head appeared over the lip of the trench. "Did you find something to tie it to?"

"Scaffolding," came the reply. "I was worried it wouldn't reach, but it should be all right."

Mark gripped the rope with both hands. "It's fine!" He pulled hard and levered himself into a standing position. The mud was so slippery that as soon as he tried to move his feet went from under him and he was flat on his back again. There was a clanking sound from far away as he hit the ground.

"Be careful!"

"I'm trying!"

Mark pulled on the rope again, getting himself into a kneeling position first this time, then a crouch, and finally into an upright stance.

"I'm standing up!"

"Great. Can you climb out?"

Mark pulled on the rope and tried to put his right foot against the wall of the trench. It sank in halfway up to his calf. He tried to pull it out but with only his left foot to balance on he was soon on his back once more.

"It's too slippery! You'll have to help pull me out!"

"Okay." Jason was standing at the edge of the trench again. "Stand up and we'll do it on three."

It took what felt like hours for Mark to get on his feet again. This time he clung to the rope even more tightly. If his mum wanted to know why he was picking fibers out of his hands for the next week he would have to make something up that wouldn't be as ludicrous as the real reason.

"Ready!"

"Okay, but you're going to have to help me."

Mark wasn't sure how he could, but he braced himself as he felt the rope go taut.

Then it went slack again.

"You're not helping." Jason sounded out of breath.

"What do you want me to do?"

"Try and climb while I pull."

"I can't!" Suddenly the whole thing seemed hopeless. "I've already tried!"

"Well you're going to have to try again. Otherwise you're going to be stuck in there all night until the builders come in the morning."

Whether it was the fear of being found by the workmen, or the sheer terror of what his mum would say when he failed to come home all night again, the next time the rope went taut Mark threw himself at the trench wall, plunging both feet into the crumbling mud and levering himself upward. Each time he had to take another step, his foot came free with a sucking sound, and each time a few more gobbets of wet mud and a few more clusters of tiny wriggling creatures found their way up his trouser leg. He closed his eyes and kept going. When he opened them again, Jason's silhouette was much closer.

"Come on, mate." The other boy seemed to be looking behind Mark for some reason. "Not much further."

Mark gave another tug on the rope. There was that clanking sound again, closer this time. Mark could feel his feet slipping. But he was so close! With a Herculean effort he pulled himself up another few inches.

Which is when everything went wrong.

First, there was a crash that was like the clanking sound only ten times worse. This coincided with the rope going loose and Mark falling backward to land once more in the slime and horror of the pit.

Then Jason landed on top of him.

Then the loose scaffolding poles Jason had tied the rope to landed on top of both of them.

For a moment, all was silent.

"Jason?"

The flashlight had fallen into the trench as well. Now its beam was outlining the bulk of the taller, heavier boy, who groaned.

"Get off me!"

But Jason wasn't moving, not without some encouragement, anyway. Mark curled his fingers into fists and beat his friend on the back. When that didn't work, he reached out to his right to grab some of the stinking mud he had been trying to stay away from. He meant to rub it in the other boy's face.

What he actually found himself holding, in the cold glow of the flashlight, was a thigh bone.

A human thigh bone.

Mark didn't know that for sure, of course, but it was just the right size and shape, and after all he'd been through already this evening it was enough to make him yell at the top of his voice.

That woke Jason up.

"What the fuck are you screaming about?" the boy mumbled, pushing himself off his friend and sliding into the muck adjacent to him.

Mark grabbed the flashlight and shone it on the bone.

"Where did you find that?"

Still incapable of speech, Mark pointed to the hole he had tried to gouge in the mud.

"Maybe there's more!"

Jason leaned over and pushed his hand deeper into the muddy sludge. "Yes," he said, feeling around and ignoring Mark's petrified gaze, "there's something else in here, but it's stuck. Give me a hand."

Mark shook his head.

"You are so useless." Jason was leaning right over Mark now and had both his hands in the hole. "At least shine the flashlight over here so I can see." With a final effort Jason pulled hard on whatever it was he had a hold of. It came free, but was so slippery that it fell from his grasp and tumbled into the pit, coming to rest close to Mark's face.

"Go on then," said Jason. "Shine the flashlight on it."

When Mark finally plucked up the courage to do so, two hollow sockets stared back at him.

That was when both boys screamed.

"A skull!" Jason had forgotten all about them keeping their voices down. "We're in a grave with a fucking skull!"

The hole he had widened in the side of the trench suddenly collapsed in on itself, covering Mark's right arm in more mud, more crawling things, and more bones.

There was something else there too.

Something wrapped in sacking.

"What's that?" Jason was already reaching over to pick it up.

"I don't care," said Mark, finally finding his voice again and pushing himself into a sitting position. "I'm going home."

The smaller boy grabbed hold of the nearest pieces of scaffolding and pushed down on them as hard as he could. Wedged at an angle inside the open pit, the poles sank into the soil a little and then held, enough for him to get onto his hands and knees and try them with his full weight. Satisfied that they weren't going to budge any farther, Mark used the metal shafts to clamber up and out of the trench.

"Don't you want to find out what it is?" Jason was still down in the pit. He was unwrapping the sacking and revealing what looked like a large clay urn.

"Fuck that." Mark wiped a mud-smeared hand across his face. "We've made so much bloody noise, if we stay here any longer we're going to get caught."

That was when the dark figure standing behind him laid a heavy hand on his shoulder.

Mark took in the security patrol uniform and the flashlight that was about to be shone in his face and realized they just had been.

SUPERMARKET SHIVERS!

Two young boys playing on a building site on monday night got more than they bargained for when their mischievous antics unearthed the skull and bones of an ancient corpse

Building work for a new branch of Sainsbury's has been stopped while the police investigate what has already been suggested as a crime that might date back hundreds of years.

Chief Inspector Raymond Partington of the Metropolitan Police gave a press conference earlier today and had this to say: "It has already been confirmed that these bones are just a few fragments, and that they are very old. Any crime that may have caused them to end up here is probably more a case for the British Museum than the local constabulary."

A spokesman for Everett Construction said, "Building sites are not playgrounds, and these boys should not have been there. Needless to say we are making every effort to examine our security arrangements to determine how they got in."

The two boys were taken to Farnborough Hospital. Neither they nor their parents were available for comment, but we understand that apart from some cuts and bruises they were unhurt.

The demolition site where the boys were discovered is part of plans by the Council to modernize the High Street and included the building where the famous author H. G. Wells, known for his science fiction novel *War of the Worlds*, was born in 1866. A plaque commemorating his birthplace is due to be included in the new supermarket that will be erected on the site.

TWO

Friday, October 21, 1994. 1:33 P.M.

THERE WERE THIRTEEN DEAD flies on the windowsill.

Bob Chambers knew this because he'd already counted them twice. He was considering counting them again when his friend finally returned from the bar carrying two pints of brown bitter. Once he had put those down, the man opened his mouth. The packet of peanuts clenched between his teeth dropped to the polished cherry wood surface of the small circular tabletop, narrowly missing both glasses.

"Glad you could come, Bob." The other man took a seat while Chambers sipped at his pint and allowed his taste buds to adjust. British beer always came as a bit of a shock after what he was used to back in Washington. "You've no idea how much you're helping me out with this."

"I haven't said I will help yet, Malcolm." Chambers put down his glass. "Whatever it is, it can't be too important if you're only willing to buy me beer and nuts."

Malcolm Turner gave him an uneasy grin. "The British Museum's on a budget too, you know. If you were a visiting dignitary, or we were negotiating you letting me have three hundred terracotta warriors for the Summer Exhibition, I might have taken you to the Italian place down the road."

"But not an old university friend you haven't seen in years? One who's just got off a crappy seven-hour flight where he spent the entire time crammed into coach? I just get some nuts?"

Malcolm tore open the packet. "Want one?"

Chambers shook his head. "I ate on the flight." He hadn't but he could wait.

It was just after lunch, and the Princess Louise pub was emptying out. Those who had chosen to dine there, or just pop in for a swift half-pint, presumably all had jobs in Holborn they needed to get back to.

Turner shook a few nuts into his cupped right hand and then gulped them down, aiding their passage with a swallow from his glass. Then he sat up straight, attempting to tidy himself up by tugging at the folds of his crumpled brown corduroy jacket and smoothing down what little hair he had on either side of his otherwise bald head. He leaned forward as if what he was about to say was not for the ears of those still on the point of leaving.

"I might have something of interest to your . . . department."

Chambers nodded. Even though he was far from home, it was still best that no mention was made in public of the Human Protection League, nor of the specific scientific department he worked for. The Cthulhu Investigation Division had researched cases worldwide, and the enemy could be listening in anywhere. It had been some time since there had been an incursion in Britain, but they all knew it was only a matter of time before something unspeakable was raised again, given this tiny island's eldritch history.

From what his friend had told Chambers over the telephone, that time could be now.

Turner reached into his bag and pulled out a battered tabloid. He handed it over.

"Local newspaper," Chambers noted. "How did you come across this?"

"I live in that part of London," the other man replied, taking another mouthful of beer. "I was reading it on the bus coming in to work yesterday morning when I noticed the report tucked away on page six."

Chambers turned to the relevant section. "I'm guessing you don't want me to read about the closing of the local library?"

Turner sniffed. "At the bottom." He waited while Chambers read. "I think you ought to take a look at them."

Chambers handed the paper back. "You've asked me to come all the way over here to look at a few moldy old bones? I know my field is forensic pathology, but surely the British Museum must have their own expert for something like that?"

"He's on leave." Turner looked embarrassed. "Permanently."

Chambers shook his head. "What happened?"

"I'll get to that." Turner shifted uncomfortably in his seat. "It wasn't pleasant."

"But surely you must be getting a replacement?"

"Doesn't start for another month."

"And let me guess, you need the lab space these old bones are taking up for some other major project that the Museum desperately needs to get going on?"

"Something like that." Turner took another sip of his pint. "I really hate having to exploit our college friendship like this, but I'm in a jam, and when someone said the bones could be hundreds of years old, I thought of you."

Chambers raised an eyebrow. "This doesn't sound worth me coming nearly four thousand miles, Malcolm."

Turner leaned forward, his voice almost a whisper. "That's because I haven't yet mentioned the most interesting part."

Chambers sighed, took another gulp of beer, and grimaced. Next time he'd ask for a bottle of Budweiser. "Go on then, I really can't take the suspense any longer."

"It's possible these bones have some sort of effect on the mind. Have you ever heard of anything like that?"

"No." But this was more like it. "Tell me more."

Turner shrugged. "There's not much else to say. The boys who found them are apparently both nervous wrecks. They keep going on about slime and wriggling things coming to get them. Mind you, the security guard who found the boys handled the bones and he's been fine, and so has almost everyone else who has come into contact with them since. I only looked into it because of what happened to Dr. Trent on Tuesday night..."

"Your forensic pathologist?"

Turner nodded. "He will never examine bones, or anything else, again. When we found him he'd stabbed out his eyes and was trying to cut his own throat with a scalpel. But the worst thing was what he kept screaming, over and over again, about how his self-mutilation hadn't made any difference. He could still see *them*, could still feel them plucking at him." He took another swig of his beer. "Like I said, not pretty."

"What do you think he meant by 'them'?" asked Chambers intently, his interest now piqued.

"I have absolutely no idea." The other man put his glass down heavily on the table. "He was barely coherent when we found him."

"Did he have any prior psychiatric history?"

"He did, as a matter of fact." Turner looked uneasy. "Problems with depression and alcohol. Sorry, it's certainly possible I brought you here on a wild-goose chase, but I thought I should be careful."

"You did the right thing." Even if the bones turned out to be harmless, Chambers was grateful for his friend's caution. If more people were like Malcolm Turner, that whole problem with the shoggoths at the Chilean Museum of Anthropology in Santiago could have been avoided.

There was a pause as both men considered their pints. Eventually Turner looked up.

"I've had everything sealed away. It's all being hushed up at the moment, and to be honest nobody wants the matter taken any further. The bones were found beneath the house where H. G. Wells used to live, and as a result the British Museum is stuck with them. Which means I'm stuck with them. And I need your help. Ideally I'd like you to take the damned things away with you, although I know that might be difficult."

Chambers nodded. It might also be the right thing to do. But still, he was here now, and if the British Museum had its own laboratory . . .

"Let me make a call to my Division in Washington and see how they want me to proceed, and then I'll get back to you. Probably after I've gotten some sleep."

Malcolm Turner visibly relaxed. "Thanks Bob. I knew I could rely on you. So if I tell the journalist you'll have something for her by Monday, will that be all right?"

Chambers put his pint down. "What journalist?"

Turner was unfazed. "The one who's covering the story, of course. She wanted me to tell her when we had any more information." He sucked up another nut with a sound that made Chambers glad he hadn't bothered with lunch. "You've no idea how relieved I'll be to get her off my back."

"I don't want to talk to any goddamned journalist, Malcolm." Chambers got up to leave, half the dark liquid in his glass untouched. "I've had enough run-ins with their type in my line of work to know to steer well clear."

That got a reaction. Turner was on his feet in a second, a pleading look on his face.

"You just have to give her your findings. Just a line or two for her story. If it makes you feel any better I'll call her to say you're busy and won't be able to talk to her for more than five minutes."

Chambers shook his head. "Makes no difference with that type. Shaking them off can be more difficult than . . ." he tried to think of something that wasn't related to the otherworldly monstrosities he had been fighting for the last five years, but it was no good. He had been doing the job for too long ". . . lots of things. Tell your journalist that I'm not going to talk to her for more than a minute."

"Two minutes?"

"All right, two."

"In that case," Turner swallowed the rest of his pint in one gulp then reached out to shake his friend's hand, "you're on. It won't be that bad— you'll see."

Chambers wasn't so sure. Bones that might exacerbate mental disorders? Found buried beneath the house of a man who had written about time travel and alien invasion?

Oh no, he wasn't so sure at all.

THREE

THE ROOM WAS BLINDING white.

So harsh was the glare that attacked him as he stepped inside that Bob Chambers wished for a moment that he had brought sunglasses. As his eyes adjusted, he saw the three workbenches, arranged to radiate outward from the apex that was his point of entry. The benches were white as well, and each had an overhead fluorescent light for extra illumination. In the wall opposite, heavy-handled doors led to cupboards that presumably contained any equipment he might need to assist his examination.

The things he was intended to examine were on the middle bench.

In his career, Chambers had become used to the stink of death in all its varieties, from those recently deceased of natural causes, to the burn victim dumped in a river and then dragged out weeks later. However, since joining the Cthulhu Investigation Division he had seen more death by more bizarre methods than he had ever dreamed possible.

The bones on the table in front of him, however, had a stink all of their own.

He had noticed it as soon as he came in, a smell not just of earth and of the grave, but something else. An insidious sickly sweetness that caught in the back of his throat and made him cough. It was hard to believe that a few fragments of long-dead bone could cause such an odor, but at least it explained the absence of anyone else in the room.

As well as the skull, the single long bone, and the few other fragments that had been unearthed, the clay pot the boys had found had been left for his inspection as well.

"In case it's of interest," Malcolm Turner had said.

"I don't know anything about pots." Chambers wasn't having any of it. "When I next speak to Washington I'll ask if they want to send someone over to take a look at it."

"Up to you," came the reply. "Just leave it with all the bits and pieces when you've finished."

Chambers removed his jacket and hung it on the peg close to the door. On the phone last night Marcia Anderson, the team's psychiatrist, had reassured him that, despite what Malcolm had said, he was unlikely to be affected by coming into contact with anything that had been retrieved from the pit.

"A susceptible adult and two impressionable children?" She hadn't sounded impressed. "Even the slightest Cthulhian influence has been known to drive such individuals insane. That's why we only recruit people with a strongly stable mental state."

"It's possible there is some malign influence in the bones, then?"

"It's possible." She was still unimpressed. "But in view of what you've told me, and the fact that most people who have handled the bones seem to be unaffected, I'd say the chances are less than fifty percent."

He decided to wear gloves anyway.

He pulled a pair of pale blue latex ones from a cardboard box crammed with the things, and then replaced the box in its holder above a sink, the chrome lining of which was so highly polished it looked as if it had never been used.

He retrieved his Dictaphone from his jacket pocket, and switched it on. In the loud, clear voice he reserved for the purpose, he dictated the date, his name, and a reference number his department could use for the case before switching it off again.

Then he tried to pick up the skull.

It was more difficult than he had expected, and he couldn't for the life of him understand why. The dull brown bone, its eye sockets packed with earth, the nasal cavity cracked and bearing traces of a dirty green fungus, was just a skull, like many others he had examined. Admittedly it was a lot older, but that shouldn't have made any difference.

But nevertheless, there was something . . . wrong about it. Something that made his hand tremble as he reached for it, that made his eyes smart and a lump form in his throat. By the time his fingertips were almost in contact with the scoured surface he was close to vomiting.

He withdrew his hand and the feeling subsided.

When he tried again it came back.

Chambers shook his head and blinked. This was ridiculous! It was an old and possibly diseased piece of bone. He'd handled worse in his career. Perhaps some part of the material packed into the eye sockets was causing his reaction?

Let's try another bone, then, he thought, reaching for what looked like the top half of a femur.

The same thing happened. If anything, this time it was worse.

Ridiculous, he thought. Perhaps someone had foolishly dunked the bones in an excessively powerful preserving fluid, and that was what was making him feel dizzy. If that was the case, he needed to move quickly, or there wouldn't be any tissues left for him to examine at all.

He gritted his teeth and made another grab at the skull with both hands. This time he succeeded in lifting it from the workbench.

It was difficult to work out what happened next. Even later, after several hours of thinking about it. The sense of nausea returned with a vengeance of course, assaulting his senses like a battering ram to his brain. But something else happened as well, something even more horrible and infinitely more terrifying.

A cloud of insidious darkness descended upon his vision, and a thick deafness clogged his hearing. He felt as if he was falling backward even though he was sure he was not moving. This progressive and methodical ablation of his senses did not abate until he could feel nothing.

Then the visions began.

They were worse than anything he had experienced so far. Shapeless things clutched at him out of the blackness; spider-thin fingers crawled from the right eye socket of the skull he had just laid his fingers on, a thin and shapeless hand following it that was so abnormal in its elasticity that it made him dread to see the individual to whom it belonged.

The image before him changed to a distant church atop a howling hill, the only feature on the powder-dry windswept plain on which he found himself. The sky above was red as an arterial fountain. Then he was looking at a man nailed to a cross. No, not a cross, just the image of it, painted on a stone wall to which the man had been pinned in a hideous travesty of the crucifixion, metal spikes placed through both hands and feet and into the crumbling mortar beneath. Something had wrapped itself around the man's body—not a toad as such because its pale, diseased body possessed rudimentary, flipper-like legs. Something older, then? Something from a time when evolution was still trying to decide on its final path?

More images—a goat's head with seven eyes arranged in a cruciform pattern, the emerald iris of each glinting with a terrible and arcane knowledge, made worse by the creature's body being that of an anatomically perfect young woman. The thing before him raised its hands, palms upward. A dove flew upward from each and fluttered toward him, so he could see the creatures' bleary compound eyes and the insectoid mandibles that clicked and clacked from their ill-formed mouths.

Then he was falling, leaving the horrors he had been shown behind, tumbling past pictures, walls, rock, past time itself. Everything was being lost to him. Everything he had ever known, everyone he had ever met, had ever loved. None of these mattered anymore. None of them had ever truly mattered.

The only thing of importance was what lay at the bottom of the pit.

He could see it now, coming up to greet him. A plain of gray dust that shone with a pale luminescence. The featureless landscape promised nothing but a purgatory without end, an eternal prison that needed no bars because there was nothing but the prison, and nowhere to run to but the never-ending nothingness of all that surrounded him.

His landing was surprisingly gentle, and as he got to his feet the goat-woman appeared to him again. This time her hands were tapering claws and they held in their chipped and dirt-encrusted grasp the urn he had told Turner he was going to have nothing to do with.

She held it out to him.

He took a step back, only to collide with the same girl behind him, to his left, to his right, in every direction he looked. An infinite number of beautiful young girls, each with the head of a monster, urged him to take the burden each of them was holding.

He closed his eyes and tried to push them away. His senses now fully restored, he could feel the softness of their skin, smell the rot on their breath. As his fingers came into contact with their claws he felt them crumble beneath his flailing hands, the nails coming apart like rotten tree bark.

One urn dropped to the ground, causing the anemic dust to puff around it before settling once more.

Another fell, and then another, stirring up more of the desiccated soil until the resultant cloud was so thick that even when Chambers opened his eyes again he couldn't see the myriad bodies that thronged around him.

The urns were continuing to fall, landing upon one another and making sounds like dry bones breaking as they discharged their contents into the dirt. The cloud that enveloped him was too thick to see what it was they contained, nor did he want to. It was only when the dust began to clear and the broken shards of pottery were piled high enough, that he began to understand they were intended to contain *him*. As he watched they smoothed themselves, fusing together to create a chamber he knew would enclose him forever.

Chambers put his hands out again, battering at the newly formed clay walls, beating at them with his fists until, finally, they too began to crack. In the spaces he could now see only darkness beyond, and yet he knew that darkness contained the worst of all. Suddenly something came rushing toward him. It was blood, a frothing ocean of it, containing every dreadful thing he had ever feared, and every terrible thing he had ever done, all in one mighty, overwhelming wave of despair, misery, and horror. As it enveloped him, swamped him, drowned him, Chambers could do nothing but scream, only for his open mouth to be filled by the scarlet wave.

"Are you all right?"

Chambers was on the floor, but at least it was a floor. A nice, solid one with no trace of dust or monsters or anything else that shouldn't exist in a sane, rational, normal world. He gasped and looked around him. He was back in the British Museum laboratory. Not that he had ever left it, of course.

He got to his feet. It wasn't as easy as he had expected, and he had to lean on whoever must have found him in this rather embarrassing situation.

"I'm fine," he said. His voice made him sound anything but. He turned to look at the person on whose arm he was leaning. "And you are...?"

He caught a glimpse of a kind face framed by red hair that swept down to just above the young woman's shoulders. Her green eyes were filled with concern.

No, not green—emerald...

Chambers shook his head and tried to dismiss the image of the goat girl from his mind.

"...worried about you right at this moment," the girl replied. "I was waiting around outside when I heard a crash. I came in and you were flat out on the floor, mumbling all sorts of nonsense."

"Nonsense?" Chambers eyed her with concern. What might she have heard?

Her expression softened now she could see he was all right, and her face broke into a smile. "Don't worry," she said, "you weren't saying anything I could understand. They weren't even words, really. To be honest I was worried you were having a fit, and I wouldn't have had the slightest clue what to do about that."

Chambers leaned against the bench and did his best to return her smile. "You're not a doctor, then?"

"Oh Christ, no." She held out a well-manicured hand which was nothing like the crumbling claws the girl in his vision had possessed. "Karen

Shepworth. I'm covering the story about the bones being found under H. G. Wells's house for the *News of Britain*."

Chambers flinched without meaning to before gently shaking her hand. "You're a reporter?"

"I prefer 'investigative journalist.'" She was rummaging in the brown leather tote bag that was slung over her left shoulder. "I've got a card in here somewhere . . ."

Chambers held up a hand. "Don't worry about that," he said.

"Oh, but you're going to need it," she said, finally locating one and handing it over. "How else are you going to get in touch to give me your final report?"

Realization dawned.

"You're the one doing the story—"

"—about the bones found on the building site, yes." She finished his sentence for him with a smile he did not share. "Why else would I be hanging around the arse-end of the British Museum on a Sunday?"

"Why indeed?" He was beginning to feel better. "Well I'm sorry to have to inform you Miss Shepworth, but I haven't had a chance to get started yet."

She insisted he call her Karen. "But you have made a start on the pot those boys dug up along with the bones, I see."

Chambers had no idea what she was talking about, nor why she had such a mischievous smile on her face. Then he followed her gaze to the bench where the skull lay, along with half a thigh, and the other fragments of bones.

But no clay urn.

Because it was on the floor.

In pieces.

"Shit." His first reaction was guilt. He must have knocked the thing over during his faint. He was already dismissing that as a result of the preserving fluid, the bright lights, and the jet lag. It still wouldn't be a good enough excuse to give Malcolm, though.

"I'm guessing you didn't mean to do that then?"

Chambers was already down on his knees and picking up the pieces. *I don't even remember doing it* he was about to reply, and then he thought better of it. Anything he came out with in this girl's presence could be in the papers tomorrow morning.

"More fragile than it looked," he said, as he placed the broken fragments back on the bench.

The contents were still on the floor.

It was the first time he'd noticed them, and now he wondered if perhaps they were too delicate to be picked up by his untrained hands. There were three rolls of what looked like parchment, each tied with a fine piece of maroon thread, flecked with gold. They also seemed to be in far too good a condition to have spent much time in the ground.

"Aren't you going to pick those up too?"

He wasn't, but there was no way now he could get out of it. "I'm guessing these are something more suited to Malcolm and his team." He picked each one up individually, and laid it gently on the work surface.

"We could have a look." Already she had a pair of nail scissors out and was advancing on the one closest to her.

"I think we should leave it to the experts," he said, but it was no good.

"Oops," she said as she snipped through the thread. "It must have come off in the fall."

Almost as if the parchment approved of her actions, it unfurled before them, revealing a document of such beauty that they both took in a breath.

"It looks like a page from a medieval Bible," said Chambers, peering at the ornate, beautifully lettered script, complete with an intricately illustrated drop capital that began the text. The colors used could not have been any more vivid if they had been applied yesterday.

"It's like a work of art," said Karen, reaching out to pick it up.

Chambers pushed her hands away. "You'd better not touch it," he said. "Apart from the fact that these old paints and inks can contain toxic compounds, there's always the possibility that we've got something priceless here."

That took a moment to sink in. "Priceless? How can you tell?"

Chambers gestured to the rest of the specimens. "They were buried with this poor chap, whoever he may be, and even a rudimentary examination suggests the bones have been in the earth for a very long time, possibly hundreds of years."

Karen looked intrigued. She also took out her own Dictaphone and switched it on before continuing. "How can you tell that?"

Distracted by her presence, Chambers picked up the skull without thinking. This time he felt no ill effects. No dizziness, nothing. He coughed to conceal his relief and continued. "Some of the signs are obvious, others are more subtle. The bone itself has a density that you only get when the minerals of the bone matrix—mainly calcium and phosphate—have been leached out into the soil by rainwater. As a result the bone ends up porous. The older it is the lighter and more porous is the tissue. And this skull is very light indeed."

He held it up to the light. "If you look carefully you can see a lot of tiny lines over the surface." Karen came close. "The best place to look is the calvarium—the top of the skull. Can you see?" She nodded. "Well, those are formed by creatures that live in the earth—worms, beetles, and suchlike, moving against it. The thing is, the wearing away of the bone like that takes time."

Karen held the recorder close. "How much time?"

Chambers shrugged. "Difficult to say, but again we're looking at hundreds of years rather than decades." He picked up the femur. "You can see the lines on here as well, which helps confirm this is probably part of the same body the skull belongs to."

"Anything else you'd like to add?"

Chambers put the femur down. "Not at this time," he said.

"Okay." She smiled and switched off the recorder. "One last question, the answer to which I promise you will be off the record."

Chambers wasn't about to let his guard down. "Go on."

"What on earth were you doing on the floor when I came in?"

"Oh that? It was because when I went near the skull I—" He stopped. He had just been handling the bones with no ill effect at all. That made no sense, but then neither did much else that had happened this afternoon.

The only thing he was sure of was that he must not let this reporter pick up on how disturbed he was feeling right now. "No good reason," he said with a sheepish smile. "I just took a step back from the bench and missed my footing. Promise you won't tell anyone?"

She offered him a sunny smile that had probably gotten her more than one good lead. "I promise. That particular secret of yours is safe with me." She turned to the opened parchment. "Although how about in return you don't say anything to Malcolm Turner about me opening this?"

"Okay," he agreed. "But that's probably a slightly bigger favor, don't you think?"

"A hard negotiator. I like it." She was putting her Dictaphone away. "Okay—I'm ever so slightly in your debt." Now she'd taken out a tiny pocket camera. "Stand back, would you?"

Chambers was about to protest but by the time he'd opened his mouth the flash had gone off and an image of the parchment had been committed to film.

"Thought I'd better do it before you stopped me," she said, tucking the camera out of reach. "Fancy finding out what it all means?"

Chambers had to admit he was interested. "But how are you going to—?"

"You said it could easily be several hundred years old, yes?" Chambers nodded. "Well, one of my teachers at Oxford was an expert in Medieval English. If he's still there he might be willing to translate it for me. I can guarantee it'll be a hell of a lot quicker than getting them to do it down here. And he'll keep his mouth shut. For a price."

Chambers didn't want to know what the price might be.

"But you're interested?"

He nodded. The C.I.D. team in Washington might like to get their hands on it first, but he couldn't pass up the chance to let an Oxford University lecturer take a crack at it.

"Fine, in that case, we can do a swap. You tell me what other information you get from those old bones, and I'll tell you what I can get out of my old tutor. We could discuss it over dinner next week sometime. Deal?"

It was only when she had gone that he realized he might just have been asked out on a date.

FOUR

Thursday, October 27, 1994. 6:30 A.M.

HE WAS DREAMING AGAIN.

The church was nearer this time, and the blood-red sky was darker. There was no rain but the hoary damp stink suggested a heavy storm would soon be battering the landscape.

He reached down to touch the ground. The dust was so fine it turned his fingertips white, and he immediately knew this was not dust but ash, from some cataclysmic catastrophe that had scoured this land and rendered everything barren.

He was surrounded by bodies.

He wondered if he was being witness to the site of a battle, but if that were so, whatever conflict had been fought here was long past. The bodies were rotten, desiccated, their outlines softened by the white dust in which they lay.

Then the bodies began to move.

Frozen to the spot by unseen forces, he was helpless to do little else but watch as the army of the undead rose to its feet. Scraps of withered muscles hung from bones that should not have been able to move without them, and yet they could. Crumbling hip and shoulder joints were in such a terrible state they should not have been able to bear even the weight of a feather, and yet they held firm as the creatures looked around them, regarding their surroundings through eyeless sockets.

He stood at the center of an ocean of the undead, newly risen and, as yet, unfocused and purposeless. He was expecting them to begin shambling awkwardly and haphazardly in random directions, but they didn't.

Instead, they all turned and looked at him.

Even though he could only see the closest of those that surrounded him, he knew that all the others were regarding him, too, their skulls balanced on crumbling spinal columns, the gentle rocking movement either the tremor of anticipation, or merely the method by which they prevented themselves from falling to pieces completely.

He felt something brush his feet. Looking down he saw more of them, the ones who had no legs but were just as eager to make their presence felt, dragging themselves toward him with bony claws of fingers, or ragged stumps of broken bone where arms had been snapped off, or, he thought with a shudder, eaten.

He was about to cry out when, as one, the grisly army looked toward the church. There was more shuffling, and a hideous grinding noise that reminded him of intricate but badly oiled machinery as they moved.

As they parted to form a path.

That led to the church on the hill.

He stood at one end of an avenue of the undead. They waited, anticipant, filled with an unearthly hunger, with the desperate need to tear the living flesh from his bones. And yet they did not.

Instead they stood there, the gentle rocking motion seeming to urge him down the path, toward the building that lay at the end of it. Chambers stayed where he was, terrified and still rooted to the spot, knowing that whatever fate was intended for him, it would be worse than dying at the hands of these monsters.

Black lightning snaked across the sky, and then a crack of thunder louder than anything he had ever heard caused him to look up.

When he looked down again, he saw, in the distance, that the church doors had opened.

And something was waiting for him inside.

Bob Chambers glanced at the half-empty bottle of whisky on his nightstand and resisted the urge to pour himself another glass. Drinking scotch at seven in the morning might have been a sign of high spirits when he was a student, but at the age of thirty-five it was the sign of a problem, jet lag or not.

He put the bottle in the cupboard, hoping that out of sight would lead to out of mind as well. If only that would work for the nightmares.

The bloody nightmares.

He still found it hard to believe it was only four days since he'd been at the British Museum laboratories and had sparked off whatever it was that was now haunting his dreams, gnawing away at his sleep like a rat that wouldn't let go. It was always the same and, for a dream, was surprisingly logical—if an army of the undead trying to force him into a church that looked as if it was on another planet could be considered logical.

He pulled on the jacket of his blue serge suit. At least this afternoon he should be able to finish up the work on Malcolm's bones. He resolved to stay at the British Museum labs until his report was finished, even if it took all night. Perhaps then the dreams would go away, and even if they didn't, at least if he was up working he'd be spared the misery of sleep.

He checked his pocket for his hotel room key, and something scraped his hand as he did so. It was the business card that girl had given him. He took it out and stared at it. He was convinced the nightmares were important, and Washington had agreed. His new instructions were to find out as much as he could about the manuscript. All major resources were being directed toward a rising of Deep Ones off the Baja Peninsula, so the League didn't have anyone spare to send over. He was on his own. He didn't mind that, and as he seemed to be personally involved in this (or at least, his subconscious was), he was eager to find out what the scrolls said. Perhaps, he thought as he left the hotel and made his way to the London Underground station, they spoke of a curse that would befall the first person to touch those bones or smash that pot.

And if that was the case, hopefully they could tell him how to rid himself of it as well.

It wasn't until later that night that Chambers remembered he had to call Karen. Sitting in a cramped office at the back of the British Museum, with the final write-up on the bones in front of him, he knew he needed to speak to her before passing his report to Malcolm in the morning. More than that, he needed to know more about what it was those two boys had found, and the only place he was going to find answers was in the manuscript.

"Karen?"

"Yes."

He had expected the voice on the other end to sound sleepy but it was anything but.

"I'm sorry to disturb you so late. It's Bob Chambers here. You remember? Malcolm Turner's colleague." He was still doing his best to keep his background details secret. "The one he asked to look at the bones." Silence. "You came in after I'd knocked that pot on the floor at the British Museum."

"Oh shit, yes, I remember you." She gave a nervous laugh. "How are you doing?"

"You're sure I'm not bothering you?"

"God no, I'm a night owl, and a day owl, and an every-hour-God-sends owl when I'm working on a story." She certainly didn't sound annoyed, which was a relief. "What can I do for you?"

Chambers took a deep breath. He was shocked at how difficult it suddenly was for him to come out with his next question.

"Have you managed to meet with that tutor of yours yet? The one who was going to take a look at that manuscript for you?"

The line was quiet for a moment before Karen spoke again. This time her voice was quieter, less sure of itself. "No. Why?"

"It's just that . . ." God, why was this so difficult? Was it because it all sounded so ridiculous, or because it seemed to be affecting him personally? "... I've got the results on the analyses performed by the team here, on the skull and ... the other parts."

"Great." It didn't sound as if Karen actually thought it was great at all. "Why are you calling me about this now?"

Chambers picked up the document, still written in his own spidery hand. He had thought it best not to dictate it in case speaking any of this aloud aroused the attention of forces he had no wish to come into contact with. Not until he knew more about them, anyway. He read the summary paragraph at the bottom of the fifth page for the umpteenth time before speaking again.

"Karen, according to the mass spectrometry, radio-carbon dating, chromatographic analyses, and electron microscopy, the bones found on that building site could be up to six hundred years old."

"You're kidding."

In some ways, he wished he was. "No. Six hundred years. Of course you have to bear in mind the error factor with these sorts of things, but that doesn't change what I've said."

There was a pause during which he imagined he could hear her scribbling down what he'd just said. "That still doesn't explain why you're calling me about it now."

"Those scrolls we found, the rolled-up parchment. There's a chance they could be just as old, and if they are, I'd like to know what they say."

"What makes you interested in medieval manuscripts all of a sudden?"

It was a fair question, and one which he didn't feel at all comfortable answering over the phone.

"When are you meeting your teacher?"

Again he sensed a creeping uncertainty. "He's not there anymore. The head of the department sounded very nice and was actually very helpful, though. I read a few words out from what I'd photographed, and she said we could meet up tomorrow." Her hesitant speech finally ground to a halt.

"Karen," Chambers could sense her uneasiness, "what's the matter?"

"Promise you won't laugh?"

In this office, at this moment, he couldn't think of anything that would even raise a smile. "Absolutely."

"To be honest I was thinking about canceling it and chucking in the story. Since we met the other day I've been having these . . . horrible dreams. Like you wouldn't believe."

Oh, he could. "Try me," he said. "I promise I won't laugh, and I promise I won't make fun of you. You may find this hard to believe, but I've been having some dreams of my own. They're part of the reason I called you."

That got her attention. "What dreams?"

He shook his head. "You first."

And so, hesitatingly, haltingly, Karen began. The story she told was horribly familiar. The blood-red sky, the church, the army of the dead.

The thing waiting just inside the door.

"It's actually the real reason I'm still up," she said. "Please don't tell anyone, but it's getting so I'm afraid to go to sleep. I'm trying to bury myself in work, in anything but this bloody story, but I just can't stop thinking about it."

"Well now it's my turn to sound crazy." Karen's outburst had rendered him far more willing to talk. In fact it was a relief to speak his thoughts aloud. "I've been having the same nightmares you've just described. Exactly. Right down to the doors opening and that thing waiting inside." It was safe to tell her that much. In fact there was the chance it might save her life if the visions got worse. He didn't want to reveal too much about himself, though. Not just yet. He still wasn't entirely sure he could trust her. "This may sound weird to you right now but you don't know how good it's been to hear you tell me all of that. It means I might not be going nuts after all."

"Me too." Karen's voice sounded a little brighter now, and a little more relaxed.

"We need to get those manuscripts translated. Whether it's some sort of curse or demonic possession, or we just got a big dose of some weird hallucinogenic drug that no one's discovered before, our best chance of finding an answer is in those scrolls."

"Scroll—singular," said the voice on the other end of the phone. "I only took a picture of the one, remember?"

That was right. "Do you think your tutor would mind if I brought pictures of the other two along?"

"Can you?"

Of course he could. "I'll do my best," he said. "I take it you aren't going to mind me coming along with you tomorrow?"

"No." She sounded relieved, or at least a little part of him hoped so. "No, not at all."

"Great. And you can take me out for that dinner you offered me last time we met."

"That would be nice. And you can tell me everything about the tests you did on the bones."

He grinned. Having someone to share all this with was doing his mood no end of good. "I will, which makes me guess you've decided not to chuck the story yet?"

"Not just yet," came the reply. "Not now that I've just uncovered a very promising new lead."

How promising it would turn out to be, of course, remained to be seen.

FIVE

THE WEATHER IN OXFORD was terrible.

In Pelham College, the conifer trees that lined the quad were being buffeted by an angry wind, their normal uniformity blown out of tune like a discordant choir in which every member was slightly out of step with his neighbor. Chambers was permitted one more glimpse of the outside world through the beveled windowpane before a dark red curtain of heavy fabric was drawn rudely across, blocking out the gray daylight.

He heard the click of a switch, and the screen that had been set up was illuminated by the sterile light from the slide projector behind them.

"And you say no one else has seen these?"

The words came from behind them as well. Rosalie Cruttenden was Pelham's Reader in Medieval Studies and looked as if she had spent the majority of her fifty-plus years in the cloistered world of academia. Her tweed suit was a little too tight, as was the wiry gray hair that had been uncooperatively pulled into something resembling less a bun and more a cottage loaf. Her eyes remained bright and enthusiastic, however, and her voice was cultured, no doubt as a result of her background. It was also deep and rasping from far too many cigarettes. There was one in her hand right now, the smoke particles swirling in the projector's beam before drifting to become embedded with millions of their fellows in the books, woodwork, and plaster of the study's smoke-stained walls.

"No one who would be able to understand them." Chambers coughed. "Would you mind if we opened the window?"

"Oh, is it this?" She indicated her cigarette, and Karen joined him in nodding. "Sorry—I forget myself sometimes." She dropped it into the half-empty cup of coffee she had been drinking, where it extinguished itself with a hiss. Chambers hoped she didn't forget and drink from it later.

"Let's look at the first one, shall we?"

Dr. Cruttenden pressed a button and words filled the screen. Chambers had to give her credit—upon their arrival they had been taken straight to a state-of-the-art photographic department where the images had been transferred onto high-resolution glass slides. "That should allow us to get a really good look," Dr. Cruttenden had said as she'd taken them back to her study.

"How can you tell it's the first?"

It was obvious, really, but Karen was probably asking to be polite and—as is always most important when dealing with anyone in academia—to show interest in their subject.

"The document begins with this especially ornate drop capital." Dr. Cruttenden unsheathed a telescopic pointer and indicated the immense letter "T" that filled the top right-hand corner of the screen. "It was not unusual for texts of great worth and intended permanence to be decorated in this manner. A bit like royalty for language, if you like."

"So what does the title actually say?"

Despite their size, Dr. Cruttenden still had to peer at the letters. "A rough translation would be 'The Soothsayer's Tale.'"

"Soothsayer." Karen had her notebook out. "You mean like a fortune teller?"

From the way Dr. Cruttenden was shaking her head she obviously didn't. "Fortune tellers were the staple of traveling fairs, offering comfort, solace, and outright lies for the outlay of a few coins. The tradition of the soothsayer goes back to ancient Rome and quite possibly beyond that. An individual blessed—although many would say cursed—with the ability to foresee future events, good or ill. According to certain texts, these unfortunate individuals would often be haunted by the events they had predicted until those events took place."

"Or they went mad first—like Cassandra?"

Dr. Cruttenden flashed an encouraging smile Chambers assumed she usually reserved for her students. "Precisely, Professor Chambers. Now, let's see what the rest of this first page is about."

She adjusted the focus so that the blackened letters, looking more as if they had been forged in iron than with ink, stood out more boldly. She began to read through the text, mumbling to herself. At points the mumbling grew loud enough to pass for an attempt at a commentary.

"Much of what we have here is just setup for the story to come. The individual who is telling the tale claims that he is a man of God, by which the text means that he probably held some position in the church. He is on his current journey because of the visions which plague him, and which have plagued him 'since his inception,' which we can presume means birth. 'The solace of the Holy Father' apparently wasn't sufficient to stop the 'voices and demons which persisted in his mind' and so his church . . . no . . . more like a monastery actually—sorry—gave him permission to take part in this pilgrimage to . . ."

There was silence as Dr. Cruttenden stopped and stared, open-mouthed, at the screen. For a moment there was nothing but the sound of the window-glass being rattled violently. It was as if something immense and unseen was trying to get into that room. Was it Chambers's imagination or had it gotten darker?

Finally, it was Karen who broke the spell.

"Can you not read what it says?"

Dr. Cruttenden had presumably forgotten there was anyone else in the room. She abruptly turned around while lighting a fresh cigarette and blowing out the smoke straight at the word she had been staring at on the screen.

"No, my dear, I can read what it says perfectly. I just can't believe it, that's all."

Karen leaned forward in her chair. "Can't believe what?"

Dr. Cruttenden pulled herself up to her full five-foot four-inches, poked at the screen with her pointer, and said a single word.

"Canterbury."

Chambers's eyes widened. "You don't just mean as in 'Archbishop of,' do you?"

The Reader in Medieval Studies shook her head. "No, I most certainly do not. I mean as in *Tales*, as in Geoffrey Chaucer, as in—" she paused taking in the true possibility of the implication of the moment, "—the missing story from *The Canterbury Tales*."

Karen was busy writing it down. "Can you be sure?"

"Of course not. But what I can say is it's certainly worthy of further study. Which is what we are going to do right now. Let's move onto the next slide."

She pressed the changer and the screen was lit up with script that was smaller and more cramped. It was no less meticulous, but seemed a little more hurried than the previous page.

Karen leaned over to Chambers. "How did you get hold of that again?"

He still didn't feel confident enough to tell her the truth. Not yet, anyway. "I made up some story Malcolm had to believe about the bones possibly having some infection risk. I was convincing enough that he's had everything sealed until I can get a translation from our friend here."

"You must remind me to buy you an extra glass of champagne this evening."

"I'm glad you said *extra*."

"*If* you two have quite finished chatting—" the lecturer was back and wielding the pointer, "—we can start to take a look at this second page."

Karen and Chambers sat quietly while Dr. Cruttenden examined this new page of the manuscript. She mumbled much more quietly this time, and when she turned around to face them once more the wind seemed to have gone out of her sails somewhat.

"I am sorry to have to tell you that, after my initial enthusiasm, this document cannot be anything other than a hoax. A very good hoax, in fact a quite brilliant hoax, but a hoax nevertheless."

Karen's shoulders sagged and she put down her pen. "Why?"

"Because after a most promising beginning, with perfect period language and detail, whoever wrote this then goes on to have his soothsayer talk of things about which he could not possibly know."

Chambers frowned. "Such as?"

Dr. Cruttenden slumped into a worn but comfortable-looking armchair upholstered in red velveteen. She took a long drag from her cigarette before continuing. "Most scholars believe *The Canterbury Tales* to have been written sometime around 1380. Chaucer himself disappears from the historical record around 1400. It would therefore be the act of only the most supremely ignorant and stupid of individuals to include historical events such as 'crook-backed Richard III lying in defeat' which must refer to the Battle of Bosworth Field. That took place in 1485— pretty much a hundred years later. But then there's worse—we get talk of a 'Great Fire' that decimates London. That didn't happen until 1666. And as for the 'Worlde War to Ende all Wars' . . ."

She was already lighting another cigarette, despite the current one being only half-smoked.

Chambers was trying to keep up.

"So you're saying that this is a manuscript that is perfect in its language, in its font, and in its presentation."

Dr. Cruttenden nodded. Smoke billowed from her nostrils as she spoke. "To be honest, it's absolutely marvelous. Usually I can spot the fakes, but this one looks perfect in every way. I would have to look at the original manuscripts of course, and get some dating done on the paper this is written on, but otherwise it's quite remarkable."

"And it's called 'The Soothsayer's Tale'?"

Dr. Cruttenden laughed out loud now, most likely to cover her obvious disappointment. "It is, isn't it? I should have seen that coming, shouldn't I? Serves me right. Even when you've been in this business as long as I have you can still be taken in."

Chambers shook his head. "That's not what I'm getting at. Look, I'm a scientist in my own field as you are in yours. I can vouch that the bones that were found wrapped around that manuscript were easily six hundred years old, and possibly older."

Dr. Cruttenden shrugged but Karen was catching on.

"Doesn't it seem a bit weird that someone would go to all those lengths for a forgery, right down to finding some very old bones to help verify the story? Where the hell would they find old bones, anyway? And to go to such lengths just to write something that would get their overly elaborate plan dismissed by the first person who reads it?"

The lecturer gave them both a quizzical look. "I have no idea what either of you are trying to get at."

Chambers and Karen exchanged looks.

"Is it not possible," said Chambers carefully, "that what we've stumbled on here is a document from the fourteenth century that really does predict events that took place hundreds of years later?"

"You must think I'm an idiot, Dr. Chambers."

Chambers shook his head. "No, believe me, I don't at all, and I agree with you entirely that we need to verify the actual manuscript before we can start to draw any formal conclusions, but it is something to consider isn't it? Just as an outside possibility?"

"A frankly ludicrous possibility."

"But improbable rather than impossible?"

"I suppose that depends on how much daytime television you watch."

"He's right, Dr. Cruttenden." It was Karen's turn. "I know you won't listen to me because I'm just a journalist, but if Bob says those bones are six hundred years old then I believe him. Surely that hugely increases the odds of this being the real thing rather than someone somehow being able to fake it?"

There was a pause as Dr. Cruttenden blew more smoke heavenward. "If I thought you were wasting my time I would have already asked you to leave," she said. "However I do now feel that any more time that we expend on this could be better spent on other projects."

Chambers got to his feet and grabbed the remote for the slide projector. His finger hovered over the ADVANCE button that would bring up the third and final slide. "Could you please at least tell us what the end of the manuscript says? It might actually be important."

Dr. Cruttenden refused to shift her gaze from the ceiling.

"Please," said Karen. "We promise we won't bother you any more after this, and we certainly won't mention your name in connection with any of it."

"As I hope I have already made clear," Dr. Cruttenden still appeared to be addressing the roof, "I no longer wish to be a part of this charade. I hope you understand that if you were to mention my involvement, the subsequent lawsuit would definitely find in my favor. Now, are you happy to see yourselves out or do I need to call security?"

Karen was on the verge of getting out of her chair, but Chambers wasn't finished yet.

"Well I want to see what it says even if you don't," he said.

His thumb came down on the button.

And all hell broke loose.

Within a split-second of the words appearing on the screen, there was a thunder crack outside the building as loud as that in Chambers's dream, followed by a gust of wind so violent that it drove the rain against the windows like bullets.

But only for a second.

Because then the windows exploded inwards.

The drawn curtains did little to dampen the howling hurricane that followed. Instead, they flapped and billowed from the onslaught as if a pair of caped fiends was standing either side of the windows, presiding with glee over the ensuing chaos. Books fell from shelves, were flipped open, and had their pages torn from them by unseen hands. Other documents joined the defiled paper in the building tornado inside Dr. Cruttenden's study. The uncapped fountain pen on her desk rattled against the leather, was lifted into the air, and flew straight at her, narrowly missing its target and embedding itself in the upholstery as the lecturer dived to her right and covered her head with her hands.

A vase on the mantelpiece exploded, scattering lilies that were scooped up by the whirlwind. Other items adjacent to it followed—a glass bowl shattered, the door of a gilt carriage clock was torn off its hinges and the dial hands bent out of shape. A belch of flame erupted from the fireplace where no fire burned. It disappeared almost as quickly. Dust and crumbs of plaster began to fall from the ceiling as the building was shaken as if by a giant.

But that was not the worst of it.

The three of them crouched on the floor, arms over their heads as debris rained down upon them, as rain lashed at them, as objects were thrown at them. But such physical protection did not extend to their minds, and it was their minds that were the main object of attack.

The visions were terrible.

They were images of the events described on the final page of the document. Images of horror and despair, of disease and of chaos. They saw the thing that lived within the church, high on its hill beneath a crimson firmament. They saw it give life to things that should not live. But it was not real life, vivid and active, productive and colorful. This was the opposite— an un-life, a living death. The creatures that were vomited forth from the church were worse than diseased, more terrifying than pestilence, for they were not mere random, aggressive vectors of a terrible kind of death. They could think. They could reason. And they had a purpose.

There was a crash as the slide projector fell to the floor. It stayed switched on, the words now at an angle and displayed against the collapsing bookshelves, words of chaos causing actual chaos.

Chambers felt pain in his right hand. He looked at it and could scarcely believe that the rain was now hammering so hard and so viciously that the tiny razor-sharp droplets were capable of drawing blood.

Then he realized it wasn't the rain that was causing it at all.

Other things were now being swept into the room with the force of a hurricane. Thousands of them, in fact.

Maggots.

As a snowstorm of curling white dots they came, blasting across the room and coming to lie on the carpet, on the shelves, on the clothes of the three individuals crouched helplessly on the floor. They formed writhing heaps that quickly collapsed and added to the shifting sea that was beginning to build around them, an ocean of unending, voracious, wriggling hunger.

Chambers reached out and, ignoring the hundred tiny mouths biting into the skin on the back of his hand, grabbed the projector's electrical cord and yanked it with all his might.

It refused to budge.

He reached out with both hands, trying to ignore the fact that both were now streaming with blood, and tried again.

And again.

One last try, he thought, blinking away the crawling things that were trying to get to his eyes and spitting them from his mouth. *One last try and then we run for it.*

The cord came free.

There was an ear-splitting pop and flash from the toppled machine, and then the projector lamp dimmed.

Bob Chambers, Karen Shepworth, and Rosalie Cruttenden suddenly found themselves crouched on a perfectly normal carpet in the middle of a perfectly normal study. Outside, the storm had calmed.

The projector, however, was beyond repair. All that remained of it was a carapace of blackened plastic and some exposed wiring. The slides were gone.

Good thing too, was Chambers's first thought as he surveyed the damage and the scorched area surrounding it.

Karen was getting to her feet, while Dr. Cruttenden was still brushing frantically at her hair.

"It's all right," Karen said, laying a hand on the older woman's shoulder. "They're gone. It's all gone." She flashed a glance at Chambers. "Whatever it was."

The lecturer looked up at her with terrified eyes. "You saw it too?"

Karen nodded, but Chambers wasn't so quick to agree. "That all depends, Dr. Cruttenden," he said, helping her up and back into her chair. "What do you think you saw?"

She obviously wasn't eager to revisit the images. "Horrible . . . horrible. That church, those . . . things, and then the windows burst open and—" She got up and ran to the curtains, drawing them back with a savagery that surprised him.

Outside was an unremarkable gray Oxford day. The conifers in the quad were uniform once more, and the paving stones of the perimeter path weren't even damp.

Dr. Cruttenden backed away. "But it was raining!"

"We know," said Chambers.

"Pouring!"

"We felt it too," said Karen.

"And then the rain changed into . . . into . . ." She looked at the cracked remains of the projector. "It's ruined. You've no idea how hard it is to get equipment like that for my department."

Karen put an arm around her and led her back to her seat. "My paper will see that you're reimbursed, Dr. Cruttenden, don't you worry."

"Will it? Oh, thank you—most kind."

"Well, if nothing else we've learned one thing today." Chambers was pulling the curtains back fully to allow as much natural light into the room as possible. "Malcolm Turner has what might amount to a time bomb in the British Museum vaults."

Karen was crouched beside Dr. Cruttenden, holding the lecturer's quivering hands. "The manuscript, you mean?"

Chambers nodded. "Either it's just the last page, or a cumulative effect as a result of reading all three pages in order."

"But we didn't read them." Karen squeezed the older woman's hands. "Dr. Cruttenden did."

Chambers shrugged and spread his hands. "Well, we looked at it. Perhaps that's all it takes. I'm afraid I can't offer any scientific explanation, but then what we just witnessed wasn't very scientific."

"He was a sorcerer . . ." came a quiet voice from the chair.

They both stared at her.

"Who was?" Karen asked as gently as she could.

"Geoffrey Chaucer. I mean, he was a lot of other things as well, but it was rumored by the Royal Court of King Edward III—of which he was a member, I'll have you know—that one of his many activities involved the study of the arcane arts."

Karen raised an eyebrow. "I thought he was just a writer."

"So did I," said Chambers, drawing up a chair.

"If he had been just a writer, we would have known far less about him." Talking about her subject seemed to be the best way of calming herself, so they let her continue. "Writers were of little interest to those who kept the historical records of the times. However, someone who studied law at the Inner Temple, someone who was appointed Comptroller of Customs for the Port of London, someone who then went on to become Clerk of the King's Works and was responsible for various building projects including repairing Westminster Cathedral, now that is someone the historians considered worth taking note of."

"And Geoffrey Chaucer was all those things?" The revelation of these facts was proving as much a salve to Chambers's nerves as it was to Dr. Cruttenden.

"Oh, those and much more," she said. "He was extremely well-traveled, you know. In 1374 Edward granted him 'a gallon of wine a day for life' for services rendered. It's believed when Richard II came to the throne it was changed to cash but still, that would have been quite a lot of cash in those times."

"For services rendered?" Karen asked.

The lecturer patted her hand. "No one really knows, but at least one major voyage abroad—in 1377—was for reasons no one to this day has been able to ascertain."

"Maybe that was when he wrote *The Canterbury Tales*?"

She shook her head. "It's generally accepted he started work on them in the 1380s, after that voyage but before instigating the repairs on Westminster Cathedral."

"And initiating other building work as well, I should imagine." Chambers was looking thoughtful.

"Well yes, naturally."

"And that would have included other churches?"

"Yes, of course. Why?" A streak of fear crossed her face. "Oh. I see what you mean."

Karen looked worried. "You think the church we all saw might be a real place, then?"

Chambers thought so. "I'm almost certain of it, just as I'm almost certain that the documents we've just been looking at were created to warn us."

"Warn us of what?" Dr. Cruttenden started to tremble again. "Armageddon? Ragnarok? Some kind of impending apocalypse?"

"I don't know." *And I don't really want to find out*, Chambers thought. "Was there anything in the two pages you were able to translate to suggest where it might be?"

Dr. Cruttenden frowned, trying to concentrate.

"Here." Karen lit one of the lecturer's cigarettes and passed it over to her. "This might help."

"Oh, thank you." She took a deep drag and angled the exhaled smoke away from her two companions. "As well as the description of major world events that convinced me the document was a fake—I apologize about that, by the way—"

"No need," said Karen with a friendly smile.

"—apart from those there were several paragraphs describing fairly minor events, but all in the same place, an area called Blackheath." She looked at them. "I don't suppose either of you know anywhere with that name?"

"There's a Blackheath in London," said Karen.

"South London, I think." Chambers was tapping his chin. "And I'll bet there's at least one church there with a history of weird goings-on."

"There's bound to be." Dr. Cruttenden was up and searching her shelves. "It's not my field of course, but I'm sure that's the area where Nicholas Hawksmoor must have had some influence on church design. Or if not him then his acolyte, Thomas Moreby."

She found a heavy volume, took it down, and began to leaf through the pages. "The 1700s was one of the periods I studied for my undergraduate degree, many years ago now. If I hadn't settled on the medieval period that's probably what I would have gone for, although—" and here she chuckled to herself, "—I have to say that most periods in history have their appeal to me, except perhaps the twentieth century."

Karen and Chambers waited until she found the right page.

"Here we are," she said finally, pointing to a picture that caused all three of them to shudder. "It does rather look like the place, doesn't it?"

The black-and-white photograph that took up the top left-hand quarter of the page was old. A caption identified it as having been taken in 1901. The surrounding area was different—instead of a desolate plain there were buildings and crowded streets. But there was no mistaking the building, standing on the hill of Blackheath like some demented overlord watching those over whom it had power. Dark, silent, deadly.

"All Hallows Church, Blackheath." Karen read the words aloud but they still sounded like a whisper to Chambers.

"All Hallows." Dr. Cruttenden suppressed another shudder. "And there we are," she said, reading on, "I was almost right. It wasn't designed by Hawksmoor but by Thomas Moreby, his apprentice, in Hawksmoor's late Baroque style. The original building was destroyed by fire in 1850, but Moreby's undercroft and crypt designs remain, apparently. The rest of it was rebuilt in Portland stone with flying buttresses—presumably to help keep the thing propped up."

Karen was frowning. "The church I saw looked like that one."

"I think the church we all saw looked like that one," said Chambers.

"But that doesn't make any sense. If it was built in Victorian times, all those streets and buildings were probably already there. What I saw was much older."

"Or much newer," Chambers said, and suddenly wished he hadn't. "Much more in the future, if you like."

"'The Soothsayer's Tale,'" Dr. Cruttenden breathed as she closed the book.

Chambers took it from her and laid it on her desk. "You mean Chaucer wrote it to warn us?"

The woman shrugged. "Who knows? Wrote it, imbued it with some special power, and then hid it?"

"But why?" Karen was shaking her head. "Why hide it if he wanted to warn the world?"

"Maybe he didn't hide it," said Chambers. "Maybe someone else hid it. And him."

Dr. Cruttenden was nodding. "Despite every academic fiber of my being telling me I'm being ridiculous for harboring the notion, the same thought had occurred to me."

"What?" Karen asked, finally sufficiently recovered that her journalistic instincts were having her reach for her notebook. "Are you saying that what those boys found is an undiscovered story by Geoffrey Chaucer and that it was buried with his bones?"

"Either him," said Chambers, "or someone who lived and died during his lifetime."

"Or was murdered," Dr. Cruttenden added.

"Whatever," said Karen, "it's going to make the most brilliant story."

The others stared at her in disbelief.

"You can't be serious," said Chambers.

"I am serious." She was defensive now. "This is the most amazing story I've ever come into contact with, and it's mine. Surely you can't possibly think I'm not going to write about it?"

"But the danger!" spluttered Dr. Cruttenden. "We have to warn Professor Chambers's friend at the British Museum! Get him to lock those things away!"

"Or get them properly studied so that whatever apocalypse we are being warned about is averted." Karen was shaking her head. "Either way the public has a right to know, and no one can stop me telling them."

"I can." It was time to tell her. To tell both of them. Chambers reached into his pocket for his wallet. He took out his Human Protection League identification card and showed it to both her and Dr. Cruttenden. "By the power invested in me by the FBI I am asking you to not make this information public."

Karen peered at the badge and snorted. "Human Protection League? What the hell is that supposed to be?"

Chambers could tell this was going to be difficult. "I know you're going to have trouble swallowing this. Some people call us 'The Lovecraft Squad,' and the simplest way to explain it is that Hell is exactly what my department was created to protect the world from."

Now it was Dr. Cruttenden's turn to give a splutter of disbelief. "Dr. Chambers, what on earth are you going on about?"

He had both their full attention now, and he knew the next few minutes would be vital if he was to get them on his side. "There have been incidents like this before. Many of them, all over the world. Occasions when dark powers have tried to break through, evil forces that exist just on the other side of our reality and want to make this world their own." It wasn't working. "We could all be in grave danger!"

"Dark powers?" Dr. Cruttenden was shaking her head. "Evil forces?" Now she was turning away.

Karen wasn't, but if anything the look on her face was even worse. "I think you need to have a long lie down in a darkened room. And after that you should probably get on a plane back to where you came from. You may be able to fool your fellow Americans with this bullshit, but it won't work here."

"It's true." Chambers didn't know what else to say. "You can call Washington. They can tell you what kind of things we've been fighting against for almost the past sixty years!"

Karen raised a hand as if to slap him across the face, then seemed to think better of it. As she was making for the door, Chambers grabbed her wrist. "Think about it, Karen! Even if you haven't believed a word I've said, think about what just happened in this room, what might happen if you make all this public knowledge. Panic, mayhem, anything!"

"Or just possibly a nine-day wonder that sells a lot of papers before dying down. Papers with my name on every single article." She yanked her arm away. "No, I can't pass up this opportunity. It's too good. No one but the most eminent, sane, British experts deserve to examine those scrolls, and because of me they will get to examine them, rather than let them molder in some dusty old cupboard in Holborn." She glared at him. "I take it you don't want a lift to London?"

Chambers was shaking his head. "I think I'll make my own way back."

He didn't need to say it twice. Karen turned on her heel and was closing the door behind her when Chambers called after her.

"What if we were meant to find those scrolls? What if that was part of someone's plan?"

But Karen had already gone.

SIX

Monday, October 31, 1994

THE STORY BROKE ON Halloween.

To give her due credit, Karen had moved fast, faster than the bureaucrats in both Washington and Whitehall who might have been able to put a stop to it all. Chambers leafed through the morning paper, the *News of Britain*, going straight to the FULL STORY that had been promised on PAGES 3, 4, AND 5! by the headline. The front page had been enough to make him wince, with its screaming white on black of IS THIS THE REAL GEOFFREY CHAUCER? above one of the photographs Karen had taken when they had first met in the museum. Along with several million Britons that day, he had purchased a copy and thereby ensured that there would be more news about the find over the next week, and perhaps even longer than that.

Inside were more of the snapshots she had taken on that first day. Thankfully he wasn't featured in any of them. Neither were there any shots of the text of the scrolls, possibly because Karen had more sense, but more likely because the paper wanted to keep its readers in suspense. Instead there were tantalizing glimpses of the parchment, the silk threads that had bound them still intact.

Chambers rubbed his eyes and wished the seals had never been broken.

Perhaps he didn't wish it as much as Malcolm Turner, though. The phone call had come through to Chambers's hotel room at just after ten o'clock that morning. On the other end had been an angry director of the British Museum demanding to know how on earth "that bloody journalist" had been able to conjure up such a collection of conjecture and hearsay. In no mood to be shouted at by someone who was at least partly, if not wholly responsible for the whole mess, Chambers had answered calmly that the "bloody journalist" in question had been put in touch with Chambers by Turner himself, and that conjecture, hearsay, and outright lies were pretty much that newspaper's stock in trade.

"I had no idea she was going to be writing for . . . that!" had come the outraged response.

"I suspect she didn't either until it dawned on her that this was something she could sell to the tabloids." Chambers was trying hard to remember what the broadsheets had been carrying as their headlines and couldn't, which said it all, really. "I think she got lucky with a quiet news day. If I were you, I'd forget about causing a fuss and it should all blow over in a few days." He certainly hoped so.

Turner refused to be quelled. "And what if it doesn't? My secretary is already being inundated by demands to know what those scrolls show. If we get many more inquiries I may be forced to tell them."

Chambers gripped the receiver so tightly he heard it crack in his grasp. "Don't do that," he said, more strongly than he intended. It wasn't the best approach.

"Why ever not? Although I have to confess I don't really know what else to do. I'll have to show them sometime—there's really not going to be any way around it."

"You mustn't." Chambers had to convince Malcolm somehow. "Those scrolls need to be kept safe until I can get a team of experts to analyze them." Although heaven knew when that would be.

There was a pause. "My dear fellow, what on earth are you talking about?"

Chambers sensed cross purposes at work here, but he pressed on anyway. "The scrolls," he said. "I think it's best to keep them covered and sealed away until an appropriate team of experts can be assembled to decide what to do with them."

There was a hint of tired laughter in what Turner said next. "But that's my whole point! We don't have them anymore! At least not in any read-able form. Something happened to them three days ago."

Chambers had to repeat that in order to process it. "Three days . . ."

"Yes, when you were on that little jaunt of yours to Oxford with Miss Shepworth in tow. One of my technicians was transferring the first scroll to an airtight container when, according to her, it crumbled in her hands. When we checked the others, the same thing had happened to them as well."

Chambers didn't know whether to feel relieved or horrified. He ended up feeling a mixture of both.

"And that's not the worst."

"What was?" Chambers was already wishing he hadn't asked, but he had to know. Was the technician lying in a hospital bed somewhere now—dying of some hideous rotting disease and all the while mouthing apocalyptic predictions?

"The bones are gone too. Or rather, they're nothing more than dust. Can you believe that? All that time in the mud and it must have been acting as some sort of preservative. The air must have done for the bones in the same way it dissolved the scrolls."

That sounded ridiculous but Chambers wasn't tempted to tell him that.

"Mind you, neither I nor anyone I've discussed this with has ever heard anything like it, so I'd appreciate it if you'd keep it under your hat for the moment. I'm sure you now realize the problem I have."

Chambers knew only too well. The British Museum (and its potentially historically significant discovery) had made front-page news. And now they had nothing to back the story up with.

And, of course, neither did Karen.

Almost right away, the realization hit him that when she, and her paper, found out that Turner had nothing to show them, Karen would cite Chambers himself as the only one who could corroborate her story. Dr. Cruttenden had seen slides, but she hadn't seen the real thing, or the bones.

Media attention would swing very swiftly from Malcolm (who would claim not to have anything tangible to show) to Chambers himself, who would then find himself in the unenviable position of having to make a public statement on behalf of the Human Protection League. There was no way he was going to go public with what had happened to them in Oxford, much as Karen might want him to. Scenes of late-night talk shows filled his head, programs where he and Malcolm were pitched against each other—the British Museum director who didn't know how to look after relics and the American forensic pathologist who had seen crazy things after handling the items now apparently lost. It would all make fabulous trash television and any chance of it happening had to be stopped.

At least, he thought, the scrolls were gone. He had put the lack of nightmares over the last three nights down to his experiences in Dr. Cruttenden's study. Perhaps it was because the scrolls themselves were destroyed that he was being allowed to rest more easily.

Perhaps it was all over.

Or it might be just beginning.

Chambers started going through his pockets, hoping that he still had Karen's business card.

It was the first thing he found. Trying his best to ignore the idea that unseen forces had placed it in his hand, he dialed her number.

"I have to admit you're the last person I expected to hear from." Karen sounded confident, if a little shaken by the sound of Chambers's voice.

"I'm surprised you're at home." Chambers couldn't resist that. "I had assumed you'd be with the rest of them, trying to get Malcolm to show you the scrolls."

"I've the rest of this week's articles to get finished. I haven't time to bother with that right now," she said. "I think I managed to get quite enough to write about in Oxford that the British Museum can wait a while. I don't see him releasing them anytime soon, anyway."

"Or ever." Chambers told her what had happened. "I'm actually beginning to think that's why the nightmares have stopped."

"You too? I was hoping it was because I'd found something to keep myself busy. Nothing like working twenty hours a day to give you a really good night's sleep for the other four." She sighed. "I must admit I was hoping to get another look at them, something to round off the series of features the paper will be publishing over the next week. Now I'll have to try and find another angle."

"That's kind of why I was calling," Chambers licked his lips. "I was wondering if you might consider making whatever other angle you choose nothing to do with me."

Karen sounded amused. "I had no idea you were so scared of the Press, Professor!"

"To be honest with you, I don't know if it's the Press I'm scared of or just the events of the past few days. Either way I'd be grateful if you'd keep me out of it."

"Sure," she said, surprising him no end. "I promise I won't involve you again unless I really need to, but only on one condition."

"Which is?"

"Was all that stuff you told me true? About you being the member of some kind of crazy religious group that thinks it's defending the world against demons and other nonsense?"

Chambers couldn't resist smiling. Perhaps it would be better to let her believe that. But he couldn't. "We're not crazy, and we're not even religious, at least not in the way you mean. Our organization was created in the mid-1930s by J. Edgar Hoover himself to combat otherworldly invaders."

"This isn't convincing me. Why haven't I heard about any of this before?"

Chambers took a deep breath. "You will have, if you're a fan of weird fiction."

"I don't follow."

"Have you ever read H. P. Lovecraft?"

There was a giggle from Karen. "There used to be a shop near Leicester Square called that. I had one ex-boyfriend who wanted to buy me all sorts of pervy stuff from it. I told him I drew the line at the handcuffs and those weird leather mask things."

"Not Lovecraft as in a sex shop, I mean H. P. Lovecraft, the fantasy author."

"Fantasy author as in books?"

"Yes."

"Meaning fiction? As in stuff that's made up?"

This wasn't going the way he intended. "You know those four hours a night you've reserved for sleeping? Spend a bit of them reading his story 'The Call of Cthulhu'..."

"The call of whatahullu?"

He sighed and pronounced it for her. "Ka ... *thoo* ... loo. But as you do, just imagine the words to be true. He did make these things public, only they had to be dressed up as fiction or they would never have seen the light of day."

"Okay ..." From the hesitant tone of her voice it didn't sound okay at all, and it certainly didn't sound as if she was going to do what he'd said. Perhaps playing the crazy card would have been a better option.

"Just forget everything I've said, Karen. With any luck your story will do very well for you, I'll be able to go back to the States, and we can forget any of this ever happened."

He heard her sigh of relief as he put the phone down. For all he knew, it was all over. He'd call Washington in the morning. They'd probably ask him to stay another couple of days, just to make sure everything was blowing over. Then he'd be able to go home.

He truly hoped it was all over.

But of course, he was wrong.

WIN FOUR NIGHTS IN THE MOST HAUNTED PLACE EVER!

Creepier than Dracula's Castle . . .
More terrifying than The Overlook Hotel from *The Shining* . . .
More thrilling than any haunted house . . .
This place is scarier than all of them put together.
And it's REAL!

Do some REAL ghost hunting with a team of REAL experts—right here in the United Kingdom!

Yes, your great value *News of Britain* is giving YOU the chance to spend four nights inside All Hallows Church—the MOST HAUNTED place in the country!

Two lucky, lucky winners will join the *News of Britain*'s intrepid team of expert ghost hunters for one of the most intensive investigations into the paranormal ever performed! And YOU could be right there alongside them!

All you have to do for a chance to win is answer the trivia question we've set you below. Then either call our competition hotline number, or write your answer on the back of a postcard and send it to our usual address. Competition closes one week from today, after which the lucky winners will be notified!

Have a go! You KNOW ghosts are fun!

Here's the question: What is the name of the haunted hotel in the classic film *The Shining*?

SEVEN

ALL HALLOWS CHURCH.

Father Michael Traynor allowed the taxi that had brought him to this place to disappear down Blackheath Road before turning to face the building, almost as if he didn't want any witnesses to his entering it. Certainly there didn't seem to be anyone else around at this time on a Thursday morning—not even a jogger straying from the tried and trusted paths on Greenwich Common. But then there were enough stories about this church that all but the most foolhardy stayed away. Like the tale of those two boys last year who had disappeared. The whereabouts of one of them was still a mystery, and the other was undergoing psychiatric counseling that as far as he knew had so far been unsuccessful.

Father Traynor had wanted to arrive before the rest of them anyway. In fact he had been requested to, by powers he simply could not refuse. A distant clock tower chimed six as he hefted the heavy bags he had brought with him and approached the perimeter fence. The tower of the building in front of him remained silent—thirty feet of black Victorian stone, dead to the world and all its concerns.

No, he reminded himself, not dead. Not if what he had been told before coming here turned out to be true.

He had no reason to believe the stories he had been briefed with, other than that they had come from the highest authority the Catholic Church had as representation in the country, and that individual had received his instructions directly from the Vatican itself.

Father Traynor still found it difficult to believe that it had only been a week ago that he had been called into the office of Cardinal William Thomas, better known in most circles as the current serving Archbishop of Westminster Cathedral. The elderly man, resplendent in his scarlet robes of office, had bade his younger associate sit even though his attendants—two men also of advancing years and garbed in more restrained black vestments trimmed with scarlet cord—had not been granted such an honor; and while they addressed their Archbishop with all the respect due a man of his station, Michael could see they had nothing but jealous disdain for the little priest who had been permitted to sit in his presence.

"Father Michael," the old man's words were kind but firm, and his eyes betrayed the seriousness of this situation, whatever it was. "How long have you been with us?"

The priest had been unsure exactly what the Cardinal meant. "Do you mean Westminster, or the Catholic Church?"

"I mean, how long is it now since you were ordained?"

He had to think about that, not because he was unsure, but because it still seemed so recent that individuals like Cardinal Thomas still greatly intimidated him. He took a sip of water from the crystal goblet on the desk in front of him before answering.

"Five years."

The attendants' feathers were ruffled by that. It was all but imperceptible, but he had more than once been complimented by his educators on his empathic nature, and he could tell they weren't happy.

"Five years."

The Archbishop leaned back in his chair. The studded upholstery creaked with the sound of the finest and most expensive oxblood leather stretching gently. "And you have been with us in Westminster for just two of those, is that not so?"

Father Traynor nodded.

"In that case you may find the request I am about to make of you somewhat curious, but let me assure you this has been discussed among the highest and most eminent of our Holy Mother Church. And, after due meditation and consultation with Our Lord and the Most Holy Virgin Mother, it has been decided that you, Father Michael Traynor, are the one whom God has selected to take on a most challenging of burdens."

Traynor's mind was already racing as to what the request might be. He could not believe that he was being sent to a parish in the needy East End, or even further afield to Africa or South America. The attendants were too unsettled for that. Suddenly, and for no reason he could fathom, he was reminded of the parable of the prodigal son, with himself playing the role of the fatted calf. The opulence of his surroundings, the comfort of the chair, the fineness of the goblet from which he was drinking, the very attitude of the Archbishop himself made him wonder if this was all preparation for some extremely honorable, but nevertheless extremely unpleasant, undertaking.

Cardinal Thomas took a sip of the wine that had been poured for him. Then he fixed Father Michael with a steely gaze, and said three words.

"All Hallows Church."

An uneasy silence fell upon the room, made all the more so by Father Traynor's fidgeting as he tried to remember where he had heard that name before. Eventually, he had to give up trying and just sat in awkward silence, much to the delight of the two attendants.

"I take it you are not familiar with it?"

Traynor had assumed that was probably obvious by now. "I am afraid not, Your Grace," he said, trying to sound as humble as possible. It wasn't difficult.

"The Lord has an important task for you to perform at All Hallows Church, one that will require all of your courage, resourcefulness, and compassion for the poor souls destined to enter within its walls." The Cardinal had finished his glass of wine and was being poured another. He raised an eyebrow and repeated the offer he had made when the priest had entered the room. "Are you sure you would not like one?"

Yes, yes, he would love one, but that was all behind him now, and he was not about to succumb to temptation in front of the only man he had more respect and love for in the entire world other than Pope John Paul II himself.

"No thank you," he replied, praying that God would give him the strength not to be forcing the words out between gritted teeth. "But some more water would be most welcome."

The fatter of the two attendants—a Father Carlo—was awarded the unasked-for honor of refilling Father Michael's glass. His scowl remained concealed from everyone but the person for whom it was intended. Father Michael responded with the nervous smile he always employed in confrontations.

"All Hallows Church is in Blackheath, south London. It has an . . . *eventful* past." The Cardinal was sitting back again now, his fingertips touching to form a pyramid above which he regarded the young priest. "It isn't in use now. In fact it hasn't been in use for the past twenty years. A perimeter fence of barbed-wire five feet high surrounds it, and the gate by which the grounds may be accessed is secured with a heavy length of chain that I am reliably informed is so old the links have rusted and become welded together by the damp of twenty of our winters, followed, as surely as night follows day, by the heat of twenty summers. The key to the padlock is not locatable and the situation is likely to remain that way."

Traynor was intrigued, even if he was still not entirely sure why he was being told all this. "It's desanctified, then?"

The Archbishop nodded. "It was a more difficult ritual than one usually encounters in such cases, but the details of All Hallows' desanctification can wait for another time. We need you to go there."

That came out of the blue. "You do?" Traynor's response came haltingly and was immediately followed by "Why?"

"Do you read the popular newspapers?"

He didn't and he was quite proud of the fact. He didn't say that, though. Instead, he just shook his head.

"Then you won't be aware of this."

The Cardinal held out his right hand. His gloves were the same shade of scarlet as the rest of his garments. The thinner of the attendants, a

Father Daniel, handed him a copy of a tabloid newspaper which he proceeded to pass to Father Traynor.

"'Top Team to Enter Most Haunted Place in Britain.'" Traynor read the headline aloud, assuming that was what the Archbishop wished his attention drawn to. "Do they mean All Hallows?"

"They do indeed." Cardinal Thomas lowered his voice to almost a whisper, as if even he was a little embarrassed about what he was about to reveal. "All Hallows Church was a place of Catholic worship until the mid-1970s. It was eventually closed because of a number of incidents that had occurred in and around its location. What the Catholic church might describe as 'Significant Incidents,' taking place over the preceding one hundred and fifty years."

Traynor blinked. "One hundred and fifty years? You mean since—"

"Since the 1800s, yes, when it was rebuilt after a fire destroyed much of the main structure. The Victorians gave All Hallows a fine rebuild, but unfortunately even the very best granite and a series of priests dedicated to the care and protection of their parishioners couldn't prevent the terrible things that have happened there."

A twinge of fear clutched at Father Traynor's insides. "Terrible things? Like what?"

"It is . . . best you do not know." From the tone of his voice it sounded as if even Cardinal Thomas was reluctant to repeat the catalog of atrocities that must have taken place there. "Suffice to say that by the time the church was closed, a considerable amount of antireligious, and specifically anti-Catholic fervor had been fomented in the surrounding area." He leaned forward, his voice a dry rasp. "They thought it was *our* fault, you see. How could God exist in Blackheath if He allowed such terrible things to take place? How could His priests be so powerless? How could the Devil be so strong? They were dark times for our church in that part of London, dark times indeed, and it is only with the passage of time that such things have been . . . *mostly* . . . forgotten."

"These terrible things—" Traynor was still trying to imagine what they could possibly be, "—they stopped when All Hallows was closed?"

"And desanctified—yes. At least . . . for the *most* part. But the Church is worried that if people once again cross its borders and walk within its walls, the old troubles may be stirred up. There is also the concern that, somewhere within the building, perhaps even hidden within the undercroft or the crypt, there may be records, documents written by the priests who were brave enough to shoulder the heavy burden of responsibility of looking after that difficult parish."

The Cardinal paused there, both to take a breath and a further sip of wine. When Traynor made no indication that he wished to speak, the Archbishop continued.

"Can you imagine what a potential disaster it could be if those documents were discovered?" He pointed at the newspaper. "By people who write the kind of thing one can find in this . . . rag? It could prove very difficult for all of us. Very difficult indeed."

Father Traynor looked at the newspaper, then he looked at the Archbishop again. The attendants were smiling now. Obviously they had not been privy to the plan Cardinal Thomas had for him.

"You want me to go to All Hallows?"

The Archbishop tapped the newspaper with a finger sheathed in red silk.

"You haven't read closely enough, have you?"

Traynor picked up the newspaper and began to read in earnest. Following the amazing discovery of what was being postulated as the missing story from Geoffrey Chaucer's *The Canterbury Tales*, as well as bones that could well be the actual remains of the writer, lawyer, minister, and member of the court of King Edward III, a team had been assembled to investigate what many believed to be the most haunted place in Britain, if not the world.

The scrolls on which the story had been written were in the care of the British Museum, which was still declining to comment at this stage. However, thanks to the tireless efforts of journalist Karen Shepworth (Father Traynor couldn't help noticing it was her name on the byline as well), many of the salient points of the story, entitled "The Soothsayer's

Tale," had been obtained and verified thanks to the assistance of sources at Oxford University who preferred to remain anonymous. Many of the events described in the tale centered around the area of Blackheath in general, and the site where All Hallows Church would eventually be built in particular. It was even rumored that the tale, which could not have been written later than the year 1400 (the presumed year of Chaucer's death, or possibly even murder), described All Hallows Church itself, and predicted some of the terrible events it had been witness to over many decades.

Since the scrolls were not available, and were not likely to be made so for some considerable time, according to officials at the British Museum, the "Brave and Enterprising" *News of Britain* had therefore decided to launch a detailed investigation into the place "The Soothsayer's Tale" had described as playing a key role in the country's future.

A team consisting of the paper's very own investigative reporter Karen Shepworth, a parapsychologist, a scientist, an expert on Medieval English studies, a priest, and of course the two lucky winners of the paper's "Win Four Nights in the Most Haunted Place Ever" competition, would be taking part in the biggest ghost-busting investigation ever to be covered by a major newspaper.

The team would enter the church on Thursday, the 22nd of December and would remain inside for four days and four nights, emerging on Boxing Day morning to exclusive press and television coverage from the *News of Britain* and the Stratus TV Channel, both members of the Bromsey Group of Companies. Each member of the team had been profiled in detail in the paper's special "Ghostly Pull Out" section.

"It would probably be in your interest to take a look at that too." He waited for Traynor to find the right pages and read through them. When he got to the relevant part, the Cardinal chimed in with an explanation.

"We could not allow such an expedition to take place without one of our own being part of it," he said. "And so, once we had learned that this . . . investigation was to take place we contacted the appropriate bodies and explained that it would be only right that a member of our Holy

Mother Church be present on what used to be God's sacred ground." He gave a tiny chuckle. It was the first real expression of emotion Traynor had seen him betray since the meeting had begun. "Can you believe they hadn't actually thought of including a priest in their group? We were told some nonsense about how we had not been approached because 'it was assumed that the Catholic Church would not wish to be associated with a publicity stunt' and that 'All Hallows has not been a place of worship for at least twenty years anyway.'"

·"I must confess," Traynor said, finally finding his voice again, "in all my time as a member of the priesthood, which I appreciate has been nowhere near as long as your many years of devotion, I have always understood that our Holy Mother Church prefers not to involve itself in events such as this."

The Cardinal nodded. "In most cases, ninety-nine percent of them in fact, that would be true. But, as I hope I have already explained, All Hallows Church is a special instance. A very special instance indeed."

Traynor frowned before he could stop himself. He didn't feel as if anything had really been explained to him at all.

"So you wish me to join the team investigating All Hallows Church?"

"We do."

"And you wish me to keep you informed as to how their efforts are progressing?"

The Cardinal shook his head and tapped the newspaper again. "If you read on you will see that, as part of their 'show,' the *News of Britain* has decreed that you will all be sealed inside the church for the four-day period. You will not be able to communicate with us, nor with anyone else from the outside world, during this time."

"So . . ." Traynor was still unsure of his brief. "What do you want me to say when we come out?"

"Nothing controversial, obviously, but I am sure we can all trust you to be sensible about that. To be honest, it's not how you behave when you emerge that is of concern to us, but more the activities you undertake once you are inside."

"Inside? Am I to offer succor to the other members of the team?"

"If you feel it appropriate, but the most important task with which we, and therefore our Holy Mother Church, and therefore God, are charging you is to make sure no member of this team finds anything that might bring us into disrepute."

Traynor's throat had dried up again. He took another sip of water and wished dearly that it were something stronger.

"What kind of things are you concerned they might find?" he asked.

"Images, writings, the documents I mentioned earlier. When All Hallows was desanctified, a group of our Holy Brethren was charged with the searching of the place. Unfortunately, due to tragic events that befell two of them, their efforts remained peremptory at best. A further visit was planned, but it was difficult to recruit individuals willing to go there. Their faith simply wasn't strong enough." He gave the priest a steely look. "I trust that is not going to be a problem here?"

Father Traynor had no idea. "I hope it will not be, Your Grace," he said, as honestly as he could. "I will pray for humility, and for the strength to be guided through the task our Church has considered me fit for. I can do no more than that."

"Nor can any of us." Cardinal William Thomas seemed pleased. "One final thing. Should you yourself discover anything of a . . . controversial nature, it is the wish of the Church that it be destroyed by you, and before you leave that place. Is that understood?"

After years of faithful devotional service, Father Michael Traynor suddenly realized he had never felt so unsure of anything in his life. "Are you certain, Your Grace? Should I not bring it back here so that it might be studied by our scholars?"

That was not the correct answer. Cardinal Thomas's expression darkened to the point where the color of his face began to resemble his garments. "On no account must you bring anything out of All Hallows Church." His voice was quivering now, more than Michael's had been earlier, in fact. "Except, of course, yourself—alive and well and with nothing to report to anyone who might ask you questions when you emerge. I hope that is understood? It would be a shame to lose such a promising young member of our Westminster priesthood because such simple instructions could not be followed."

Traynor gulped and nodded. "Of course, Your Grace. I understand perfectly. I will join the team, destroy anything I find, and anything that they find too. On Boxing Day morning I will say that all is well and that, through the protection of God and our Holy Mother Church, those under my care were seen safely through this most Holy of festivals."

"That all sounds splendid." The Cardinal seemed satisfied. "It is almost as if God himself has placed the words in your mouth, just as he has placed the thoughts in your heart."

"And then I presume you wish me to come back here and tell you what I found?"

"That will not be necessary. What is necessary is for you to swear on the Holy Cross that you will never tell a single living soul of any of the events you witness, or items that you or others may find, within the confines of All Hallows Church."

"Never?"

"No."

"Not even you?"

"Not even me. We will, of course, all be praying for you while you are in there, but everything that happens to you inside All Hallows Church during those four days will be a matter for you to resolve with Our Lord in the fullness of time."

The Cardinal stood, and his attendants moved aside to allow him to come around to Father Traynor's side of the desk. "Have faith!" he said with a smile. He laid a comforting hand on Traynor's shoulder. "You have been chosen by Our Lord for a most important task, as was Saul of Tarsus who became St. Paul on the road to Damascus. Do not underestimate how valuable our Holy Mother Church considers you to be. There are few who would agree to this heavy burden. We will all be praying for you."

There was nothing Father Michael Traynor could do other than give his Archbishop a weak smile and promise that he would do his very best.

That had been a week ago.

Now, after seven days of prayer, contemplation, and numerous unsuccessful attempts to rid himself of self-doubt that had, in the last twenty-four hours, escalated into mounting terror, here he was, standing outside All Hallows church at six o'clock on a freezing December morning.

This, too, had been part of the Cardinal's instructions. He was to ensure that he was the first to arrive, the first to break the chains that held the rusting iron gates together, the first to step inside the place for nearly twenty years. It was a task he had been anticipating with nothing other than a gnawing horror that clutched at his insides every time he contemplated it.

Of course, it hadn't helped that, in order to prepare himself for his task, he had thought it best to familiarize himself with the history of Blackheath in general and All Hallows in particular. The Catholic National Library in Hampshire had nothing on the place. Neither did the other libraries he and his fellow priests were allowed access to.

A couple of local Greenwich libraries did, however.

They had been the last resort, a final desperate attempt to glean more about the place where he was to be locked in for four days and four nights with only six other people, none of whom he would likely have anything in common with. It was there, among stacks of dusty books and crumbling box files, that he found them.

Considering they were from a time when newspaper articles were meant to be more about reportage and less about sensationalism, the stories were still pretty horrific. Too horrific, in fact. Many were hearsay, scraps of stories gleaned from those who had lived in the area all their lives and had lost friends and loved ones in the catastrophes that had befallen those who ventured too close to the church "when the stars are right" as one old woman had put it.

There were the usual stories of strange noises or lights coming from the building, but it was the details in some of the tales that had caused his fingers to tremble and his mouth to turn as dry as the paper he was holding by the time he had finished the articles. A strange, luminous hopping thing with flesh whiter than moonlight that had been seen amid the gravestones on summer nights; horrible sounds that seemed to come from deeper than the church foundations could possibly go; a multitude of twisted human-like creatures seen simply in silhouette and from a distance, their shambling march stopped only by the boundary wall that had apparently been constructed with the purpose of keeping things in rather than others out.

For the few tramps who had dared spend the night near the church's walls the story remained the same—they were invariably found dead come the morning, their eyes opened wider than any normal man's, the orbs bulging from their sockets, "as if something had tried to suck them out" to quote a local publican of the time.

There were other stories too. Worse stories, concerning things Father Michael wished he had never read, so deeply embedded had they become in his consciousness. These were the tales he did not wish to revisit, even though he had been forced to for the two sleepless, nightmare-ridden nights he had had to endure since he had read about them.

Only the Cardinal's parting words had stopped him from picking up the telephone to let them know he wouldn't—no, *couldn't*—go. If he failed in this, if his anxious nature got the better of him and stopped him from embarking on this task which the Lord had set him, then what kind of a priest was he? And worse, what kind of a man was he?

If he failed in this, he would consider himself to have failed in life. And then there would be only one way out.

There he stood, before the building that, until a week ago, he had never known existed. Now he wished it had never been built.

In his right hand was a suitcase containing his personal effects and changes of clothes. In the left was a heavier, sturdier bag of deep brown canvas held together with a number of straps. This contained equipment and tools his seniors had considered to be essential to aid him on his journey. He knew there were crucifixes, bottles of holy water, altar cloths, and other items sacred to his religion. There were also five canisters of lighter fluid and several boxes of matches, in case he came across anything that needed to be destroyed leaving no trace. There were other items, too, and he had not yet had the chance to see what they were as the bag had been in the taxi that had been sent to collect him at five o'clock this morning. The bulkiest item in there, however, was a sturdy set of bolt cutters. From the look of the heavy rusted chain that was coiled between the iron bars of the church gate, he was going to need them.

He gave the gate a shove. It refused to budge even an inch. The light from the flashlight he had taken from his pocket and another, heavier push revealed that the metal of the gate had not become welded to the snaking chain solely by the elements. It was stuck solid to the gate-stops embedded in the flagstones at his feet as well. Even if he could get the chain off, he wouldn't be able to open the gates without the aid of a battering ram.

Father Traynor sighed. Perhaps this, too, was a sign from God? Perhaps the most important sign of all? The one telling him not to go in there, the one that, if he did not heed it, would lead to his certain death and eternal damnation?

To his left, the barbed-wire fence that had been erected on his side of the boundary wall creaked in the chill morning breeze, the blackened points of lethal tetanus-dosing steel just visible in the orange glow from the street lamps. The stonework adjacent to the gate had crumbled sufficiently that it might be possible to squeeze through, and definitely possible if he used the bolt cutters.

If you don't do it now, the others will when they get here, a voice warned him. *And they'll wonder why you didn't when you had the bolt cutters and, as far as they are aware, you volunteered to accompany them on this ordeal.*

He reached down, and unzipped the canvas bag. He rummaged around inside until the cold metal of the bolt cutters met with his searching fingertips. The handles were colder than he expected them to be and the sudden shock made him gasp, his breath steaming before him in the lamplight.

They were heavier than he expected as well, and he had to use both hands to get them out of the bag. It was a struggle to fit them around the top strand of wire, and even more difficult to orient them so they would cut, but eventually, after a lot of straining, he managed it.

He had thought the strand of barbs would snap as he cut through it, but instead the broken ends flopped limply to the ground with barely a sound, all resistance gone out of them many years ago. The strand below had a little more fight in it, and he had to twist the bolt cutters more savagely to make the wire finally break. One more, and there was enough space for him to clamber through.

Father Traynor threw his bags across the gulf of crumbling stone. That was what the black outline of the collapsed segment of wall made him think of. A gulf, a barrier of nothingness between the normal, natural world outside, and whatever it was that was waiting within the rotten edifice that lay before him.

The bags landed with a dull *thump* on the other side. An early morning mist had gathered during his efforts, and now the graveyard was wreathed in a low-lying fog. He could just make out where the bags were, but he would have to hurry if he wasn't going to lose them.

He placed a hand on the wall on either side of the gap. The stone felt clammy in the early morning chill, the surface gritty beneath his quivering palms. He could feel something else as well, something more than just the moisture from the dew. It was sticky, and as he pulled his left hand away the lamplight caught the outline of numerous slime trails, glistening orange in the artificial light. Without thinking, he wiped his hand against his coat before realizing he was just going to have to put his hand there again if he was going to get across.

Get on with it, then.

He could already feel his nerve failing and he wasn't even inside the church boundaries yet. He gripped the walls again and took his first step. His right foot landed somewhere within the gulf, the fallen stones beneath his shoe rocking back and forth as he tried to find a firm surface. When he saw there was none he leaned back, balancing all his weight on his left foot, and then vaulted himself across. At the last minute, he felt something grab at his leg and he almost went sprawling as he landed in the graveyard. He recovered his balance and caught his breath, coughing to clear the gritty feeling at the back of his throat. Was it his imagination or was even the air of a different quality on this side of the wall?

He looked for the bags. They had landed close to the wall, somewhere to the right, and in the direction of the church. But the mist had thickened now, and he could no longer see them. It felt as if he was standing on bare, hard-packed earth and, as he took a step forward, his foot caught in what he presumed was a tree-root, even though the landscape before him appeared bereft of vegetation apart from a skeletal apple tree he could just make out in the far distance, beyond the heavy buttress that was propping up the left-hand wall of the building.

Between him and what he hoped was a tree were the graves.

He hadn't been able to see them from the road, so small were the stones and many of them so low lying. Now they revealed themselves, teetering stone heads rearing in the mist, poking through the carpet of fog that was failing to conceal them. He was tempted to examine a few, to see how recent the newest grave was, but he reminded himself that he had been charged with getting into the church before the others arrived.

Somewhere inside the canvas bag was the heavy iron key that would open the main door. If that didn't work, he had been told there was a separate side entrance on the right. In case the key for that didn't work, he had been assured it could easily be forced using the crowbar they had also given him. He hoped it wouldn't have to come to that.

But first, the bags. He took a step to his right, something brushing over his foot and scuttling away as he did so. He pointed the flashlight at the ground and, leaning over, swept at the mist with his free hand.

Nothing.

They had to be here! This was where he had seen them fall! He coughed again, what he was breathing feeling more like smoke than air. It didn't smell like smoke, though.

It smelled of the dead.

Stop thinking like that, he told himself. *It's just earth, that's all. Earth and rotting grass and the damp stirring everything up. Now get back to looking for those bags.*

They were still nowhere to be seen.

He widened his search, even though he knew there was no way they could have fallen this far from the wall. To his right All Hallows Church loomed, its beckoning shadow inviting him to search within the blackness of the mantle it cast over the ground close by.

Perhaps he had miscalculated? Or maybe the ground had been slippery and the bags had slid farther away? The beam of his flashlight began to flicker and he started to panic. If he had to wait until sunrise, the others would be here and how ridiculous would he look then? He kicked at the ground and looked over at the teetering headstones to his left.

Was it his imagination, or were they now nearer?

Stop thinking like that.

He turned around to face the church once more. The towering black, monolithic outline seemed almost to be defying him. *You're never going to survive this ordeal,* it seemed to be saying. *Not if you can't even get inside the building.*

His search became more frantic. He started again, back at the boundary wall and the torn fence he had pulled apart. He traced the trajectory of the bags once more, one step at a time.

Nothing.

They had to be here!

Father Traynor took a step back, took a step closer to the church, closer to the shadow cast by the church.

Suddenly, just as he imagined he could see something through the distant mist, the ground gave way beneath his foot and he fell, striking his head on something. The shadow of All Hallows Church embraced him, and then everything was darkness.

memo

From: His Eminence Cardinal William Thomas, Archbishop of Westminster Cathedral

To: The Office of the Secretary to His Holiness Pope John Paul II, and subsidiary members of The Vatican Advisory Committee on The Incidents at Blackheath

Most Holy Father and Fellow Brethren,

The priest has been despatched with God's blessing. As we discussed, I still believe it to be highly unlikely that we will hear from him again. It is therefore my sincerest hope that all of you in Vatican City will join me in praying for his safe passage, at least until he is able to locate that which I have charged him with destroying. We live in trying times. Few things are sacred, and little can be kept out of the watchful eye of the media. That attention should have been drawn to All Hallows Church is regrettable, but it is my hope that the matter will be dealt with appropriately.

They will be inside that place for four days.

Surely no one will be able to survive in there for that long?

I remain your most humble servant,
William of Westminster

EIGHT

NOT QUITE DARKNESS.

Not quite.

Father Michael Traynor lay in the damp silent black for several minutes before he realized that he was still conscious, that he was still breathing, and that the overbearing might of All Hallows Church had yet to consign him to the hell he had been convinced he was destined for.

Not quite darkness.

But certainly different.

When he opened his eyes again, the cemetery was not as he remembered it, but then neither was the world. The landscape he now beheld possessed an eerie green glow, a dull emerald sickness that tainted the lightening sky as well as the land that was gradually being revealed by the dawning rays of a pallid sun.

He placed his palms against the ground, ignoring the chill feel of the earth beneath his skin, and levered himself upright.

Something was wrong.

Horribly wrong.

The mist that swirled about his feet seemed too thick to be the ordinary moisture of a chill winter's morning. The breeze that blew was tainted with the slight but bitter stink of corruption as it assailed his nostrils. It wormed its way to the back of his throat and hung there, tickling a little, causing him to cough, the mucus that was expelled into his mouth tasting even worse. It was as if he had swallowed something rotten, a thing of flesh that had been long in the grave, that had tried to rot to a dry nothingness, but had been prevented from doing so by the very mist that was plucking at his trouser legs.

Father Traynor spat, trying to rid his mouth of the taste of wet, long-dead flesh. But no matter how hard he tried, and how raucously he coughed, the actions just made the taste more intense.

What was happening?

He took a step out from the shadow cast by the steeple. Then another, and another.

If he craned his neck he could see the moon above him now, a distorted clown's face of painted silver, smeared by the inky darkness of a cloud covering its lower half, like a surgical mask for the undead. The moon, too, held a greenish tinge, as if the sky itself was wasted and sick.

He must be dreaming.

Then wake up! he told himself, running his hands over his face in the hope that when he uncovered his eyes again the world would be back to normal.

Instead, it was worse.

Ahead of him stretched the cemetery, the gravestones leering at him through the mist, seemingly jostling each other in their efforts to move, to get closer to him, to smother him with stone, encase him in granite and bury him alive beneath engraved sarcophagi, their epitaphs to those long gone from this world marking the passing of many others, but not him. Never him. Even if someone were eventually to find his body, crushed beyond recognition, flattened into the mud by the weight of a hundred of them, he would be unrecognizable, denied the Christian burial he needed and banished forever to spend eternity in a purgatory somewhere like this.

Somewhere like this.

He coughed again, the rancid taste in his mouth and nostrils even stronger now. A thought struck him, one so awful in its implication that he barely dared give it further consideration. And yet it was impossible not to. Was that what had already happened? Had that fall killed him? Had he fractured his skull? Broken his neck? Was his body in an ambulance right now, hapless paramedics working frantically to bring him back, pushing air into his lungs, trying to get his heart pumping?

A noise distracted him up ahead, close to the stunted, twisted tree he had seen on his way in. A grating, jarring noise, like two heavy surfaces grinding against one another.

Like the sound of stone against stone.

The gravestones seemed nearer now. In fact, it was almost as if they were moving, shifting slowly from side to side.

Or were being shifted by what was beneath them.

Panic gripped him and he was rooted to the spot. He rubbed his eyes but that only made things worse because it confirmed that this was no optical illusion. The gravestones were being moved, were being pushed up from below. Before his terrified gaze, to his left a monolith ten feet tall fell over with a muffled thump, revealing dirt-stained fingertips clawing at the air, ragged nails chipped and torn from the effort of scrabbling at the imprisoning stone. Elsewhere, smaller upright markers were being pushed until they toppled, while their flatter, broader counterparts were being lifted aside. In the middle distance, the memorial marker to a family of four was being raised sufficiently high so that Traynor could see three pairs of rotting adult hands, and one pair of tiny infant hands, attempting to work their way out.

With infinite slowness, the dead began to rise, bringing with them the accoutrements of the long-deceased. Ragged, hairless corpses pulled themselves free of the crumbling earth, their skulls gleaming in the unearthly greenish light. Scraps of muscle and clothing still adhered to the limbs of some and the ribcages of others, but the occupants of this graveyard had been here a long time and there was very little left that was not bone. Despite this, maggots tumbled from every orifice—from eyeless sockets, nasal cavities, from ear canals and mouths from which the lower jaw had long been dislocated and lost. Earthworms disturbed from their slumber wriggled free from these feeders of flesh, dropping in long, undulating coils to the ground and seeking the darkness from which they had been so rudely disturbed. Beetles fell with them, shiny black jewels that scuttled and vanished as the moonlight struck them.

Traynor tried to move, but fear held him in its grip as each and every burial plot gave birth to a twitching, crumbling creature. Some were missing arms, others legs. The final corpse to clamber forth was a semi-humanoid remnant of a human being that possessed neither arms nor legs. Once it had finally burrowed its way through the surface and, almost free of its prison of earth, toppled to one side to remain half-in, half-out of the place that had been intended to contain it forever, Father Traynor found himself faced with over a hundred of the undead.

Who then, as one, turned to look at him.

There was a horrible creaking noise as they did so, the sound of a hundred skulls grinding against a hundred dry vertebrae, all support and lubrication of the neck joint long since gone, leaving a treacherous and painful-sounding balancing act.

Father Traynor tried again to lift a foot, but it was useless.

The dead remained where they were.

Something else was happening now, though. As well as spiders, beetles, and countless wriggling things with no legs at all, something else was falling from the rotting corpses, something so fine as to resemble carmine dust in the moonlight.

But dust did not have a life of its own.

Dust did not crawl; dust did not jump.

Dust did not hop with purpose toward the spot on which Father Traynor was rooted.

Fleas.

Thousands of them.

Like a storm of crimson snow, a swirling mass of tiny bodies bounded toward him, gaining numbers as it did so. And now the maggots and worms and other crawling creatures were following in the wake of this living tempest, this pestilential swarm that had been buried for centuries and had only now been brought to the surface.

As one they jumped, as one they crawled, as one they squirmed. Soon it was difficult to tell the individual bodies apart as they came, from left and right and far in the distance, congregating before the terrified priest. Congregating, and coming to a halt.

As more of them arrived, they jumped and crawled on top of those already there. Soon a teetering pile of writhing parasites stood before Traynor—two feet of squirming, wriggling creatures, none of whom showed any desire to leave the companionship of their pestilent brethren.

Three feet.

Four.

Now the mound of seething activity was as high as Traynor's chin and still it grew, beetles upon grubs, spiders crowned with fleas, maggots entwined with earthworms. Still the mound grew.

And began to take on a shape.

Before Father Traynor's disbelieving gaze the mass of living horror not two feet away from him began to organize itself. A pair of outpouchings two thirds of the way up became rudimentary arms. The lower half of the mound split in two, the gap between giving it the appearance of shimmering legs. At the top, a protuberance swiftly rounded itself into a head that stretched itself a little lengthways before developing a broad mouth, a Roman nose, broad-set eyes.

And this *arthropodal homunculus* was not yet finished. The creatures were now reconstituting themselves so that it seemed that the figure standing before Father Traynor was wearing clothes. Not modern-day clothes, however. The man before him appeared to be clad in garments perhaps two hundred years old or more. A greatcoat with heavy cuffs cut to hang open and reveal the buttons of the waistcoat beneath. Was it his imagination or were the maggots coiling at his wrists intended to resemble lace cuffs and, on his head, not hair, but worms coiled into the semblance of a Regency wig?

Father Traynor knew he had to be dreaming now, or dead, or both. Even so, nothing prepared him for when the ungodly apparition before him opened its mouth and began to speak.

"You transgress."

Its voice sounded like something that had been underwater for a long time, the larynx folded in on itself, the vocal cords gone to rot.

Traynor coughed and tried to say something himself. Something apologetic, something humble, but the words would not come.

"Why are you here?"

Traynor tried again, and failed again, to speak.

The thing (he could not think of it as a man) took one step forward. It was a weird, ethereal, shimmering movement, catalyzed by the creatures of the earth, but it was obvious now that they were slaves to this monster's will.

"I asked you a question, sir."

The last word was spat out, along with a centipede that dribbled over the thing's lower lip and scuttled away to contribute to some lower part of its anatomy.

Struggling, almost choking, Traynor finally found his voice, although it was as if he had little control over the words that finally emerged from between his lips.

"There are others coming . . . four days . . . inside the church . . . I must . . . protect."

"Oh, must you indeed?" The thing took another step forward. Now it was so close he could see the eyes—tiny black ladybird-like beetles balancing on top of broader, blue-shelled relatives. The eyelashes were the spiny limbs of harvestmen, the lids rolled maggots that twitched and squirmed to give the semblance of blinking.

"Tell me . . . have they yet found the scrolls?"

Traynor, too paralyzed with fear to shake his head, or shrug, or do anything, tried once more to find words.

"I . . . don't . . . know."

The thing of worms and fleas appeared to be thinking for a moment.

"They must have," it said, eventually. "Which means the heavens are almost aligned. All this waiting and soon the time will be upon us again." The thing looked him up and down, the movement of its head causing a handful of tiny white larvae to become dislodged from its crown and go tumbling to the ground. They rapidly made their way back to the thing's feet. "You are a minister? Of the Catholic faith?"

It was a Herculean effort, but the priest was finally able to summon the strength to nod.

"Excellent!" The thing raised an arm. Worms and beetles fell as a rudimentary finger pointed over Traynor's shoulder. "I have need of a representative in there, someone who can ensure that nothing untoward is disturbed . . . until the time is right." Its centipede lips stretched into what passed for a smile. "Congratulations. I do so appreciate a willing volunteer."

The outstretched hand fell to Traynor's shoulder. At its touch, the fingers became detached, and the earwigs that had formed them began roaming over the material of his black priest's gown, seeking ways to penetrate beneath the material and be one with his flesh. One found its way in down his neck, another between buttons. Still more made their way down his sleeve and up the arm beneath. A piercing agony seared his flesh as each of the creatures made contact with his skin, their hooked legs burrowing into the tissue, burying themselves beneath the subcutaneous fat, hooking onto his nerves and causing almost unendurable pain.

"Remember . . ." said the thing, already coming apart now that its job was done. ". . . I shall be watching you."

Father Traynor fell to his knees, his arms over his head. There was nothing he could do but scream and scream and scream.

He was still screaming when he woke up.

Damien Childs: [M.S. CAMERA 2] And that was Sam with the weather. Nice to know it's not going to be too chilly over the Christmas period.

Emma Byfield: [M.S. CAMERA 3] But I wanted snow! I think we all want snow at Christmas really, don't we? [C.U. Camera 1] But seven people in particular are probably going to feel very relieved that the weather over the next few days is going to be mild, although who knows if that's going to keep the ghosts away? [back to Camera 3] All Hallows Church in Blackheath, London, has long been considered a place of spooky happenings and ghostly sightings. Many local people believe it to be haunted and now, in one of the most in-depth and prolonged paranormal investigations ever, a team of seven experts is going to spend the next four days and nights locked inside the church in the hope they get to witness some demonic goings-on.

Damien: [C.U. CAMERA 2] I'm not sure if they're going to be hoping for ghosts or just be relieved when they don't find any. But it's not strictly seven experts, is it, Emma?

Emma: [C.U. CAMERA 1] No Damien, that's right. Two of the group are the lucky winners of a competition run by the newspaper the *News of Britain* to spend four days in the most haunted place in the country! I wonder if they're regretting their choice now?

Damien: [M.S. CAMERA 2] Well let's see, shall we? Laura Sprackling, our girl on the scene, is outside All Hallows Church right now. Laura, can you hear us?

Laura Sprackling: [O.B.] Hi Damien. Well, despite what Sam said, it's actually freezing out here and you can probably see that it's quite blowy as well. I'm here with newspaper reporters, radio broadcasters, and others to give the team of ghost hunters organized by the *News of Britain* a good send off and wish them the very best in their investigations over the next few days!

Emma: [2-SHOT CAMERA 3] Are they not there yet, Laura?

Laura: [O.B.] Ah, not just yet. We understand they're being brought by armored car from the *News of Britain* offices where they have under-gone rigorous checks to ensure they aren't bringing anything with them other than approved equipment. There really has been every effort made to ensure that this is a genuine and scientific investigation.

Damien: [2-SHOT CAMERA 3] So there's no one in the church at the moment?

Laura: [O.B.] We understand that one of the team is already inside. A Father Michael Traynor, who is to be the representative of the Catholic Church in this project. Older viewers may remember that All Hallows used to be a place of Catholic worship until it was closed down in the 1970s. Father Traynor is there by kind permission of Westminster Cathedral, which has been kind enough to loan the project his services so that there is at least one person who knows their way around the church.

Emma: [M.S. CAMERA 1] And keep a Godly eye on everyone?

Laura: [O.B.] That's right, Emma. Because they want as few people in there as possible, he's checking right now that the electricity provided works, and that there are enough supplies for the four days. When he's happy, and the others have got here, he'll be the one to give the all-clear that they can go in.

Damien: [M.S. CAMERA 2] Laura, did they have to get special permission from the electricity company to get the power up and running again? If it's been empty for so long—does anything still work in there?

Laura: [O.B.] I asked about that earlier. To be completely safe they're not going to be relying on any external source of power. A generator has been set up in the basement, and I understand lighting will be provided by freestanding lights that have been set up throughout the building—floodlights for the larger areas and smaller lamps for more intimate places. It will also power the cooker and the microwave that have been installed, and cables have been run through the building to power electric points so they can boil a kettle.

Emma: [M.S. CAMERA I] They'll be able to offer the ghosts a cup of tea, then Laura?

Laura *(laughing)*: [O.B.] Oh yes, no shortage of tea or coffee. Alcohol will be a strict no-no, of course.

Damien: [C.U. CAMERA 2] They've got water, though?

Laura: [O.B.] The plumbing still works and there's a kitchen in the undercroft so, yes, that shouldn't be a problem.

Emma: [M.S. CAMERA I] Damien won't have thought about this because he's a man but, how are they all going to keep clean? It's not as if these old churches came with all mod-cons bathrooms. Have they got baths and showers?

Laura: [O.B.] No baths, I'm afraid Emma, but if they go downstairs to the undercroft they'll find showers have been set up by plumbing directly into the pipes that run underground. Apparently they're not the most luxurious, but they'll do the job.

Damien: [M.S. CAMERA 2] Mixed showering, then?

Laura: [O.B.] Is that all you can think about? They're individual cubicles separated by opaque Perspex partitions, so there should be no way you can see what your neighbor's up to.

Emma: [C.U. CAMERA 1] What about communication with the outside world?

Laura: [O.B.] Well that's perhaps the most controversial part of all of this. For the entire period that they are in there, no one is going to be permitted contact with anyone on the outside. The church has no telephone, and the team is not being allowed walkie-talkies.

Damien: [C.U. CAMERA 2] Why not?

Laura: [O.B.] Well, according to Dr. Peter Chesney, the parapsychology expert on the team, the bandwidth that these radios work on can interfere with the equipment he is bringing in, so he has personally insisted that they not be used.

Emma: [C.U. CAMERA 1] So what happens if there's a disaster?

Laura *(pointing behind her)*: [O.B.] I don't know if you can see from where you're watching, but if you look at the main entrance to the church a security system has been set up to the left of the door. There's a panic button inside the building, and if there's any concern from any of the inmates they can push that. It will set off the alarm by the door, lights will flash, and whoever is on duty out here will be able to go in and get them.

Emma: [C.U. CAMERA 1] Only in the event of an emergency, though?

Laura: [o.b.] That's the idea, yes.

Damien: [M.S. CAMERA 2] Inmates.

Laura: [o.b.] I'm sorry?

Damien: [M.S. CAMERA 2] You just called them inmates. Asylum or prison?

Laura *(slightly flustered):* [o.b.] Er . . . let's hope neither, shall we?

Damien: [M.S. CAMERA 2] Sorry Laura, just a little joke. Is there any sign of them yet?

Laura: [o.b.] Well it's funny you should say that, Damien, because I think I can see the armored car coming now. Yes, yes, it's definitely them. I'm going to see if I can have a word with them before they go in.

Damien: [2-SHOT CAMERA 3] Well we'll leave it there for the moment, but we'll go straight back to Laura if she manages to get any of the team aside for a moment for a quick chat. *(turns to Emma)* Dr. Peter Chesney—is he the same one we had on the program last year?

Emma: [2-SHOT CAMERA 3] Yes Damien, he is. If you recall at the time he and his team had just been performing the most exhaustive investigation ever into Brigham Priory.

Damien: [M.S. CAMERA 2] Another famous haunted location, and as he's well known to be a stickler for being in charge of his investigations, I'm guessing he must think All Hallows Church might be even more haunted than Brigham to be willing to go in there under someone else's rules.

Emma: [M.S. CAMERA 1] Well we can ask Laura more about this if she comes back on. But I read in the paper this morning that access to All Hallows has been refused to any and all parapsychological research teams for the last twenty years. The Catholic Church still claims ownership for it and, well, with its history, I'm guessing they wouldn't want to be thought responsible for any more deaths.

Damien: [C.U. CAMERA 2] Wait . . . Laura's coming back on. Can you hear me, Laura?

Laura: [O.B.] Yes Damien, hi! I can just about hear you. I haven't got much else to tell you, I'm afraid. We didn't get much of a look-in. The van pulled up outside the church—in fact, it's still here and you can probably see it behind me *(she stands slightly to one side as the cameraman zooms past her)*—the van pulled up, the team stepped out of the back and were immediately kept away from the rest of the press by the *News of Britain*'s security team. These are the people who will be keeping a round the clock watch on the church during the next four days. *(pull back to reveal Laura)* Anyway, this team allowed *News of Britain* photographers to take a couple of group photos and then they were quickly ushered inside the church, where we understand they are now going to remain. We all know the newspaper has secured exclusive rights to this story, but it's still a bit disappointing that we didn't get to talk to any of the team members before they began their mission.

Emma: [C.U. CAMERA 1] Never mind, Laura, I'm sure you did your best.

Damien: [2-SHOT CAMERA 3] Best get out of there before they stir up any spooks, Laura!

Laura: [O.B.] Yes, I will, don't worry. Bye!

Emma: [2-SHOT CAMERA 3] Bye!

Damien: [2-SHOT CAMERA 3] Bye! We'll take a short break now, but be sure to join us on our return when our resident chef, Marjorie Marsden, will be giving us advice on how to cope with those last minute Christmas cooking nightmares...

Emma: [2-SHOT CAMERA 3] ... and I'll be talking to soap opera heart-throb Danny Styler about what it was like to come out of the closet. We'll see you soon!

[SOUND ONLY OFF-AIR RECORDING DURING COMMERCIAL BREAK]

Damien: Didn't someone die during that Chesney guy's last ghost-hunting thing?

Emma: Two people, actually. That's why we had him on—he'd just been found not guilty of the manslaughter charge. Only he and one other person crawled out of the place alive, and Marion Peters is going to be in an asylum for the rest of her life. *(the rasping sound of a cigarette lighter being used)* Thanks. Mind you, if he wants to go back into one of those sorts of places he must be pretty mad himself.

Damien: Pretty stupid as well.

Emma: You mean he's pushing his luck? He's survived one battle with ghosts and now he's just going back for more?

Damien: I mean if ghosts really existed, wouldn't his team members be haunting him up the arse by now? Some people never learn.

Emma: You don't believe, then?

Damien: No, it's all bollocks. All done to get attention, which is exactly what's going on here. I didn't expect the *News of Britain* lot to be such a bunch of bastards they wouldn't let us get a look in, but there you go. No such things as ghosts, and no bloody point to this other than to sell papers. That's why they held that bloody competition as well.

Emma: Shit! We didn't mention the competition winners!

Damien: Yes you did—I remember you saying. It was on the autocue.

Emma: But I didn't mention their names or ask Laura about them! I'll probably get it in the neck from Simon about not exploiting the public interest side of things...

Damien: In case you hadn't noticed, we were overrunning as it was. Our dear producer had been giving me the "Cut to a Break" signal for the last thirty seconds. Don't worry—we went on about that old bollocks for long enough. If people want to know more about the two luckless idiots who've won themselves four nights in a freezing cold church just before Christmas it's all in the article the *News of Britain* published yesterday. Now put that cigarette out—we're back on in ten seconds.

[END OF TRANSCRIPT]

SPOOKY SUCCESS!!!

THE ANSWERS ARE IN AND THE DECISION HAS BEEN MADE!

We'd like to thank each and every *News of Britain* reader who entered our shivery competition to Win Four Nights in the Most Haunted Place Ever!

A spook-tastic 83,256 of you couldn't wait to get your hands on some real live ghostly action, and got phoning and writing to let us know the answer to our ghost-tastic trivia question.

But there can only be one winner—In OTHER newspapers, that is!

Because your super-reading, great value *News of Britain* made sure there were TWO!

TWO, that's right, TWO lucky winners will be joining the *News of Britain*'s Paranormal Research Team when they enter All Hallows Church tomorrow. They'll be there right alongside our team of experts as they uncover the unknown, probe the paranormal, and examine the eerie.

And our winners are: Paul Hale, 22, an unemployed bricklayer from South London, and Veronica "Ronnie" Quesnel, 44, who is a professional medium and spiritualist in her spare time.

Paul entered our competition on a dare from his mates but says he's always liked scary movies. His favorite horror film is *A Nightmare on Elm Street*, which he first saw on home video when he was thirteen. Not sure what the censors would have to say about that, Paul, but we promise we'll keep quiet. Let's hope Freddy's not waiting for you in All Hallows Church!

Ronnie told us she's been into paranormal and ghostly activity for as long as she can remember, and has seen many strange things during her lifetime. Let's hope the best is yet to come for Ronnie over the next few days! "My only regret," she tells the *NoB*, "is that my cats won't be able to come with me. They're my lifeline to the cosmic universe, my companions and soul mates. I have proof that some of them are the reincarnations of those with past lives and they have often aided me in detecting places with abnormal psychic activity."

Unfortunately the rules have stipulated that no animals are to be allowed into All Hallows for the period of this current study. But your ever-caring *News of Britain* has ensured that all of Ronnie's pets will be looked after until her safe return. We're sure you'll join us in wishing Paul and Ronnie, and the rest of the team, the very best of luck as they prepare to take on the WORLD OF THE WEIRD!!!

NINE

Thursday, December 22, 1994. 11:03 A.M.

THE FIRST DAY.

Bob Chambers paused, the nib of his pen still poised over the fresh creamy paper of page one of his notebook. He was tempted to add *Hour One*, and for that matter *Minute One* as well. After all, they had only just arrived and, while he had no intention of documenting everything that happened during the next four days (despite Washington instructing him to do just that), it was a way of preventing the others from bothering him for the moment. And he needed that—just a few moments to himself so he could get used to the place.

Who was he kidding? He leaned back in his seat in the rearmost pew and looked around him. He could probably spend days here and not get used to the interior of All Hallows Church, but it was a passable distraction while the others explored their new surroundings.

The notebook—two hundred pages of blank letter-sized vellum bound between two stiff boards beautifully covered in pale blue marbling with slick navy leather down the spine—had been a gift several years ago from a grateful student. It was one of the few personal possessions he had brought with him.

The rest of his stuff included medical supplies. He had been asked to bring whatever he thought might be useful and so he had included a first aid kit, a few drugs (mainly antibiotics and painkillers) and a few small items of surgical equipment (a scalpel and some sutures) because he wouldn't have been happy going to a place like this without them. Other than that there were a few changes of clothes and other personal items packed into the heavy black Samsonite suitcase that was presently still standing near the main door, along with everyone else's bags.

Looking at what some of the others had with them, he was grateful that was all he had needed to bring along. At least he hadn't required half a library's worth of ancient-looking volumes on the history of this place from Roman times up to now, but that was what Dr. Rosalie Cruttenden had insisted on having brought in here. At the moment they were still in tea chests, stacked at the back of the church just to the right of the font. The lecturer was currently prizing open her second crate with gusto, using the crowbar that, curiously, Father Traynor had brought with him.

That had been the first odd thing. The rest of them had met at the *News of Britain* offices in Fleet Street earlier that morning and been assured that everything they had asked for had been delivered to the church over the preceding three days. They were then driven to the location in the back of a van that smelled as if its last cargo had been overripe pears; and when they had finally been allowed to emerge into the chill light of dawn, the security the paper had seen fit to employ had shielded them from the mass of journalists gathered in anticipation of getting a few words. Exclusive obviously meant exclusive to the *News of Britain*. Chambers had felt sorry for the pretty girl with the *Wake Up Britain!* microphone who had almost had to be pushed out of the way to let them through the gates. In many ways, however, it had been a relief. He couldn't think of anything to have said to them anyway, other than that he thought the whole thing was a ridiculous idea and that he felt stupid for having agreed to it.

He wasn't going to put that in his journal. He was, however, going to make a point of noting that the chain on the gates had looked almost melted, that the gates themselves had not so much been pushed open to allow them entry as pulled apart, and that the doors to the church had opened at their touch as if the hinges had been well-oiled.

But the strangest thing of all had been Father Michael Traynor, standing there in the aisle to welcome them.

"I thought no one was supposed to be in here." Karen had looked annoyed until the pale-looking priest had explained who he was, and even then she hadn't been entirely happy.

"My Cardinal thought it only right that I be here to welcome you," Father Michael had replied, "and to ensure that this building which, after all, is still God's house, was fit for you to enter."

"I thought the blokes who brought the stuff in and connected up the electrics were supposed to do that." Paul Hale, thin and lanky, his spiky white hair suggestive of a rockabilly style that had been trimmed back for the occasion, was obviously picking up on the unhappy vibes of the woman standing next to him.

"Oh, they did, before vacating the premises as quickly as they could." Father Traynor had smiled with the obsequiousness of a politician who hopes his latest misdemeanor will remain undiscovered. "But nevertheless the Catholic Church felt it was its duty to ensure its representative in this party was the first to be here."

Karen hadn't been happy, but instead of protesting further she had suggested that, as Father Traynor presumably knew the layout of the place, he show them around. The priest had readily agreed to this, and that was what most of them were preparing to do now. Dr. Cruttenden had been too anxious to ensure her books had arrived safely, and had elected to stay behind. Chambers had found a pew at the back of the church that looked safe to sit on, and had flipped open the brown leather briefcase he always carried with him. It usually contained his latest research papers and data, but now it held a couple of novels and the journal. With nothing better to do while he waited for the guided tour, he had started to write.

On the pew opposite sat Karen, speaking quietly into a Dictaphone. Her luggage had consisted mainly of cassette tapes, notebooks, and journals, plus more AA batteries than he had ever seen in his life.

"If you'd ever been in the middle of a civil war and run out you'd understand," she had said, to which he had nodded politely.

He still found it difficult to believe she had wanted him to come, and had in fact asked for him by name. Once they had learned of the proposed "Ghost Hunt" Washington had insisted that, as their man on the spot, Chambers had to be a part of it. Just as he had been about to pick up the phone, Karen had called him.

"I read that story of yours, that one about the dreaming god that rises up out of the sea," she said.

"And?"

"And I don't believe a word of it. But we need someone with medical qualifications to come into All Hallows with us, and you're the least boring doctor I know. Besides, while you might be crazy I think you're probably harmless."

"Appearances can be deceptive," he replied. "But I promise to be on my best behavior."

He was surprised she had asked Dr. Cruttenden to come along as well, and that the Oxford University lecturer had agreed. Karen later told him that Dr. Cruttenden had initially refused, but after she had realized they would be going in with or without her, she had relented, saying she would rather be in the thick of history in the making, being able to do something about it, rather than simply suffering its aftermath.

Chambers hadn't actually wanted to go near the place, despite the insistence of his department, and over drinks in a bar a few days before they were set to leave he had told Karen as much.

"But aren't the nightmares back?" she had asked.

They were.

"And aren't they worse than ever?"

That was true too. Since getting back from Oxford, every night had been a journey to a hellish otherworld, where the undead roamed and the living fell victim to them. All except him, that was. Powerless to do anything, Chambers's dream-self had been forced to stand by impotently while populations had been ravaged and turned into more of the insatiable, ever-consuming zombie horde. He had seen cemeteries turned into cathedrals, and cities into tombs, and he had not been able to do a thing about it. *If only agent Randolph Carter was still around*, he thought to himself. *He would have known what to do.*

No, he hadn't wanted to go anywhere near All Hallows, but he knew he had to. If what he was being shown during the hours of darkness was some dreadful vision of what was to come, and if All Hallows Church was something to do with that, then even though it was the last place in the world he wanted to be, he had to be there.

The others didn't seem to have been similarly affected, although Father Traynor had looked distracted and anemic in the light from the floodlight that had been positioned halfway up the aisle on the left-hand side. Paul Hale had seemed excited by all the press attention while the other winner, Ronnie Quesnel, had said very little so far. She had arrived in a flurry of voluminous gypsy skirts (which would certainly keep her warm, Karen had remarked in the van) and equally voluminous curly brown hair. Her voice had so far made less noise than the many beads around her neck and the bangles on her wrists. Right now she was drifting up and down the aisle, her face upturned to the cracked and broken ribbed vaulting of the ceiling. Every now and then she would stop, spin around daintily on one toe, and begin walking in the opposite direction.

She had already bumped into Peter Chesney twice.

He called himself Dr. Peter Chesney, but when Chambers had asked him at which university he had obtained his doctorate, Chesney had changed the subject. Despite pressing him on it for the short spell they were in the back of the van, Chambers was still none the wiser as to whether Chesney's doctorate was scientific, medical, or if it had been scribbled on the back of a cereal box and sent to him in the mail. Chambers was well aware that there were a number of disreputable institutions willing to cash checks for middling amounts of money and dole out a degree or two to those who wished to live under the delusion that the certificate they now had framed on their wall somehow made them better than those to whom they showed it. The fact that the very opposite was the case was something Chambers hoped he would be able to keep from announcing. At least until the last day, he thought with a smile.

Chesney was not happy, and Ronnie repeatedly bumping into him had not helped to improve his mood. Apparently the equipment he had asked to be delivered wasn't working properly.

"Have you ever seen such incompetence?" he snarled to nobody in particular as he waved around two pieces of tubular aluminum that until recently were probably just one, judging by the jagged ends. "How am I supposed to construct my psychic detector now?"

"I have some Scotch tape in my bag." Ronnie's voice was soft and deep, as if she had never had to speak above a whisper in her entire life. "If that would help."

"A soldering iron would help," Chesney replied, "I don't suppose you've got one of those in that carpet bag of yours?"

"Father Traynor might." Paul diverted the parapsychologist's attention. "After all, he had that crowbar, and a whole load of other stuff."

That was enough to send Chesney scurrying off toward the vestry as Karen came over, obviously with the intention of chatting.

"Making a record of us all, then?"

Chambers closed the book and put it back in his bag. "Just something to pass the time," he said.

She sat next to him. The old pew creaked with the weight of both of them. "Are you going to come on the tour?"

Chambers nodded. "I usually like to find my own way around, but it's probably worth letting Father Traynor show us around. I'm still finding it a bit weird that he was here before us, though."

"I know." Karen looked around at the others, all finding nothing to do as they waited for the priest to emerge from the vestry. "Any second thoughts?"

"About what?"

"About coming here. About what we might find here."

Chambers resisted the urge to snort derisively. "My second thoughts were ages ago, along with my third and my fourth. But you're right. If we're ever going to get a good night's sleep again this is where we need to be."

Karen's brow creased. "Especially as . . ."

He nodded again, knowing what she wanted to say. ". . . as from the outside this looks like the place in the dream. I mean the hill isn't as high, and there are a few buildings here and there to break up the landscape, but it could easily be the same location."

"Lots of churches look alike."

"I don't think there's a church in the world like this one, and you know it too."

Karen held up the tape recorder. "Would you care to put that on record?"

Chambers smiled. "You know, the last time a reporter waved one of those at me they weren't being quite so friendly, so you'll forgive me if I have an aversion to them."

"Journalist if you don't mind." She sighed. "Well you're going to have to agree to be interviewed sometime. Lots of sometimes, in fact."

"Okay." He took the machine from her and switched it on. "This is Professor Robert Chambers MD, trapped in a church for four days with—" he gave her a knowing look, "—a journalist, a priest, a lecturer, a bricklayer, a fortune teller and . . . someone else."

Karen's eyes narrowed. "You don't like Dr. Chesney, do you?"

"Because I'm not convinced he is a doctor, and for all his self-proclamatory spiel about the paranormal investigations he's been involved with, he's the only one of our group who gives me the profoundest feeling of insincerity."

Karen had to laugh at that. "Why, Professor, I'm honored!"

"Honored?"

"That you should consider me sincere."

"Oh you're sincere all right—sincere that you want to be rid of these nightmares, that you need us all here to help that happen, and that if you can get a story out of it then so much the better."

"Not just a story." She was putting the tape recorder away. "*The* story, the one that's going to make my career."

"If you live long enough to have one."

She laid a cool palm on his cheek. "Are you going to be this optimistic all the time?"

"Oh, no. I may well become quite miserable as the hours drag on."

"In that case I hope the undead do appear to liven things up a little."

"If they do I'll assume you've provided them specially."

There was a commotion at the front of the church.

"Come on." Karen held out a hand. "It looks like Father Traynor's ready to show us around."

All Hallows Church was in a terrible state.

There had been a rudimentary attempt to clean the place up, but when a building has been deserted for twenty years, a few days' tidying can do little but remove the worst of the broken pews, brush away the most bothersome dust and cobwebs, and push any fallen masonry into corners where it might be hoped it won't be noticed.

"I wonder why all the pews are still here?" Karen had taken the lead as they made their way up the central aisle, with Chambers in tow and the others following behind. "You would think the furniture reclamation people would have had some of these."

"They would usually." That was Paul. "But no one wanted to take anything from here."

"How could you possibly know that?" Chesney seemed determined to be made unhappier with every passing minute. "There's nothing in any documented records about it."

"Before I was a bricklayer I spent a couple of months working at the reclamation company that was asked to take a look at this place," came the reply. "I had the bright idea that there might still be some good stuff worth having, but when I suggested it I just got looked at as if I was stupid. Turns out they had tried coming in, years ago, but one of the blokes had an accident. Something to do with the pulpit over there." Paul indicated the dusty booth to the right of the pews, the wooden steps leading up to it looking perilous even from a distance.

"He was trying to unscrew the steps when something happened and he fell. He died in the hospital three days later."

"Died?" Ronnie's soft tones came from the back of the group. "How?"

"Blood poisoning apparently. He'd cut himself on a splinter and had never had his tetanus shots. Bloody awful what that can do to a bloke. That was what made me go and get mine from the doctor—there was no way that was going to happen to me."

"Well I hope everyone here has had one." Chambers made sure his words were loud enough for them all to hear. He took the mumbled response for assent.

"Are you all ready?"

Father Traynor, his face as gray as the surrounding walls, was standing on the edge of the single step that demarcated the border between the nave and the choir. His dark hair and gown made his skin look that much whiter in the glare of the floodlight to his left.

"Sorry, Father," Karen apologized on behalf of the group. "It's very good of you to show us around."

Father Traynor's tones were soft and he spoke almost in monotone. "We felt it appropriate that the task should fall to me. There's not much for me to say, really." He raised his arms and looked around him. "You can see most of what is left of this lovely old church, which has sadly been allowed to fall into ruin."

"I wasn't expecting it to be so large," said Ronnie, the echo of her voice making her jump.

Father Traynor did his best to smile but there was little life in it. "It served quite a sizeable population in its day, which is why it's easily twice the size of the typical village parish church of the period."

"Of what period?" shouted an elderly female voice from the back.

"I beg your pardon?"

The group parted to allow Dr. Cruttenden to come to the front.

"I wanted to know what period you were referring to."

Father Traynor looked confused. "I'm not sure I . . ."

"I had been led to understand that this church suffered a catastrophe in 1850?"

The priest nodded. "That's correct."

"In fact it was burned to the ground?"

"Yes."

Dr. Cruttenden looked around her. "And prior to this disaster it was designed and built by a . . ." she consulted the notebook she had managed to produce after rummaging through the voluminous pockets of her tweed jacket ". . . a 'Thomas Moreby,' is that not so?"

"It is."

"Whose dates, I believe, were 1702 to 1803?"

The priest shrugged. "If you say so."

She looked at him over her horn-rimmed spectacles. "Oh, I do say so, young man. I do indeed. I also understand that he was a disciple of Nicholas Hawksmoor and designed All Hallows in Hawksmoor's late Baroque style."

Father Traynor nodded again.

Dr. Cruttenden looked around her and sniffed. "This doesn't look late Baroque," she said. "This looks positively medieval—twelfth or thirteenth century at the latest."

"That's because after the fire it was discovered that All Hallows had been built over the remains of a much older church. The Victorian architect who supervised the rebuild thought it only respectful to base the new building on the plan of the older one."

That seemed to please Dr. Cruttenden no end. "Well you've passed the test," she said, allowing him the briefest of congratulatory winks. "Carry on."

If Father Traynor had been at all bothered by the interruption he did not show it. "There is very little left of the choir behind me," he said, as if the incident had never happened.

He was right about that. The choir stalls had rotted and collapsed, and there were great gaping holes in the screens on either side. To their right, a battered two-manual pipe organ looked very sorry for itself, its exposed keys clotted with cobwebs and the pipes teetering at angles and clogged with dust.

"I'd like to hear someone try and get a note out of that thing," said Paul with a chuckle.

"You might before our time here is out," said Karen with a grin. "It all depends on how bored you get."

Chambers raised an eyebrow. "You play, then?"

"Only the piano," she said, blushing. "But the principle's the same."

"If you look farther behind me," Father Traynor continued, "you will see the altar. Of course it has been desanctified now, but we would ask that you nevertheless treat it and the rest of this building with respect. This place was home to many years of worship before it was closed down."

Chambers peered over the priest's shoulder. The altar didn't look like anything special—just a block of pale gray as dusty as everything else around it.

"What I mean is—" the priest seemed to be searching for words, "—we would appreciate it if you did not stand or lie upon the altar, even in jest. Especially in jest."

"Well I don't know about the rest of them," growled Dr. Chesney. "But I am here for some serious scientific research. And when I'm not doing that I'm going to need to get some decent sleep."

"Yes," Ronnie said, picking up on that. "What are the sleeping arrangements?"

"As you can imagine this building was never designed to accommodate such a number of individuals used to the conveniences of modern living for such a length of time." Father Traynor looked at Karen. "Your paper contacted me and asked my advice on this and I suggested the following."

He pointed to his left. "Two of the men can sleep in the south transept. There is enough room for two of the cots that have been left, as well as room for changing and small lights for reading. I would suggest Dr. Chesney and myself." He pointed to his right. "Professor Chambers and Mr. Hale can sleep in the north transept where similar arrangements have been made. I've examined both areas and the drafts are nowhere near as bad as in the main part of the building."

"Sounds all right to me." Actually, it sounded a bit rough, but Chambers was happy to make the best of it and took the lead, doing his best to sound a lot more optimistic than he felt.

"If you don't mind my snoring, Prof," said Paul with a cheeky grin, "I can put up with that."

"Well, I can't." Dr. Chesney appeared to be approaching apoplexy. "There's no room over there for the amount of work I will need to have with me. I need a desk, I need filing space, recording space, and I intend to be keeping irregular hours and most certainly do not want to be disturbed when I am trying to sleep!"

Father Traynor remained calm in the face of the outburst. "In that case," he said, "might I suggest that you take the south transept for yourself? I am sure we have been provided with sufficient materials to construct an appropriate draw curtain that will keep you separated from the rest of us when necessary."

Not everyone was able to stifle a giggle at that, but by the time Dr. Chesney looked around it was impossible to determine who was responsible.

"I suppose that will have to do," he said, in the tones of someone who didn't really think it would at all.

"What will you do, Father?" Paul asked.

"There's a small vestry off the north aisle. You'll see the door to it when I show you where the ladies are to sleep. It's not very clean but it will serve my purpose."

"No way," said the bricklayer. "You sleep with the Prof—I don't mind getting all dusty."

Father Traynor smiled. "I assure you I will be fine. Now, if you would care to follow me I will show the rest of you where you are to sleep."

The priest stepped down from the choir and led them across the north transept and through a small door into the north aisle. He turned to the right, leading them past a small wooden door set into the stone on the left-hand wall.

"The vestry," he said by way of explanation.

He continued around until they found themselves walking along the east wall.

"Now we are at the very top of the cruciform that the building forms," he said, before pointing to three discrete outpouchings of stone. "And here, as you can see, are three small chapels."

"Ah," Dr. Cruttenden was nodding. "Apsidals."

Father Traynor gave a little bow in acknowledgement. "As you say, Dr. Cruttenden. I thought these three small rooms would provide the most satisfactory accommodation for the three of you. Miss Shepworth, you will find that each has been equipped by your newspaper with a cot and appropriate accessories for your needs."

"Please call me Karen," she said as she drew back the heavy black curtain that hung across the first apsidal. Chambers peered over her shoulder. The stone cubicle beyond was just large enough to contain a small altar with space for three people to kneel. A metal-framed army supply cot had been set up in the space and he presumed that the Catholic Church wasn't too bothered about the altar in here being used as a storage shelf.

"Small place but it's home," he said encouragingly.

"Oh believe me," Karen replied, "I've stayed in far worse."

"So have I," echoed Dr. Cruttenden as she examined the second apsidal chapel. It was the same as Karen's.

"I've been to the Glastonbury music festival five times," said soft-voiced Ronnie as she inspected the third. "This will be absolutely fine—thank you."

Father Traynor seemed pleased. "I therefore take it that everyone is happy with the sleeping arrangements?"

Dr. Chesney snorted. "Well, I wouldn't exactly say I was happy, but—"

"I think we'll all be fine," Karen cut in before Chesney could complain any more.

"Good. In that case we can move on to view the bathing and cooking facilities."

"I didn't spot anything on the way around," piped up Paul. "Are they up in the bell tower or something?"

Father Traynor shook his head. "The very opposite, Mr. Hale. The shower rooms and kitchen are downstairs, in the undercroft."

Dr. Cruttenden's voice rang out from inside her apsidal. "You mean you want us to wash in the crypt?"

"The facilities have been constructed in the area before one gets to the crypt proper." Father Traynor was already on the move. Karen pulled back Dr. Cruttenden's curtain and told her to come on. "The generators are there too, so that area should be the warmest in the building."

"What do the generators run on?" Paul had caught up with the priest as he led the way down the south aisle on the other side of the church.

"Petrol, I believe, although I could be wrong," came the reply. "Why?"

"It means that as well as being the warmest place it's probably also going to be the smelliest," said Paul, "especially if the ventilation isn't good. Plus we'll need to be careful cooking if there are petrol cans around."

"I can't say I fancy taking a risk like that," said Ronnie. "I'd rather eat cold stuff."

"There is plenty of canned food should you feel so inclined." Father Traynor had stopped by a small door in the south wall. It was just past the south transept and led off the part of the south aisle that ran parallel to the nave. He withdrew a heavy iron key from his robes and fit it into the lock. With a little persuasion it turned, eventually.

"I'm presuming that will be left open?" Chesney snapped.

"It will." The priest pulled on the wrought iron handle that had been fashioned in the shape of an upside-down heart. If anyone was expecting the door to open with a creak they were to be disappointed. A flight of stone steps led down to the right.

"Recently oiled," Father Traynor added.

Chesney raised an accusatory finger. "What's that other door for?"

Sure enough, beyond the opening and the steps was another door, similar in size and shape and firmly barricaded from the inside by means of bolts both top and bottom, and a heavy oak beam across its middle that looked as if it hadn't been moved in years.

"It leads to the outside," Father Traynor explained. "A side entrance that was used many years ago but, as you can see, has been locked for a long time. It was thought best to leave it as such for security reasons. Now, if you would all be kind enough to follow me?"

The staircase was narrow and they had to go single file. A single bare bulb suspended from the stone halfway down allowed just enough darkness remaining in the corners to be unsettling. Now Traynor had opened the door, the noise of the generator was obvious.

"We're barely going to be able to hear ourselves think down there." Dr. Cruttenden was doing her best not to slip.

At the bottom a narrow archway led into the undercroft—a rectangular space roughly fifty feet long. Or at least that was as far as the two bare bulbs would permit them to see. To the left were two cubicles with rudimentary water pipes leading to shower attachments. On the right was a cast iron sink complete with two dripping taps and a draining board turned a rusty orange by the leakage of water from the feeder pipes. Far away from them the generator rumbled away in the darkness. At the near end were numerous bright yellow gas cans to keep it going. Above the sink and to its right and left were a number of cheap-looking storage cabinets. All had been filled with a quantity of food designed to last longer than four days.

"It's like a bloody bomb shelter!" Paul had a smile on his face. "My Grandad used to tell me about these but I never thought I'd actually see one."

"Who's going to keep the generator going?" Ronnie asked.

"We can take turns," Paul replied. "I can show you how. Unless you'd rather cook my dinner for me."

"I shall be far too busy working to be bothered with a generator." That was Dr. Chesney. Of course.

"Okay," said Paul to the parapsychologist. "You can cook my dinner for me, then."

"I'm sure we can work out some sort of rotation," said Karen. "It's not as if there really has been an apocalypse and we're down here forever."

Despite the heat coming from the generator and the number of warm bodies crammed into the confined space, a chill suddenly descended on the group.

"Fascinating how things can take on a more sinister meaning in the right environment, isn't it?"

Chambers laid a hand on Dr. Cruttenden's shoulder before he replied softly, "I think it's just beginning to sink in that we're here for the duration," he said.

"And wasting precious time while we're about it." Dr. Chesney was making for the stairs. "I need to set up my equipment. I shall speak to you again when I need you."

Paul waited until the parapsychologist was out of earshot before speaking. "Oh he will, will he?"

"At least he's away from here for the moment," said Karen. "I was getting close to all I could stand of him."

"Well, it was your paper who asked him to come along," said Chambers with a wry grin. "In his absence I would have expected you to be the one defending his honor."

Karen pointedly ignored that. "I wouldn't be surprised if ghosts refuse to appear when he's around just to piss him off." She caught the priest's eye. "Sorry, Father."

"Well I think I've seen enough for now," said Ronnie. "Is there anything else you need to show us?"

Father Traynor shook his head. "Now you know as much as I do about the building. We will be discovering everything else together."

As they made their way back up the stairs, something in what the priest had said didn't ring true for Chambers. Maybe it was simply that the man's manner had seemed a little unnatural the entire time he had been showing them around, or perhaps it was just that because of Chambers's experiences with the Human Protection League he held an innate mistrust of those who represented religion. It wasn't just that, though. He couldn't help but feel that the Father knew more than he was letting on, and that if they should end up confronted by some hostile spectral apparition during their time here, it wasn't necessarily clear whose side the priest would be on.

He also couldn't help admitting to himself that he would be more than a little interested in finding out.

TEN

Thursday, December 22, 1994. 11:42 A.M.

"IS THAT A SEISMOMETER?"

Dr. Peter Chesney raised his head. The floodlight behind him gave his wavy, tightly cut silver hair an almost angelic appearance. The glowering eyes behind the black-rimmed spectacles, however, looked anything but.

Ronnie Quesnel wasn't sure if he'd heard her. Or perhaps he didn't know what one of those was? "You know, for recording earthquakes?"

His hands came away from aligning the delicate, ink-filled needles on the reel of graph paper.

"A seismograph," he said between clenched teeth.

"I'm sorry?"

"A seismograph is what is used to record tremors of the earth."

Ronnie peered at the flat sheet of paper and the needles poised above it. There were five of them, each connected to a wire that led to a machine beneath the low table upon which Dr. Chesney had placed the recording device. "Is that what it is then? A seismograph?"

The parapsychologist shook his head, causing Ronnie to be intermittently blinded by the lamp. "No," he replied and then, when it became obvious that such an abrupt answer wasn't going to make her go away, he added, "it works on a similar principle, but instead of detecting disturbances of the physical plain, this detects disturbances of the ether."

Ronnie nodded. She had read about that in some of her husband Terry's old books. "You mean that medium through which the ancient Greeks thought light traveled?"

Chesney nodded. "Sound, light, the entire electromagnetic spectrum. Of course it's not a term used in common scientific parlance these days, but I use it to refer specifically to that part of the atmosphere through which spectral, ethereal, and paranormal activity is propagated."

Ronnie pointed at the device. "And this is meant to pick them up?"

Chesney nodded again, obviously eager to get back to his adjustments. "I designed it myself," he said, not without a certain amount of pride. "It showed some remarkable results at Borley Rectory, as well as at numerous other locations in the UK known for their psychic phenomena."

"Has it picked up anything?"

Chesney answered with an exasperated no. "I haven't plugged it in yet, because I haven't calibrated it yet, and I won't be able to, either, if I keep being disturbed!"

Ronnie finally took the hint and left the parapsychologist to his devices. The seismograph, several sets of microphones, a complicated-looking aluminum framework and what looked like a small portable generator took up, along with Chesney's cot, most of the available space in the south transept. No wonder Father Traynor had been happy to sleep in the vestry, she thought, even if it was cramped and dusty.

She took a swig from the bottled water they had found an ample supply of downstairs. Turning on the taps to the sink had resulted in something a rusty brown color being ejected from both spigots. It had refused to clear, despite their running it for several minutes.

"Maybe that's just what the water's like down here," Paul had said. "It can happen sometimes."

"Well I'm not drinking it," said Karen. "And I can't imagine they would have thought we would."

A quick search in the darkness near the thrumming generator had revealed a refrigerator/freezer amply stocked with drinks.

"Shame there's no booze here," Karen had said.

"There is," Paul had replied, "if you like scotch." He had been searching the cupboards and had found two bottles of J&B whisky.

"Not for me," Karen had said wrinkling her nose. "I'll wait until I'm out of here and then I'm celebrating with as many dirty martinis as I can drink."

"Me neither," Ronnie had piped up. "A glass of wine every now and then is about my limit. I never touch anything stronger."

If she didn't find something to keep her occupied Ronnie could see herself trying a tipple or two, though. She skirted two large fallen cornice stones, the intricate sculpted scrollwork still visible despite the obvious trauma they had sustained. She looked up to see the gap where they had fallen from. There were other spaces too, but no more stones nearby. Perhaps they had been cleared away in preparation for the team's arrival, she thought, but it was rather odd that these two had been left here.

At the back of the church, sitting in the rearmost right-hand pew, Professor Chambers was scribbling away in his journal. Ronnie wished she had brought a journal, or at least something to write in or on, but it had been such a rush getting here. She had never been the most organized of types, and Terry was even worse. It was only when her husband was reminding her of the various client appointments she would need to change two days ago that she had remembered the competition she had won. She had packed her bags hastily. Changes of clothes, toiletry kit, her favorite, oldest and most trusted Tarot deck, and a couple of books had all been crammed in. To be honest, she had assumed there was going to be more of a showbiz element to it, that the paper would have laid on a program that they would be following, rather than this hanging around waiting for something to happen.

Professor Chambers was still scribbling. Behind him, close to the west door through which they had entered, stood a font. It was without question the most beautiful piece of work in here. It appeared to have been sculpted from a single piece of blue-veined marble, and the quality of the stone was such that it had refused to succumb to the ravages of time, dust, and decay. A brown stain around the drainage hole in its base showed that it had indeed been used for baptisms and the like in years past. Now it stood there, empty, a reminder of All Hallows' former glory.

Ronnie looked at her watch. It was hard to believe it was only two o'clock in the afternoon. Perhaps it was the windows. There were four of them on either side of the nave, each consisting of three narrow rectangular stained-glass panes. Ronnie wrinkled her nose. Stained was right. The newspaper's tidy-up job had not extended to cleaning the windows, and the glass was so filthy it was almost impossible to make out what the illustrations depicted. It also meant that, no matter what time of day it was, or how bright the sunshine might be outside, inside the church was perpetual gloom.

Ronnie crossed the nave and entered the north aisle to take a look at the four windows there. She was wondering why the glass had not been smashed by vandals years ago, but on closer inspection the heavy metal meshwork over each pane became apparent. There was probably similar rusting grillwork on the outside as well, all that protection a significant barrier to any natural light.

What did the glass depict? She studied the more easterly of the four. Even now she was so close it was virtually impossible to make anything out. She thought she could see a hill, possibly with angels surrounding it. But surely, if they were angels, shouldn't they have wings? And should they be so horribly thin? And to the right, were those meant to be shepherds? If they were, someone had made a terrible mistake with their flock—it looked as if some of the sheep had six legs, and they almost seemed to be jumping at the humans that were supposed to be tending them.

Ronnie shook her head. Perhaps some answers could be found elsewhere.

The most westerly of the four windows in the north wall was fifty feet away. In between lay the two other windows, their glass completely shrouded by grime, separated by an expanse of bare wall. Much of the graying plaster was still intact, with the stone beneath only showing through in a few places.

As Ronnie walked past them she felt a sudden shock, like fingers of ice touching the back of her neck.

She stopped and turned, rubbing the skin. Had she been bitten? That was ridiculous—it was hardly the time of year for insects that did that sort of thing. Perhaps there was a leak in the ceiling and she'd been dripped on? She looked up but could see nothing, then she looked down but there was no suggestion that water was pooling anywhere.

Yet still the chill sensation on the back of her neck remained. It was less intense now but she could still feel it, preventing her from thinking it was just her imagination.

She took a step back from the wall and its pair of obfuscated windows.

The feeling diminished.

She took a step forward.

The feeling became more intense.

Almost immediately regretting it, Ronnie took a stride closer to the plain, unremarkable, plastered wall of the north aisle.

The icy, spiking pain in the back of her neck nearly made her fall to her knees. She fought the urge to vomit as she backed away, the feeling subsiding as she put distance between herself and the stone. As soon as it was tolerable, she looked up at the wall.

Nothing.

Yes there was, she told herself. There was something there, but she just couldn't see it.

"Be careful while you're in there," Terry had said to her. "You know how sensitive you can be."

"That's only when I'm with people who need my help," Ronnie had replied. "I'm a psychic empath, remember? I feel the pain of those in distress, those who come to me for help, and through the cards I try to give them that help."

Terry hadn't been so sure. "I've seen you sometimes," he'd said, "when you don't think I'm looking. It's not just people you have empathy with, it's places. All Hallows is a bad place, and it might be especially bad for you."

"I'll be all right," she had tried to reassure him. "And besides, I don't know if you've noticed, but business hasn't exactly been booming lately. Glastonbury's started to become overrun with people claiming they can do readings, and there are only so many clients to go around."

"You're doing it for the publicity, then?" Terry hadn't seemed too impressed with that either.

She had admitted that had been one of the reasons, yes. "But it's not just that. All my life I've felt alone, even with you, even in a place like this where I've found more like-minded people than anywhere else. But loneliness runs deep if you experience it young enough and long enough. This is a chance for me to . . . oh, I don't know . . . to reconfirm that it isn't all in my head."

He had held her then, tightly, and for a long time. "You know I love you, don't you?" She had nodded, her face buried in his shoulder. "And you know that, no matter how much I might worry, I would do anything for you?"

"I know," she said at last, "and that's why I need you to let me go and do this. I need to be with these other kinds of people they've described in the newspaper, I need to be with them in a place like that, to prove to myself that it isn't just all incense and nonsense—that I have an ability and that I can use it to make a useful and valuable contribution to the work of others. I even see the fact that I won the competition as a sign that I have to go."

And so he had let her, and now here she was, rubbing the back of her neck and staring at a blank wall in a freezing cold church, convinced that something was trying to communicate with her, that she had picked up on something but at that precise moment she had no idea what it was.

She looked over at Dr. Chesney, fiddling with his machine, and at Professor Chambers, staring off into space. She thought of Karen Shepworth with her tapes and Dr. Cruttenden with her books, of Father Traynor with his faith and Paul Hale with his cheery goodwill and willingness to help out with the practicalities while he waited for the monsters to turn up.

She would tell none of them.

This was hers and she would tell none of them until she was absolutely sure, until there could be no doubt that there was someone, or something, in this wall. She would find out why it was there, and what it was that it wanted. Then, and only then, would she tell them.

She smiled despite the pain. Finally she had found something to do.

ELEVEN

PETER CHESNEY, AMATEUR PARAPSYCHOLOGIST (not that there was any other kind) and guest on a number of British television programs profiling the paranormal and those who investigate it, was not a real doctor.

Neither medically nor scientifically qualified to the level where he could have been offered a doctorate, he had earned the appellation by mistake. And, like all mistakes that can dog an individual for the rest of their lives, he had failed to deny his title right at the beginning, when he should have. Now he was stuck with it, and while it had opened doors, the constant fear that he might one day be revealed to be a sham in a field known for charlatans and tricksters was one that weighed more heavily on his soul with every passing day.

It was the television show that had caused it. After that he hadn't been able to live it down. Three years ago he had been contacted by Central TV to ask if he would like to appear on an edition of its popular late night debate program, *Central Weekend*.

"It's very popular in the Midlands," the girl had said. "We get a forty percent audience share on a Friday night. We're doing an edition on whether the paranormal really exists. I did a bit of searching and found your name. Would you like to be on?"

Chesney had said yes without even thinking about it. He had been a dabbler in parapsychology for ten years, and had been refused access to most of the UK's allegedly most haunted sites. He had attended the few conferences on the subject that had been held, but his attempts to talk to the lecturers afterward had met with little success.

He was sitting in his Nottingham flat one dreary Monday evening, holding the letter that explained why he was being "let go" from his management position at the Broadmarsh Centre branch of Our Price (the store was closing due to a management buyout and besides, there were already two large record shops nearby and no need for a third one) when the telephone call came out of the blue. He had nothing to lose and so of course he had said yes. It was only later that he discovered that the researcher had contacted over twenty people before him, and had simply been working her way down the attendance list of the Birmingham conference he'd been to the previous month after she'd tried the guest speakers. He was annoyed at first, then immensely grateful that he had a surname close to the top of the alphabet. He was the only one whistling when he signed on at the unemployment office that Wednesday, but that was only because he thought he had reason to. With any luck, an appearance on *Central Weekend* would be the springboard he had been waiting for. Perhaps then publishers would stop turning down his nonfiction book, *Ghosts Everywhere*. They might even offer him a contract to write another one—filled with pictures he would be taking at their expense. A nice, glossy hardcover of the type he regularly perused in Dillons bookshop.

It hadn't turned out quite the way he was expecting.

First, he had arrived at Central's Nottingham Studios fully expecting to be shown into some sort of greenroom where the guests would have access to plentiful drinks and nibbles. Instead, a young man whose only achievement in life had probably been to learn to chew gum and talk at the same time had told him that he was mistaken, that he was not on the guest panel, and that he was, in fact, a member of the audience.

"Are you the skeptics or the weirdos?" he had been asked.

"I beg your pardon?"

The young man indicated the near-empty auditorium into which he had guided Mr. Chesney. "Skeptics on the right, weirdos on the left. That way if there's a fight it looks better on camera."

Some may have been lost for words at this point but not Peter Chesney, who let rip with the full indignation of someone who has been disappointed to the point of considering violence. Of course, such individuals rarely act on their desires, and Mr. Chesney was no exception. With a grumpy expression and the gait of a defeated man, he took a seat near the back.

The auditorium was almost full when the next unexpected thing happened.

Chesney felt a tap on the shoulder and turned to his left to see a young woman wearing glasses, carrying a clipboard, and bearing an apologetic expression.

"Dr. Chesney?"

"It's Mr. Chesney," he said, correcting her for what would turn out to be the first and only time, "and if you're here to apologize for the mix-up don't bother, Miss . . ." he peered at her name badge, ". . . Sandra Bellingham. I'll stay for the first half but then I should probably be going."

Sandra Bellingham looked even more worried. "Oh, we couldn't have you leaving us, Dr. Chesney, not halfway through the program, and certainly not if you could see your way to doing us a small favor."

He had heard about questions being planted in the audience of programs like these. Well, if she wanted him to do the program's dirty work and ask something that made him look stupid he had another cascade of vituperative bile ready just for her.

"What sort of favor?"

"Well, first of all I have to admit this is a little embarrassing." Sandra actually did look uneasy, but it was probably an act. "But I was the one who asked you to come here."

He recognized her voice now. It no longer endeared her to him.

"I'm really sorry about the mix-up, about you thinking you were going to be on the panel and everything."

"That's all right," he said. It wasn't, not at all, but he was saving his rage for what he imagined she was going to ask him next.

"No, it really isn't all right, and if you turn me down now, I shall quite understand."

Turn her down? Was she going to ask him out? The slip of a girl had to be half his age if she was a day! No, that couldn't be it.

She took his silence as permission to proceed. "It's just that one of our experts hasn't turned up. It's possible it's because of someone else who is here, but anyway," she took a deep breath, "the fact is we're a panel member short."

"Well, what do you want me to do about it?" Suggest someone else? Give her their phone number?

"We were wondering if you would be kind enough to fill the missing place. I appreciate it's short notice and, well," the girl gave a little gasp of embarrassment that was suddenly most becoming, "we've messed you around so much, but you really would be doing us a tremendous favor."

Chesney remained silent, temporarily speechless, unable to believe his luck.

This time Miss Bellingham mistook his silence for reticence. "We will of course pay your expenses and, as a panel member, you will be entitled to a night's stay at the Royal Hotel in the middle of the city."

Chesney was still processing the information.

"There are a couple of well-known people on the panel—including author Ramsey Campbell, who, as well as writing all those terrifying horror stories, has actually written an article about certain psychic research activities himself. There are also a couple of people for the skeptics' side, but we could really do with another expert on the paranormal." She looked at him with eyes trained to melt men's hearts. "Would you? *Please.*"

Chesney managed a nod and was immediately offered a hand to help him to his feet.

"Thank you so much, Dr. Chesney, you have no idea how much you're helping us out."

Actually he did, but he still hadn't found his voice to tell her that, or indeed to correct her as to his title. He had another reason for remaining silent now, one that he hadn't counted on when he had arrived at the studio.

Complete and utter stage fright.

What were they going to ask him? What was he going to say? He had seen at least one of the experts speak before. He had even read a couple of that Campbell chap's novels, and if he was anything like his books the man was unlikely to be sympathetic to a parapsychologist who couldn't hold his own in a discussion.

So he would just have to, wouldn't he? His mind raced back to all the conferences he had attended, all the people he had met or tried to meet, all the books he had read and the one he had actually written. It was no good. He couldn't do this. Even as he was being introduced to the other panel members he knew he couldn't do it.

No, Mr. Peter Chesney couldn't.

But *Dr.* Peter Chesney could.

In that moment, that split-second when he had to decide between telling Miss Bellingham it just wasn't possible and running for the exit, and taking his seat on the couch next to the experts, something happened. A new persona was born, full-formed and ready to take on the world. It was not Peter Chesney, ex-manager of a failing Our Price record store, that took his seat on the couch between a famous vampire-hunter and a famous horror writer. It was the soon-to-be just as famous Dr. Peter Chesney, parapsychologist and investigator into the paranormal.

Which was just how they introduced him.

After that it was easy. Chesney had learned much just by watching those whom he now understood he had idolized. Not just for what they knew, but for how they handled difficult questions, how they prevented themselves from being forced to give answers on controversial topics and, most importantly, how they turned their personal experiences into stories that held the audience enraptured.

All in all, by the time the program came to an end he was quite proud of himself. Afterward he ignored the other "experts," who had been difficult all night, and told Ramsey Campbell how much he had enjoyed *The Doll Who Ate His Mother* (the horror author had turned out to be extremely amicable after all, and just as fond of a glass or two of wine as the "newly qualified" Dr. Chesney was). He then proceeded to drink more than he should, safe in the knowledge that a Central TV taxi was waiting to take him to the Royal Hotel in the middle of the city.

The next morning, his pounding hangover was worsened by the ringing of his telephone. It was Sandra, sounding none too bright herself.

"The show was a success! The ratings were fantastic!"

"That's good to hear," Chesney mumbled from beneath the sheets.

"My producer has asked me to call you this morning to see if you'd be interested in appearing in a new show, one about paranormal investigation around the country. He's kind of into it himself and has wanted to get something like this off the ground for months. The problem has always been that there's never been anyone reliable enough to front it."

Most of that passed in a blur, but he did manage to catch the last sentence. "Who is going to front it, then?"

A pause. "We've got a couple of great celebrity choices we're considering. But what we really need is an expert to come on each week and give advice, some background, all that sort of stuff. If you'd be willing."

Chesney didn't exactly sober up immediately, but he made a very good attempt. "Would this be for a series?"

"Yes." She still sounded apologetic. Perhaps that was just her normal tone? "For six episodes to begin with. We'd see how those went before thinking about renewing it. Are you interested?"

Of course he was, and he told her so.

"Great. They wanted me to catch you before you left the hotel in case you were off on some sort of long-term ghost-hunting thing. Would you be able to come in on Monday to discuss contracts?"

Chesney said yes and wrote down her phone number, very carefully and in large numbers so he couldn't possibly get it wrong. After she had gone and he had managed to make himself presentable, he was doubly glad of that slip of paper because otherwise he would have been convinced he had dreamed it.

Thus had been born Dr. Peter Chesney, parapsychologist and investigator into all things paranormal. Nobody at Central TV had asked him for proof of qualifications and besides, he had never claimed to possess any. It was everyone else who was eager to believe he was an expert, and he wasn't going to argue with them if it got him access to places denied him as a plain old "Mr."

And now he was here, in All Hallows Church. One of the newspapers had called it "the Mount Everest of haunted buildings," and if the stories were to be believed, it had certainly earned that reputation. After its closure in 1972 there had been two concerted efforts to investigate it, both illegal in that no permission was given for the site to be trespassed upon, and both ending in disaster. The injuries, deaths, and cases of incurable insanity that had followed those episodes had not cowed Dr. Chesney, however. They had both been expeditions that had been poorly planned and executed—groups of amateurs who had little idea what they might be getting into. True, there had been parapsychologists and mediums involved, and even a physicist in the second case, but no provision had been made for medical aid nor the aid of a higher power should it become necessary.

Chesney's eyes darted over from his equipment to Professor Chambers, seated at the back of the church. The fellow was a pathologist, but they all had to go through basic medical training, didn't they? The man had instantly riled him by asking where he had been trained. Chesney had successfully dodged that for now, and despite the fact that they had started off on the wrong foot he was pleased that there was a medical man here to help the injured, so Chesney wouldn't be called upon to. He was similarly relieved by Father Traynor's presence, even though the man seemed a little distant and, curiously for a Catholic priest, was yet to give any blessing to the group, or even offer up a prayer for their protection. Perhaps that was what he was doing right now, tucked away in his vestry.

The reporter girl Chesney could have done without, but it was difficult to feel too much animosity toward her when she, and her newspaper, were the reason they were all there. Dr. Cruttenden could be nothing but an asset—a lady of letters who would be able to translate any obscure writings they might come across. Chesney had already been impressed by her observations concerning the church architecture. He had been intending to bring that up himself, but she had beaten him to it.

Finally, there were those competition winners. He could almost hear his internal voice sneering at the words. The woman obviously had connections to the world of the paranormal. He had seen the Tarot deck among her possessions and she had mentioned Glastonbury—one of the most powerful and significant places of psychic power in the country. She might be of some use to the group. Right now she was staring at the wall of the north aisle, tilting her head back and forth. Perhaps there was something there no one else could see. He made a mental note to check the area for psychic energy once she had gotten out of the way. Then hopefully he could make a formal announcement about it before she said anything and claim the discovery for himself.

He turned his attention back to his machine. He had insisted on a number of items of equipment being supplied for his use. Most of them were far too expensive for him to own and he had relished the opportunity of being able to use them. The device before him was, as the woman Ronnie had intimated, a seismograph, but one that had been designed to detect psychic disturbances rather than physical ones. He wasn't exactly sure how it worked (he wasn't entirely sure how any of the equipment worked even though he had done his best to read up on the relevant papers in the parapsychology journals beforehand) but the principle was that any release of abnormal energy would be registered by the needles on the graph paper. Something minor like a ghostly breath, or slight movement of furniture—any of the commonly accepted attempts to communicate from the Beyond—would register at the low end of the scale, never any higher than a three. A spectral apparition would rate halfway up the scale at a five or a six. A full-blown demon from the gates of Hell would rack the needle up to ten. While the prospect of such an occurrence filled Chesney with terror, there was also a small part of him that knew he would be made for life if he survived to tell the tale. And there were plenty of people here who could be encouraged to get in its way while he made good his escape.

Of course he also had more protection than they did, he thought, as he eyed the half-constructed framework of aluminum tubes in the corner. It was based on the design of the electric pentacle used by the occult detective Thomas Carnacki in the stories of William Hope Hodgson. The author, who had spent a considerable amount of time at sea, had discovered something akin to it on his travels and had "updated" it by adding the use of electricity in his books. Chesney's device didn't need power, but had been developed such that, when they were assembled, the aluminum tubes formed a three dimensional pentacle large enough to contain a man. Each of the tubes was filled with holy water. Chesney had wanted the tubes to be made from silver, but the budget hadn't been able to stretch. He hoped that the water and the pattern of the pentacle itself would be enough to protect him from supernatural horrors should the need arise. As for the others, well, they would just have to take care of themselves, wouldn't they?

As he worked, he kept his eye on them. Chambers and Karen at the back, Ronnie mooning over that wall, that Hale chap carrying stuff around and helping to set up the cots as if he thought he was being useful. Father Traynor had cleared off to the vestry, presumably to try and make it livable. On reconsideration, Chesney wouldn't have minded sharing the transept with the priest, who certainly might come in useful if the pentacle needed urgent blessing. Plus, demons often tended to have a preference for priests, or so he'd read—something about the challenge and the crushing embarrassment they imagined would have to be endured by God if they won.

Which meant there was only one person whose whereabouts were unaccounted for, Chesney thought as he made a final adjustment to the middle needle and prepared for a test run.

What was Dr. Cruttenden up to?

TWELVE

DR. ROSALIE CRUTTENDEN HAD been busy.

The fifty-eight-year-old Oxford lecturer had initially been trepidant about agreeing to come on this expedition, as she preferred to think of it. Not an expedition into foreign lands, but one into history. All Hallows, and the ground on which it had been built, had an awful lot of that, much of it from the last couple of hundred years poorly documented because it was difficult to distinguish facts from hearsay. Oddly, All Hallows as well as the area of Blackheath that surrounded it, was one of those rare instances where as one went further back into the past, the historical records became more detailed, almost as if, as the centuries had gone by, attempts had been made to conceal what had happened here.

And what, for all she knew, might still be happening.

She still found it difficult to accept the concept of the supernatural as something that actually existed, but over the last few weeks she had been witness to enough evidence to suggest otherwise. The episode in her Oxford study where she, the reporter girl, and that nice professor had been subjected to a hailstorm of wriggling horror had only been the beginning. Since then her dreams had been plagued by visions of this place. She hadn't been sure until she had arrived, but one look at the building had confirmed it. A tiny part of her had wanted to run in the other direction, as fast and as far away as possible and screaming as she went.

But Dr. Cruttenden was made of sterner stuff than that, and besides, this was probably going to be the last big project that she would work on before retirement. Oh, she knew colleagues who just couldn't leave Oxford, or their life's work alone, who returned in unpaid *emeritus* positions and carried on as before. But it wouldn't be the same. No students, no exams, no formal lectures. Some found this a blessed relief, but the youth, vitality, and enthusiasm of her students were among the main things that caused her to delight in her job.

She was already in the process of composing the first part of the lecture she would deliver on her experiences in here. Perhaps, at the end of the day, she was just a bit of a show-off. If she was, she was too old to start caring about it now. In two years she would retire, and that would be an end to it. It would be lovely to go out with a bang, she thought, and getting rid of those bothersome nightmares would be most acceptable too.

So here she was, in an allegedly haunted church built on land with connections going right back to the time when Geoffrey Chaucer was appointed Clerk of the King's Works in 1389, and possibly even before that.

The apsidal was quite snug. Her cot fit close to the curve of the far wall, under a narrow window that admitted a slip of gray light. To the left and right were two low tables, piled high with the books she had spent the last half an hour carting in. There were even more volumes underneath, which was just as well, as the stained wooden surfaces were on the point of collapsing from the weight and in dire need of being propped up.

The cot was currently home to several notepads. She could have brought a Dictaphone, but she preferred to work in longhand. As well as being more pleasingly tangible, it also made it easier for her to refer back to items of importance.

A small wooden stool completed the furniture in the cubicle and she was sitting on it right now, sorting volumes into alphabetical order, with works dealing with pre–seventeenth century history beneath the tables and more modern works on top. The light from the tiny window was minimal. In the right-hand corner, next to the head of the cot (a small pillow signified that), an upright lamp cast a harsh glow upon that side of the room. Rosalie sat in shadow. For some reason she felt more comfortable there than in the light, perhaps because there was less chance of something finding her.

Sitting here, in this tiny, poorly lit chilly room, with only a few rude pieces of furniture for rough comfort, she was struck by sudden feelings of sympathy for the many nuns who must have survived in conditions either similar to, or worse than, this. Of course they had the inner comfort of the promise of Heaven, she thought, something an atheist like herself had attempted to entertain many times during her youth (and with the aid of her overly religious parents), but somehow the Message had never sunk in. After a horrendous failed relationship when she was only seventeen, she had given herself up to the religion that was academic study, isolated herself from society within the sort of confines only an institution like an Oxford college can truly offer, and devoted her life to seeking more secrets from the past while trying hard to conceal her own from herself. And on the whole she had succeeded, feeling safe behind the walls of ivory towers, only venturing out now and again in the name of research. It had not been a bad life, even if it had been a somewhat uneventful one.

She was squeezing her copy of G. M. Trevelyan's *History of England* next to van Thal's two-volume work on Britain's prime ministers when there was a noise from behind her, over in the far corner.

Behind the lamp.

She squinted, but it was difficult to see because of the brightness. Was there something?

"Hello?"

She had no idea why she called out. It wasn't as if anyone could have been able to sneak past her and get behind the lamp while she had been working, was it?

And yet, it looked as if there was a figure standing there, or at least the outline of one. A figure wearing a cloak and a cowl. That had to be what it was, because no living thing could have a head that shape.

"Father? Is that you?"

Rosalie got to her feet, but the angle of the lamp's glare just made the figure all the more indistinct.

Until it moved.

Its head swayed a little, from side to side. Rosalie frowned. Was it saying no? Or was the priest perhaps in some kind of trouble?

"Father Traynor? Are you all right?"

She took a step forward. The figure stayed where it was. She could see its outline a little more clearly now, or at least she thought she could. The shimmering had to be caused by the light, as was the way in which the surface of the figure's garment seemed to undulate softly, as if there were things beneath it that writhed and squirmed in the darkness of the cloak's embrace.

"You're going to burn yourself if you're not careful." Rosalie reached out and grasped the thin black cable that ran to the lamp, keeping her eyes on the figure as she felt her way down to the switch.

Click.

It took her eyes a moment to adjust to the gloom, to the insipid gray dimness caused by the feeble light entering the tiny slit window.

It took her a moment.

Then, as the figure rose to its full height, she wished she couldn't see anything at all, and most certainly not the worm-ridden, rotten face of the thing that had entered her room, that perhaps had always been there.

Rosalie backed toward the door, but she was only just getting used to the room and she miscalculated, finding herself pressed against solid stone.

The corpse-thing took a shambling step forward, its lower limbs obviously in an even worse state than its face.

Its face . . .

It was the last thing Rosalie wanted to look at, and yet she didn't dare take her eyes off it. It was the narrow, thin, wasted visage of something terribly old, something that should be dead but somehow wasn't, that could offer little resistance to the creatures that feasted on what was left of its flesh and yet still possessed enough life to part those maggot-chewed lips to reveal the swollen tongue within. As it leaned forward to speak, Rosalie noticed other things about the figure, noticed the simple black habit, stained with the dirt of the grave; noticed the wimple that could be seen now that the cowl had fallen back a little.

The nun leaned farther forward, tottering a little, and took in a breath. The air rattling through the rotted larynx and inflating what was left of her lungs sounded like dry leaves being shaken in a paper bag. Her face was very close now, just inches from Rosalie's own. She could see tiny lice crawling in the creases of the thing's parchment-thin skin, worms wriggling in one nostril, and as for the eyes . . .

There were no eyes.

When the thing finally spoke, the words came out as a crackling whisper, the ravages of time and the grave having taken their toll on vocal cords that were almost too dry and too scarred to form intelligible sounds.

"Nine . . . circles."

The thing's breath stank of the charnel house. Rosalie held her own for as long as she could, until the pounding in her ears and the pain in her chest became almost unendurable. She exhaled with a gasp and took another breath. The stink nearly made her gag as the thing spoke again.

"The . . . Gates . . . of . . . Hell."

Rosalie felt something clutch at her. Her arms were raised in front of her, hands balled into fists. She looked down to see her right forearm in the grip of weathered claws, bare and brittle bone stained brown from cemetery earth. The cracked fingertips were digging into her sleeve. She could feel chill tendrils probing her mind, her thoughts being lifted and overturned as if by the limbs of a curious spider seeking its prey.

"Don't . . . dig . . . down . . . below . . ." the thing said. But this time its mouth had stayed closed.

And then it was gone.

It took a moment for Dr. Rosalie Cruttenden to realize what had happened, another to switch the light on, and then a third to scream.

THIRTEEN

Thursday, December 22, 1994. 12:25 P.M.

BY THE TIME BOB Chambers got there, with Karen close behind, Peter Chesney was already on the scene.

"Are you all right?" Chambers asked.

Dr. Cruttenden nodded as Chesney, who had sat next to her, patted her hand. Her cot was creaking under their combined weight.

Chambers took her pulse. Bouncing along at a regular ninety beats per minute, which was to be expected in someone who had received a mild shock.

"I'm fine, really," Dr. Cruttenden insisted, "I'm just a silly old woman who gets spooked too easily sometimes."

"What spooked you?" Karen, ever the journalist, had her Dictaphone on and was holding it up to record the lecturer's words.

Chesney answered for her, his eyes glinting with fanatical zeal. "Dr. Cruttenden has witnessed an apparition, our first genuine sign that something is actually here!"

"I'm not so sure about that," Rosalie replied. "It could well have been my imagination."

"What did you see, Dr. Cruttenden?" Chambers released her right wrist while her left continued to receive the unwanted attentions of the parapsychologist.

"Well, I thought I saw . . . I thought I . . ."

"A nun." It was the first time Chambers had seen Chesney smile. "She saw a nun. In this room! And it spoke to her."

"What did it say?" Karen still had the Dictaphone switched on.

"I'm not really sure." Dr. Cruttenden was obviously shaken but trying to keep calm. "To be honest it didn't make much sense."

"The dead seldom do," said Chesney, unhelpfully, "until we understand the context in which they are trying to communicate with us."

Chambers flashed him a glare but it was going to take more than that to shut him up. "It might be helpful if you told us anyway, Dr. Cruttenden," he said.

Rosalie briefly repeated what the nun had said to her. "It doesn't make much sense, does it? I mean, it's not as if we're intending to do any digging while we're here."

"Not physically." Ronnie was peering in through the narrow doorway, and Chambers could see Paul Hale's youthful face behind her as she continued, "But what about spiritually? Or even historically? There are more ways in which to disturb the past than by simple physical means."

"What did she look like?"

Rosalie turned to face Karen, licking her lips before answering the question. "She was very old. So old that quite a lot of her wasn't there, if you see what I mean."

"Like the things in our dreams?" asked Chambers.

Rosalie nodded.

Chesney frowned. "What dreams?"

"We'll tell you later." Chambers spoke calmly. "Rosalie, you don't have to tell us any of this if you don't want to, but did she look like the things that guard this place in the dreams?"

"I couldn't see much of her, of course," Dr. Cruttenden continued, "just her face, or rather what was left of it, and her hand. Her left hand." She rubbed the forearm where she claimed the thing's fingers had gripped her. "It was so cold, her touch, so cold. Perhaps that was what made me cry out." She frowned. "No, no that's not right. I cried out after she had gone, I think."

Chambers did his best to reassure her. "You've had quite a shock," he said. "It's completely understandable that you might get your facts muddled for a while. It sounds clichéd, but the best thing for you to do is get some rest."

Rosalie looked around her tiny, book-lined cubicle. "Oh, I couldn't possibly," she said. "I mean, what if it should come back?"

"Take my room," said Karen. "There's precious little of my stuff in it yet anyway. And I'll stay in here so if anything does appear I'll be able to verify your story."

"I really think I should be the one to stay here," Chesney sniffed. "It's a shame that my equipment won't fit in this room, but I have had to rely on my own eyes and my innate sensitivity before. In fact, I have prior experience of a similar event."

"Really?" Chambers raised an eyebrow. "Where was that, then?"

"Brecon Cathedral. It is a very well documented case. The remains of a number of nuns were found bricked-up in the walls of the Cathedral. Their ghosts roam the building, cursed to remain there because of the violent nature of their deaths."

"And you saw them?"

Chesney seemed reluctant to discuss the matter, with Chambers at least. "I felt them, Professor Chambers, as did other members of my party."

"It's certainly possible to feel such unhappy spirits," said Ronnie, "especially if their death was unexpected."

Chambers turned to her. "And did you feel anything?"

"When?"

"Just now, when Dr. Cruttenden saw what she thought she saw."

Ronnie shook her head. "No."

"She was too far away," said Chesney.

"And did your equipment pick anything up?"

Chesney looked uneasy. "It isn't calibrated properly yet."

"So I'll take that as a no." Chambers could see Karen's chastising gaze out of the corner of his eye. "I'm just trying to establish the facts here, that's all. I wouldn't want you recording a distorted version of what actually happened."

"I believe what I saw, Professor Chambers." Dr. Cruttenden got to her feet. "And I believe it strongly enough that I am convinced we are going to discover the meaning behind those dreams the three of us have been having."

That made Dr. Chesney even more cross. "Three of you?"

Karen raised a hand. "Me as well, I'm afraid. We'll tell you all about them later."

"Anyone else?" Chesney was looking at Ronnie and Paul now. "Anyone else had weird dreams about this place that they have neglected to inform me of?"

They both shook their heads. Paul looked relieved. Ronnie did not.

"I would appreciate it if you would all keep me informed of any paranormal activity in the future," Chesney snapped. "There is precious little point in my being here if I cannot rely upon all of you to report your observations. Now, I shall stay here while Dr. Cruttenden sleeps in Miss Shepworth's room. Hopefully our ghostly nun will elect to make a further appearance for me this time."

As Chambers stood back to let Dr. Cruttenden out, he could not help but think that the last person any ghostly spirit would want to appear in front of would be this self-important little man. He and Karen made sure Rosalie was all right before joining Ronnie and Paul back in the nave.

"Where was Father Traynor during all of that?" Karen asked.

"Probably still sorting out his vestry," Chambers replied, pointing to the little door as they passed it. "The walls are pretty thick and the wood of that door most likely is too. He probably didn't hear a thing."

"Lucky him," she said. "Besides, there were quite enough of us in there. Any more and Rosalie would probably have fainted from lack of air rather than from seeing a ghost."

Chambers agreed. "Once she's gotten over the shock we'll have to ask her more about it, hopefully without Chesney there."

"You really don't like him, do you?"

Chambers knew it was obvious. He had never been able to hide his true feelings about things from anyone. "I don't know how to describe it," he said, "but he has that aura of insincerity about him that you get with stage magicians, dodgy faith healers, and other charlatans."

"You'd better not let Ronnie hear you say that." Karen was leading the way now. "I think she's quite big on all that psychic stuff back in Glastonbury."

Chambers shook his head. "She strikes me as sincere. Whatever she feels, or thinks she feels, she completely believes it. She isn't trying to fool anyone."

"And what about you?"

Chambers stopped, his eyebrows raised. "What about me?"

Karen gave him a cool look. "Here you are judging everyone on their absence of psychic ability, of sensitivity, and yet you're basing the conclusions you've drawn on your own feelings, your own intuition. Surely that's the same as what they do?"

"Ronnie perhaps, but not Chesney. I get the feeling . . ." Chambers paused and flashed a guilty smile ". . . that he doesn't have a sensitive bone in his body."

"You may be right, but we still have nearly four days to spend in here, so don't start being rude to him just yet."

Chambers looked at the red button rigged up near the west entrance. "We can always push the panic button if it gets too much."

"And then the nightmares might never stop. Do you really want to risk that?"

Of course he didn't. "I was only joking. And I promise I'll do my best to behave in front of 'Dr.' Chesney."

"Good." Karen smiled. "And if you address him take those quote marks off—I can tell it pissed him off a lot when you called him that in the van."

There was another surprise awaiting them on the wall of the north aisle, one that brought Dr. Chesney running at the possibility he might be missing out on yet another potential paranormal phenomenon.

"I knew there was something there," Ronnie breathed. "I knew it."

"I saw you staring at it earlier." Chesney took a step back to get a better look. "Could you see it then?"

"No," came the reply. "But I could feel it."

High up on the wall, very faded but definitely there, was an artist's rendition of a skeleton. It wasn't exactly anatomically accurate, Chambers thought. The skull was too small, the neck too long, and the radius and ulna of both forearms seemed abnormally thickened. With muscles to match around those bones he imagined the figure would be incredibly strong. The misshapen skull meant it probably wouldn't look very pretty either.

The left elbow was bent, the forearm at right angles to the body. As Chambers stared he realized the figure was leaning on something.

"What is that?" he whispered to himself.

"It looks like a spade," said Karen. "Or at least the handle of one. The blade is buried in the ground."

"And no one saw this before? No one saw this when they came in here?'" Chesney had brought his camera over now and was taking picture after picture, the flash blinding the rest of them.

No one gave him an answer.

"You," he pointed at Ronnie. "You said you could feel it? How could you 'feel' a painting of a skeleton?"

"I didn't 'feel a painting of a skeleton.'" Ronnie looked hurt but stood her ground. "I just knew something was there, underneath the plaster, almost as if it were trying to get out."

"It definitely wasn't there before," said Paul. "I would have seen it. Hey, we all would. Who's going to miss a huge skeleton like that?"

"You'd be surprised what people can miss if they're not looking, Mr. Hale." Chesney took his umpteenth photograph and finally seemed satisfied. "I'll be interested to see if anything different shows up on the film."

"You'll have to wait until we get out for that though, won't you?" said Hale.

Chesney shook his head. "In addition to my other equipment, I asked for all the appropriate developing materials and chemicals to be supplied. All I need is somewhere dark enough to process them."

"Well, that won't be difficult." Hale raised his hand. "In here I can barely see this in front of my face most of the time."

"The undercroft will do nicely," said Chesney. "Have you all eaten?"

The rest looked at him blankly before Karen volunteered a slightly confused "No?"

"In that case I would ask that you all please hurry and have your lunch. After that I would ask that no one enters the undercroft while I am down there. I want to get these pictures developed as soon as possible."

Before any of them could reply, Chesney dashed back to Dr. Cruttenden's apsidal, keeping the camera with him.

"Can we lock him in?" Hale asked.

"Well, we get two choices," said Chambers with a grin. "The apsidal or the undercroft. Which do you think he deserves?"

"Stop it, both of you," said Karen. "He might still be able to hear you."

"Who made him boss anyway?" Hale didn't look impressed.

"No one's the boss," said Karen. "We're all here for different reasons, and we all have to give each other the appropriate respect."

"The only respect that bloke has is for himself," said Hale. "He could do with being a lot less of an arse."

"It's not finished," said Ronnie quietly from behind the three of them.

They turned to see her still gazing at the picture. Karen laid a hand on her shoulder.

"How do you mean?"

Ronnie shook her head. "I'm not sure, but it's not finished yet. It has more to say, more to show us." She gave Karen a helpless smile. "I can't say more than that I'm afraid."

"It looks old," said Hale. "Maybe Dr. Cruttenden might know something about it."

"I think Dr. Cruttenden has seen enough for now." Chambers was looking at the painting. "But I agree we should ask her to take a look at it once she's over the shock."

"It's amazing, though, isn't it?" Ronnie took a step closer and stared at it, as if she was willing the painting to show her its secrets. "First Dr. Cruttenden's apparition and now this." She turned to look at the others. "The church obviously wants us here."

"I'm not sure I find that thought entirely comforting," said Chambers.

An uneasy silence followed. It was finally broken by Karen nodding in the direction of the undercroft.

"Right, well," she said. "Shall we get ourselves some lunch before the kitchen gets turned into a darkroom for the afternoon?"

The others readily agreed, relieved to have something else to occupy their thoughts. Karen volunteered to take some food to Dr. Cruttenden.

"While you're at it you can drop some off with our parapsychology colleague," said Chambers, not unkindly.

"All right," she said. "But only if you agree to get Father Traynor."

Chambers shrugged. "I'll do my best."

"That leaves you and me to start looking through the cupboards." Ronnie already had Paul Hale by the sleeve. "Come on, let's see how good you are at peeling potatoes."

"Serves me right for not volunteering for one of the easier jobs," said Hale with a grin as he started to follow her. "Lead the way."

Karen followed, leaving Chambers on his own. He stayed there for a moment, enjoying the calm. It wasn't long, however, before the silence and the solitude began to feel unfriendly. The others hadn't gone far, and yet the few sounds they were making suddenly seemed miles away. He resisted the urge to look at the painting again but it was no good. A skeleton in the process of burying something.

Or digging something up.

He tried not to dwell on that thought, instead turning his mind to how it had gotten there, or rather, how no one had noticed it before now. A change in humidity causing damp to bring out the pattern? Or perhaps the angle of one of the floodlights had been altered, casting light in a slightly different direction and simply making it more apparent?

Neither explanation fit, and the thought of that chilled him to the marrow as he made his way to the vestry door. He knocked hard, twice, but received no answer. The third time he called Traynor's name and rattled the handle of the locked door.

Nothing.

For some reason, it made what he was thinking seem all the more terrifying.

All Hallows Church knew they were here.

And it was pleased.

FOURTEEN

Thursday, December 22, 1994. 12:46 P.M.

BEHIND THE VESTRY DOOR that Chambers was at that moment knocking on cowered a terrified man.

At least he was a man at that moment, Father Traynor thought. A terrified, impotent, waste of a man but a man nevertheless. One who was increasingly unable to account for his words or his deeds, and one who, it seemed, could no longer rely on the protection of the Lord inside this damned place.

That was the worst of all.

He had barricaded himself in this room, the voices in his head getting louder all the time. Especially that One Voice, the one that belonged to that . . . thing he had seen or hallucinated in the graveyard before coming in here. Telling him what to do and what to say, where to tell the others to sleep, to cook, to eat.

To die.

No, no, no! He refused to be a part of that. He would not play a part to murder. He was a man of God and no power on Earth could change that.

Oh, but my power stretches beyond Earth, the voice said, still privy to his thoughts. *Far beyond and deep beneath. So deep it reaches all the way down, all the way through.* It suddenly seemed amused. *Do you wish to know what lies beyond this place, on the Other Side?*

Father Traynor shook his head.

It is known as the "Sea of Darkness." It lasts forever, in all directions, and the harder you try to escape it the stronger its hold on you becomes. Does the prospect of immortality in such an unending limbo terrify you?

The priest nodded.

It is much as I thought. Spineless fools such as you who will be your religion's undoing, and mine own salvation. I think I shall keep you alive so that you may see it in all its hellish glory.

And then the inside of his head was silent once more, once again granted temporary respite while the demon within him faded, rested, went about business elsewhere for all he knew. Still too afraid to move, he stayed where he was, crouched against the vestry door, his fingers clawing at the intricate carvings in the wood.

He looked at them more closely. They resembled no religious iconography he was aware of, no biblical story or tale of martyrdom. Instead, each row of carvings depicted the same thing—an unending plain on which wandered tiny figures, all far from one another and going in no specific direction. Some were walking, others were crawling. Every now and then one must have fallen into a swamp or something because they appeared to be buried up to the waist. Or they possessed nothing below it.

Perhaps it was something from Dante's *Divina Commedia*, or adapted from one of the hellish landscapes of Hieronymus Bosch? But even if it was, what priest would have chosen to have that to decorate the inside of his vestry door? A never-ending reminder of the tortures of the pit that awaited sinners? In his life he had known priests who were very fire and brimstone in their sermons, and others who had led private lives that certainly deserved such constant chastisement, but few were those who would entertain such images in the house of God.

Perhaps it was the Sea of Darkness.

He wiped the sweat from his face and looked around the room he had made his prison once more. It was small, no bigger than twice the size of the apsidal chapels he had been instructed to show the women to sleep in. Stone walls with a tiny slit window to the north overlooking the cemetery.

And a trapdoor in the far left-hand corner.

The voice had urged him to lift that up, to go down there and explore. But the tones had been mocking and his fearful response had merely made it laugh all the more. Presumably it, too, led to the undercroft, just like the flight of stone steps on the other side of the church. If that were true, though, it meant that the undercroft had to be huge, spanning the width of the church at least, and extending who knew how far north and south?

There was nowhere for him to sleep.

He deserved that, the priest thought. He deserved it for being weak. Everyone knew All Hallows was a cursed place, and yet he had simply followed his Archbishop's orders, had not questioned them once, had not said that if he was coming into such a place, surely he needed help? That there needed to be more than just one of him? If there had been another priest with him perhaps they would have been able to save each other from the horror in the graveyard. Now he was trapped in here and something had damned his soul.

What was it the Archbishop had wanted him to find? Incriminating documents? There had been no sign of any such thing so far, and he would have assumed the vestry to be the repository of any records that had been kept.

Unless they were . . . underground.

Something drew his attention back to the carvings on the door. The Sea of Darkness itself appeared to be the work of an artist, as did some of the figures. However, now that he looked closely, some of them weren't. Some of the tiny men and women crawling across that hellish landscape looked as if they had been added later, and often by hurried hands, so much so that one or two of them were little more than scratches in the wood.

A terrifying thought struck him. Was this the "document" Cardinal Thomas might have been referring to? Was the fate of those who had entered this place and never come out recorded on this door?

It lasts forever. Does the prospect of immortality in such an unending limbo terrify you?

Was that where they had ended up? In the Sea of Darkness, which could be accessed through this building? His eyes turned to the far left-hand corner again.

Perhaps through that trapdoor?

But what was he supposed to do? Wrench the door from its hinges? Chop the thing into firewood and burn it? There was no axe here for him to do that.

There might be one down below, a voice whispered in his head. *Everything you need might be down below. An axe ... fire ... salvation ...*

He shook his head and tried to stop the tears welling in his eyes. *More like damnation*, he thought.

You will not be able to resist me forever, said the voice. *Why endure such pain and torment now, when you could make it so much easier upon yourself? The task for which I have brought you here remains unfinished. Go below, fetch forth the instruments of their sacrifice and earn yourself a place at the right hand of darkness.*

So that was why the voice came and went! Father Traynor felt a flicker of hope. He had not been aware that his efforts had met with any success, but the voice had betrayed itself. It could be resisted, it could be fought. He took a deep breath and levered himself to his feet. He had been ill-prepared the first time, when that worm-ridden thing had appeared to him in the graveyard, and he had allowed it to overwhelm him, to take control and use him to arrange the hapless individuals outside into positions in the church that were to its liking. Perhaps it intended them to have their fates recorded in the wood as well, sacrifices to its dark domain.

He gripped the doorframe and stared at the carvings. He would not let those who had been placed under his protection by the Holy Mother Church fall to the evil within his head. He would not surrender them to the Sea of Darkness, and he would not destroy this door either. Perhaps there was still a chance that the souls engraved on the wood could be saved as well, that they could be liberated from the eternal Hell they had found themselves consigned to, and delivered safely into the hands of the Savior.

He gasped three Hail Marys, and then followed those with the Lord's Prayer for good measure. He was just uttering the line about not being led into temptation when the voice returned, a roaring tumult inside his head.

Do not presume to test me! I have been patient with you. I have shown you part of my domain, for indeed it is only a part, and yet I can see you need a more considerable demonstration in order to curb these petty rebellions of yours. Very well. Look upon my works, oh ye petty creature, and despair . . .

At first Father Traynor thought he was shrinking. His clutching fingertips were torn from the doorframe as it moved away from him, as the door before him seemed to grow. Then he realized that the carvings were staying the same size—it was the canvas on which they had been inscribed that was expanding, gaining height and depth and stretching to the right and left as far as his eyes could see.

He hung in limbo in front of the Sea of Darkness. Not the real thing, just an artist's impression of it, wandering souls immortalized in wood, bodies carved into oak, millions of them, all in pain, all suffering.

No matter how high he looked, or how far from side to side, the monstrous depiction of Hell went on forever, and as he gazed upon it, he was struck by a horrific realization. Hell was not like he had been taught at all. There were no devils, no fiery pits, no mutilating tortures. Just an unending ocean of wandering, of searching, of lost ambition and disillusioned fulfillment, going on forever and ever, until all sanity was lost and all hope dashed. And still it went on.

The real place is, of course, much worse, said the voice.

That was when he started to scream.

FIFTEEN

"DID YOU HEAR SOMETHING?"

Chambers shook his head and Karen knocked on the vestry door again, calling out this time as well.

"Father?"

"Father Traynor?" Chambers added his voice. "Are you all right?"

After his first attempts to rouse the priest, Chambers had joined the others in the undercroft kitchen, where he and Karen had volunteered to do the first round of food deliveries to those who were too unwell (Dr. Cruttenden), too "busy" (Chesney), or too locked in their own vestry to be able to come and eat with everyone else.

Karen looked at the tray of food Chambers had just placed on the floor so he could knock. "Should we just leave it there?"

Chambers shrugged. "I can't think of what else to do with it."

"Perhaps he's hurt."

Chambers rattled the handle again and gave the solid oak a shove. All it did was hurt his shoulder.

"Whether or not it's been bolted from the other side I can't tell," he said. "I suppose he could have locked it and gone wandering. He might be around somewhere and we just haven't bumped into him yet."

"But if he's not?" Karen was insistent. "What if he's had a heart attack? Or something's fallen on top of him and he can't move?"

"There's no way anyone is getting through that door without the aid of a battering ram." Chambers was rubbing his shoulder. "So if you want to go in there I suggest we either hit the panic button now, or start looking around for something suitably heavy."

Karen pinched her lip. He knew it would be disastrous to abort the project only a few hours in, and it would probably be highly embarrassing for her as well. Now she had labored the point, he was starting to wonder if the priest was all right himself.

"Okay," he said after he'd allowed her to procrastinate for a moment, "now you've got me worried. It could be any of the things you've said, and I agree we haven't seen him since he gave us his guided tour." He looked toward the west entrance. "I say we abort and get some equipment in here to get that door open."

"Wait!" Karen called him back.

"We need to get him out, Karen." Chambers was already halfway to the door, and the red button that had been attached to the right of it.

"I can hear something!"

Chambers stopped. "You can?"

Karen nodded, her ear pressed against the wood. "It's very faint but there's definitely someone in there."

By the time Chambers was back and listening as well the sounds were a little clearer. They were very faint, but were definitely words.

"I . . . am fine . . . thank you. Just . . . busy."

Karen looked up at her colleague. "He sounds a million miles away."

Chambers nodded. "Or buried under about twenty mattresses." Once she was out of the way he cupped his hands to shout. "Father Traynor? Are you sure you're all right?"

There was a delay before the reply, as if Chambers's words had needed to be relayed down a telegraph line to somewhere distant. The words seemed to come from somewhere just as far away.

"I am . . . fine. Please . . . do not . . . worry. Much . . . to do."

Karen didn't look happy. "He sounds weird."

Chambers thought it all seemed strange, but he couldn't offer anything other than, "He didn't come across as exactly normal when we met him."

"We're leaving a tray of food for you here, Father!" Karen shouted. "Dr. Chesney wants to use the undercroft as a darkroom for the next couple of hours so we're having lunch a bit early."

Silence.

Chambers crouched down and rattled the tray, as if that would make any difference. "We'll leave it here for you then," he said. "Don't let it get cold."

"There's nothing hot on there," Karen hissed, pointing at the chunk of cheddar cheese, the slices of ham, and the dollop of coleslaw. The two pickled onions stared back at Chambers accusingly.

"He doesn't know that," he replied. "And in view of what's already happened to two of us I'd be happier seeing him in the flesh, and sooner rather than later."

Karen nodded agreement, and gave the priest some encouragement of her own. "We'll be back to pick it up later, Father, all right?"

They waited, but this time there was no answer at all.

"Let's give him the benefit of the doubt for the moment." Chambers didn't know what else to do. Besides, there was another patient he was eager to check up on. "Come on, let's get back to the kitchen and get the tray for Dr. Cruttenden. I'd like to see how she is."

"Bet you won't be so eager to take Dr. Chesney his tray." Karen was already grinning.

"You can take that one yourself."

"Oh, no." She was shaking her head theatrically in a way that was actually quite becoming. "You agreed to do this with me and that means all of it. No chickening out. Or are you a man who doesn't follow through with his promises?"

"Never." Despite his general dislike for anyone associated with the media, Chambers was starting to warm to her. "At least not if there's no way I can get away with it."

"Very honest of you, professor. Would you care to put that on tape?"

"I think you know the answer to that," he said with an even more theatrical grimace. "Come on, let's get our university lecturer her salad."

Dr. Cruttenden seemed to welcome the intrusion, and was already levering herself off Karen's cot as they drew back the curtain to bring in the tray.

"You're supposed to be sleeping," said Chambers with a twinkle in his eye.

"Have you ever tried to rest after seeing a ghost, Professor Chambers?"

Chambers could see her point, and at least she seemed to be recovering her good spirits. "All I really want to do is get back to my books and see if there's any mention of such a person in the historical record."

"You might not be able to get in there for a while," said Karen, shifting the tray to make sure none of them tripped over it. "Dr. Chesney has set himself up in your room."

"That ghastly little man?" Dr. Cruttenden appeared to be rolling up her sleeves. "I'll soon have him out of there."

Karen grinned. "You may have a bit of a job. I think he's hoping to see the same thing you did."

"Maybe it'll cart him off with it while he's at it." Dr. Cruttenden broke off a chunk of cheese and chewed it absentmindedly. "Mind you, he's welcome to it, whoever or whatever it is. I'd be happy if I never saw it again. Ugly bloody thing, and that voice!"

"What sort of a noise did it make?" asked Chambers. "Groaning? Hissing?"

"No." Rosalie almost looked offended. "And it wasn't rattling a chain either. It spoke to me."

Karen pushed a stray strand of hair back over her right ear. "You vaguely told us before, but what exactly did it say to you?"

"Yes. I'm sorry I didn't elaborate, but that's because I was in something of a state of shock, for which I must apologize."

Karen shook her head. "No need," she said, reaching for her ever-present tape recorder. "But I would really like to know everything it said."

"Not much." Rosalie had picked up one of the pickled onions. She gave it a heavy crunch and then swallowed the whole thing. It almost made her cough. "Just something about digging. Or rather, not."

"I'm sorry?"

"'Don't dig down below,' it said to me. It was quite emphatic about it. Said it a couple of times." She shuddered and frowned. "At least, I think it was a couple."

"'Don't dig,'" Karen repeated and then switched the recorder off. "I wonder what that could have meant?"

"The graveyard, presumably." Chambers was peering out through the slit window of the apsidal. "There's nowhere you can really dig in here, is there?"

"Of course there is, you silly man." The other pickled onion disappeared and that just left the ham. Rosalie stamped on the floor. Her foot made hardly a noise on the dull stone. "What do you think lies beneath here?"

Chambers shrugged. "The undercroft?"

"Possibly. It's rumored that this church possesses an unusually large undercroft, with hidden chambers and passages, some of which have been closed for over a hundred years. But what lies beneath *that*?"

"Earth? Rock?"

Rosalie shook her head and popped the final strip of cold meat into her mouth. "Plague victims."

Karen's mouth opened at that.

"Don't do that my dear, you're actually very pretty and a look of bovine stupidity most certainly does not become you."

"Plague victims?" Karen refused to be distracted. "You mean from the Great Plague of London?"

"Oh yes, from 1665, and possibly victims of the Black Death which, of course, was much earlier."

"How much earlier?" Chambers asked.

"Around 1350, although there were still cases in the latter half of that century and the first half of the next. Of course, I have no idea if bodies were buried here over that entire length of time, but we have it on good authority that this place, and much of Blackheath, was used for the burial of plague victims in the fourteenth century as well as the seventeenth."

"How do we know?" Karen had the tape recorder on again.

"Well, I'd show you but that . . . man is in my room at the moment. Anyway, it's all down to you and your discovery, otherwise I would never have read up so much about Geoffrey Chaucer."

"How does he figure into it?" Chambers was paying more attention now.

Rosalie gave him the withering look of a teacher who is extremely displeased with her star pupil. "If you recall, we covered this back in Oxford."

"I'm afraid Professor Chambers has been through a lot since then," said Karen, "and so have we all. Could you possibly repeat it again for the official record?"

Dr. Cruttenden made a noise that sounded a bit like a *hrumph* before continuing. "In 1389 Geoffrey Chaucer was appointed the official Clerk of the King's Works. His main task was to organize repairs on Westminster Palace, but it is claimed that the reason he was given the position in the first place by King Richard II is that he did such a marvelous job supervising the clearing and burying of plague victims from the streets of London town."

"Burying them *here*?" Chambers was pointing a finger at the ground.

Dr. Cruttenden nodded. "And sealing them in stone so that . . . oh, what did that book say? Something like 'So that in future times a church might be built on this place to seal in what evil Satan may wish to revisit upon the world.' It's quite a famous quote, actually, and he said it in 1377." She looked at them as if the date was supposed to have significance. When Karen and Chambers continued to look at her with blank faces she rolled her eyes. "The year 1377? When he went on a mysterious sea voyage abroad? A journey for which many possible explanations have been offered but none have been accepted as fact."

"So bodies have been buried on this site for more than seven hundred years." Karen spoke so quietly it was possible to hear the squeak of the cassette tape as it ran over the recording heads.

"Buried, moved about, dug up again, buried again. It's been a curious site for that sort of thing." Rosalie chuckled. "You wonder where they managed to find room for them all."

"Perhaps the undercroft goes a very long way down." Chambers had intended it as a joke but here, in this tiny, chilly room, it didn't sound funny at all.

"Or perhaps they had magic to help them." Rosalie didn't sound as if she was even trying to joke.

"What do you mean by that?"

The lecturer gave Karen a reassuring smile. "Only what it says in the history books, my dear. According to the Medical Faculty of Paris at the time, the Black Death was thought to be due to a conjunction of three planets in 1345 that caused 'a great pestilence in the air.' Perhaps some other 'conjuration' helped them dispose of all the bodies."

"I've never really understood this," said Karen, "were the Black Death and the Great Plague caused by the same thing?"

Chambers coughed to draw attention. At last here was something he could talk about. "On the whole, yes. *Yersinia pestis* was the organism, and it was spread by fleas that lived on rats. *Yersinia* obstructs the flea's mid-gut, which basically causes it to starve and makes it incredibly hungry. So it feeds aggressively, drinking as much blood as it can. But the gut is blocked so its food doesn't go down. Instead . . ."

". . . it vomits up a mixture of the ingested blood and the *Yersinia* into the wound it's feeding from," finished off Dr. Cruttenden. "All rather disgusting, really."

"Yes," said Karen. "Really disgusting."

All three of them were suddenly looking at the floor.

"They couldn't still be down there, could they?"

"What, my dear?"

"The fleas." Karen had gone pale. "They couldn't still be down there? I mean, like, hibernating or anything?"

"I'm afraid I'm not an expert." Rosalie looked to Chambers, who responded with a shrug. "However, I imagine they would only be able to live for several hundred years if they themselves had been given magical powers."

"So that means maybe."

Chambers stepped over and placed his hands on Karen's shoulders. "Are you okay?"

She gave him a weak smile and nodded. "I felt very sick there for a second, but it's gone now. I'll be fine, thanks."

"Well, I think that's enough talk of things that are long dead." Chambers picked up the tray. "Are you going to try and sleep some more or come along with us?"

"Ghosts, plague victims, and fleas?" Rosalie shuddered. "I think I'll come along with you if you don't mind. I'm guessing nothing else strange has happened since my little visitation?"

Karen and Chambers exchanged looks.

"So something has, then?"

Karen spoke first. "While we get Dr. Chesney's lunch you might like to take a look at the picture that's appeared on the wall of the north aisle."

"A picture?" Rosalie was brightening again. It certainly didn't take much to cheer her up. "What of?"

"Oh, you'll love it," said Karen. "It's a skeleton."

"Marvelous!" Dr. Cruttenden appeared overly enthused, but Chambers guessed this was her own way of compensating for the situation they seemed to be finding themselves in. "Is there any writing with it?"

"Not as far as any of us could see," he said. "But your trained eyes may be able to do better."

"Of course, of course." She was on her feet and pushing past them. "If you will excuse me, I shall see you both a little later."

They only managed to make it as far as the door to the undercroft when Rosalie called out from the other side of the church.

"I thought you said there were no words with the picture?"

"None!" Chambers called back. "Not a single letter!"

"Well that's odd," came the reply, "because there are definitely some here now."

SIXTEEN

Thursday, December 22, 1994. 1:59 P.M.

THEY ALL CAME RUNNING at that. Karen and Chambers from the top of the steps, Ronnie and Paul from the undercroft, even Chesney from Dr. Cruttenden's room. Father Traynor remained noticeably absent.

"What have you found now?" Chesney sounded mildly irritated, as if he was starting to become jealous of Rosalie for discovering the things he ought to be.

"Look." Dr. Cruttenden pointed to the wall mural. "Miss Shepworth and Professor Chambers told me there were no words associated with the image of the skeleton. But now, as you can see, they are quite apparent."

Ronnie stepped forward to take a closer look and the others made way for her. It had been her discovery after all.

MEMENTO MORI

One word was to the left, the other to the right of the image of the skeleton, each in letters easily twelve inches high. She read them aloud slowly, as if they had no meaning for her.

"Remember you must die." Karen's voice was barely a whisper.

"And this wasn't here before?"

"No, Dr. Cruttenden, it wasn't." Chesney was already taking pictures with his camera.

"More work for your darkroom, eh?" said Hale, only to be rewarded with a glare.

"The skeleton's different too," said Ronnie.

"Is it?" Chambers looked at it carefully. She was right, of course. How could he not have seen it before? The image was more, well, solid.

Whereas before it had appeared faded, the product of the work of centuries past, now the picture seemed clearer, the bones more solid, the outlines stronger. The pits that passed for eye sockets in the malformed skull seemed all the blacker. And the skull itself. Was it his imagination or was it even more misshapen than when they had first seen it?

"It looks like some bloody monster," said Paul, summing up succinctly what everybody was probably thinking. "Not just that huge skull, but the arms and legs as well. They don't look like they belong to anything human. Like some huge toad that's all messed up."

Now that he mentioned it, Chambers thought, he had a point. The proportions of the bones of the arm—humerus, radius, and ulna—were all wrong. Too large, too thick. And the lower limbs were the same. Most telling, however, were the digits. Long arachnodactylic fingers stretched out, as long as the thing's arms, possessing far too many finger bones for them to be considered human. The same went for the toes, which made the thing seem almost amphibious.

"What is it?" Karen breathed.

Chambers licked his lips. Could it be intended to represent the great toad god Tsathoggua? Here? In an English church? "Can we all agree that it's not what we originally saw an hour or so ago?"

He was rewarded by fitful, tentative nodding from most of those present.

"Mr. Chesney," Chambers continued. "I'm relying on you to give us proof of that." He pointed to the undercroft door. "Were you serious about getting those photographs developed this afternoon?"

Chesney did not appear at all happy about being addressed in that way. "Of course I was," he sniffed. "And I still intend to."

"Good. It'll prove that this isn't some kind of group hysteria." He looked at the others. "I can't begin to explain what's going on here," he glanced at the door, and specifically at the red panic button, "but I'll understand if anyone thinks we should leave now, before things get any weirder."

It was a calculated gamble. Chambers didn't want to leave, and he knew that neither he, nor Karen, nor Dr. Cruttenden could leave, not even if they wanted to, but it would be unthinkable to drag innocents along simply because they had wanted to take part in a newspaper publicity stunt.

"Well, of course I'm not going," Chesney replied, much to Chambers's disappointment. "There's definite evidence here of paranormal activity, and I have no intention of leaving before I have had the chance to fully investigate it."

"I can't go," said Dr. Cruttenden. "I need to be here as much as you two."

"What do you mean, you two?" Chesney flashed a look at Rosalie, and then at Karen and Chambers. "What are the three of you up to?"

Chambers sighed. There was no point in holding anything back, not if they were going to be staying here. He looked at Karen, who nodded in agreement, and so he told them. Everything. From the discovery of the Chaucer manuscripts, to what happened at Oxford, to a detailed account of the dreams they had been plagued with since they had first been exposed to the scrolls.

"You knew all of this, and didn't plan on telling us?"

"We *are* telling you," said Karen. "Right after having given you the chance to leave."

"But I should have been told about this at the beginning!" He was starting to splutter. "It could have affected what preparations I needed to make, what equipment I needed to bring—"

"And what would you have done differently, had you known?" said Karen. "Other than not come at all?"

That was too much. "I resent that remark. In fact, it's exactly the kind of thing I've come to expect from your kind of reporter." Chesney's eyes narrowed. "Even though you have evidence of the supernatural you would prefer to keep your discoveries to yourself rather than share them with an expert. Well, two can play at that game." And with that he turned on his heels and made for the undercroft steps.

"I think you've pissed him off," said Paul once Chesney was gone.

"I'm pretty sure I have," said Karen. "But it needed doing."

"I'm not leaving," said Ronnie.

They turned to look at her.

"Are you sure?" said Chambers. "You don't have any need to be here, and it could become dangerous."

Ronnie smiled. It was quite possibly the most serene thing he had ever seen. "I'm sure, Professor Chambers. All my life I have wanted to make a difference. All my life I've seen things, heard things, known that there are forces outside the bounds of our normal reasoning. All my life I've been trying to help people, from telling the fortunes of friends in the schoolyard right up to my humble little place in Glastonbury. If things might get as bad as you seem to think, how could I possibly be anywhere else?"

Chambers resisted the sudden urge to hug her. Instead he turned to Paul Hale.

"I'm guessing you'd like to get away from here?"

The young man surprised him by shaking his head. "I don't like Dr. Chesney much, I don't like the idea of things scaring Dr. Cruttenden, and I don't like that ugly bastard up on the wall there," he said. "But if you think I'd leave you all here to deal with it and wimp out like some useless piece of cowardly shit you're wrong." He gave them all a grin. "I'm in, if you want me."

Ronnie squeezed his hand and smiled.

"Right," said Chambers. "In that case that's settled. We see this thing through to the end."

"If there is an end," said Ronnie.

"What about the priest?" That was Hale. "Shouldn't we ask him?"

Karen shrugged. "We can't get into the vestry. He's locked himself in."

Dr. Cruttenden looked concerned. "Is he all right?"

"He's talking," said Chambers. "Or at least we heard someone speaking behind the door."

"Very quietly," Karen added. "Or rather, as if he was very far away."

"Well, it's not fair we don't ask him," said Hale, making for the vestry door. He hammered on the wood. "Father?"

No reply.

"Father Traynor, we need to talk to you."

Nothing.

"Did you say it was locked?"

Karen nodded.

Hale took a couple of steps back, and then thrust himself at the door, twisting the handle at the same time. Everyone jumped when the door opened with little effort and the man went careering through. Chambers helped him up while the others stayed in the doorway and peered into the room. There was silence for a moment, before Ronnie was the first to state the obvious.

"There's no one here."

Hale brushed off his trousers as he and Chambers regarded the bare stone floor, the forbidding stone walls, the damp-stained plaster ceiling.

The open trapdoor in the far corner.

"Do you think that's where he's gone?" Karen asked.

Chambers crouched by the hole in the floor and peered into the yawning darkness. "If he has, he's probably broken his neck by now. I can't see a thing down there."

"If it's multichambered under there he may have passed into a different area and . . . closed the door behind him?" Dr. Cruttenden offered.

"True." Chambers looked at the trapdoor itself—worn planking with a few scraps of fading pinkish paint still adherent. When he tried to move it the door refused to budge, the hinges clogged with rust. "And he certainly couldn't close this behind him. Or open it in the first place for that matter."

"I'm guessing no one wants to go down there, then?" Hale had joined Chambers and was gazing into the void.

"He could be hurt," said Ronnie.

"He could be waiting for us with an axe," said Hale.

"That's a bit melodramatic." Dr. Cruttenden had ventured in and joined the two men.

Chambers had to smile at that. "I wouldn't call what's already happened understated," he said. "We've only seen Father Traynor once, and even when he was showing us around I thought he was a bit odd. Who knows, he might have his own reasons for wanting to be here?"

"If they're down there," said Hale, "I think we should let him get on with it."

"Are you just going to leave him down there, then?" Ronnie was in the room now, having followed Karen in. "In view of what's been happening up here?"

Hale sniffed. "*Because* of what's been happening, don't you think? How do you know that giant thing that's been painted on the wall isn't waiting down there for us?"

"Well, there wouldn't be much room for it to move around," said Dr. Cruttenden. "Unless, of course..."

Chambers's ears pricked up at that. "Unless of course...what?"

"There are documents suggesting that some churches were built on top of natural caverns, places where townsfolk could escape to as a final retreat in times of conflict. If that were true, there could be caves with ceilings a hundred feet high down there."

"How can you build a church on top of a hollow structure?" Chambers asked. "Surely it would subside and eventually collapse?"

"Not if the cave was deep enough and the rock on which the building was erected was solid enough. It has been done before, which is how we know about the concept."

"I thought plague victims were buried under here?" That was Karen again.

"Oh Christ, this just gets better and better." Hale took a step toward the door. "Maybe pushing that panic button isn't such a bad idea."

"I wasn't saying there definitely was a cave system directly under here," said Rosalie. "And even if there is, the ground wouldn't be entirely level. There could be pockets of the dead buried between the church and any cavern system that might exist."

"But they were *plague* victims?"

"It was a long time ago," Karen said to Hale, who was starting to look nervous. "They'll have rotted to nothing by now."

"You don't know that," Hale continued. "What if they didn't rot? What if they . . . changed? What if one of them is still alive, something that looks like that thing on the wall out there. What if it's living under here right now, in those caves Dr. Cruttenden's talking about?"

"Then it won't be able to fit through that tiny trapdoor, would it?" The situation was starting to get out of hand and Chambers was anxious to defuse it. "Come on, let's get out of here. If anyone's really anxious about something coming up from down below we can lock the door."

"But what about Father Traynor?" Ronnie asked.

"He was happy enough when he'd locked the door himself, wasn't he? He'll just have to knock to ask to be let out."

Hale was still looking panicky. In fact he seemed to have suddenly gotten worse as he had edged toward the door.

"What's the matter, Paul?" Chambers could see he was staring at the back of the door.

"There's no keyhole." Hale's voice was trembling.

"Then he must have bolted himself in."

Karen had joined Hale now, and was looking puzzled. "There's no bolt either," she said, near-closing the door so the others could see.

"That's impossible." But Chambers couldn't see any way of locking the door either.

"Perhaps he unscrewed the bolt before he went down?" Ronnie suggested.

"No screw holes." Chambers scratched his head. "Perhaps he wedged it shut."

"Bob," said Karen, "you tried that door. I watched you. It wasn't just wedged, it was locked solid."

"In that case I have absolutely no idea how he did it," said Chambers. "And I suggest we leave here now in case the door somehow magically locks with us all inside."

That got people moving. On her way out, Dr. Cruttenden said, "I hope that whatever Father Traynor is doing down there, he's not digging."

Ronnie was following her out. "Why not?"

"Because that's the very thing the guest in my room was trying to warn us not to do, of course."

The others heard that, and silence descended upon the group.

It was only broken when they heard Dr. Chesney's anguished cry from the undercroft.

SEVENTEEN

PETER CHESNEY KNEW HE was probably overreacting, but he had never been able to deal with conflict well, and while he would have preferred to be liked, he preferred even more to have the opportunity to further his career in parapsychology.

So far, whatever lived in All Hallows had seen fit to reveal itself to people other than himself. It was difficult to be jealous of Dr. Cruttenden—she had qualifications and academic training. She could understand and appreciate the momentousness of such a materialization. Judging from her attitude, it didn't seem to have entirely sunk in yet, but he was sure it soon would.

However, that moon-faced Quesnel woman had now been allowed a glimpse into the other world. She was the one who had been permitted to be the first to see the painting on the wall. And he was jealous. This sort of thing never happened to him. In the Brecon Cathedral case it had been the idiot-savant son of a local woman who had insisted he could see monsters climbing out of the walls, and Chesney had had to take his word for it. At Nottingham Castle the specter of a ghostly lyre player had been seen by numerous drunks and nightclubbers during the midnight hours, but no matter how much time he had spent crouched in the darkness by the battlements, he had seen nothing. In Aberdeen a medium had insisted that he was being followed by a tall individual with no face. That was the one that had spooked him the most.

"He is always there," she had said. "I am surprised you have not felt him."

Of course it was difficult to know who were charlatans and who were genuine. As time had gone on, however, he had come to the sorry conclusion that he lacked any kind of paranormal sensitivity, and that he was about as likely to see a ghost as he was to fly unaided.

It still didn't stop him from being jealous of the people who *could* see, though.

It was the lack of respect that was the worst. Here he was, having decided to devote his life to the study of the paranormal, having made quite a name for himself as a crusading investigator into the unknown; and now, at one of the most haunted sites in Britain, he was being treated as an extraneous member of the team. Ignored, forgotten about, shunned.

That was why he had lost his temper with that bloody reporter woman. How dare she suggest that he, Dr. Peter Chesney, champion of the occult, would have turned down the invitation to investigate this place had there been the suggestion of danger!

Danger.

He hadn't gathered it might actually be dangerous, he had to admit that. All the sites he had previously visited had been quiet, unremarkable, with just a few stories of strange goings-on in the distant past to keep them on the paranormal investigators' map. All Hallows Church was different. He hadn't expected it to be, but it was.

All Hallows Church hadn't just been haunted in the past. It still was.

What worried him was that the realization of that fact should have filled a specialist like himself with eager anticipation, but it didn't. It didn't at all.

Peter Chesney was terrified.

He couldn't admit that, of course. To do so would be to push the self-destruct button on a career built on lies and half-truths; and if he lost that, he would lose everything. The real reason he had exploded at Karen Shepworth was because she had been right. If he had known that three people had been plagued with dreams of this place surrounded by an ocean of the undead, of something hideous that lurked within the building of which they had only been permitted occasional glimpses, and that those same three people had been witness to an event in Dr. Cruttenden's rooms that was on a par with one of the biblical plagues, he might just have decided that he had been prebooked for a different event that he could not possibly postpone.

But he hadn't, and now he was here, standing in the undercroft of this hateful place, away from those dreadful people who probably knew his secret and despised him for it. He had claimed he was going to sit in Dr. Cruttenden's apsidal in the hope that the ghost she had seen might materialize for him, and to some extent that had been true. But he had known before he had gone in there that it would be useless. He never saw anything. The real reason he had stayed in there for so long was the same reason he was down here in the undercroft now. He needed to get away from the others because he had come to realize that they were all against him.

At least one of them—most likely that Chambers bloke—knew the truth about him and had told the others. And because Chambers had "real" qualifications and had respect for doing what they considered a "real" job, they were bound to believe him, weren't they? It hadn't been so bad when they had first entered the building but now, even just a few short hours later, he knew they had turned against him. He only had to be close to them to feel their disdain.

He took a pint glass down from the cupboard to the left of the sink and half-filled it with water. It tasted strange, brackish, a mixture of earth and the rust from the pipes. He drank as much as he felt able, and then poured the remainder into his cupped left hand, using it to wash his face. The liquid felt cooling and reassuring, especially when he rubbed it into his eyes. When he looked at the dim chamber again, it didn't seem quite as forbidding.

Perhaps I am just overreacting, he thought. *Perhaps it's this place. It's making everyone else on edge, so why not me?*

Because I am a professional? the conceited part of him reminded. *I am the one these people will be turning to for reassurance, for guidance, for advice on what we should do next, and I haven't the slightest clue.*

They will not ask anyway, said another voice.

They all hate me already, he conceded, *and even if I was to suggest anything they would just laugh in my face.*

And what would you do if they were to do that? asked the other voice. *If they were to laugh in your face? Would you punish them?*

Shouldn't you?

Chesney froze. That wasn't internal dialogue. That was a voice, an actual voice, entirely unlike his own. Deep, authoritative, commanding.

And yet it still seemed to come from inside his head.

"Who's there?" He didn't know what else to say. His voice sounded dull in the gloom, soaked up by the stone rather than resonating off it.

Silence.

"Who is it?" He wished he could turn the light up, instead of having to rely on that damned solitary bare bulb hanging from the ceiling. If only there was a way of having more light in here.

It was only when the buzzing of the refrigerator next to him started to interfere with his strained attempts to hear a reply that he found he could open the door. A blast of chill air made him shiver as the middle third of the undercroft-cum-kitchen was filled with a pallid blue glow. The ends of the room were a little better illuminated as well, but for the most part were still in shadow.

At the end furthest from the door, where all the food cartons had been stacked, something moved.

Chesney heard it rather than saw it, a flickering movement of something long and fine and thin, almost spider-like in appearance but much too large to be such a creature.

"Hello?"

There was no response from whoever had spoken to him, nor any reaction from whatever was crawling among the boxes. *Because they could not possibly be one and the same.*

His throat had suddenly gone dry.

Could they?

He pulled the refrigerator door wider, propping it open with a two-liter bottle of soft drink. It did little to make the room any lighter, but now he could move forward without fear of it shutting.

As he did so, there was a muffled *pop*, and the bulb above him burned out.

"Shit." The word came out as little more than the breath that steamed before his trembling lips. The fridge light was still working, but that just meant that now the room had taken on the appearance of a blue neon-lit nightmare. He knew the way out was on the opposite side of the room and just to the left, but for some reason he couldn't see it. The entire wall had disappeared into blackness.

There was the noise again, a loud scuttling and scraping, as if something with spindly, insectoid limbs was scrabbling to be free of the boxes that were keeping it trapped.

Oh God, help me.

There was nothing else to do—he was going to have to feel his way toward the exit. He walked to where the wall should be, and stretched out his arms, expecting to feel chill stone.

Nothing.

He took another pace forward.

Still nothing.

He turned back to see the blue fridge light, much farther away than it should have, or could possibly have been. He reached out for the wall once more, but his groping fingers only connected with nothingness.

Go back, he told himself. *It's the only thing you can do.*

Slowly, his arms held out before him, Peter Chesney made his way back to the source of light.

Or rather, he tried to.

Because now the light was receding. For every step he took, the light seemed to move even farther away. In three shaking steps it was reduced to a size where he could blot it out with his outstretched thumb.

And now the scrabbling sound was coming from behind him.

He started to run, the light leading him on, something terrible in pursuit. As he ran on into the blackness, not caring whether he was about to tumble off the edge of some supernatural precipice, he could not help but feel how unfair it was. One of them had seen a ghost, another had sensed a painting. Why did he have to be the one who was being dragged to Hell?

He was too panicked to be able to draw sufficient breath to cry out. All he could do was run, on and on, toward the only marker in this purgatory of a landscape. The ground beneath his feet had changed also. Stone slabs had been replaced by a fine dust that was more difficult to run on than dry sand at the height of summer. It was finer, too, as if he were trying to run on chalk, or ground wheat.

Or ground bones.

His stomach lurched at the thought. Could it be true? Was he running on the accumulated dust of a billion damned souls? Would he run forever until he tired, and rotted, and his bones, after thousands of years, eventually joined the remains beneath his feet? And would he still be conscious? Still aware? As his eyes fell from his face, his ears shriveled and closed; as his skin and muscles withered and his bones became exposed to the wind that even now was beginning to whip up around him?

He stopped in the darkness, the light ahead of him now just the merest of pinpricks. He knew he had tears on his cheeks because the wind had chilled them. What could he do? Was that thing still chasing him? He crouched down and lifted a handful of dust, feeling the powdery consistency of the ancient dead sift through his fingers. Was that thing still following him? He couldn't know. His own footsteps made barely a sound on this surface, so any crawling, scuttling, hopping thing would be silent also. There was no light for it to find him, but somehow he suspected it would have other ways of detecting its victim.

Exhausted, terrified, and close to giving up entirely, Peter Chesney sank to his knees, dust puffing up around him and making him cough. He resisted the urge to cry, although he didn't really know why. There was no one here to ridicule him, like there had been in school.

Don't think of that or maybe you'll get sent there next, he thought.

For he had no doubt now that he was in Hell, that somehow he had died. Perhaps in his anger and shame he had tripped and fallen down the steps to the undercroft. Or perhaps he had never entered All Hallows Church at all. Perhaps the entire thing had been some elaborate form of purgatory for past sins before his final, eternal punishment.

Why not cry, he thought, *if it makes you feel better?*

But he couldn't. All he could manage was a dry, pitiful croak that came from the back of his throat and was sucked up by the abyss of darkness around him. He tried again, and this time no sound came out at all.

Then he felt something on his shoulder.

Something thin and hooked and lined with bristles that dug into the fabric of his shirt.

He raised a hand to brush it away and then stopped. What if it didn't brush away? What if the hooks caught on his hand? Buried themselves in his skin? Tore his flesh from his bones before he could even draw another breath?

So he stayed there, on his knees in the darkness, the feeling of something large, insectoid, and alien behind him. What might it look like? Mandibles the size of garden shears? Black, multifaceted compound eyes the size of saucepans that would stare dispassionately as the thing picked him to pieces?

If he inhaled too deeply he could smell its musty scent.

And if he listened carefully, there was the faintest sound of clicking and wheezing, as the creature itself drew breath through its spiracles.

You are right to fall to your knees, especially as one so miserable and insignificant as you has been afforded so great an honor.

There was the voice again, the one that had spoken to him in the undercroft. It had probably only been moments ago, and yet it already felt like an eternity. It took all his strength to reply.

"An honor?"

The moment the words left his lips they were absorbed by the cloying darkness, but if he imagined they had fallen on deaf ears, he was mistaken.

Yes, honor. It is rare for one to be touched by Him as you have been.

Chesney tried to rise, but the claw pressed down on his shoulder, holding him there.

You dare to rise in His presence? Do you dare risk arousing His displeasure?

He still couldn't tell if the voice was inside his head or coming from elsewhere. As the pressure on his shoulder increased and he felt himself being forced toward the ground, he coughed more words into the emptiness around him.

"Where are you? Are you in my head?"

Chesney was almost bent double now, the pressure almost unbearable. As his face made contact with the ground, he turned his head to one side to avoid smothering in the dust. Still the pressure worsened. He could feel the barbs of the thing that held him piercing the material of his shirt, digging into his skin. They felt like pinpricks at first, then tiny daggers, each one digging into his flesh and piercing his nerves. When they scraped his bone he screamed.

I am everywhere and nowhere. I am both the cause of your damnation and your only hope of salvation. To earn that salvation, you must answer one question and answer it truly.

"What?" The pain was almost unbearable. He could feel blood running down his sleeve and trickling from his wrist onto the lifeless surface beneath him. He imagined a thousand tiny hungry mouths erupting from whatever depths of Hell lay below the dust and sucking away greedily at his life. His head was beginning to sink into it too. Soon he wouldn't be able to say anything, much less answer a question.

Will you serve Him as His chosen servant?

What else was he going to say? As far as he was concerned he was damned anyway. If there was the slightest chance of him getting out of this, he was going to grab it with both hands.

"Yes!" He spat dust. "Yes! I will!"

At once the pressure was gone. Chesney wiped dust from his face with hands sticky with blood, and lay there for a moment, crouched in the near-darkness, resisting the urge to weep.

At least it was no longer total darkness. Whereas before there had been nothing but unending void, now it was possible to see . . . something. By the time he had levered himself to his feet there was yet more light, gloomy and dim but nevertheless enough for him to make out where he was.

And it filled him with horror.

It was the unendingness of it that was the worst, the way the gray, dusty plain on which he found himself standing seemed to go on forever, with little variation in the landscape other than occasional spots where the dust had become heaped into low dunes. It reminded him of the desert, but a desert where the sun never shone and where, he knew, souls came to spend eternities.

I felt it only appropriate to show you, said the voice.

Chesney turned around, expecting to see the creature that had held him down, had made him bleed, had forced him to make obeisance to it, but there was nothing. Just more of the same. Unending, unchanging.

Unbearable.

Chesney coughed and wiped his face once more. He could see the blood on his right hand now. The crimson rivulets that glistened between his index and middle fingers looked gray in this light, but then so did his skin.

So did everything.

"What is this place?" he breathed, the words snatched from him by a cool but fetid breeze that played with the dust piles and was presumably responsible for forming them in the first place.

It has many names, some of which you will be familiar with, came the reply. *Its true name cannot be spoken properly in your tongue, nor should it be. It is a word of too great a power for any human to be permitted to wield. You may think of it as the Sea of Darkness. Never-ending, a repository for the souls that have been sacrificed in His Master's name.*

"His Master's name?"

The one whom you now truly serve, whose servant Himself has blessed you with his touch and put his mark upon you. Should you ever have second thoughts concerning your devotion to His will, that mark will cause you unendurable agony. I would suggest that you remember that.

Chesney clutched at his right shoulder. It felt curiously numb, as if the life had been drained from it, and the flesh felt strange through his shirt. Puffy, boggy.

Dead?

"I'll remember," he said, more to himself than the voice that had offered him up for enslavement. "And who are you?"

I am merely a vessel, a conduit for His power to reign upon the Earth. I have had many names throughout history, though I see no reason why I should give you any one of them, as none are my true name.

"And what is your true name?"

Another word that is too powerful for you to know. I shall not give you my name, but I will give you His, so that you might know who it is whom you now ultimately serve. He is the Mighty One, the Powerful One, the Bringer of Death, and the Giver of Life Anew. He is the Great God Cthulhu, and it is time for you to gaze upon his visage!

Even as the voice cried out its litany of appellations, Chesney became aware of something rising up behind him, erupting from the dust and at the same time being fashioned from it. He could feel it rising higher and higher, this thing that had been fed with the souls of billions that had fallen and been sacrificed in its name. As high as a mountain, as over-bearing as a tidal wave, and vaster than both. He didn't want to look. To gaze upon such a thing would surely be to invite eternal madness.

He was unsure as to whether unseen forces were turning him to look at it, or if the ground beneath his feet was being rotated to achieve the same effect. Either way he suddenly found himself unable to move, his eyes forced wide open. He felt the whites of his sclera beginning to burn even before he saw the many-tentacled thing that towered over him, the creature to whom he was now a hapless servant.

The God to whom he had promised his soul.

And it was with that realization that he finally let out the longest, loudest, and most despairing scream of his entire life.

EIGHTEEN

THEY FOUND HIM COWERING by the open refrigerator, bathed in the blue glow of its internal light.

"The bulb's gone." Paul Hale was flicking the overhead light switch with all the manic energy of someone who believed the electricity would come back on again if only he tried hard enough.

"He's freezing." Karen was already trying to help Chesney up.

"Of course he is." Chambers came to her aid. "He's been lying next to the fridge."

"But that can't have been for very long." They had only moved Chesney just far enough to be able to close the fridge door and already the two of them were having to blow on their fingers. "He's ice cold!"

"And injured." Chambers pointed to the blood on the back of Chesney's right hand. "I need to take a look at him. We'd best get him upstairs. Paul, can you give us a hand?"

Hale seemed distressed to leave the light switch, but he grudgingly came over to help take the weight of Chesney's shoulders with Chambers. With Karen and Ronnie taking the feet, they began to carry him up the steps.

"What was that?" Ronnie asked when they were halfway up.

"I didn't say anything," said Hale. "It came from him."

Chesney mumbled something else. "... *Ph'nglui mglw'nafh R'lyeh* ..."

"What language is that?" asked Ronnie.

"If it even *is* a language ..." Karen pointed out.

"Not far now," said Chambers, concentrating on carrying Chesney upstairs. "Not far, and then we get to have a proper look at you."

That didn't seem to calm him down.

"I think you're making him worse," said Paul.

"Do you think he might have given himself tetanus?" Karen asked as they heaved the body over the top step.

Chambers didn't think that would be the reason for his confusion. "Not just yet, anyway. It's certainly grubby enough down there, but I would be very surprised if tetanus acted that quickly. Let's get him onto his cot."

Dr. Cruttenden moved some of Chesney's equipment aside so they could lift him up. The parapsychologist groaned and tried again to speak as they righted him on the bed. The words were still unintelligible to most of them.

"... *Cthulhu wgah'nagl fhtagn* ..."

Chambers immediately recognized the litany and got to his feet. "I'll get my medical bag."

"I can do that." Paul was already making his way over to their sleeping area.

"What are you going to do?" Karen asked.

"I need to cut his shirt off so I can take a look at his injuries."

"Oh, you bloody doctors, always wanting to use a knife when common sense will do." She looked at Ronnie. "Help me get his shirt off."

The job was done impressively quickly. By the time Paul got back, the rest of them were staring at Chesney's right shoulder.

"What's wrong with him?"

Chambers was pulling on a pair of latex gloves. "I have no idea," he said. "But I don't want anyone touching this in case it's contagious."

"I can't imagine why any of us would want to touch it." Ronnie was already backing away.

"You'd probably all best keep a distance until I have some idea of what this is." By now Chambers had donned a surgical mask as well.

The others were quick to make their getaway, but Karen insisted on staying, stating as her reason that any story she was going to write she wanted to be as accurate as possible.

"Well it's up to you," said Chambers, "but make sure you keep out of the way. I don't want two patients on my hands." He also didn't want anyone asking any more questions about Chesney's ravings.

"I'll keep my distance," she said, looking as if she was going to do anything but. "So you don't have to worry."

The wounds Chesney had sustained were obvious—four jagged puncture marks arranged vertically down the outer aspect of his left upper arm. The bottom two had crusted over, while the others were still leaking a little blood that had yet to clot. What was strange was the color of the surrounding flesh. From his shoulder to his elbow joint the skin had assumed a pale blue pallor, with a sharp demarcation between that and normal healthy tissue at either end.

Chambers prodded at the skin over Chesney's shoulder. He grimaced when his finger sank into tissue the consistency of wet putty.

"Does that hurt?" he asked.

"No." Chesney seemed to be rapidly returning to his usual, irritable self. "But it does feel a little strange. Of course it would feel a lot better if you would just stop poking it about."

"What about this?" Chambers had his fingers on the flexure of Chesney's left elbow now. He only exerted a slight pressure but it left the impression of his fingerprints in the boggy tissue.

"Fine," Chesney snapped. "Well no, not fine exactly, but annoying. You're annoying me."

"Just doing my job." Chambers checked Chesney's pulse and compared it with the other side. "Do you have any established vascular diagnoses?"

"Like what?"

"Subclavian Steal Syndrome? Coarctation of the aorta?"

"Nothing." Chesney pulled his arm away from Chambers's touch and rubbed at it. Even he seemed surprised at how it felt. "I'll be fine."

"Are you up to date on your tetanus shots?"

"Had them before I came in here. I thought we all did."

"Thought I'd better check anyway." Chambers was unfurling a length of bandage. "I'm going to dress the wound with some antiseptic cream and then put this around it." He gave Chesney a serious look. "And you are not to disturb it, understand? I'll inspect it again later, and in the meantime if your symptoms change you're to tell me." He secured the bandage with a piece of micropore tape.

"I don't know what you're making such a fuss about." Chesney tried to get up. On the second attempt he managed it. "I'm perfectly fine." He began to struggle back into his shirt.

"What happened down there?" Karen was waving the tape recorder in his face.

There was no answer. Peter Chesney's features had gone blank. He stared off into space for a moment, and then said, "Nothing. The light bulb blew and I didn't know what to do, so I opened the fridge door. I slipped on something and must have cut myself."

Chambers narrowed his eyes. "There wasn't anything near you that could have caused wounds like that."

Chesney glared at him. "Then it must have fallen somewhere when I slipped." He was buttoning his shirt now. "Honestly, I do not see what all the fuss is. I just had a tiny accident, that's all."

"We were worried about you," Ronnie said. "You weren't yourself at all."

Chambers backed her up. "It's easier than you might think to pick up an infection off all this old stone."

"And that's all that happened?" Karen was still after her story. "You just fell and cut yourself?"

Again that pause before his reply. Not as prolonged this time, but very definitely there. "That's all." He got to his feet. "Now if you don't mind, I have work to be getting on with."

"Developing those photographs you mean?" said Hale, gesturing to the steps that led back down to the undercroft. "It's nice and dark down there now for you."

"No." Again Chesney was lost for words for a moment. "No, that can wait until later. I'd be a fool to go down there now and injure myself again. Perhaps you might like to make yourself useful and go down and replace the bulb?"

Whatever Hale said in reply was muttered under his breath.

"If you don't mind all getting out of my way," said Chesney to the crowd still assembled in the south transept, "I have work to do." The tremor in his voice suggested he wasn't as confident as he was trying to sound.

"Are you sure you're going to be all right?" Chambers thought he had better try once more before leaving the man to it.

This time Chesney was emphatic. "I will be fine, just as soon as you all stop bothering me."

"All right." There was obviously no point in pursuing things further. "Just as long as I have your assurance that if you start to get any symptoms you'll let me know."

There was something about Chesney's reply that made it sound more like a threat. "Don't worry, Dr. Chambers. If anything happens to me, I promise to make sure you'll be the first to know."

NINETEEN

THE FIRST EVENING.

Paul Hale looked at his watch again just to confirm it. Three minutes past seven. He still found it hard to believe they were yet to spend a night here. So much had already happened, culminating in Chesney being injured.

Hale didn't care how much the guy told them to stop fussing—that shoulder had looked wrong, almost as if the blood had stopped flowing through it, or the flesh had died. He had thought about mentioning it to Professor Chambers, but he figured the doc knew what he was doing, and he had done his best to convince Chesney he needed to rest. It hadn't made any difference, though.

There he was now, fiddling with that earthquake device thing of his over on the other side of the church. At least he was quiet. They were all quiet, in fact. Ronnie and Dr. Cruttenden had gone back to their—what had someone said those cubicles were called? Apsidals? The Prof had gone with Karen back to the vestry, presumably to wait for Father Traynor to pop his head out of that trapdoor they'd found.

The whole business with Father Traynor still bothered him. Even though it was possible the priest was exploring the depths of the church crypt or something, shouldn't he have come up for air by now? Or at least to reassure everyone he was all right? And where had all that stuff come from that Hale himself had blurted out? He'd never been the type to have much of an imagination—even in school the best he could manage with his mates was to pretend to be something from *Star Wars*. So how the hell had he come up with what was in his head right now?

He lay on his cot and shivered. The worst of it was that he could see it vividly—the thing he'd been trying to describe to the others. He could see it down there, but it wasn't in a cave. It was creeping around a plain covered with gray dust, a plain so far away and so deep down that you'd have to sink a mineshaft down from the trapdoor to get to it. A huge place, the size of a desert and then some, lit by a kind of purplish glow in the sky that caused eerie shadows to be cast by the ranks of small dunes where the dust had gathered.

The more he tried to shut out the idea of something living far beneath the church, the more it refused to budge. Every now and then his imagination allowed him a glimpse of it—all shiny and glistening, clutching at the land as it tried to gain purchase on the dust with its weird, three-fingered hands.

No, not hands. They were more like claws—tapering claws crowned with bristles, and as the thing heaved along, he could see that it had more than one pair of them.

Jesus Christ, what the fuck was in his head?

Suddenly he wished the others hadn't left him alone. Suddenly he wanted to run to the main doors and push the panic button. Never mind what anyone else had said—he had to get out, he had to get away from this place, far away where none of the things that lived here and under here could get to him.

Calm down, Paul, mate, calm down.

He held his breath the way he'd seen people do on TV and waited for his heart to stop pounding in his chest. Then he exhaled slowly. It seemed to work a bit, so he did it again and felt even better the second time. God, he could be an idiot sometimes! It was a good thing he hadn't gone running to the door, or he would have ruined it for everyone. Father Traynor hadn't really been gone that long—only a few hours. It just seemed longer because being shut up in this place was starting to feel like he had been imprisoned for an eternity.

Stop thinking like that. It's only the first night. You've got three more of these to go, and you're going to look bloody awful for the cameras if you keep yourself awake dreaming up this sort of bullshit. If you can't think of anything else to do, read your book.

It was an idea. Paul wasn't much of a reader, but he had figured this would be the ideal time to discover if it was something he might like to do more of. He'd asked Dave Maskell at work for some recommendations (Dave always had a book open on the bus or during the lunch break), and now he reached into his bag and took out the first paperback that Maskell had suggested he might like. It was a new one about the Special Air Service, and apparently Dave thought it was great. Mind you, Dave had watched *Rambo: First Blood Part II* over a hundred times, and once had been enough for Paul. Still, he hadn't known anyone else who could recommend anything, and so he turned to page one of *Bravo Two Zero* by Andy McNab and started to read.

He managed three pages before he put the book down again. Was it his imagination, or had it suddenly gotten much colder? The glare from the lamp next to his cot seemed to be duller as well. He rubbed his eyes and looked up. Dr. Chesney was still over there in the corner, fiddling away, but now his previously well-defined outline had changed to a murky blur.

It's because you're not used to reading, Paul told himself. *Pick the book back up and keep going—it's not as if there's anything else for you to do.*

He tried again, getting as far as page five before he stopped again, and this time it wasn't because he was bored. It was because the page he had just turned had been blown back over by a draft of freezing air. Paul shivered and put the book down. If that kept up he wasn't going to spend the next five minutes here, never mind the next three days and nights. He would either have to find the source of the chill breeze and stop it up, or move his cot elsewhere.

As soon as he was on his feet he found himself face to face with Dr. Chesney. Paul jumped and did his best to stifle a gasp of shock. It wasn't entirely successful.

"Startled you, did I?" The parapsychologist's voice sounded odd, but Paul put the tinny vibration at the end of every word that was uttered down to the acoustics here.

"A bit." Paul shivered again. "That's because it's cold, though, so I'm a bit jumpy anyway."

"Cold. Yes." Chesney didn't sound as if he understood at all, even though he was nodding his head. "That will probably be because of what they've found in the vestry."

"Who? Professor Chambers and Karen?"

Again that sense of a lack of understanding, despite the almost mechanical nod. "That's right. They wanted you to come and see. They've finally managed to locate Father Traynor, but he's stuck and they were thinking maybe you could help them get him out."

"Stuck?" Paul's brow furrowed. "You mean in the trapdoor?"

Dr. Chesney took some time considering this before he eventually replied. "No. Underground."

"They've gone under the church to find him?"

"Yes. You must come. You must help."

Of course Paul would. In fact he was secretly delighted to be of some use for a change. He followed Chesney around the corner and into the north aisle. The vestry door was open, but beyond it lay darkness.

"The lights are a bit dim here," he said, looking around him.

"Problem with the power," came the reply. "Should be fixed soon."

Paul leaned in through the vestry doorway. "I can't see a thing in there," he said. "We'd probably better go back for a—"

He never finished the sentence because the blow to the back of his skull sent him tumbling into the room. He heard footsteps follow him in, and then the creak and slam of the vestry door. Then all was darkness.

No, not quite darkness.

It took a while for his eyes to adjust to the greenish gloom, and once they had it was possible to make out, in the center of the stone floor, the gaping hole of the open trapdoor.

Paul rubbed his head and turned to see Chesney's outline behind him. "What did you do that for?"

Chesney remained silent.

"I'm serious." Paul pulled himself to his feet. "What did you do that for?"

Chesney knocked him down again.

Paul wasn't sure what shocked him more—the fact that the parapsychologist had hit him or the power of the blow. Either way, he decided to stay down, the cold stone damp beneath his fingers.

Now Chesney was pointing to the trapdoor entrance.

"Down there."

"Yes, I know he's down there, you've already told me." Paul tried to crawl in the opposite direction, but Chesney's raised foot warned him otherwise.

"You go down there."

There was no way he was doing that.

Chesney emphasized his insistence with a well-aimed kick to the base of Paul's spine. "You go down there. Down . . . below."

"No." The word came out as a strangled gasp. Paul would never have thought a blow to his back could cause so much pain.

"Don't make him . . . come up here."

"Who?"

No answer.

"Do you mean Father Traynor?"

Nothing.

"And where are Karen and Dr. Chambers? Are they down there too?"

Dr. Chesney remained silent, guarding the door and only changing his position if Paul made a move in the wrong direction. Eventually, after what felt like an eternity, he spoke again.

"He . . . is . . . coming."

There was nothing at first. Then, from deep down below, Paul could hear the faintest noise of scraping. Something heavy was moving beneath the church, coming inexorably closer.

Paul tried to back away from the trapdoor, but every movement was met by another blow to his spine. The noise was getting louder—a lurching, scraping sound, as if something with too many legs was dragging itself across stone. It got as far as being directly beneath Paul, and then stopped.

A new sound replaced it. That of footsteps on iron rungs. One after the other, the rhythmic clanging of leather against metal rang out, getting louder and louder until, in the filthy gloom of the vestry, something appeared through the opening in the floor and turned to look at Paul.

Father Traynor.

Paul's sigh of relief was short-lived as the priest levered himself up out of the hole. Paul hadn't had much chance to study the man's face, but he knew it was not as he remembered it. Even in the near-darkness of the room in which he had suddenly become a prisoner, he could tell that there was something wrong with Father Traynor.

The priest approached until his bile-stained boots were inches from Paul's head. A pale, emotionless face regarded the prostrate man on the floor, and the voice that emerged from between maggoty lips was a cold monotone.

"He is the one?"

The words were meant for Chesney, who nodded. "Yes," he said. "Flesh for the Body."

The lips stretched into a smile. Blood leaked from the cracks that appeared as a result of the flesh being put under such tension.

"Good. More flesh for He Who Waits Beneath."

Paul tried again to get up, but the other two were too quick for him. Traynor gripped his arms while Chesney held his legs. He screamed, wondering why he hadn't done so before.

"They cannot hear you," Chesney said.

"You are not longer of their world," Traynor added by way of explanation. "You belong to us now."

Struggling every inch of the way, Paul could do nothing to stop himself being dragged on his belly toward the trapdoor. He felt both knees clatter against a raised slab as they bruised heavily, the joints filling with blood. The harder Chesney gripped his ankles the more he twisted them as well, until the ligaments tore and blood vessels ripped, causing a susurrus of pain that encased Paul's feet until he lost all sensation in them. He screamed again, not because he thought it would gain attention, but because he couldn't help himself.

He kept on screaming as his body was bundled through the trapdoor and allowed to fall into the pitch darkness. He hoped that when he landed it would be all over. He was wrong.

His two captors were beside him again, faster than it would have taken for either of them to climb down the ladder. Father Traynor had a lantern now, holding it up so Paul could see it was still them and not some new tormentors. The priest moved to his left and hung the lantern high on a rusty iron hook driven into the stone wall.

Paul tried to twist himself, better to see the room he was in, but every movement sent needles of pain shooting through his knees and ankles. Then he was being lifted roughly onto a broad table with a lead surface. Restraining straps of damp worn leather were applied to his wrists, which were dragged up over his head. Then his swollen ankles were strapped in the same way. When these were tightened he screamed again.

"The sacrifice is ready." Chesney spoke first. It was not a question but a statement, and Father Traynor's response was merely intended as a confirmation.

"The sacrifice is ready."

Then the priest gripped his left ankle, and Dr. Chesney his right. They remained like that for a moment, long enough for Paul to realize that his surroundings had changed. He was no longer in a dim chamber enclosed by stone. Now a fetid breeze buffeted his body, stirring up the gray dust on the plain that seemed to stretch for miles in every direction. In the far distance, where charcoal sky met pallid dunes in a hazy semblance of a horizon, he could see figures. Hundreds of them. If he turned his head the other way he could see the same—an army of shambling, stumbling things, barely human and yet driven by a hunger, by a need, that scared him even more than the two men who were holding him down. Even though they were miles away he knew they were coming closer, slowly but inexorably, to converge upon his helpless form.

Paul screamed again. This time, rather than echoing off the walls of his prison, his voice mixed with the wind. The sound faded quickly, whisked away over the barrenness, an anguished cry that would live for eternity in this never-ending hell.

He howled more loudly when Traynor and Chesney began to tug at his ankles. They pulled so hard that at first it felt as if they were trying to dislocate his hips. Then, as the skin around his groin began to tear free, he understood it wasn't what was covering his lower limbs that they wanted.

It was what lay beneath it.

Pain such as Paul had never experienced before wracked his body as both his legs were degloved, the skin coming away from each in sheath-like flaps of tissue. Paul raised his head to see what damage Traynor and Chesney had wrought. He expected to see shining muscle, bloodstained nerves, and glistening fat. What he actually saw was far worse.

His legs were no longer human. From the waist down the skin had been ripped away to reveal, instead of normal tissue, barbed multi-jointed limbs of insectoid chitin. Paul stared in horror at this alien half of his body, at the way the limbs scrabbled for purchase on the shining black surface, at how they bent in places normal limbs never should.

"Oh God, what have you done to me?"

Traynor and Chesney ignored him. They had moved to the head of the table, where now they were gripping his wrists. Paul felt the same wrenching pain close to his shoulder sockets as the skin of both his arms was torn free. He couldn't see, but he knew his arms were now the same as his legs—dark brown, lined with spiked barbs, and utterly inhuman.

Now the two men were either side of him—Traynor on his left and Chesney on his right. The parapsychologist leaned over him.

"Nearly finished," he whispered. "Not much more to do now."

They were tugging at his flanks, grabbing the flesh of his loins and pulling it outward on either side. Paul didn't move, didn't resist, all hope of escape gone. He lay there in mute stillness as the flesh was torn from his sides and his ribs were unfolded to form another pair of segmented, scrabbling, multi-jointed limbs.

Father Traynor returned to the head of the table and gripped Paul's chin. He looked at Chesney.

"For the Anarch," he said.

The other man nodded. "For the Great God Cthulhu."

Paul felt the skin slide from his face, felt his ears tear from his head, knew that his eyes were coming away too, even though he could still see, through multi-faceted compound eyes that regarded this land of desolation in a different way than he had before. Where once he had seen hunger and horror, he now saw appetite and promise.

So much promise.

He rose to his full height and nodded to acknowledge his servants' obeisance, as well as the approach of his armies as they edged ever closer. The chitinous joints of his neck glinted as his bristling antennae tasted the air—so deathly, so sweet, so perverse.

There was still much to do.

TWENTY

"I CAN'T FIND PAUL anywhere."

Ronnie was poking her head through the vestry doorway. It was obvious from the way she was acting that she didn't want to come in.

"We left him ten minutes ago," said Chambers. "He told us he was going to try and read and then get some sleep. Is he not on his cot in the north transept?"

Ronnie shook her head. "And that's not all. Dr. Chesney's vanished as well."

"Well, they didn't come this way," said Karen, rising from her crouching position near the trapdoor and putting away her tape recorder. "We've been here the whole time and we've seen no one."

"So still no sign of Father Traynor, either?"

"No." Chambers was getting increasingly worried about the priest.

"So that's three people potentially missing, then."

"Paul and Chesney must be around somewhere," said Karen. "Have you checked the undercroft?"

Ronnie had. "I've checked everywhere. I don't want to spoil things for anyone but I was thinking, perhaps you could come and search again with me, and if we still don't turn anything up maybe we should be thinking about hitting the panic button?"

Chambers had to agree. The thought had occurred to him several times over the past few hours, especially when Chesney had suffered his injury. He gave Karen an apologetic look. "I have to say I agree with Ronnie.

We're not even twenty-four hours into this and Father Traynor has been gone for too long. We're only assuming he went below the vestry, and that he's still there. Anything could have happened to him, and I don't think it would be safe for us to go after him."

Karen didn't look happy. "He could be, though," she said. "He could have found church records, ancient books, anything. You know what these types are like once they get engrossed in something."

"Even so, it's part of his responsibility to the rest of the group to let us know where he is and that he's okay." Chambers looked at Ronnie. "Come on," he said. "Let's look for Paul and Chesney, and if they really have gone then it's time to call this a day."

Karen chased after them. "You're making a fuss over nothing! Father Traynor is probably buried in documents. Dr. Chesney bumped his shoulder. He told you he was okay afterwards. And nothing's happened to anyone else."

Chambers kept walking, out of the vestry and down the north aisle toward the west entrance. "Something's happened to the building though, hasn't it?"

"What do you mean?"

"Well in case you hadn't noticed, since we came in here a painting of a ten-foot-high skeleton has appeared on the wall with the words 'Memento Mori' daubed across it."

That was the point at which Ronnie screamed.

The painting had changed. Considerably. Where before the twisted bones and elongated skull had suggested the semblance of the skeleton of a human being, now something else entirely had taken up residence on the wall. Something alien, something insectoid.

Something cruel.

"Jesus Christ." Karen looked at the thing in horror. "What is that?"

Chambers took a step back so he could get a better look. It wasn't the toad god Tsathoggua at all. This thing had huge compound eyes, six jointed limbs, a bristled carapace behind which seemed to be concealed the merest hint of wings. And yet it appeared to be standing upright, as a man would, its two foremost limbs raised while the middle two hung at its sides. The weight of its entire body seemed to be supported by the back legs, which looked much stronger and more powerful than their counterparts.

"It's an insect of some kind," he said. "If I didn't know better I'd say it looks like . . . like . . ."

"A flea," said Rosalie Cruttenden's voice from behind him. "Carrier of pestilence, vector of death, responsible for more misery and suffering worldwide than anything else until man's technology caught up with God's."

"That . . . thing, is not a creation of God's," Ronnie whispered. "More likely it was made by the Devil."

"Or indeed it could *be* the Devil." Dr. Cruttenden's academic interest was obviously outweighing any revulsion she might be feeling. "Don't forget Beelzebub, the Lord of the Flies. Images of insects as representations of evil have existed ever since ancient man dipped his fingers in the blood of a kill and found he could use it to paint on the walls of his cave. But this . . ." she pushed past Chambers ". . . this is worrying."

"Why?" Karen had her recorder out again. Chambers didn't know whether to admire her professionalism or tear the thing out of her hand and stamp on it.

Dr. Cruttenden pointed to the bottom of the painting. "Do you see what's here?"

"Looks like a collection of tiny black dots to me."

"That's because you have to come closer, Dr. Chambers. Don't worry, it's only a painting. It can't hurt you. Not yet, anyway."

Chambers did as he was told, even though every fiber of his instinct was telling him to keep his distance. He had to get right up to the wall in order to see it, and when he did he wanted to run away even faster.

People.

Thousand of tiny people, their numbers densest around the rear legs of the thing.

"Do you think they're running away from it, or toward it?" he asked.

Dr. Cruttenden peered even more closely at it, narrowing her eyes through her spectacles. "I don't believe you can tell. Not at the moment, anyway. But I would find either concept equally terrifying, wouldn't you?"

"The spelling has changed as well," said Karen from behind them.

Dr. Cruttenden turned to acknowledge her. "I beg your pardon?"

"The words." Karen pointed. "It used to say 'Memento Mori,' but now the second word is different."

Chambers looked up with the others. Sure enough, the word to the right of the insect god no longer referred to the inevitability of death.

"What does 'Memento Moreby' mean?" he asked.

"'Remember Moreby,'" Dr. Cruttenden breathed. "Of course. I should have guessed that. Stupid of me, very stupid indeed."

"What is 'Moreby'?" Ronnie had finally regained her voice, but it still sounded weak and thready.

"You shouldn't be asking 'What,' my dear, but rather 'Who.' Thomas Moreby was . . . something of an enigma."

"I'm guessing from the way you're saying it that he was a bad kind of enigma?" Karen still had the recorder on, but her grip on it wasn't as sure as it had been and the machine had slipped a little. Despite the chill in the building, Chambers could see traces of sweat on the black plastic casing.

"The very worst kind," Dr. Cruttenden replied. "You remember I told you he built this church?"

Chambers nodded. "And that it was destroyed by fire."

"In 1850, yes, but the undercroft—the place we've been using for our kitchen—is still the same, and the crypt also." Dr. Cruttenden seemed to be considering whether or not she should continue. "He was a strange man, a very strange man. He believed that the body lived on after death, and that it could be made to rise again if exposed to something he called 'pure humors.'"

Karen had regained her grip on her recorder, and now she was holding the machine so close to the historian that it was almost in Dr. Cruttenden's face. "'Pure humors?'" she asked. "What does that mean?"

Dr. Cruttenden shrugged. "Who knows? I don't think he was taken terribly seriously, except by a few who became part of the Well of

Seven—sort of like his disciples, if you will. They're all buried at St. Pancras Old Church."

"Along with Moreby?" Chambers hoped so.

"Oh, no." Dr. Cruttenden's face was grave. "He was committed for a while to Bedlam, raving about how he had seen the Other Side, and that the newly revived dead would inherit the Earth because they had purer souls. Upon his death, the exact date of which is not exactly clear, he left instructions to be interred here."

"Here?" Karen spoke loudly, presumably to ensure the tape picked it up.

Dr. Cruttenden nodded. "Somewhere in the crypt beneath us. There was another odd thing." The others waited for her to continue. "No one knew how old he was when he died. As I mentioned before, if records are to be believed, he must have been over a hundred years old, and yet apparently he looked little more than forty."

No one spoke for a moment. The atmosphere suddenly seemed to have gotten even colder. Karen shivered, and when she switched off her tape recorder the click echoed around the church's empty walls. Everyone's breath steamed in the lamplight. Chambers was sure it couldn't be seen before.

There was a crash from behind them. They all turned to see a chunk of plaster had fallen away from the portion of wall beneath the bottom of the painting and shattered on the stone floor.

The plaster had revealed something.

The symbols probably formed a word, but it was written in a language with which Chambers was unfamiliar. Daubed in red streaks against the pale Portland stone beneath, its purpose could be nothing other than to describe the creature painted above, or perhaps even to name it.

ANAPX

"What does it mean?" Chambers guessed Dr. Cruttenden knew. "It doesn't actually say Anapx . . . does it?"

"It's classical Greek." Even Dr. Cruttenden was starting to sound nervous now. "In our language it would be pronounced 'Anarch.'"

"You mean as in anarchy?

"It can mean that, but it depends on the situation. Here I very much suspect it to mean 'Without Beginning,' as in something that is eternal."

"Something that's existed since the beginning of time?"

"Perhaps. A more literal translation would mean 'That Which Exists Outside of Time,' which of course makes little sense. It is interesting, though."

"Why?" Chambers could sense she was holding something back. "What else does it mean?"

"Oh, nothing. It's just that Thomas Moreby was rumored to practice black magic of a sort, and that he had a familiar."

"Like a cat?"

"No, nothing like a cat at all. But very much like . . ." she pointed a bony finger at the image on the wall.

"A . . . *flea*?" Chambers spluttered. This was starting to get ridiculous. "Thomas Moreby had a flea for a familiar?"

Dr. Cruttenden shook her head. "It was much larger than the insect you know. Some say it was as big as a dog, sometimes bigger. Moreby was rumored to feed it the blood of children. Some believed that the creature was actually the master, and Moreby the slave, that it was a constant reminder of the true power he served. A power even greater than the Anarch itself, otherwise described as the 'One Who Watches in Darkness' in the *Liber de Nigra Peregrinatione*."

It was almost too much, but Karen had to know. "The what?" It was the first question she had asked without having her recorder switched on.

Dr. Cruttenden looked more and more uncomfortable as she was pressed to continue. "The *Book of the Black Pilgrimage*. It's one of those fabled volumes like Alhazred's *Necronomicon*, Ludvig Prinn's *De Vermis Mysteriis*, or the *Book of Eibon*. They all turn up on dealers' lists from time to time, usually as a joke because the books in question are so rare that all copies are thought to be in the possession of individuals who would never for a moment consider parting with them.

"To be honest with you, I can't remember much of what it's meant to be about. I believe, however, it details a journey taken to the fabled city of

Chorazin, and of a Black Cathedral wherein dwelt some terrible power. Moreby's familiar allegedly came from there."

"When was this book meant to have been written?" asked Karen.

Dr. Cruttenden seemed thrown. "I . . . I'm not sure. Possibly the sixteen hundreds, possibly earlier. Why?"

"Because you told us that Geoffrey Chaucer went on some mysterious sea voyage, didn't you?" Chambers could tell Karen was getting excited now, and he wasn't altogether sure that was a good thing. "And while it may have been three hundred years earlier, isn't it possible that might be where he went?"

"It's possible," Dr. Cruttenden conceded. "But there are a thousand other places he would have been more likely to have gone. What made you mention him?"

"Because he's the reason we're all here!" There was no stopping her now. "It was the discovery of that story of his that brought us all together. Surely that can't all be coincidence?"

"Coincidence or not, we've got three men missing, too many strange things happening, and we're only just starting our first night here." Chambers had little choice now but to alert the League as to what was occurring here. He had made up his mind and no one was going to stop him. "I think it's time we called a halt to this whole thing."

Only Karen looked upset, but even she didn't move as he strode to the door. His hand hovered over the panic release for a moment as he considered asking the rest of them if they were in agreement. If anyone did have any objections, however, he didn't much care.

He brought his palm down on the red button.

TWENTY-ONE

Thursday, December 22, 1994. 7:37 P.M.

NOTHING HAPPENED.

He tried again.

The same thing.

"Is it some kind of long distance thing?" Chambers called back to the others. "Does it set off an alarm in one of the vans outside or something?"

"It's supposed to release the door immediately." Karen was at his side now. "In case there's a fire or if anyone's hurt."

"Maybe I just didn't hear it unlocking." Chambers took hold of the wrought iron door handle, and pulled. Then he pushed. Then he pulled again.

"You don't have to push the button a certain number of times or something, do you?" He was already doing so without waiting for her reply.

"Of course not." Now Karen was looking as worried as he felt. "A single push should release it."

"Perhaps you're not pushing it hard enough," said Ronnie from behind them.

Chambers stood out of the way. "Be my guest."

All four of them took turns pushing the red release button as hard as they could and then rattling the door handle.

"Did anyone bring in one of those handheld phone things?" Dr. Cruttenden looked at each of them and finished on Karen. "Or a radio?"

"No." Karen looked as if she was kicking herself for not doing so now. "That was the point, remember? No contact with the outside world. No one could get out, and no one could get in. We wanted to make it virtually impossible for anyone to be able to rig up a hoax."

"And by doing so you've made it actually impossible for us to leave." Chambers resisted the urge to hammer at the door in frustration, then thought there wouldn't actually be any harm in it. The others followed his example, all except Dr. Cruttenden. When they started to shout for help, her voice cut through their pleas for assistance.

"It won't do any good, you know. Do you know how thick those doors are? You're wasting your breath."

"Well, what else are we supposed to do?" Ronnie's words were choked with tears. "We can't just sit here."

"All you're going to do if you beat on those panels is exhaust yourself and injure your hands."

"Dr. Cruttenden's right." Chambers's fists were already starting to hurt from him battering them against the weathered oak. "Is there any other way out of here?"

The lecturer shook her head. "Not if Miss Shepworth's team has arranged for the side entrance to be barricaded." Karen gave a guilty nod at that. "In that case we are truly trapped. At least we won't starve to death."

"But something else might get us first." Ronnie glanced back to the painting of the Anarch, or whatever the hell it was. "Yes . . . something."

Chambers was doing his best to remain rational as his training as an agent finally kicked in. "Well, before we all give up and consign ourselves to whatever might be living in—or under—this church, I suggest we make a concerted effort to search the entire building, both for another way out and . . ." he suddenly found it difficult to say, now that he was facing up to the reality of it ". . . and for any evidence of Father Traynor, Dr. Chesney, or Paul Hale."

"They've gone, haven't they?" Ronnie was looking at Dr. Cruttenden. "They've gone to be a part of that picture."

"We don't know that." Karen laid a hand on Ronnie's arm, but the woman pulled away.

"We *do*! Haven't you noticed? The picture has changed each time something has happened to one of us. Paul disappeared with Dr. Chesney and that . . . thing appeared on the wall, with all its worshippers or whatever you want to call them." Ronnie looked around her, trembling now. "They're still here, you know. All around us. So is that thing. Deep down, deep down below. That's where they all are. Waiting. Waiting for us to make them seven again. It's a very powerful number, seven. Powerful in all kinds of religions, all kinds of cults. And since at the end of the day only one religion can be the true one, if it's *that*—" she pointed at the picture of the Anarch once more "—then seven's going to be important to it, isn't it?"

"That's enough, Ronnie." Chambers intended to calm her down but the words came out as a bark.

"No it's not. We're trapped in here because we were meant to be here, all of us. You three and your Chaucer documents, Chesney and his parapsychological past, me and Paul winning that competition. We didn't win anything. There is no chance, no luck. Everything's been planned. By that thing on the wall, lording it over all of us and waiting, biding its time."

"Biding its time until what?" Dr. Cruttenden seemed more interested than distressed by Ronnie's outburst.

That threw her. "I don't know . . . not yet."

"If it wants worshippers," Dr. Cruttenden persisted. "If it wants us, then what for?"

Ronnie looked at the image once more and began to cry. "It wants everything. Us, this land, this world, everything and everyone. And even that won't be enough. And no one is going to be able to stop it. No one."

"Perhaps we can," said Chambers. "If it needs us, we must be important to it, mustn't we? And if we're really part of a plan stretching back over six hundred years to when Geoffrey Chaucer, or whatever his real name might be, journeyed to some dark and ancient city and brought something terrible back to this country, then we must be *really* important."

"Time has no meaning to it," said Ronnie. "It's existed forever."

"Outside time," Dr. Cruttenden whispered. "I think she may be right.

Time has no meaning for it. Three days or three thousand years are probably the same to it. In that way at least, it's exactly like an insect, merely waiting until the right moment to take its prey."

"Will you listen to yourselves?" Karen almost screamed the words. "A flea god? A master plan? Thousands of years old? You're being ridiculous!"

"All right, Karen," Chambers couldn't help but notice she wasn't recording any more. "Let's consider the reality of the situation. We are trapped in here and will be for the next three days if we don't find a way out. Three of us are missing. Three out of seven. I still suggest we mount a search for them, and in case anyone's worried, we are absolutely not going to be splitting up.

"Since we came in here a number of weird things have happened. Dr. Cruttenden saw an apparition that warned her not to 'Dig Down Below.' Ronnie was the first to spot that picture on the wall, a picture that we all agree has changed while we have been in here. Father Traynor disappeared almost as soon as we came in after showing us where we were all to sleep . . ."

"At strategic points around the church, which could also be important," Dr. Cruttenden interjected.

"Right. Now I agree we should only deal with facts, but the facts are that something is going on here that is outside the bounds of normal scientific rational thinking. It involves that thing on the wall over there—the Anarch, or whatever it likes to call itself. And I think we can all agree that its intentions probably aren't beneficial toward humanity."

"It could still be a hoax," said Karen. "Father Traynor, Dr. Chesney, and Paul could all be in on it. They could be laughing at us right now. That picture could have been painted onto the wall before we got here, in special layers that dissolve over time to make it look as if it was changing."

"You know that's not true, Karen." Chambers resisted the urge to shout. "You were there in Oxford. You witnessed the storm just like Dr. Cruttenden and I did, and you've had the dreams just like we have as well. And you know those dreams must be linked to what that thing on the wall wants. An apocalypse of the undead, spreading out from this land to infect the world. And the source, the starting point, will be *here*." He stamped his foot to make the point. "In this church."

"Or under it," Dr. Cruttenden added.

"Or under it. We have been granted a vision of the future as that thing wants it to be. It's up to us to make sure that doesn't happen. And I suggest we start by finding out what's happened to the others."

Ronnie was drying her eyes but her voice was still wracked with sobs. "That means going through that trapdoor, doesn't it?"

It probably did. "We'll search everywhere else first," said Chambers. "And remember—stick together. I don't want this to turn into some bloody horror movie where the straggler at the back of the group gets picked off by monsters hiding behind pillars."

"That won't happen. Not if you behave yourselves."

The voice came from the choir. They all turned to see Father Traynor standing before the altar.

"Father Traynor, are you all right?" Ronnie was making her way up the aisle toward him before Chambers could stop her. The others followed, but kept a safe distance. They all came to a halt at the altar step.

The priest spoke in a voice not unlike his own, but it was tinged with a metallic burr. "As you can see, I am well, as will all of you be if you listen to His word."

"Where's Dr. Chesney?" Karen called out.

"He is here as well."

As if on cue, the parapsychologist stepped out from behind the priest and stood to his left.

"I have seen below," Dr. Chesney said, his voice possessing that same tinny abnormality, "and it is a place of wonder."

"It doesn't look as if it's done your left arm any good though, does it?" Dr. Cruttenden was staring at the man's hand. As Chesney raised it, Chambers could see what she meant. The flesh of his fingers had become discolored, along with the heel of his palm. Both now looked an unhealthy mustard color, but that was not the worst. In places the skin had broken down to reveal darkened muscle beneath. Chambers knew dead tissue when he saw it.

Dr. Chesney's hand was rotting.

"This?" The parapsychologist barely seemed to notice it. "A gift from Him. You may not fully appreciate its glory now, but that is because your eyes have not yet been opened."

"That is why we are here," said Traynor. "We are both His servants and His messengers, and we wish to bring His glory to you."

"Where's Paul?"

Chesney lowered his left hand. Thick greenish fluid dripped from it onto the stone floor. "He is still below."

"He is Most Blessed," said Father Traynor. "He is One with the Anarch now. You shall join him, and us, in His worship."

"And if we refuse?"

Traynor glowered at Chambers. "If you do not come to the Anarch, then we will bring you His word."

"I think I'll take my chances."

"You will all come with us."

"No, we won't." Dr. Cruttenden was shaking her head. "I'm not quite sure where you've come from, or even who you both are anymore, but we'll make our own minds up about what we wish to do."

"I'm staying too," said Karen, stepping behind Chambers for good measure.

"Veronica Quesnel, He has picked you as His messenger as well."

Ronnie shook her head as Traynor leered at her. "I can't, I can't."

He took a step forward and held out his hand. "Come with us and be spared the pain these fools will have to endure."

"No. No, I . . . get away from me!"

Traynor's face was inches from Ronnie's own now. He turned his palm flat and held it before his mouth. "In that case, you will be the first to receive His gift." With that, he took a deep breath, and blew.

A handful of tiny red particles leapt from his hand and onto Ronnie's face. As soon as they landed Chambers could see they were alive—tiny wriggling, biting creatures that jumped across her skin searching for the best place to penetrate her flesh.

Fleas.

As the insects took hold and began to bite and to burrow, Ronnie raised her hands to her face and screamed.

"If you will not come to Him, we bring His message to you," Traynor said once more.

"Stay away from her!" Chambers shoved Karen sideways as she went to help the kneeling Ronnie, who was now clawing at her cheeks, at her forehead, at her eyes.

"They burn!" She screamed. "Oh God, they burn!"

"We've got to help her!" Karen tried again, but Chambers pulled her even farther back.

"Can't you see they're infected with something? If you touch her you're just going to end up the same way!"

Holes were already beginning to appear in Ronnie's face, punched-out ulcers rimmed with yellowing necrosis. The flesh beneath was already darkening.

"What is it?"

"Some accelerated version of the plague, I should imagine." Chambers took Karen's hand and glanced at Dr. Cruttenden. "We have to get away from here."

Traynor and Chesney had moved now, and were standing by the exit that led to the vestry.

"Your only salvation lies with us," gargled Chesney in a voice that was sounding more insect-like all the time.

"The undercroft I think," said Dr. Cruttenden.

Chambers nodded. "Me too."

They kept away from the two figures at the vestry exit, taking care to circle Ronnie and give her a wide berth. Karen clamped a hand over her own mouth as she saw the state of putrefaction the woman had already reached. Ronnie's face was now a mass of weeping sores, deep enough to reveal shining white bone. Her cheeks had come apart and her exposed jawline revealed teeth that were already loosening in their sockets. The hands that had clawed at the diseased flesh were now just as discolored, each finger's joint swollen and purple with disease, the fingernails the color of old tree bark or lost entirely. She still had eyes but they had collapsed within her skull, like rotten puffballs left out in the rain.

They were apparently still good enough for her to see with, though.

"Don't leave me!" The tangled knot of leathery decay that was her vocal cords was still capable of uttering intelligible words, but when she tried to stand and follow her friends, her right leg gave way with a sickening crunch, the knee collapsing as the ligaments that held bone to bone fell apart. The shearing stress of tibia grinding against femur tore the main artery, and blood the color of old engine oil sprayed across the floor.

"Don't let that touch you!" Chambers pushed them back toward the wall of the south aisle. "Chances are it's all infected."

"How can she still be alive?" Karen hissed as they edged their way to the undercroft door.

"Those injuries must be agony." Dr. Cruttenden was close behind them, her resolve close to breaking.

The horrific state Ronnie was now in wasn't preventing her from trying to get to them, however. With rotting fingertips, all now bereft of fingernails, she was pulling herself along the stone floor toward them. Her previously intelligible words had now degenerated into a series of fluid-guttural groans. As she dragged herself toward the undercroft door, a slime of necrotic tissue trailed behind her.

And she was moving quickly.

"Come on!" Chambers ran to the door and held it open for the others. Dr. Cruttenden made it through first. "Be careful on the steps!" Chambers yelled after her.

"We have to do something!" Karen was hesitating in the doorway as what was once Ronnie edged rapidly closer.

"We can't do anything." Chambers pushed Karen through. "It's not even Ronnie anymore."

The crawling creature was nearly upon them.

"How can you say that? How can you—"

Chambers backed into Karen and pushed the two of them through the entrance to the undercroft steps, slamming the door behind them.

"Thank God there's a bolt," he said, drawing it across.

Almost immediately there was a wet pounding from the other side.

"Let . . . me . . . in." The voice was nothing like Ronnie's. In fact, it was nothing like Chambers had ever heard. "Let . . . me . . . in . . . or . . . suffer."

"I think we'll take our chances, don't you?" Chambers's words had little effect on Karen other than to make her even angrier.

"You bastard! How could you leave her out there?"

"Let's get down the steps."

"I'm not going anywhere until you tell me how you could leave a living, breathing human being suffering out there like that!"

"Well, for one, she wasn't breathing, and for another, I'm not even sure she's human anymore."

There was more thumping from outside that soon changed to a scraping sound. Chambers imagined the dead flesh of Ronnie's wrist had worn through and that she was now thumping at the wood with exposed bone.

"Karen, please, let's get downstairs where we can discuss this—that noise is making me very nervous."

"Good! I hope it fills you with guilt for the rest of your days! I hope it reminds you what an utter bastard you were to leave an innocent defenseless woman to die in a freezing cold church, all alone and with no one to help her!"

Chambers let the fury boil off her for a moment. Then, doing his best to ignore the horrible scraping noises that were still coming from behind him, he looked her in the eyes and said, "We are going to get out of here, you know."

Karen lowered the fist she'd raised to strike him.

"We will. But we have to stick together, and we have to be on our guard for danger. Otherwise we're going to end up like . . ." He suddenly found it difficult to say her name ". . . Ronnie." He had no idea there were tears on his cheeks until Karen wiped them away.

"I'm sorry," she whispered. "I'm so sorry."

"So am I." He considered putting his arms around her, but there would be time for that later—he hoped. The pounding on the door stopped for a moment, then resumed with greater ferocity and strength. Either the Ronnie-creature had gained some energy, or there were more things out there now. He decided not to mention either possibility to Karen.

"Come on," he said. "Let's get down into the undercroft and plan our next move. We should at least be safe down there for a while."

As he followed her down the stone steps, he hoped and prayed that he was right.

TWENTY-TWO

Thursday, December 22, 1994. 8:05 P.M.

THEY BARRICADED THE LOWER door to the undercroft as best they could in case Ronnie, or whatever Ronnie had now become, managed to break through and get down the steps. Then they sat down and tried to pretend they couldn't hear the noises she was making.

"It was a good idea, coming here." Dr. Cruttenden was looking around her. "Plenty of food, a water supply. Whatever's going on up there—and I'm still having trouble accepting any of it—we could survive in here for days if we needed to."

"We could." Karen didn't look so sure. "Providing Ronnie doesn't manage to get in here, and providing Chesney and that priest don't have some secret passage they can slip in through."

Dr. Cruttenden seemed unperturbed. "I'm sure they came up through the vestry trapdoor," she said. "It's the most logical explanation."

"But from where?" Karen hissed.

"Why, from that 'down below' we keep hearing about, of course. I can't say exactly what that is, mind you, and I have absolutely no desire to find out, but I don't doubt that's where they've come from. Where all the evil here has come from." She was rubbing her chin as she looked at Chambers. "I very much suspect that Anarch thing is down there too."

Chambers nodded. "With Paul. In fact, I got the impression that Paul had somehow become it."

"Did you?" Dr. Cruttenden didn't seem so sure. "I got the distinct impression that it—whatever 'it' is—needs all of us to . . . I don't know—return to life? Have its power restored?"

"Rule the world for all we know." Chambers had his ear against the door. The banging upstairs seemed to have subsided a little.

"I think rule the world is the least of it." Karen was hugging herself against the damp chill. "It wants to consume, whatever it is, to consume and change every living thing so that it becomes one of those tiny dots on the wall painting—mindless, hungry, and utterly driven by the instinct that thing has put there."

"It certainly could be one of the Elder Gods." Chambers was looking at Dr. Cruttenden, who shrugged.

"If it is, I'm surprised we haven't heard of it before, except in a few obscure and forgotten tomes like the *Liber de Nigra*. But that might just be because it's been sleeping for a very long time."

"But there must have been priests? Followers? This thing can't have just been asleep for thousands of years and suddenly woken up?"

Karen wanted Chambers to give her answers, but he couldn't. Whatever was happening here, neither he nor anyone else in the Human Protection League had ever encountered anything like it, so far as he knew.

"Surely you need followers to keep things on track?"

"Who's to say that hasn't happened?" Dr. Cruttenden was rubbing her chin again. "We know for a fact that the architect of this church, Thomas Moreby, had a mysterious past, and a mysterious end."

"Perhaps he was the priest?" Chambers checked the barricade once more. "Or one of them?"

"Like I said, it was rumored he consorted with at least one strange creature—said by some to be an insect as large as a wolfhound—and kept it alive by feeding it the blood of young children. There was some discussion at the time as to who was the master and who the servant. Up until an hour ago I would have said with all confidence that we would never know the answer, but now I'm not so sure."

"You mean Moreby might be down here too?"

"I mean he *is* down here . . . somewhere." Dr. Cruttenden pointed to the pile of packing crates stacked against the west wall. "This is only a very small part of the undercroft, you know. No one really knows how far it goes on for, but Moreby could have had himself interred here in a secret chamber after his death." She gazed into the darkness, her breath steaming as she spoke. "He's in there, somewhere, I'm sure of it, and who's to say this isn't all part of some occult plan to bring him back too?"

"But we're okay, aren't we?" Karen looked from Chambers to Dr. Cruttenden and back. "I mean, all we have to do is stay here and nothing will happen—no Moreby, no flea god, nothing."

Dr. Cruttenden nodded. "If we can stay here for three days and three nights, with no further attempts by the other four members of our group to try and get in here, then the doors to the west entrance will be opened..."

"... and we'll be saved? Right?" Karen was looking to the others for agreement, but wasn't getting any. "Right?"

"I think what Dr. Cruttenden is getting at," Chambers had to force himself to continue, so horrific was the implication of what he was about to say, "is that rather than the outside world coming in to save us ..."

Dr. Cruttenden nodded. "Those who have already become slaves to the Anarch will be released *into* the world. And there are bound to be other suitable subjects out there. It won't matter if we've survived or not."

"You mean right now the only thing that's protecting this world is the fact that we're shut in here?"

"Yes. And rather than having to last three days and be saved, we only have three days to stop whatever has started here and save the world from apocalypse."

They were silent for a moment, but that just served to emphasize that the hammering against the upper door had recommenced.

"That's not going to hold forever." Chambers was already debating unplugging the fridge and adding that to the downstairs barricade.

"And the lower door is a lot flimsier." Dr. Cruttenden sighed. "Despite our best efforts, if they can break down both of those they're not going to have much of a problem getting past packing cases, chairs, a table, and a fridge—are you going to add the fridge, Professor Chambers?"

He shook his head. It suddenly seemed rather pointless. "We have to get out of here, don't we?"

Dr. Cruttenden nodded.

"But there's nowhere to go!" Karen looked at them in horror and then followed their gaze over to the west wall. In any other situation the disbelief on her face would have been comical. "Oh, you're not serious? Go farther *into* the crypt? We could get lost in there and never come out."

"It's better than getting killed in here, or . . . worse." Chambers still felt uncomfortable mentioning Ronnie's name.

Karen was about to say something else, but she was interrupted by a crash from upstairs.

"And from the sound of it, I'd say we haven't got long." Dr. Cruttenden heaved herself to her feet and made her way to the back of the improvised kitchen. "I hope at least one of you is going to help me move these crates?"

They both did, once they realized that they were staring at the door and that the nasty, slapping sounds beyond it were only going to get louder the longer they procrastinated.

It didn't take long to shift the boxes. Karen had the helpful idea to pile them up against the door as an extra barrier to whatever was trying to get in.

"It might hold them for a few more seconds," she said.

"And that might make all the difference." Dr. Cruttenden was wheezing with the effort.

"I hope you're going to tell me you've remembered any inhalers you take." Chambers didn't let his concern slow him down, but he knew *she* would slow them down if she couldn't breathe.

"Don't worry." Dr. Cruttenden produced a mint green inhaler from her jacket pocket and took two puffs. "Plenty in here to last me. It's the dust, you know, my body never was on friendly terms with it."

"Keep out of the way, then." He meant it kindly. "We can shift these, there aren't many of them left, anyway."

It only took another couple of minutes, which was just as well as once the final packing crate was moved, there was a heavy thump and a crack appeared in the door to the undercroft.

"Okay." Karen wiped her hands on a rag. "What now?"

Dr. Cruttenden was examining the far wall. "By all accounts there should be a way through." It was almost pitch-black and she was feeling her way. Chambers looked around for a portable light source, but there was none.

There was another thump, followed by another crack appearing in the door. And now there were voices as well.

"You . . . have . . . to . . . let . . . us . . . in."

Was that Ronnie? Or what was left of her? The words sounded like air being squeezed across rapidly rotting vocal cords, lending them a liquid quality that was simultaneously nauseating and terrifying.

"You must, you know." That was Chesney. "He is waiting for you. For all of us. And the longer He waits, the more He will be displeased."

"Accept your salvation," said Traynor. "Accept it and revel in the Holy Putrescence that is His Holy Glory. Embrace the Anarch and He Whom He Serves and learn true salvation! True immortality! There is an after-life! There is life everlasting! No pain, no fear, just inviolable appetite, unending consumption, eternal satiation! Why prolong the agony?"

Because we still want to be ourselves, Chambers resisted crying out to the things now pounding at the rapidly splintering door. He shouted at Dr. Cruttenden instead. "Have you found anything yet?"

Her response was not what he wanted to hear.

"Not really. A few loose bricks, but that's all they are—there's solid stone behind them."

A chunk of the door flew into the room. Behind it was something that would live in Chambers's nightmares for as long as he lived.

If it was Ronnie, there was very little left of her face to identify it as her. The skin was gone, the muscle had liquefied and her left eye had fol-lowed, trickling in a snail trail of postulant necrosis down what was left of her cheek. Loosened teeth rattled in her exposed jaws, and what was left of her tongue had to be pushed against the roof of her rotting mouth to make any kind of intelligible noise at all.

"You can't escape ... join us ... join Him."

The two dark shapes behind her echoed her words as they, too, reached through and clawed at the air in the undercroft with rotting hands and leaking fingers, nails gone, bone poking through fingertips.

"Embrace ... His ... salvation," gargled the thing that had been Father Traynor.

"Could you hurry up and find the way out?" Chambers kicked at one of the crates. Then he kicked it again. Eventually a shard of splintered wood big enough to wield broke off. He gripped it tightly, even though it was probably the most pathetic weapon in the history of conflict, but he didn't know what else to do.

"There might be something here!" Karen was crouched next to Dr. Cruttenden. "It's small, but it feels like a door."

The way in to the undercroft finally gave way completely. Three unrecognizable figures that only a few hours ago had been their colleagues began to push aside the furniture and crates that had been piled up there.

"If you could hurry and get it open, that would be great." Chambers didn't know whether to face the onslaught or get behind the two women, so he remained standing midway between them and the door.

"It's definitely a door," said Dr. Cruttenden.

"But it's stuck," said Karen.

Chambers was gripping the wooden stake so hard he could feel the splinters digging into his skin. "Do you need a hand?"

"We might actually."

He had no idea if it was Dr. Cruttenden or Karen who spoke, but as the last of the crates were pushed aside and the three rotting things that had once been their colleagues shambled into the room, Chambers leapt to where they were crouching, groped for the small square of moist-feeling wood, and punched it as hard as he could.

Once.

Twice.

The rotting things were almost upon them as, on the third blow, the wood collapsed inwards. Chambers pushed Dr. Cruttenden through the tiny doorway, then Karen, before picking up the broken shards of wood and throwing them at the creatures that were staggering toward him. Then he grabbed a flashlight and followed the other two through the opening.

TWENTY-THREE

Thursday, December 22, 1994. 8:26 P.M.

"IT LOOKS AS IF it goes on for miles."

Chambers wished Karen was exaggerating, but he was beginning to feel the same way. He shone the flashlight ahead of them as far as the beam would allow. All he saw was more of the same. The same flagstone-paved floor, dusted with grit and chips of stone that had fallen from a ceiling only inches above their heads; the same cylindrical pillars of red brick, the ancient cement that held them together and oozed out between the cracks when the bricks were first laid; the same sarcophagi.

No. Not the same.

Many had only minor differences: a different name on the tarnished brass plaque that had been affixed to the lid of pale gray stone; a slightly different design to the scrollwork carved into the edges; a few more cracks and cobwebs adorning the casing here and there to signify they had been here longer than their neighbors.

A couple, however, turned out to be very different.

Chambers shone the flashlight at his watch for a moment. They had been walking down here for the better part of half an hour. Every now and then they stopped and listened, but there was no sound to suggest they were being pursued. The tomb adjacent to the entrance they squeezed themselves through had been crumbling sufficiently that a good push caused it to collapse, sealing up the hole.

Let them try and dig their way through that lot with their rotting flesh and diseased bone, Chambers thought, before remembering that some of those shambling forms were people he had been conversing with not much more than an hour before.

Karen had not been impressed. "How are we supposed to get back through?"

"We're not supposed to get back through."

Dr. Cruttenden interrupted before Karen could snap back a reply. "I don't think any of us will be wanting to retrace our steps in the near future, do you?" The wet gargling noises behind the mound of rubble sounded farther away than they actually were, but they were still loud enough to make them get moving. "Besides," she continued, as they began to feel their way forward, "that can't be the only entrance to this place."

"Unless no one was ever meant to come down here."

"Oh, great." Chambers could tell Karen was glaring at him even if he couldn't see her. "If you have any other ideas like that, would you kindly keep them to yourself?"

They had resumed their journey in silence, walking forward because heading west, toward the main road, seemed the most sensible idea. They circumvented the sarcophagi they encountered. Every now and then a rat scurried across their path, and once, Karen jumped as an especially fat spider plopped from its disturbed web onto her bare neck.

They only stopped when they came to the first statue.

Chambers couldn't think of a better name for it. Whereas all the other tombs they had passed so far were of the same, functional design, now they suddenly found themselves faced with a structure roughly the same shape as the church from which they had escaped, but in miniature. It rose almost to the height of Chambers's shoulder and seemed to have been carved from several pieces of interlocking granite. The detail was lacking, but attempts had been made at carving windows and doors.

"Can you see a name anywhere?" Dr. Cruttenden asked.

Chambers shone the flashlight around it but could find nothing. "Is it important?"

"It might be."

"Why?" said Karen. "Because someone paid for an over-the-top method of being buried here?"

"Because it may not be a tomb at all." Dr. Cruttenden waited for Chambers to take the lead again before continuing. "And don't forget that Thomas Moreby is rumored to be buried here somewhere. I think it's highly likely that if he had any intentions to return from the grave, he would have left some kind of mechanism to effect that."

"If it is the only one here, I'm amazed we came across it," Chambers replied, shining the flashlight from side to side. "This place seems to go on in all directions."

"So we could easily get lost."

"We could, Karen, but we're not going to." Dr. Cruttenden was bringing up the rear now. "Carry on, Professor Chambers!" Her words were bristling with too much enthusiasm, but Chambers preferred her attitude to Karen's pessimism.

The second church was made of wood.

It only became obvious when they were right upon it. It was probably oak, or something else resilient enough to stand the test of time and the freezing damp down here. A much better effort had been made at carving the windows and doors, and this church had an interior as well. As Chambers shone his flashlight in, he could see there was more inside it than just a hollowed-out interior.

"I think I can see something in there."

Dr. Cruttenden bent down to investigate, and Karen did the same. Their eyes followed the beam from Chambers's flashlight.

"Someone's done a model of the inside of the church," said Karen. "There are pews and there's the pulpit. You can see the altar. And on the far wall is . . . is . . ." she screamed and pulled away. Chambers grabbed her wrist to stop her running off.

On the far wall, in exactly the same place as the actual life-sized church they had recently left, was a picture of the same thing that had appeared to them, with the same Greek word written beneath it.

"So someone did plan all this, then." Dr. Cruttenden leaned on the arm Chambers wasn't using to keep Karen close to them for support. "I'm afraid I can't see what you mean by something inside, though."

"Look at the center of the model."

Dr. Cruttenden followed the flashlight beam as Chambers moved it around within the structure of the church. She gasped as she saw he was outlining a shape.

"What is that?"

Chambers shook his head. "I don't know. But someone—or perhaps *something*—could be buried in that model."

"And inside the granite one too?"

Chambers breathed a silent sigh of relief that Karen seemed to be recovering from her scare. "Who knows? I guess it's possible."

"But why?"

"All kinds of reasons." Dr. Cruttenden straightened up, and Chambers heard several joints pop in her back as she did so. "The simplest would be that this, and its predecessor, are merely extremely ornate sarcophagi, monuments to the dead buried within them."

"But this is All Hallows Church," said Karen, "which means . . ."

". . . it's more likely that these are based on John Verney's original designs."

"Who was John Verney?" Chambers moved the flashlight beam away from the model's interior.

"He was the maker of Thomas Moreby's architectural models. Before any large building is undertaken, a scale model is usually constructed. Verney was the one who built such things for Moreby."

"And he was mixed up in the things Moreby was?"

Dr. Cruttenden frowned. "Much of his life is as mysterious as Moreby's, and as tragic at the end. Verney also died in a lunatic asylum. In fact, Moreby visited him on several occasions before his death. Records of the time state that Verney claimed to have found a way to travel between worlds, and he made no secret of it to Moreby when he visited at the end."

"Did these records of yours say how he was able to do that?" Karen was becoming her old self again, now, and her voice echoed off the surrounding stone.

"Not exactly . . . but they do mention that the main reason he was there was because of the things he ate."

"Ate?" Somehow Chambers knew this wasn't going to be pleasant.

"It's nothing too disgusting. He didn't feast on the flesh of children or anything like that."

"Well, that's a relief," said Karen. "All the more for Moreby to feed to his giant flea-slave-thing, then."

"It was fleas that he ate." As Dr. Cruttenden spoke, Chambers could swear the air got even colder. "Fleas and other insects, and sometimes spiders. But fleas more than anything else. And not the entire insect. He would crush them between finger and thumb and suck at the fluids that burst from them."

"Thank you so much for that image." Karen shivered. "I needed something else to scare me as I was starting to feel just a bit too comfortable down here."

"Don't mind Miss Shepworth," said Chambers, returning the journalist's glare as Dr. Cruttenden started to look upset. "She has her own way of dealing with the stress of this, as we all do. So you think these models could be part of some plan of Moreby's?"

The lecturer nodded. "He's probably down here somewhere, and I think these models may hold the key, either to where he is or how he plans to come back. I wouldn't be at all surprised if the bodies in those models are sacrifices that had to be specially prepared before they were interred and these constructs placed around them."

"But why build more than one?" said Karen. "And sorry for being sarcastic."

"That's all right. I think we're all feeling rather stressed right now." Dr. Cruttenden gave her a reassuring smile and Chambers angled the flashlight so that Karen could see it. "There might be more than one because whoever did this was trying to get it right, but a more likely explanation is that more than one is required for any transportation ritual to work."

"So what do we do?"

"We keep going," said Chambers, shining the flashlight ahead of them. "The plan is to get out, remember? Without releasing those things that we've hopefully trapped in the church. Then the authorities can deal with it."

"You really think they'll know how? That they'll even believe us when we tell them what's happened?" Karen's voice cut through the darkness. "The first thing they'll do is open those church doors and then what's left of Ronnie, Chesney, and Father Traynor will be out. And there'll be nothing anyone can do to stop them."

"What should we do, then? Find Moreby's coffin and destroy it?" Chambers had never felt so lost in his life. He just hoped he didn't sound it. "And what about Paul? And what they said he'd become? Should we try and find him, or it, as well, and . . . I don't know . . . kill what he is now?"

"How do you know it *can* be killed?" Dr. Cruttenden's voice was calm to the point of cold detachment. "How do you know any of this can be stopped? Perhaps it is as inevitable as the seasons, or evolution. Perhaps this is merely the next step in the life cycle of the Earth, and the final step for the human race, and there's nothing we can do."

There was silence from both Karen and Chambers as the horrible realization sank in. Eventually, Chambers spoke. His voice was a dry croak.

"Perhaps," he said. "But seeing as the alternative is sitting here and either starving or freezing to death, or going back the way we came to literally join our former colleagues, I think I'd rather try keep fighting for now."

Dr. Cruttenden clapped him on the shoulder. "That's the spirit! Now, even though we're looking for a way out of here, I think the best thing to do on our journey is try and find out how many of these models there are."

The third one was made of black marble.

The stone was so dark Chambers walked straight into it, even though he had the flashlight held in front of him. Was the light getting dimmer? He hoped not.

"My God," Dr. Cruttenden breathed as they examined it in more closely. "It's absolutely exquisite. It must have been sculpted from a single block. Look at the detail!"

The model was perfect, right down to the layering of individual roof tiles. Within, there were not just pews but a couple of people sitting on them, listening to a priest the size of a matchstick frozen in mid-gesticulation standing on the altar step. On the wall of the north aisle was the image of the Anarch, and on the altar lay something indescribable, made all the more twisted and hideous by the flickering shadows cast by the flashlight. The outline of the inhabitant contained within the construct was more difficult to make out, but it was there.

"What's that on the altar?" Karen was peering over Chambers's shoulder. "Is it human or insect?"

"It may well be both," Dr. Cruttenden replied. "I'm not even sure if it's safe to look at it for too long."

"Then let's not."

They moved on. Ten minutes later they found themselves facing a wall built from heavy stone blocks. The mortar between them was damp and matted with algae. When it became apparent that the wall went on for some distance, Chambers shone the flashlight back the way they had come, to reveal something none of them had noticed.

"We've been descending."

Dr. Cruttenden was right. It was only obvious when they turned around. Gradually and imperceptibly, the ground on which they had been walking had been sloping downward.

"I wonder how far down we are now?"

The flashlight revealed that, while the floor had sloped, the ceiling had remained level. The wall against which they were standing now extended upward for more than their combined height.

"Can you hear anything?" Karen asked.

Chambers shook his head. "Why?"

"Oh, I was just hoping we might be able to hear the road, that's all."

But there was nothing—no traffic and no voices. Just the endless drip of water from somewhere that sounded very far away.

"Standing here isn't going to get us anywhere." Dr. Cruttenden was rubbing her hands together as she stated the obvious. "I suggest we get moving again, if only to help my aging circulation."

Chambers licked his right index finger and held up his hand.

"What are you doing?" Karen asked.

"I was right." He had suspected it before, but had forgotten when they had come across the first of the models. "It's been getting colder because there's a breeze in here."

Karen followed his gaze. "Could it be coming from where we came in?"

"No. Although it was still bloody cold, it was definitely a bit warmer in the undercroft than it is in here. It could be a way out, or if nothing else, perhaps part of this structure has collapsed into a nearby sewer and we can get out that way."

Karen actually laughed. "I never thought I'd be happy to hear mention of a sewer."

Their moment of levity was brief as the beam from the flashlight noticeably dimmed.

"We'd better hurry." Chambers shook the flashlight, but that didn't help.

They followed the direction of the breeze for the next quarter of an hour, until they came across the fourth model. This time it was Karen who bumped into it.

"Ouch!" She nursed the cut she sustained on her hand from the sharp angle of the roof. "Since when did stone cut like that?"

"Flint can," said Dr. Cruttenden, coming to take a closer look at the model. "But that's not what this is." She gave the body of the building a tap and was rewarded with a metallic resonance. "Steel," she proclaimed. "Or possibly iron—I'm not qualified to say which."

If anything, the steel version of All Hallows Church was as exquisite as the version rendered in black marble, and even more detailed. It was difficult to see where the individual components had been welded together, and the models within were more accurate than before.

And more terrifying.

"That could almost be Father Traynor," said Karen, pointing to the tiny metal pulpit.

"I think it is." Chambers pointed the flashlight to the south transept. "What does all that remind you of?"

"Chesney's equipment!" Karen gripped his hand. "Which means that the people in the pews are us and . . ."

"... the thing on the altar must be Paul, or what was left of him by the time they had finished."

"But how did they know?" Karen kicked the base of the model. It resonated with a deep clang that reverberated throughout the chamber. "How could they have known? This model is ... well ... it's ... old."

Dr. Cruttenden nodded. "It is," she said. "I can't say how old, but I wouldn't be surprised if it's been here for over a hundred years."

"So I ask again: how did they know?"

"Perhaps they didn't. Perhaps we've been helping shape these as events have unfolded."

Chambers shook his head. "That's ridiculous."

"No more so than a lot of what we have already witnessed here. I know I'm just thinking aloud but please, it may offer us either a chance of escape or a chance of stopping this thing. Hopefully both." Dr. Cruttenden was staring at the steel church. "Imagine these models being placed here, imbued with some power that allows their interiors to alter when the appropriate series of events is put in motion."

"You mean us coming here?"

"Yes, or farther back. Our meeting in Oxford, or the discovery of those manuscripts. Even the original disturbance of the ground where they were buried might have been enough."

"But why?"

"If we knew that we'd be one step ahead of the game, wouldn't we? Instead of fumbling around in the shadows like we are now."

Chambers handed a handkerchief to Karen so she could bind her hand. "We've found four. Do you think there are any others in here?"

"What do you think? If we had not found this one, I would have assumed three was the end of it. But now ... four isn't a number of significance in any religion."

"What is the next number of significance?"

Dr. Cruttenden turned to Karen. "The same number of people who entered All Hallows Church, and the same as the members of Thomas Moreby's little group."

Chambers could hardly believe it. "You mean you think there are another three of these models somewhere in this crypt?"

"I'm almost sure of it. Just as I am becoming increasingly convinced that our actions are helping to shape their interiors. And once their design is complete as intended, perhaps that is when some mechanism will be unlocked that will allow the next stage in the process to take place."

"What process?"

"Moreby returning, the Anarch taking power, the world changing. Perhaps all or none of those things." The lecturer gave Chambers a weak smile. "I really have no idea. You do realize that, don't you?"

"I do, but your guesses are going to be a lot closer to the truth than anything either of us can come up with."

"Don't be so sure. I have a feeling the longer this goes on, the less the rules of the normal world are going to apply."

The next church model was made of a hard black stone that was duller than marble and infinitely more delicate.

"I think it's coal," said Dr. Cruttenden as Chambers once again shone the flashlight beam inside it to reveal a now-familiar scene.

"At least the tableau hasn't changed," said Karen.

"I suspect it won't now until something happens to us. And before you chastise me for my pessimism, young lady, might I add that the mere fact we escaped from the undercroft has probably delayed things? Shall we move on?"

Chambers wanted to say something to Karen, who was left biting her lip, but Dr. Cruttenden was already pushing ahead without the aid of the flashlight and he had to hurry to keep up.

The sixth model was made of something white, something smooth.

"Is that porcelain?" Karen asked.

"Actually, I suspect a more accurate description would be glazed clay." Dr. Cruttenden circumvented the model, which was exactly the same size and shape as the others, but was a pale mustard color, either because of the clay from which it had been made or the effects of having been down there for so long. The detail was not as good as the coal, steel, or marble churches, but it was still possible to see that the tableau within was the same. "One more to go," she said as they moved away from it.

"Even if there is," said Chambers as he followed the breeze, "there's no saying we'll bump into it."

"No, but somehow I think that we will."

"You're saying we're being guided down here?" Karen was keeping close to Chambers, as if her proximity to the flashlight might somehow help to prolong the battery life.

"We're following a trail, aren't we? Even if it's one of air rather than of breadcrumbs. And before you say we shouldn't, I don't think we have much of a choice, especially as those batteries seem to be almost dead."

It was true. The beam the flashlight was giving out was now so weak Chambers wondered if perhaps there was some other source of light that was allowing them to see. The breeze was stronger now as well, and it was turning the skin on his face to ice. Onward they went, past more of the same pillars, more of the same sarcophagi, wanting it to end but knowing when it did that there could be something worse waiting for them.

The final model was made of glass.

It was inarguably beautiful, even in the dim light of the crypt. Delicate-looking, and yet when Chambers accidentally brushed against it nothing broke off. He didn't need to shine the flashlight into one of the windows of this one—he could simply point the beam through the wall. Doing so caused the entire model to light up.

"Beautiful," Karen breathed.

"Exquisite," Dr. Cruttenden agreed. "The work of a true craftsman."

The interior of the building revealed the hazy outline of something imbedded within it, plus a familiar tableau. Except for one very important difference.

"The people have gone." Karen's eyes were searching the model. "They've all gone. I can't see them anywhere."

"It's catching up," Dr. Cruttenden agreed. "I suspect if we went back and looked at the others they would now show the same situation."

"So where are they?"

"We know where they are," said Chambers, gently. "We are down in the crypt, and the others are in the undercroft."

"They won't stay there, though," said Dr. Cruttenden. "They need us, and they'll try any way they can to get us."

"In that case I suggest we keep moving," said Chambers.

"Where?" Karen sounded as if she was about to cry. "Around and around this crypt? Bumping into these bloody models again and again as they show us how much closer those things are getting to us?"

Dr. Cruttenden laid a gentle hand on her shoulder and pointed to the right. "I think he meant through that door over there."

Chambers blinked. He hadn't meant that at all, in fact he had only come out with it because he didn't know what else to say. But Dr. Cruttenden was correct. Just ahead of them was an ornate door of thick oak, with clasps and hinges of heavy iron scrollwork. It wasn't set into any wall they could see. Rather it seemed to lead the way to a lower level, a place that lay beneath even the crypt of All Hallows Church.

And it was open.

TWENTY-FOUR

"MY WATCH HAS STOPPED."

Chambers shook his wrist a few times and then held the device to his ear. He looked confused. "It's still ticking," he said.

"Perhaps we have traveled far enough for time to have lost its meaning," Dr. Cruttenden suggested. "It is, after all, an abstract concept, one the world of man has attempted to rationalize and quantify. I have the strongest feeling we are no longer in that world."

Meanwhile, Karen was peering into the doorway. "Should we go down there?"

The steps leading down had been fashioned from the same worn black stone as the walls.

"I don't think we've got much choice." The steps were broad enough for two of them to walk abreast, Chambers noted. "Besides, the batteries in this flashlight are going to run out soon. At least there seems to be a source of light down there."

And there was—a kind of pale greenish glow given off by the phosphorescent moss that clung to the roof of the staircase, spreading to the tops of the walls and no doubt kept alive by the dripping moisture that echoed with a regular *pat*... *pat*... *pat* throughout the chamber.

"We have to go down." Dr. Cruttenden's face was grim. "This is the next stage."

"Stage of what?"

"I have no idea," the lecturer confessed to Karen. "I can only assume it's going to be unpleasant, whatever it is. But we have no choice."

"Can't we stay here?"

"As Professor Chambers said, in a moment we are going to be plunged into darkness in this crypt. Then instead of blundering around by lamplight we will spend the rest of our days blundering around in darkness."

Karen could barely say the words. "The rest of our days?"

"You don't think we're going to be allowed to stay up here for long, do you? And I don't know about you, but if we do have to face our pursuers, I'd rather do it in the light."

As if to encourage them, the flashlight chose that moment to go out, plunging them into darkness save for the green glow emanating from the staircase.

"Nothing," said Chambers after giving it a good shake. "Looks like our minds have been made up for us."

"Like they have been all along," murmured Dr. Cruttenden as she stepped through the doorway.

Chambers felt someone take hold of his left hand and he almost jumped. Then he realized it was Karen.

Who else could it be? he thought, before refusing to let his mind dwell on the possibilities. He gave her hand a reassuring squeeze as they followed Dr. Cruttenden down the steps.

The very steep steps.

Chambers hoped their rapid descent would soon level out as each step jarred his knees. He put out his right palm to steady himself and was rewarded with the curious sensation of touching wet stone that was also somehow warm.

Getting closer to the center of the Earth, he thought with a trace of amusement, before wondering just how far underground they were now. Shouldn't they be coming across water pipes, or sewers? Didn't one of the London Underground lines extend out this far? Why hadn't they encountered any of that, and even if all those structures had been cunningly constructed to avoid such things, surely they should be able to hear the rumble of trains, the rush of water? How late was it? Too late for traffic to be rumbling along the main road outside? He tried looking at his watch and then he remembered what Dr. Cruttenden had said.

"Are you all right?" Karen had picked up on his concern.

"Just wondering why the wall's warm," he replied.

"Quite possibly an effect of nature," came the voice from ahead of them. "The water table in this area has always been very high, which probably explains the constant dripping. One also has to assume that such soil, which would have a very high clay content, would probably be a great insulator of heat."

That didn't exactly explain things, though. "But the heat has to come from somewhere in the first place," Chambers said, trying hard not to slip on steps which were becoming increasingly muddy.

"No, it doesn't," came the reply. "I wonder if we shall find out."

The farther down they went, the wetter it became, and as the moisture increased, so did the temperature. Soon Chambers was pausing to roll up his sleeves and hoping his shoes were sufficiently waterproof to prevent his feet from getting a soaking.

"How much farther?" Karen was wiping sweat from her forehead.

"Who knows?" he replied. "For all we know it could go right down to..."
He stopped.

"Go on," she said.

"Go on what?"

"You were going to say 'Hell,' weren't you?"

He was. "Not necessarily."

"Well, you should have. I never could have believed it would be so bloody warm down here."

"And bright as well," said Dr. Cruttenden. "I'm sure you've both observed how the light seems to be getting better the deeper we go."

Chambers had assumed that was simply their eyes adjusting. "There is a lot more of that green algae stuff here. It must be ideal growing conditions for it."

"And handy that it's luminous," Dr. Cruttenden continued. "Of course, as you and I know, heat and light don't come from nowhere. There has to be an energy source that the algae can absorb in order to give off this kind of luminescence."

"I can't believe you're both still trying to be scientific about this." Karen almost stumbled as she spoke. "After what we've seen, everything that happened in the church, everything we had to run away from. This is all part of the same world and there's no reason why it should make any more sense than a giant flea god appearing on a wall, or people we know turning into . . . *things*."

"That's very true," said Dr. Cruttenden. "And it probably explains why the ground is leveling out ahead."

It was true. Chambers could hardly believe it, but their descent was coming to an end. The stone steps ended so abruptly that he almost fell, his legs trembling as he found himself standing on level ground for the first time in what felt like hours.

The corridor was widening as well. Now the three of them could walk side by side, as the ceiling began to lift away from them. Soon there was space for them to walk together without bumping shoulders. Not long after that, it was as if they were walking down a main road.

"I can't believe this is under the church," said Karen, her voice echoing around the rapidly expanding chamber they now found themselves in.

"We may no longer be under the church," Dr. Cruttenden replied, although she refused to be drawn further.

As they kept on walking, the ceiling rose to the point where they could no longer see it. The greenish light, however, remained.

After approximately another ten minutes of unending stone corridor, Karen grumbled. "It's like we're back in the crypt."

"Not at all." Dr. Cruttenden had an answer every time, thought Chambers, which was more than he had. "The crypt was dark, whereas here we have light. The crypt was of a different design, and it had those peculiar models. But most of all," she took a breath, "we never encountered anyone coming toward us when we were in there."

Chambers squinted and looked ahead. She was right. Coming slowly toward them, its right shoulder rubbing along the wall to their left, was a figure dressed in white. His first thought was that it was a ghost, and while he knew that was ridiculous, after everything that had already happened he was prepared for anything.

As the figure came nearer it became apparent that it was a young woman. Her long black hair clung in damp tresses to her cheeks, and it looked as if she had been crying. Chambers breathed a sigh of relief as she began to look more like a lost and lonely soul and less like something that was intending them harm.

"What should we do?" Karen hissed.

"We could start with 'hello.'" After all, Chambers reckoned, wasn't it possible that some other perfectly normal human being had managed to get lost down here and was now backtracking? Perhaps she would be able to tell them what was up ahead.

The girl beat them to it. She didn't seem to recognize that there was anyone else in the passageway with her until she was a few yards away. Then her eyes brightened, and she spoke to them.

No one could understand what it was she said. When they shrugged in reply she repeated the words. The girl took two steps forward and held out her hands. The sleeves of the gown she was wearing fell away to reveal arms of milk white skin, right the way down to her wrists and hands. Her fingers, however, were gray. The same gray as the stone that the walls had been fashioned from. She took another step forward and Chambers noticed that she was barefoot, the skin beyond her ankles the same abnormal color as her fingers. Karen was extending her own hand in greeting, but Chambers pushed it away.

"I don't think we should touch her." He pointed to the girl's hands.

"But she might be in pain."

Dr. Cruttenden ignored Karen's words and stepped forward to take a closer look. The new arrival seemed happy to let her. The lecturer frowned as she felt the girl's fingers and toes.

"If I didn't know better, I'd say this girl's hands and feet are made of ... stone," Dr. Cruttenden said.

"Stone?" Karen's voice echoed the lecturer's disbelief.

Dr. Cruttenden took out a pencil and tapped the girl's left index finger just to prove her point to Chambers. "Stone. It looks remarkably similar to the walls, doesn't it?"

And the floor, Chambers was going to add. Instead he pointed ahead of them and asked the girl slowly and directly, "What lies that way?"

The girl stared at him, wide-eyed, but said nothing.

Karen shook her head. "Well at least that proves she doesn't understand you either."

Chambers tried again, just in case, only to be rewarded with the same slightly confused and, he had to admit, slightly appealing look. The girl spoke again. The words were different this time, but no less guttural.

"I suppose it's possible that if her fingers and toes have calcified for some reason, then the same thing might have happened to her vocal cords," he said, wishing the flashlight was still working so he could shine it into her mouth. "There are conditions that can do that to you."

"None of which would explain why a young girl would be wandering around down here in a shift and with nothing on her feet," said Karen. "You know what she reminds me of? A corpse. Someone who's been buried in a shroud but has somehow dug her way out of her grave and is now trying to find her way back to the real world."

The girl flinched at Karen's words, as if they held some truth to them.

"That's ridiculous," said Chambers, although now he was beginning to wonder if the girl had a pulse. The strands of grayness creeping across her palms and encircling her wrists made him think twice about taking it, however. "I wonder who she is?" He reached out to feel the carotid artery in her neck, but at this presumed act of aggression the girl flinched and backed against the wall.

"I'm sorry." Chambers began to apologize profusely, but it was no good. The girl's bright gray eyes were filling with tears that glittered in the green light.

"Now see what you've done." Karen's tones were admonishing. "You've made her cry."

"I don't think he has, you know." Dr. Cruttenden was pointing downward. "I rather think it's more to do with that."

They both followed her gaze to where the girl's right hand had come to rest against the wall.

And saw that her fingers had become fused with the stone.

The girl was trying to pull away now, but it was no good. In fact, if anything, it was making things worse. Chambers watched, horrified, as her fingers sank into the stone as if it was the softest mud, fusing with the dark gray rock at the knuckle. When the girl put her left hand against the stone to try and push herself away, the same thing happened.

"Can't we help her?"

Chambers responded to Karen's plea by putting his arms around the girl's waist and pulling, but it was useless. They watched, helpless, as both her hands sunk in up to the wrists, and then up to the elbows. Finally, and with a calcified shriek that Chambers knew he would never forget, the girl was sucked into the wall.

For a moment they could still hear her faint wailing, then it became duller, and then it was not there at all.

"What the hell just happened?" Like the others, Karen was left staring open-mouthed at the expanse of stone where the girl had disappeared.

"I hope that's a rhetorical question because I don't think any of us can come up with a sensible answer." Chambers was rubbing his fingertips. They had been unusually chilled by his contact with the girl, whose body had been ice cold.

"No," said Dr. Cruttenden. "Not a sensible one, anyway."

That surprised Chambers, and it looked as if it surprised Karen as well. "You mean you do have one?"

"I'm not sure," came the reply. "I need to think about it for a while." She shivered. "Shall we continue our journey?"

"But that girl!" Karen was shaking. "Shouldn't we stay here in case she . . . in case she . . ."

"She's not going to be coming out again anytime soon," said Dr. Cruttenden. "Or at least I would be very surprised if she did. The only thing we can do is keep going. Oh, and whatever you do, don't touch the walls."

She strode ahead as if, Chambers thought, for all the world she knew where she was going.

"She's far too cheerful," Karen whispered. "Do you think she's going mad?"

"She's certainly going somewhere," Chambers replied. "And we'd better hurry up or she's going to leave us far behind."

A little further on they arrived at a crossroads, where two of the broad, high-ceilinged corridors met. Dr. Cruttenden barely hesitated before carrying straight on.

"Do you think you might know where we are?" Chambers asked.

"I have an idea," came the reply. "But I need to gather more data. I see no point in hesitating about it either. I have to admit I was hoping we would have come across someone else by now. If we don't in the next ten minutes or so, I hope you won't mind if we double back and try one of the left or right turns back there?"

Chambers didn't know what to say, and so he said nothing. Pretty soon it didn't matter because Dr. Cruttenden found what she was looking for. The sight turned Chambers's stomach, and Karen had to stifle a scream.

Up ahead were two people. Or rather, parts of two people. The nearer was an elderly man, dressed in a once-smart black suit that was now streaked with gray dust and pale mud. On his left wrist was a watch that still ticked, albeit irregularly. His right wrist was buried in the stone of the wall he was leaning against. Most of the rest of his body was free, but his head was close enough to the stone that his gray hair had fused to it, forcing him to tilt his head at an awkward angle. As they watched, whatever had a hold of his hair tightened its grip and pulled his head a little nearer to the wall.

"Not . . . much . . . longer . . . now," he said in a strangled voice. "No . . . more . . . waiting."

The second figure was worse, because there was so much less of it.

It was difficult to tell if it was a man or a woman as it only existed from the waist up. Anything lower than that had long since disappeared into the stone floor. Its head hung low on its chest, pulled into that position by the long strands of iron gray hair that had also fused with the ground, causing the figure to resemble an especially bloated fly caught in the web of an enormous spider. This figure emitted a low unintelligible moaning that got louder as they approached.

The three of them took great caution to avoid touching either of their new acquaintances as they carefully skirted them. Dr. Cruttenden wanted to examine both in more detail, but Chambers stopped her.

"We don't want to risk you ending up like them, do we?" he said.

"What are they?" Karen was staring at them too, fascinated.

Dr. Cruttenden didn't seem at all worried. "They are not exactly alive, but neither are they truly dead. I suppose if you wanted to give them a name you could call them 'zombies.'" She looked at Chambers. "I don't think such a fate is intended for us," she said. "Otherwise we would be here already."

"But we are here." Karen could not take her eyes off the waist-high thing, and Chambers had to take her hand to encourage her farther down the passageway.

"I know we are physically here," said Dr. Cruttenden, "but I do not believe we are spiritually intended for this place."

"What's that supposed to mean?"

It was no use. Dr. Cruttenden was already off in search of more evidence.

Very soon they encountered three more of the stone zombies, as Chambers had come to consider them. One was an elderly woman half-buried in the wall to their right. She regarded them with a single rolling eye as they passed. A little farther on was a man who had evidently succumbed to some trauma that had caused him to lose both his lower limbs. The wall to the left had sucked in his arms, but his amputated stumps still flailed helplessly against the stone floor. The last, and most disturbing, was little more than a face, staring out from the wall at waist-height. It had assumed the same pallid gray as its surroundings, but still maintained a degree of flexibility that allowed it to cry. The most horrifying aspect was that the face belonged to what appeared to be a two-year-old child.

"Does this fit in with your theory?" Chambers asked as they hurried past the last one.

"Yes." Dr. Cruttenden's face was grim. "Yes, it does. I wonder how far we are meant to go?"

"I'm guessing the answer is to keep walking until something happens?" Karen seemed resigned now, but Chambers was still worried about her.

"Are you sure you're okay?" he asked.

"As okay as anyone could be," she replied. "I'm not that delicate, you know. My job has taken me to all kinds of places in the world, and I've seen some terrible things. You just learn to cope, don't you?"

Chambers knew what she meant. "All kinds of places *in* the world, but I bet you've never been *under* it like this."

That raised the hint of a smile that made him feel a lot better. "Caves in Trinidad and mines in South Africa during an uprising. But no, nothing quite like this."

"Are you coming?"

The two of them had ground to a halt. They jumped as Dr. Cruttenden's voice came from farther up the passageway.

"Better get going," said Karen. "Our teacher's calling us."

"She is a bit like that, isn't she?" Chambers said. "In fact, I had a schoolteacher very much like her when I was five."

Karen winced, "I had a grandmother," she said. "Believe me, I think you probably got the better deal."

Ahead they reached a T-junction, with the same grotesque sight both left and right.

Projecting from the walls were human arms.

They were all different—sizes, lengths, ages. Men and women appeared to be accounted for, and children too.

And they all appeared to be made of stone.

Chambers didn't fancy turning left or right. "Do we brave one of these, or is it back the way we came?"

"There's no going back," said Dr. Cruttenden. "That would be foolish in the extreme."

It looked as if there was just enough room down each passageway for them to walk single file and not come into contact with the petrified fingers.

"Time to toss a coin?"

Dr. Cruttenden took one step into the left-hand passageway. Almost immediately there was a terrible grinding sound, and as they watched, all the arms stretched, emerging further from their prisons of rock on either side until they formed an impenetrable barrier, a mesh of petrified limbs that it was now impossible to pass.

The lecturer took a step back, and tried the right passageway instead. Nothing happened.

"It would seem the decision has been made for us," she said.

Chambers pushed Karen ahead of him. "Let's just hope they're not trying to split us up," he said as they followed Dr. Cruttenden down the passage that had been chosen for them.

The corridor of limbs lasted for twenty paces. Then they stepped through an open doorway, and into a room that seemed to have no walls. If there were any, they were too far away to see. As far as Chambers could tell, there was no ceiling either. Instead, a curtain of magenta sky hung over them, with irregular pinpricks of light that could be stars, although not in any known configuration Chambers was familiar with. A faint breeze blew, and if he concentrated he could see tiny specks on the far horizon, where the sky was redder and met the pale gray stone slabs of the seemingly never-ending floor.

"Where are we?" he breathed as he clutched at Karen's hand.

"Closer to the end than we were," said Dr. Cruttenden, looking around her.

"The end?" Karen frowned. "The end of what?"

"I could be wrong, of course, but if I'm correct I don't mean the end of us, so please don't start fretting."

"I'm not *fretting*." Karen did sound incensed, though. "Perhaps I might be a little less inquisitive if you told us what you think is going on?"

"Not enough evidence yet," Dr. Cruttenden muttered. "Not enough."

Chambers laid a hand on Karen's shoulder. "Best not to get her worked up," he whispered. "We've no idea if what she's implying has any basis in fact, or if this has just all got too much for her."

Dr. Cruttenden, meanwhile, was wandering off ahead of them, muttering under her breath the entire time.

"Has to be here..." Chambers heard when he caught up with her. "Somewhere around here ... should be obvious. Has to be here somewhere ..."

"Could it have anything to do with those shapes up ahead there?" He was trying to be helpful, and he certainly didn't expect his words to cause her face to assume a look of abject terror.

"Oh no," she said. "Oh no oh no oh no. We have to find it before they get here."

"Find what?" Karen asked. "Before who gets here?"

Dr. Cruttenden raised a shaking hand and pointed at the horizon. "*Them.*" Her voice was a dry whisper.

Chambers shielded his eyes and tried hard to focus on the tiny shapes. Was it his imagination, or did they seem bigger than before? And were they moving a little from side to side?

"We have to leave this place before they get here." Dr. Cruttenden was kicking at the stone slabs. "The way down has to be here somewhere."

Karen looked at Chambers, who shrugged. "Sounds like we need to find a way down," he said to her.

All three began to kick at the stone slabs, yielding little more than dull tapping sounds and sore toes. Every now and then Chambers looked up. The shapes were definitely closer now, shambling and rocking from side to side. If he squinted, he could make out that they were human figures, as gray as some of the parts of the poor individuals they had encountered in the corridor.

"What are they?" he asked as they continued to search.

"Souls bound to Limbo," said Dr. Cruttenden. Now she was down on her hands and knees patting at the stone. "We saw their precursors back there, in the preparation channels. Once they are absorbed, they take their place on the eternal plain to wander it forever. Only one thing can free them."

"Dare we ask?" Karen kept tapping as she spoke.

"Souls to replace them," said Dr. Cruttenden. "That's why we have to hurry, or we'll be trapped here forever."

"In Limbo?" Karen pushed hair out of her eyes and looked at the figures. Some were lurching more than others, and some seemed to only have one functioning lower limb and were dragging the other behind them. Some were crawling, and others had no limbs at all and were slowly wriggling or rolling toward them.

The ones at the front, however, were moving quickly.

"Survival of the fittest," said Dr. Cruttenden. "It's the same in Heaven or in Hell."

"Or Limbo?" Karen repeated. "Is that where we are—Limbo?"

"It's where I believe we are, and where we'll stay, forever, if we can't find the way out."

"Can't we just go back the way we came?"

Chambers looked behind them. "What way, Karen?"

It was true. The entrance to where they were had disappeared. Now the stone floor extended in all directions to the horizon.

The cursed souls of Limbo were coming from all directions as well.

"Fucking hell!" Karen beat her fist against the stone once, twice.

On the third blow she scraped her hand so badly she left a streak of blood on the stone. Chambers, already on his way over to stop her, examined the skin.

"Not too bad," he said as he looked at the scraped flesh over the heel of Karen's right hand. "But hitting the floor like that is going to do you more damage."

"Do you think I care?" she cried. "Look! Those things are getting nearer, and all we're doing is bashing our heads against a brick wall!"

She was interrupted by a loud grating sound. They all looked down to see the blood Karen had shed had trickled into the gap between two stones, which had widened and was continuing to do so. Now the stone blocks on either side were lowering, as were those next to them. As they watched, an entire section of the floor dropped, forming a broad stone spiral staircase.

"Where does it go?" Karen asked Dr. Cruttenden.

"Never mind that," said Chambers. The souls at the front were close enough now that he could see their faces and the terrible hunger in the eyes. Close enough that he could feel their loneliness, the sheer sense of isolation they felt from having spent eons trapped on this grim, empty, soulless plain. But that was nothing compared with their monumental desire to leave this place. And they were not to be cheated of the opportunity.

"Get down there *now!*"

He pushed Karen down the steps, behind Dr. Cruttenden, who was already on her way. As Chambers followed, the first of the petrified figures reached for him, and he felt a coldness worse than freezing, an emptiness greater than the gulfs of space, and a desire that was so overpowering he tripped and fell. He looked up to see that now even more of them had arrived at the brink of the steps.

As he scrambled to his feet, a multitude of clutching, ossified claws lunged for him.

TWENTY-FIVE

CHAMBERS FELT ICY FINGERS touch his skull, and he had the unpleasant sensation that his hair was turning the same shade of wiry gray as the creatures of stone that were trying to drag him back to Limbo. Then, as quickly as it had come, the feeling vanished as the blocks above closed over his head, crushing the flailing arms and reducing them to dust and rubble on the steps.

For a moment he could hear the anguished screams of those denied the salvation that had been so nearly within their grasp. Then those, too, were gone. With tentative fingers Chambers explored his scalp. The skin was numb, and felt icy to the touch. His hair was still there, but he would have to wait until the others saw him before he would know if it had changed in any way.

Rubbing his now-chilled hands together, he set off down the staircase, kicking aside fragments of petrified fingers as he did so. He made three circuits before he caught up with the others. The relief on Karen's face was obvious.

"We thought we'd lost you."

"I have to admit I thought that myself at one point." Chambers returned her hug. "Notice anything different about me?"

She shook her head. "No, but the light down here is shitty."

"At least we do have light down here." Dr. Cruttenden was, as now seemed to be the case in many ways, a few steps ahead. "You'll notice it's a different color from where we were."

She was right. Chambers hadn't had much time to pay attention, but the walls now seemed to be radiating a slightly pinkish glow.

"What does that mean?"

The lecturer shrugged. "I couldn't possibly say. I was merely making the observation. Shall we continue?"

Chambers glanced back the way they had come. "Well, I'm definitely not going back up there."

If he had been expecting the spiraling passage to open out as the corridors had in Limbo, Chambers was to be disappointed. Instead the very opposite happened, as the pink-tinged walls began to close in on them. Soon they were walking single file, and the temperature was rising as well.

"If it gets much warmer I'm going to have to lose some of these clothes." Karen had produced a tissue and was mopping her forehead with dainty dabs.

"Best not." Chambers was feeling the heat too. "That's probably exactly what they want you to do so they can plunge us into freezing arctic conditions around the next corner."

Further on the passageway became narrower and hotter. Without thinking, Chambers put out a hand to steady himself and immediately snatched it back when he felt the wall.

The stone was soft.

He examined his fingers. They appeared unharmed, and so he touched the wall again. It gave beneath his probing finger, like the softest vellum.

Or a woman's skin.

The thought had entered his head without any encouragement, and now it was there it was impossible to shift. During their descent, the walls had changed, not just becoming narrower but becoming smoother as well. Then, of course, there was the pink tinge to the light, wherever that might be coming from.

What was happening here?

They were approaching the end of the staircase, only now what they were walking on were less steps and more ridges of tissue, protuberances of flesh that supported their weight and gave with each step they took.

"I believe I see the way out."

Dr. Cruttenden might have been able to see it, but how they were supposed to squeeze through the tiny hole, beyond which a crimson glow held the promise of further horrors, was yet to be seen. Were they going to shrink? Was the hole, a puckered rim of flesh, going to expand? Before Chambers had any more time to consider how else they might get through, Dr. Cruttenden had gripped either side of the orifice and was pulling it apart with both hands.

The opening widened at her touch. Soon it was large enough for her head to go through, then her body, and finally, with a little kick of her feet, her broad pelvis slipped through, followed by her legs.

Once she was across, the hole shrank back down to its original size.

"Am I supposed to do that?" The passageway was now so narrow Karen couldn't turn to ask Chambers the question.

"I suppose so," he replied, trying to take a step back and realizing the walls weren't going to let him. "I'm afraid I can't move backward to give you any more room to try."

Karen slipped through more easily than Dr. Cruttenden, which left Chambers facing the ridged and puckered opening. Like the others, he took a firm grip on either side. The tissue—he couldn't help but think of it like that—was warm to the touch, with a slightly slimy feel. It wasn't unpleasant but, as it shrank from his hands, he knew he had only moments to push himself through or it would seal itself, this time forever. Once the opening was wide enough he pushed his head through, gripped the walls once more, and kicked against the lowermost step with both feet to propel himself through.

He imagined the sensation must be similar to that of being born. Karen and Dr. Cruttenden were waiting for him on the other side and, judging by their shared expression, they both probably had the same thoughts.

They were standing in a vast cavern.

It was well-lit, certainly enough to see the roof, and the walls, and the floor.

All were made of human flesh.

This was neither a butcher shop nor a charnel house, however. In fact it was anything but. There was not a trace of raw muscle or exposed tendon for as far as the eye could see.

There was, however, an ocean of extremely healthy-looking skin, covering a variety of body parts that undulated in a provocative manner as eyes were laid upon them. Chambers took a step forward and found himself standing on the muscled abdomen of a young man, his right toe covering the umbilicus. To his right the perfectly formed buttocks of a young woman moved back and forth softly against other body parts in a manner he found quite distracting.

"I suggest we get across this as quickly as possible."

Although she was standing right beside him, Dr. Cruttenden seemed to be speaking from miles away.

"Yes . . ." Chambers could barely remember how they had gotten there as a delicate hand with the most exquisitely beautiful fingers he had ever seen began inching its way up the inside of his trouser leg. He batted at it absent-mindedly. "Yes . . . we must . . . we . . . what?"

It was no use looking to Karen for help. She had crossed to the nearby wall and was fingering a muscular arm whose biceps was flexing and extending the more she stroked it.

"Come on, Professor Chambers!"

Dr. Cruttenden took his hand. Chambers was struck by how repulsive it was. He didn't want to hold this old lady's hand. He wanted the lovely one that had tried to climb up his leg, or the other, equally sensuous one that was creeping toward him now, rolling over onto its back and wiggling its fingers playfully at him. He tried to break free, but Dr. Cruttenden's grip was firm as she dragged him over to Karen.

"You too, young lady." She tore Karen's hand away from where she was stroking the inside of an elbow. Karen looked as if she was about to snarl at the lecturer for interrupting her. Then her face sagged as realization struck.

"What the hell was I doing?"

"Succumbing to the lure of this place." Dr. Cruttenden gripped Karen's right hand with her left and, with both of them now in tow, began to stride across the sea of slowly rousing flesh. It rippled and undulated as they walked. They made slow going across the surface, the soft sound of perfect skin rubbing against perfect skin giving a kind of whispering, sensuous voice to it as they walked. In fact Chambers was sure he could hear it talking to him.

Stay . . . with . . . us . . .

It was nonsense of course, and yet every part of him, every nerve, every fiber, and most of all, every particle of skin wanted to stay there, wanted to remain in this perfect world of perfect pleasures and become one with it. Every now and then he looked across to Karen and he could see she was feeling the same.

"Where are we going?" It was important he try and remain focused. But it was difficult.

"Away from here." Dr. Cruttenden continued to pull them forward. "Look for somewhere that's similar to the way we came in."

"I don't want to go . . ." Karen murmured.

"Oh, yes you do," came the reply. "Because those who are trapped here want you to stay even more than you do. Look."

Dr. Cruttenden was gesturing behind them. Chambers turned, to be surprised at how much distance they had already covered across the sea of flesh.

Flesh that was now rising.

"We've woken them up." Chambers had stopped, but Dr. Cruttenden was insistent and dragged him on as she spoke. "We've disturbed them from their eternal immersion in each other, their eternal obsession with the flesh. And now they want us to join them."

Slowly, clawing their way out of the ground across which the three of them had just been walking, parts of human beings were emerging. Very attractive parts, perfectly formed—a shapely female leg, a muscular male torso. As Chambers watched they began to join together, trying to create the semblance of a human form. Occasionally they got it almost right, but in many cases the results were grotesque—a hopeless mish-mash of randomly jointed limbs, orifices, and skin.

"They have forgotten what it is like to be human," said Dr. Cruttenden. "I'm not surprised they don't know how to pull themselves together."

A beautiful female body was marred by having seven limbs—four arms and three legs. The resultant fleshy creature scuttled toward them like a spider. From somewhere deep within glowed a face with the most beautiful smile Chambers had ever seen. Other creatures were more rudimentary. An arm fused to a leg, a shoulder to a hip; a handsome, impassive male head propelled along by at least twenty perfectly formed fingers projecting from the stump of its neck. One girl's head was being pulled along by the arm that emerged from her throat. Her face would probably have been pretty were it not for the twenty tiny mouths that covered it, each with perfect teeth and tongues that flickered over the pouting lips like tiny pink snakes.

And yet he still wanted to stay.

"Stop looking at them!" Dr. Cruttenden didn't let go, which was a good thing because without her, he and Karen would most likely be lost. "You're just encouraging them!"

Oh, so it's my fault, is it? The thought struck him as so funny he burst out laughing. Karen looked at him, shocked, and then she started laughing too.

"Come on," he said, "we're not teenagers."

Ahead of them was a dot of yellow light. It was the only landmark in the entire place and it could be the way out. Chambers prayed it was. As they made for it he took another look behind him, and wished that he hadn't.

The creatures had abandoned their attempts to create *homunculi* and were melding together again. But instead of an ocean of flesh, now they were forming a tidal wave, rising higher and higher and gaining on them all the time. If they didn't hurry, they would be buried beneath it.

"Run!"

The flesh beneath their feet did all it could to impede their progress. Hands clutched, legs kicked, teeth bit. As the dot of yellow light increased in size, their efforts became more frenzied. Now Chambers could hear the tide behind him, the flesh no longer offering a sensuous whisper, but a carnal roar, desperate and hungry, as hungry as those petrified souls in Limbo had been.

Because they wanted the same thing.

The yellow dot was human-sized now, a shining oval that offered them egress from this orgiastic hell. Dr. Cruttenden passed through first, pulling Karen with her. At the last moment Chambers stopped and turned. The tidal wave was almost upon him. Over a hundred feet high, he saw faces leering, fingers beckoning, flesh enticing.

And there was something else as well.

Within that concatenation of living, throbbing tissue was an image, subtle at first but more obvious now he had seen it. An image of something horned, multi-limbed, and insectoid. An image that was all too familiar, that he had seen on the wall of All Hallows Church and now seemed as large and as overwhelming as that picture had suggested.

The Anarch.

TWENTY-SIX

THE YELLOW LIGHT THROUGH which they passed was warm and comforting. Chambers had little desire to leave its reassuring embrace, and when he emerged on the other side it was with a vague sense of disappointment, and an overwhelming desire to return to the golden aura that had made him feel so safe.

It was not to be, however. The light was gone, and in its place was a long refectory table that ran the length of the chamber in which they found themselves. The room's walls were of rough gray stone, and for a moment Chambers thought they had gone back into Limbo. Then he saw the ornate windows of stained glass twenty feet above his head that met with a vaulted ceiling at least as far away again. The shades of green, blue, and red in the mullioned windows were too dark to be able to discern anything on the other side of them, but they were admitting a pallid light, mixed into a myriad hues by refraction and painting the banquet hall in shades that were not at all unpleasant.

That was what they had to be in now—a banquet hall. The refectory table that ran down the center of it had to be nearly twenty feet long and had been fashioned from polished pine. Instead of chairs, long benches of similar length had been positioned either side for diners to sit. Down the middle of the table, at regular intervals, silver candelabra had been placed. Each bore six red candles which burned with a light that seemed almost holy.

In between and surrounding the candelabra, delicious-looking food had been arranged. Roasts glistened on silver trays surrounded by crisp potatoes sizzling in the meat's juices; dishes of lightly boiled vegetables steamed on shining plates; loaves of freshly baked bread sought to escape from handsomely sized wicker baskets; and in between these large courses, delicately interpolated between the highly polished platters, were shining saucers of canapés of all shapes and colors. Everything had been cooked to perfection, and the aroma in the room was so mouth-watering it brought tears to his eyes as well as saliva to his mouth.

"God, I'm starving." Karen was already reaching out to pick up a fork from one of the many place settings, no doubt intending to plunge it into one of the slices of beef close by.

She was stopped by a sharp slap on the wrist from Dr. Cruttenden. Karen glared at her, but kept her hand at her side.

"We've no idea if any of this is safe," said Dr. Cruttenden, obviously doing her best to resist temptation herself. "After everything we've been through so far, I find it hard to believe we are being allowed to break for lunch."

Chambers had to agree. "I can't believe I have an appetite after that last room we were in," he said, "but I have. In fact, I honestly feel I could eat every scrap of what's been laid out here and still have room for more."

"Me too." Despite herself, Karen was reaching out again. This time Dr. Cruttenden grabbed her wrist and forced it away from the table.

"I'm guessing you have an idea what's going on here as well." Chambers gave Dr. Cruttenden a suspicious look.

"Possibly," she replied. "And never mind looking at me like that—once I'm sure, I promise I'll share my suspicions."

While Dr. Cruttenden was speaking, Karen grabbed a slice of ham glazed with honey. She held it up to her mouth.

"Share them now," she said, "or I'll eat this."

The lecturer tried to tear the meat from Karen's grasp, but the younger woman was too quick for her and dodged out of the way. "I mean it. Hurry up, or I'm swallowing it."

Chambers couldn't help but admire what had to have been a calculated gamble all along. The fact that he was as keen as Karen to hear what Dr. Cruttenden had to say prevented him from interfering. Eventually, after another couple of attempts to relieve Karen of the food, Dr. Cruttenden gave up.

"All right," she said, "I'll tell you."

There was a noise from the room next door. Up until then Chambers hadn't been aware that there was one but now he could see, just to the far right of the table, an archway beyond which there was darkness.

"It sounds as if they're coming anyway," Dr. Cruttenden said. "And I have to admit I have no idea what we are going to do when they get here."

"Who's coming?" Chambers listened, straining to hear. Eventually he was rewarded with a wet, slithering sound that chilled his blood and robbed him of the appetite that until a moment ago had felt insatiable.

"Where *are* we?" Karen's hunger seemed to have deserted her as well, to be replaced by a fierce determination to know what Dr. Cruttenden had on her mind.

As if oblivious to the distant sounds of squamous, slippery movement, Dr. Cruttenden folded her arms and looked around her before eventually making her pronouncement.

"We are in Hell."

"I think we'd guessed that," said Chambers.

"Well, I hadn't." Karen's eyes glistened with the trace of tears, but her voice remained firm. "What does that mean, then? Are we dead?"

"Not necessarily." Dr. Cruttenden was rubbing her chin. "We certainly shouldn't give up hope. As long as we don't give in to the temptation of any of these places, we should hopefully be able to escape them."

"You know something about that too, don't you? Exactly what kind of Hell are we in?" Karen wouldn't let it go. Good for her, Chambers thought.

"What kind?"

"Yes. Are we in Catholic Hell? Puritan Hell? The Hell of some other denomination of Christianity? Or is it the Hell of an entirely different religion altogether?"

"We're in Dante's Hell."

The stunned silence that followed was only broken by the sounds of whatever was making its way toward them through the darkness next door.

"Dante's Hell?" Chambers repeated the words just in case he had misheard them. "You mean as in the *Divine Comedy*?"

"Written by Dante Alighieri some time in the early thirteen hundreds, yes," Dr. Cruttenden was nodding now. "You know he envisioned a realm of torment consisting of nine Circles?"

Chambers had to admit his knowledge on the subject was shaky at best. "I'm afraid you're going to have to remind me."

"The *Divine Comedy* is an epic poem that details the journey of its protagonist, which is meant to be Dante himself, through Hell, Purgatory, and finally Heaven. Hell, or the Inferno as it's sometimes called, was divided into nine Circles of suffering below the Earth. It begins with Limbo and then moves onto Lust."

"The plain of stone and then that room filled with those flesh-creatures," said Karen.

"Exactly. The third Circle is Gluttony, and here we have more food than we could possibly consume, and yet when we arrived here I'm sure we all felt ourselves more than capable of eating everything in sight."

Chambers certainly had. "But we don't feel like that now."

"Because I don't believe we are intended to reside on this level. We are meant to go on. How far I don't know, but what I do know is that if we allow the souls that are imprisoned on any of these levels to trap us, then we will replace them and they will be allowed to escape."

"Don't let them catch us, eh?"

Dr. Cruttenden nodded. "Exactly, Professor Chambers. Exactly."

"Did you say the early thirteen hundreds?"

They both looked at Karen.

"Yes," said Dr. Cruttenden. "Is that significant?"

"Only because the reason we're here is because of Geoffrey Chaucer, and you said he was born in that century as well."

"He was, wasn't he?" Dr. Cruttenden was tapping her chin. "I wonder..."

They all jumped as a muffled slap came from just outside the room, accompanied by the sounds of labored breathing.

"I think we need to leave," said Chambers.

"How?" Karen kept giving the doorway nervous glances. "That's the only way out, and I think something's waiting for us out there."

It wasn't something. It was a host of *someones*, and as Karen spoke, in they came.

To describe them as obese would have been unkind to those human beings who suffer from being a little overweight. The creatures that squeezed themselves through the ever-expanding doorway were obscene, mere semblances of the human form buried in an expanse of fat, their faces tiny caricatures of pinched human expression almost lost in the folds of a sea of gelatinous lipid. Each limb was so encased in thick rolls of the stuff that they could barely bend their knees and elbows, and instead they lumbered forward awkwardly, their movements spastic and almost infantile. Tiny black eyes peered from between fat-laden eyelids oozing oil.

Eyes that lit up when they saw the food.

There were five of them in the room now, and more trying to get through the door. Bloated, obscene, almost cartoon-like versions of men and women, dressed in what looked like black kaftans, all of them distracted from the intruders in their midst by the promise of yet more food to satiate their unending appetites.

"This may be our only chance!"

Chambers tried to ignore the soft slurping sounds coming from the table beside him. "What do you mean?"

Dr. Cruttenden pointed to the door. "We have to leave now, while they're distracted!"

"But there are more of them out there, too!" Karen pushed herself against the wall as more of the soft shapes squeezed past her.

"Once they've eaten everything they'll see us," came the reply. "And then we won't have a chance."

"You mean they'll eat us too?"

"Worse." Dr. Cruttenden's face was grim. "They'll eat our souls and we will be forced to exchange bodies with them."

That was enough. Taking a deep breath, Chambers pushed past the residents of the Third Circle of Hell, followed by the lecturer. When he reached the door, he grabbed Karen's hand and together they squeezed past the seemingly never-ending parade of hungry souls keen to cram the latest offerings into their dribbling, food-encrusted mouths.

Beyond the room the horror was even worse.

They found themselves standing on another endless plain but, unlike Limbo, here the floor was mustard-colored and featureless save for the slick of food waste that coated everything and stuck to the soles of their shoes as they walked. In fact food was everywhere, but not the elegantly prepared meals of the banquet hall. Here the food was a mess of brown pulp and green fleshy gobbets, black crumbs and gray gruel.

And there were people everywhere.

They were even larger than the ones in the room they had just left. Unable to move, they mewled as they reached for morsels of fetid material that lay just beyond their reach, crawling, rolling, or sliding toward them as best they could. But their vast bulk meant that they could only move very slowly and, more often than not, by the time they reached their intended target the morsel had been snatched and gobbled up by someone slightly quicker than they. Unlike the people in the room, the gluttons out here were naked, and their maggot-like bodies were so loaded with fat that their skin had been stretched to the point of transparency. As they moved, it was possible to see the adipose tissue beneath sliding against the taut epithelium, straining to be free. These cursed souls were on the point of bursting, always hungry, and never granted any relief from the need to eat and the simultaneous desire to feel less bloated.

Karen took another step forward, slipped, and nearly fell onto the enormous body of a naked man preoccupied with licking up a sticky pink liquid in which tiny crawling insects floated. It was impossible to tell whether the putrescent smell was coming from him or his food.

"Careful!" Chambers caught her arm. "If you land in that stuff we might not be able to pick you up again."

"I can hardly breathe." Karen's coughing fit became a bout of retching. Chambers couldn't blame her. The stink in the Third Circle of Hell was unbelievable—a combination of rotting food and unwashed bodies, sickly sweetness tinged with sour sweat and other bodily excrescences allowed to ferment for an eternity.

"We have to keep going!" Dr. Cruttenden was physically pushing them forward. "They haven't noticed us yet, but when they do . . ."

They already had. Chubby, sausage-like fingers reached for Chambers's ankle and missed. The glutton zombie in question (he could think of no better term for the creature) dragged itself a little closer. He dodged it easily, but was struck at the same time by the thought that if he hadn't seen it coming it might just have been strong enough to hold him there.

"Come on!"

More of the creatures were taking notice of them now, abandoning their leaking fistfuls of squashed food, the pools of sweet-looking glutinous substances spilled on the ground. Instead tiny, hungry eyes were slowly focusing on the strangers in their midst.

"Can you see the way out?" Karen was looking around, but there was no obvious exit.

"No." Dr. Cruttenden was looking too. "Perhaps you have to cut yourself, like in Limbo."

"Why should I have to be the one to cut myself?"

"There's no glowing golden light, either," said Chambers. "But then I'm sure you'd agree that each Circle of Hell probably has its own kind of entrance and exit."

"A good point." Dr. Cruttenden hopped over a glutton zombie that was getting too close for comfort. "In that case we should be looking for something that stands out, something that's different from the rest of this place."

"That room was different." Karen dodged another slow-moving, grease-streaked crawling monstrosity. "The one we arrived in."

Chambers and Dr. Cruttenden exchanged looks. It was a good point.

"But that room is full of them now."

"It doesn't matter." Dr. Cruttenden was already on her way back. "That's where we need to go."

"But there wasn't an obvious door or anything." Karen was trying hard to keep up, avoid the glutton zombies, and not slip in their leavings.

"That's just because we weren't looking hard enough."

"There were stained-glass windows," said Chambers. "I thought that was a bit odd the minute we arrived there."

"Perhaps that's the way, then."

"But they were close to the ceiling," Karen wailed. "And the ceiling in that room is about forty feet high!"

"There's nothing that says the entrances and exits have to be easily accessible," said Dr. Cruttenden.

"Why are there exits at all?" It had suddenly occurred to Chambers. "You yourself said that these souls are trapped here, so why make it possible for people to enter and leave?"

Dr. Cruttenden shrugged. "Presumably because part of the eternal torment one is intended to endure in Hell is the knowledge that escape is possible, just highly improbable."

They were at the archway to the banquet hall now, where they encountered another problem.

"The room's full of them!" Karen was staring, wide-eyed, at the literal mass of bodies that fought over the scraps now remaining on the long trestle table.

"Perhaps we should wait until they finish, and then they'll go?"

Dr. Cruttenden shook her head at Chambers's suggestion. "If you look behind us, I think you'll find we haven't got time for that."

It was true. The glutton zombies of the third plain of Hell were all slowly making their way toward the three free souls who had intruded upon their domain.

"What about the table?"

Dr. Cruttenden looked at Karen. "What do you mean?"

"Can't we upend it? It looks as if it might be able to reach to those windows."

"It should." Chambers was constantly looking right and left, from the gluttonous plain to the room that might be their escape. "But look at the surface. We'd never be able to get a grip on it to climb up."

It was true. The elegantly placed food had been gobbled so furiously and without etiquette that now all that remained were tossed-aside plates, bones almost bitten through in the desire to consume every last morsel. Even the candles bore teeth marks. The surface of the pine table, so recently polished and clean, was now home to a slick of grease and gravy that would thwart anyone's attempts to climb up it.

"Not if we turn it over."

Karen was right, of course, they could use the legs and frame like a makeshift ladder. But it would take a hell of a lot of doing, never mind upending the thing once they'd managed to roll it. And before all that, they had to get the gluttons out of there.

Or did they?

The gluttons were still amassed along the nearside length of the table. The far side, the one that ran close to the wall with the windows, was host to only a couple, presumably because it would have taken more effort to get around there, and why bother when the food was in easy reach from here?

"I've got an idea," Chambers whispered. "You two go around to the other side of the table, and when I say so, pull it toward you with all your might."

"It's huge." Karen couldn't see where he was going with this. "We'll never be able to roll it on our own."

"We're not going to." Chambers was searching beneath the table now. "We're going to have some help."

The mess outside was testament to the fact that the denizens of this part of Hell weren't especially thorough when it came to eating as much as they could, and he had been relying on the thin hope that something in this banquet hall had been missed—a morsel of meat, a crumb of bread. Something that had escaped their notice. Finally, he found what he was looking for. A whole loaf that had somehow slipped from the table and become hidden behind one of the table legs. He grabbed it, wincing as he felt the fluid it was soaked with. He hoped it had not come from one of the glutton zombies. Then he jumped onto the table.

He almost skidded straight off again, and had to take a moment to balance himself. He waited until Karen and Dr. Cruttenden were in position and then he called out in the loudest, clearest tones he could muster.

"You've missed something!"

All eyes were suddenly on him.

It was a disconcerting moment. In fact, Chambers found it terrifying. As one, every bulky form in the room turned to look at him. Or, to be more accurate, what he was holding up in his right hand.

"I said, you've missed something!" This time he shouted to make sure the gluttons outside the room could hear as well. He wanted as many of them in here as would fit.

"What the hell are you doing?"

He darted a glance at Karen. "Trust me," he said. "And when I say pull, you pull as hard as you can."

The ones grasping at him at the front were already pushing so hard the table was starting to move, and as more bodies crammed themselves into the room the pressure increased. Chambers raised a foot and brought it down as hard as he could.

Right on the join that ran the length of the table.

He thought he heard a crack, but he couldn't be sure, so he did it again, and again.

The table was beginning to lurch now as it was pushed toward the wall with the windows.

"We're going to be crushed!" Karen yelled.

"No you won't! Grab the table when I say so!"

Chambers dealt another blow to the middle of the table and was rewarded with a satisfied cracking sound. He moved onto the half behind him. The gluttons before him pushed harder at the table, which was starting to pivot in the middle.

"Grab this side and start to pull!" he shouted.

Karen and Dr. Cruttenden did as they were told.

The effect was startling. With the combined weight of the gluttons pushing from the other side, the pivoting effect and the two women acting as a counterbalance, the far side of the table began to overturn. Before the angle became too steep Chambers jumped down to join them. He still had the bait held high, but with luck he wasn't going to need it much longer. With his free hand he helped them pull.

It happened all at once. Their half of the table tipped toward them and with a crunch came free from the other half it had been connected to. Karen and Dr. Cruttenden made sure it rolled right over while Chambers threw the bread as far from them as he could.

As one, the gluttonous residents of the Third Circle of Hell turned and went for it.

"We've only got seconds before they make short work of that." Chambers had already gone around to the length of table's other side. "Help me lift it against the wall."

"But it's still too short!" Karen was helping anyway.

"It doesn't need to reach right to the window," Chambers gasped as together they struggled to push the table upright and wedge it against the stone wall at an angle. "Our own height should do the rest."

"They're coming."

Chambers didn't waste any time looking.

"Climb up the table," he told them. "And keep your fingers crossed that it actually is the way out."

For someone who probably hadn't climbed anything more challenging than a tree when she was a little girl, Dr. Cruttenden proved remarkably agile. Soon Karen was following her up the wooden lattice. Once the lecturer was at the top, she raised a tweed-coated elbow and, with a lack of hesitation that was impressive even if it was probably born of panic, smashed through the stained glass.

"I can't see anything beyond!" she shouted down.

Chambers picked up a broken piece of table leg and hit the closest glutton zombie in the face with it. The creature was surprisingly soft, and its head burst like a rotten grape, the fat-stained fluid that leaked out spraying its colleague, who immediately began to lick it up.

"Just go!" Chambers knew he wouldn't be able to fend them off for long. "We've got no other option!"

Two more of the creatures were close enough to grab at him. Chambers aimed the bulbous length of wood at an outstretched arm and brought it down as hard as he could. The arm fell away at the elbow, greasy yellow blood spurting from the stump. He picked up the severed limb and, wincing at how very soft it was, threw the pulpy mess into the voracious crowd.

"Has she gotten through yet?"

There was no answer. Chambers looked up to see that both Karen and Dr. Cruttenden had disappeared.

Time to go.

It would be impossible for him to climb and hold onto his weapon. His delaying tactics so far had only bought him a few seconds, and he needed longer to get up there.

There was only one thing for it.

Professor Robert Chambers of the Human Protection League's Cthulhu Investigation Division in Washington, D.C. raised the piece of wood he was carrying high above his head, uttered an ear-splitting roar, and proceeded to deliver a series of savage blows to every single glutton zombie that was within his range.

The creatures burst open at his touch. Soon the floor was slick with greasy fluids, yellow fat, and bile-stained blood. The gluttons behind Chambers's victims immediately dropped to their knees and began to suck up what remained of their fallen comrades.

Chambers threw his weapon into the crowd. It had become too slippery to hold onto anyway. He wiped his hands on a shirt peppered with chunks of fat and soaked with fluids that reminded him of the hamburger bar where he had worked for a while as a student. Once his palms were as dry as he was going to get them, he turned and started to make his way up the underside of the table.

There was a cracking noise as soon as he got on it. Obviously it hadn't been made to support the effort of three people climbing. He reached up, grasped a broken support, and took another step.

Crack.

Okay, we're going to have to go very gently, but you can still do it. He didn't dare look behind him. It would only take one of those things pulling themselves on here to try and get him, and the whole structure could fall to pieces.

Slowly, but at the same time get on with it. He climbed another step, and then another.

Crack, crack.

He was nearly halfway up when there was a much louder crunch, and the length of table sagged in the middle, almost dislodging him. Regaining his hold, he looked down to see that one of the glutton zombies had crawled beneath the table and was now trapped in the angle between the wood and the stone wall. It was trying to grab at him and, in doing so, was putting an unbearable strain on the wood.

He kicked down at it once, and the table almost gave way.

Only one thing to do, he thought. Calling on every scrap of luck he might still have, Chambers took a deep breath and clambered up the remainder of the table as fast as he could. He could feel the wood collapsing beneath him as he went. He was almost at the window when the table gave way beneath him. With a final burst of energy, he leapt the last couple of feet and grabbed the window ledge.

Now he was hanging twenty feet above a room filled with creatures hungry for his flesh.

Hanging by fingers smeared with the fat and grease of their own decimated numbers.

Hanging and starting to slip.

He was about to resign himself to a horrible death when he felt hands around his wrists and arms, and his body being pulled upward. He passed through the window with surprise that equaled the shock he felt when he didn't plummet twenty feet down the outer wall of the building he had assumed they were trapped in. Instead he found himself in a tunnel with dark red walls.

Karen and Dr. Cruttenden were looking at him anxiously.

"Are you all right?" Karen asked.

He resisted the urge to laugh hysterically with relief. "I think so. But I'm in a bit of a mess."

"You are indeed," said Dr. Cruttenden. "You were almost too slippery for us to pull up."

"Well, I'm relieved I wasn't." He tried wiping his hands on the smooth surface of the tunnel. "Is this our next Circle of Hell?"

Dr. Cruttenden shook her head. "It's far too peaceful for that. I very much suspect it's down there," she said, indicating toward the receding darkness.

The lecturer seemed eager to set off, but Karen laid a hand on her shoulder, for which Chambers was grateful—he needed at least another minute to catch his breath.

"What things are we going to have to face this time?"

Dr. Cruttenden shrugged. "To be honest, I don't really know. Let's just hope it's not more of the same."

Karen's eyes narrowed. "Why? What's the Fourth Circle all about?"

The lecturer looked from one to the other of them, and waited for Chambers to stop panting before she answered.

"Greed."

TWENTY-SEVEN

THEY WERE IN A city.

Chambers thought that was what it looked like. At first impression. If you didn't look too closely. A grid system of streets down which walked somber-faced people in smart suits, moving between slate-gray skyscrapers that threatened to penetrate the dome of pallid cloud that enclosed this level of Hell. But it didn't take much to see that there was something horribly wrong with this semblance of a metropolis.

Because that was all it was—a semblance, a fake, an impression. The buildings were solid—towering cuboids of concrete with false windows and doors that couldn't be opened because there were no interiors for anyone to access. One after another, they were all the same. Chambers knew because they'd been checking them for the last half an hour, ever since they had arrived here. The only office building that was different was the one they had emerged from onto the busy city street. Their journey down the featureless tunnel from the land of the gluttonous dead had terminated in a very ordinary-looking door which, when opened, had led them onto the concourse they were now exploring.

It had seemed sensible to assume that their way out of the Fourth Circle of Hell lay through a similar-looking door in a similar-looking building, but so far their efforts to find it had proved fruitless.

"Maybe we should be looking for another way out?" Karen was keeping her voice low. So far they had been able to avoid the attentions of the inhabitants of this level. Obsessed with getting from one place to another, they were actually difficult to distract from their objective. Of course, the ironic thing was that Chambers had seen a few of them several times already, which meant that either one of the curses of this level of Hell was to be cloned, or the people he saw were simply walking around and around the same series of fake office buildings.

"Perhaps," Dr. Cruttenden hissed back. She brushed her hand against the painted door handle of a building purporting to be the headquarters of a stationery suppliers. "But another real doorway seems the most likely. Besides, there's little else on this sorry excuse for a street that has suggested itself to me."

She was right. Up and down the "sorry excuse for a street" drove sorry excuses for cars. All were of the same generic and unspecified model, all were painted the same shade of charcoal, and all had the distinct absence of a driver. Still the cars moved, at an unchanging speed that could not be faster than twenty miles per hour, up and down the street and around the corner, to reappear again a few minutes later. At least Chambers assumed they were reappearing—the lack of registration plates or any distinguishing features made it difficult to tell.

The road itself was just as bad. The tarmac was a uniform black, with no cracks, potholes, or manhole covers to mar the surface. There were no drains, but presumably it never rained here. Nor were there any road markings, but the cars seemed to keep to the correct side of the street without prompting. The sidewalk was a lighter shade of gray, but again boasted a surface free from evidence of the usual traumas such walkways would have been subjected to in a real city. There were no telephone booths, no newsstands, and nowhere to post a letter. In short, nothing that could be the way out masquerading as a street feature.

"I still don't understand why they aren't taking more notice of us." After the previous circle of Hell, Chambers was glad they were being left alone, but it was unnerving to witness the blank-faced denizens pass them by as if they didn't exist.

"I can't explain it either." Dr. Cruttenden had just tried the handle of the last door on the block. It was time for them to cross the street.

"Perhaps part of the curse of being here is that you are powerless to prevent yourself from hurrying to your next deal."

"Should we try the other side of the street, or cross to another block altogether?"

Dr. Cruttenden seemed to be debating the answer to Karen's question. "Let's try another block, shall we?" she said finally. "I have a feeling the other side of this particular street is going to prove just as fruitless."

The crossing did not go as intended.

They managed to get halfway to the other side, dodging the slow-moving cars with ease, but then they hit a wall. Literally. A moment's exploration revealed that the invisible barrier blocking their way extended for at least the length of the city block they were trying to get to, and possibly beyond. It was also at least eight feet high (Chambers tried throwing a pen over) and was perfectly smooth.

"We need another ladder," said Karen once they were safely back on the sidewalk.

"Not this time," said Dr. Cruttenden. "I very much suspect each of these blocks is the same, and each is isolated from the others so that the impossibility of going anywhere else makes the torment of repetition all the worse."

"But what if the way out is in one of those other blocks?"

Dr. Cruttenden raised an eyebrow. "Let's hope it's not, shall we, Miss Shepworth? But to be serious, all that suggests is that there must be an exit here, we just haven't been looking for it hard enough."

"The other side of the street it is, then," said Chambers, leading the way between vehicles chugging up and down and around the block from which they now knew the residents could not escape.

The office building over there also seemed to offer little other than paint and concrete. Once they had exhausted all the doors, Chambers sank down onto the step of a pretend firm of attorneys.

"We can't give up!" Karen gave him a push.

"I'm just having a bit of a rest," he replied. "And a bit of a think."

He moved over as Dr. Cruttenden joined him.

"What's on your mind?" she asked.

"I was just wondering, if we sit here for long enough, whether or not..."

"Yes?"

"Whether or not this picture is going to change. I mean, Limbo felt like limbo, didn't it? And Lust felt like lust." He looked at Karen, who blushed as she nodded. "And Gluttony definitely felt like gluttony. So I'm just wondering what wandering aimlessly around the same city street has to do with greed."

"It's a thought." Dr. Cruttenden rubbed her chin. "I had assumed we were looking at a collection of souls so obsessed by greed all they could think of was their next deal, with the result that they never got anywhere at all."

"That's what I'd thought too," said Karen, squeezing in alongside them. "Isn't that torment enough?"

Chambers nodded. "It is, but I just have the feeling that—"

The sound came abruptly, and from somewhere high above. A rich, deep resonant sound as if a bell were being tolled.

It was deafening.

"What the hell was that?" Karen still had her hands over ears, which were presumably ringing as much as Chambers's were.

"I don't know," he shouted in reply. "But keep your hands over your ears in case—"

The sound came again. The same echoing, all-pervading toll that demanded attention.

It was certainly having an effect on the souls of the Fourth Circle. For the first time since the three of them had arrived, the suited denizens were doing something other than relentlessly marching around the city streets. Or rather, they were doing nothing at all.

They had come to a complete standstill.

Some were in mid-stride, others were in the process of crossing the street, not that it mattered as the cars had come to a halt as well. After the street noise, the absolute silence that ensued following the bell toll was almost stifling. Occasionally it was broken by the clatter of a brief-case being dropped, or a portfolio being released from a loosened grip.

"What now?"

"I bet you any money we wait for the third bell," said Chambers.

Dr. Cruttenden was nodding in agreement. "There should be a third. Both history and literature are filled with—"

The third bell toll was so loud it made the ground shake and the buildings tremble. Some of the frozen souls fell stiffly to the ground. They didn't stay there for long.

As the three of them watched, the denizens of Greed began to move again, but this time it was different. Instead of the strict, driven marching of before, these movements were more chaotic, undisciplined, undirected.

No, not undirected.

As each damned soul came to, they looked around them, bewildered. Their previously blank faces were now animated, masks of overt emotion, as if all the need for expression had been suppressed and now it was finally being released.

The horror came when they looked at someone else.

As soon as the eyes of one of the damned souls of the Fourth Circle alighted upon one of their comrades, their expressions changed from bewilderment to a look of indescribable hatred. And there was something else there too.

Envy, desire, lust.

Greed.

As one damned soul gripped another and they began ripping each other's clothes, Chambers's initial confusion gave way to horror as he saw what they were doing. Once shirts had been shredded, blouses torn, skirts and trousers wrenched free, those cursed with the sin of greed began to claw at each others' flesh, burying hands within abdomens, fingers into mouths, nails into eye sockets.

And then the tearing began, the awful, terrible tearing that was the ultimate expression of these creatures' greed—the desire to possess something that is not your own at all costs, even if that meant the flesh and organs of another. Especially if it meant that.

As with any war, there were losers and victors. The losers were quickly reduced to empty, blood-streaked carcasses, lying on the pavement in pools of their own gore.

The winners were doing something very strange indeed.

Rather than holding their dripping trophies aloft, or eating them as Chambers had suspected they might, those who remained in one piece were now themselves seeking their own injuries—the gaping abdominal wounds, the rents in face and flesh—and were proceeding to cram the organs of their victims inside their own.

"It would seem they can never have enough of what belongs to others," Dr. Cruttenden breathed.

Chambers watched as one man slipped a bile-streaked liver through the rent in his abdomen. Once he had finished pushing the fleshy structure inside, the wound closed. The woman next to him now had four eyes—two crammed into each socket—and appeared to have been momentarily satiated by this. Still others had added to the muscle bulk of their arms and legs from the torn flesh of those who lay around them.

But not for long.

Because now the losers were coming back to life, slowly dragging themselves to their feet and regarding the victors with an even greater desire than they had before. There they stood, on legs of bared bone, abdominal rents gaping, an army of have-nots regarding the unwary haves with eyeless sockets.

Those with their new tissues rapidly became aware of them.

"How long do you think this goes on for?" Karen whispered as the second battle ensued.

"Who knows?" Dr. Cruttenden was watching the grotesque display with fascination. "Perhaps we have been lucky enough to witness the moment when one eternity became another."

"I'm not exactly sure we could call that lucky." Chambers got to his feet. It was the wrong thing to do.

"I think they've spotted us," he said as a sea of eyeless sockets, and heads with far too many eyes, turned to look their way.

"Perhaps if we keep still they'll go back to what they were doing."

Dr. Cruttenden's suggestion didn't work. Now they could see that there were intruders in their midst, the denizens of Greed wanted them, whatever they were. Every single piece of them.

The closest was a woman with nine eyes, a scalp almost completely devoid of hair, and legs whose red raw bones bore scarcely a scrap of muscle. Karen ran out and kicked savagely at the creature's left knee joint. It buckled backward and the woman fell to the ground with a snarl. Immediately the others were upon her.

"Run!"

They took off down the street at Chambers's command, not knowing where they were running, but knowing if they stayed still they would be the creatures' next victims. But what was the point if the streets were all the same? And if they could only circle this one block, again and again, like the cursed souls condemned to remain here, how could they hope to get away?

But as they ran, Chambers realized something.

"The doors have changed!"

Karen said it before he could. She wasn't quite right. Only some of them were different. Every fifth office door now glowed a dark blue and, if he wasn't mistaken, these special doors were resonating with a dull hum.

"Those must be the way out!" He hoped he was right. Perhaps that was the final crowning cruelty of the Circle of Greed—the way out was regularly displayed to the damned, but only when they were in this state of heightened hunger, oblivious to anything and everything but their desire to possess that which did not belong to them.

The greed zombies were gaining on them.

"Which one?" Dr. Cruttenden was fast becoming breathless and had already slowed. The creatures would be on her in moments. "Which one?"

"I don't think it matters." Chambers stopped at the door closest and hoped he was right. "And if we don't try, we're goners anyway."

He was about to step through when he was pushed aside by Karen, who was shoving Dr. Cruttenden through. He grabbed her outstretched hand and felt a chill as they passed through the deep blue of the entryway. Chambers wondered two things as he did so—whether they might die and, if they didn't, where they were going to end up next.

TWENTY-EIGHT

THEY WEREN'T DEAD.

Where they were, though, was a matter for debate. It was certainly nothing like the other circles of Hell they had so far visited. In fact, Chambers thought as he looked around him, it seemed rather pleasant.

A breeze was blowing, enough to disturb the grass that covered the gently rolling hills before him, hills that stretched as far as the line of trees he could see on every horizon. The sky was the slate gray of an approaching storm and the breeze was cold but, as far as he could see, there were no zombies, and no one intent on trying to kill him.

"Where are we, I wonder?" His question was directed at Dr. Cruttenden, who had removed her glasses and was rubbing her eyes.

"If you want an honest answer," she said, popping the spectacles back on, "I'm not exactly sure."

Karen was shivering. "What level is supposed to come after Greed?" she asked.

"Well that's why I'm a little confused. We should be on the plain of Anger."

"I don't feel angry." Now he'd seen her shiver, Chambers was feeling the cold too. "And I don't see anyone who is angry either."

"Maybe they're over the next hill?"

"If they are, then I think we'll stay here for a bit if you don't mind." Karen gave Dr. Cruttenden a friendly smile as she said it. "I could use a bit of a rest from running away from people who want to involve us in their obsessions."

"Agreed." Dr. Cruttenden gave a wheezy cough.

"Perhaps I should take a look." Chambers felt uneasy about staying still for too long. "Just in case."

"Be my guest." Karen gestured ahead of them. "But please don't go too far."

"I won't." He looked at Dr. Cruttenden. "Could there be any way we've ... I don't know ... bypassed a circle or two?"

"If we really are in Hell," the lecturer said, still trying to catch her breath, "then who knows what may or may not be possible?"

Karen rubbed the old lady's back. "What are the other circles of Hell? The ones we haven't been to yet?"

In between coughs, Dr. Cruttenden listed them. "Anger, Heresy, Violence, Fraud, and Treachery."

"I suppose it could be Fraud." Chambers had already taken a few steps away from them. "Perhaps all of this is an illusion."

"Or Treachery," said Karen. "Something's going to leap up and grab us when we least expect it."

"At least if we were in the Circle of Treachery it would be the last one," said Chambers.

His next question occurred to both him and Karen at the same time. She just beat him to it.

"What's beyond the Ninth Circle?"

Dr. Cruttenden shrugged. "Who knows? Perhaps nothing, perhaps the Sea of Darkness that was written about in the *Liber de Nigra Peregrinatione*."

"The *Book of the Black Pilgrimage*?" Chambers was impressed he remembered. "The one that talked about the Black Cathedral and that city?"

"Of Chorazin, yes. Both it and another fabled volume, the *Book of Eibon*, make reference to a never-ending plain on which wander the most damned souls of all, presided over by something vast and unspeakable, something that has been there since before the dawn of time, perhaps even existing outside of time."

"It's the thing that was on the wall."

Despite having been through so much, Chambers knew exactly what Karen was referring to. The memory of that tripod-legged insect god, towering over its tiny servants, was something he would prefer to forget, and he certainly didn't want to come face to face with the real thing. Could it be true? Was that what was waiting for them at the end of all this? And if so, was there really any point in going on?

"We can't go back." Dr. Cruttenden seemed to guess what he was thinking. "And if we stay in one place for too long, or rather one circle, we'll end up trapped there forever. I don't know exactly where we are right now, but I do think we need to keep moving. Just as soon as I've had a little rest."

Chambers left Karen to look after the lecturer. He was far too restless to stand there for a few moments and besides, they were going to have to see what was waiting for them over the brow of the nearest hill sooner or later. The grass crunched beneath his feet, almost as if it were frozen, or desiccated. When he looked down, it appeared far less healthy than when they had arrived. Instead of green, the short blades were a pale gray and felt as if they were crumbling beneath his feet.

When he reached the brow of the hill, the view beyond was only partly what he had been expecting.

The grassy, undulating landscape continued but now, dotted here and there as far as the eye could see, were wooden crucifixes, all of the same design, all composed of the same anemic wood, and each approximately eight feet tall.

Each one had a corpse tied to it.

The crucifixes may have been similar, but the bodies lashed to them were not. Men, women, even a few children it seemed, off in the far distance.

They were in varying stages of decay.

The ones closest to Chambers were the most advanced—mere mummified wisps of their former selves, clothed in a few threads of material, their eyeless skulls hanging at awkward angles if they had not already fallen from crumbling spines to lie close to the remains of bony feet. Behind those were bodies with a little more flesh still adherent to their bleached bones—mere scraps of muscle hanging from ribs, a few strand of hair stuck to fragments of scalp.

Chambers was tempted to explore further, to enter this bizarre forest of the dead and examine the more substantial corpses positioned in the brow of the next hill about a mile away. Then he remembered his promise to the others and felt a twinge of irritation. He turned on his heel and made his way back to where Dr. Cruttenden still seemed to be trying to catch her breath.

"Is there anything over there?" Karen asked impatiently. "You were gone long enough."

Was he? Surely it had only been a few minutes. "You're probably better off seeing for yourself. I wasn't gone long enough to take a good look."

"Well, it seemed like it."

Chambers shook his head. "Even if it did, that's more likely going to be an effect of where we are rather than me being selfish, don't you think?"

Karen was about to reply, but was interrupted by another bout of coughing from Dr. Cruttenden. They both glowered at her.

"Have you ever suffered from asthma?" Chambers was actually concerned, but somehow the words came out sounding far more callous than he had intended.

"When I was a child," came the rasping reply. "But I grew out of it years ago."

"Well it seems to have come back now, doesn't it?"

"That's not very nice," said Karen. "She can't help it if she can't walk."

"I can walk perfectly well, thank you." Dr. Cruttenden took two steps and had to bend over to catch her breath again.

"I don't see us getting very far with you like that," said Chambers. "Perhaps I'd better go and look for the way out while you wait here."

"Why should you be the one to go?" Karen looked incensed. "You're the doctor—you should be the one to stay here now you've finally got an actual bloody patient to look after."

"There's not much I can do," Chambers snapped. "And to be honest, I think you'd find it much more difficult getting through what's up there than I will."

"Why? What's up there? It can't be any worse than what you've dragged us through already."

"I don't need anyone to look after me," Dr. Cruttenden interjected. "Why don't you both go? To be honest, it would be a delight for me to have a break from both of you."

"Fine." Both Karen and Chambers said the word together and then glared at each other. Chambers could feel himself balling the fingers of both hands into fists.

Just as he understood what was happening.

"Anger," he said, trying to make his voice as soft as possible. It still came out as a shout.

"Too damn right I'm angry," said Karen. "I've just about had enough of you and her and this place and—"

"It's this place." Chambers still couldn't stop himself from shouting, but he tried to make himself understood anyway. "It's making us angry."

"He's right." Dr. Cruttenden gave another cough and the other two flinched in annoyance. "I'm trying hard not to annoy either of you, but I seem to be making you worse, which in turn is making me furious."

"Well, what the hell are we supposed to do?"

"We need to get out of here." Chambers was doing his best to keep his voice soft, but it seemed hopeless. In fact, the harder he tried, the more an edge of sarcasm seemed to be creeping in. "You'd better all follow me."

"Why? How do you all of a sudden know which way we should go?"

Chambers tried to ignore the rage in Karen's voice. "Because the damned souls of this circle lie that way, that's why. They're all dead, and it looks as if they won't harm us, but of course that doesn't mean once we're among them that they won't suddenly come to life, so watch out."

Karen gave Dr. Cruttenden a disdainful look. "There's no way she's going to make it."

"Don't worry about me," spat the lecturer. "I'll be right behind you every inch of the way, and if I'm not then that will be my own stupid fault, won't it?"

Chambers extended a helping hand, but it was brushed away. He bit back the words that immediately came to him and instead made a start up the hill, turning back every now and then to make sure the others were following him.

The crucifixes were still there, and as they entered the forest of withered wood and rotting, emaciated bodies, Chambers felt a sense of hopelessness descend upon him that only exacerbated his mounting anger and frustration.

"It'll probably get worse as we go forward," he said to no one in particular.

"It's probably intended to." Dr. Cruttenden's sarcastic reply came from somewhere behind him. "But if we stop now, we'll end up like these things here."

"Won't we end up like them if we carry on?" Karen still sounded profoundly irritated, but they were starting to get used to ignoring the inflections of anger in what each of them said.

"If we're not careful," said Chambers, waiting for them to catch up and join him. "Let's try looking out for each other from now on, shall we?"

They kept moving forward. Soon they were deep enough in that all they could see were crosses extending in every direction.

"Oh, that's just great." Karen sounded dejected now. "How are we supposed to know which way to go?"

"I think we follow the corpses." Chambers pointed ahead of them. The bodies tied to the crosses had begun to change subtly. Each one they passed now had slightly more flesh on its bones—rotting scraps that here and there betrayed a hint of wetness, rather than the horribly desiccated specimens they had already passed.

It wasn't long before they came to figures that were in a far less advanced state of decay, and with the sickly sweet smell of corruption to match. But that wasn't the worst of it.

These corpses were moving.

They were still tightly bound to the crucifixes, but that didn't stop those with some remaining strength from struggling against their bonds. The ones with eyes regarded the individuals passing between them from watery sockets, and those with vocal cords cried out—a mixtures of rasps and gasps that alerted their neighbors that there were newcomers in their midst.

Soon the part of the forest they were now in was filled with the cries of those banished to this circle of Hell. At first Chambers thought the sounds they were making were anguished, but it wasn't long before he could hear that they were cries of fury.

"Keep going!"

Karen had stopped and was regarding the semi-rotten body of a young woman. Most of her curled blonde hair was still present, apart from the gash that had opened up the right-hand side of her skull. Whatever blow she had been dealt had taken her right eye as well. The left, however, remained and was regarding Karen with utter hatred.

"Why are they like that?" Karen was moving again, but she could not take her eyes from the angry dead.

"My guess would be it's all part of their eternal torment." Chambers wanted to spit the words at her, and it was taking a Herculean effort not to. "They're so angry that if they weren't tied up, they would tear each other into so many pieces that no one and nothing would be able to put them back together again. This way they're just out of reach of each other, which just makes it all the worse."

"It also emphasizes why we have to try to remain calm." Dr. Cruttenden was just managing to keep up. She was stumbling along, wheezing as she went, and Chambers and Karen were going as slowly as they could to allow her to stay with them. "I very much suspect that if we were to become as angry with each other as they appear to be, we would also find ourselves lashed to one of those things."

"But the first ones we saw weren't angry." Karen was obviously struggling not to rant as well. "They were just . . . dead."

"Perhaps the curse of this circle is for you to boil away with anger until there is literally nothing left." Dr. Cruttenden coughed and the other two frowned, but they covered it up before she could see. "Then, for all we know, they get moved back to the front of the line to start the whole thing over again."

"You mean where we're heading now?"

Chambers nodded. "Let's hope so."

They had been steadily climbing a gradual incline and were now reaching the top. Chambers had expected to see more of the same on the other side, but when they reached the topmost row of crosses it also turned out to be the last.

Beyond, beneath a sky the color of blood, lay a vast pit.

More than a hundred steps carved into wet black earth led down into it, and, on the far side, a similar flight led out.

On each of the steps down was a writhing human being, lashed to a wooden crucifix. With frightening regularity a bell rang—a loud, dull monotone that Chambers was surprised they had not heard before— and the figures all moved one step up. The one on the very top step took up the space that had opened up for it at the brow of the hill and, in its angered writhings, began to tear itself to pieces as it strained against the ropes.

On the far side of the pit, each step also bore a human figure, but these were the withered skeletal creatures that Chambers had first encountered. Temporarily relieved of their burdens, these fragile wisps of humanity were tottering down the steps with the same monotonous regularity, and in response to the same urgent tolling.

It was when they reached the bottom of the pit that their transformation occurred. Gradually, as they progressed haltingly across the blackened floor of earth, the mummified remains of the souls damned to the Circle of Anger for all eternity grew flesh on their bones and then skin to cover it. Hair regrew, eyes and teeth were restored, and by the time they were close to the steps leading up to where Chambers and the others were currently standing, they looked almost human again.

Then the crucifixes were applied.

In the same way as the bodies actually progressed once they were bound up, it was impossible to see how this was done. One minute the soul resembled a healthy human being, the next they were a screaming, furious creature bound to a wooden cross and being moved slowly but surely up the wet steps to begin another round of anguished torment.

"What do we do now?"

Chambers had no idea. He hoped Dr. Cruttenden did, but she was shrugging as she caught her breath.

"Well, we haven't found the way out yet, so I'm guessing it should be just over there."

Karen pointed to the far side of the pit. "Past all those people?"

"Yes."

"All those people who are so filled with anger they want to tear each other apart?"

"Yes."

"And will probably tear us apart if we go anywhere near them?"

Chambers wrestled with the almost overwhelming urge to tell Karen to shut up. In the end he managed it by admitting to himself that she did have a point. The steps that led into the pit were barely wide enough for a single of the damned souls to stand, and the incline was steep. Even without being assaulted, the climb down was going to be difficult.

But there was nothing else they could do.

"I'll go first," he said. "Dr. Cruttenden should go second so we can watch out for her, and I need you to bring up the rear."

"You know what I want to say to that, don't you?"

"Yes." Chambers permitted himself a smile and hoped Karen wouldn't take it the wrong way. "And you know it's not you but this place that's making you feel that way."

"Oh fucking hell, let's get on with it, then."

Chambers put his foot on the top step. It sank slightly into the wet earth and something that looked like blood pooled around his shoe. When he withdrew it, the ground made a sucking noise that reminded him of a bloated maggot feeding.

"What are you waiting for?"

Chambers looked over at Karen, who had moved Dr. Cruttenden in front of her. "Just be careful as you go—the ground's very soft."

It was dangerous as well. To avoid falling into the abyss below they had to keep away from the edge, but not so far away that they came into contact with the angry dead, who snapped and snarled at the intruders in their midst.

"As long as we keep away from the teeth we should be fine," Dr. Cruttenden said, to no one in particular.

Chambers was relieved to hear she was still close behind him. The steps were too narrow for him to turn around and check the others were okay. He called to Karen and was rewarded with an exasperated response that reassured him she was still with them too.

Then Dr. Cruttenden slipped.

If she hadn't grabbed at his shoulder with her right hand, Chambers would never have known she was falling. They were about halfway down the flight of sodden steps and suddenly he felt himself being tugged backward. He turned to face the creature that was lashing at him, his features only inches from the dead thing's own, and then turned again to see what had happened.

Dr. Cruttenden was hanging from the free edge of the steps. The only thing preventing her from falling was the grasp of Karen's right hand, but that was beginning to slip.

Chambers got down on his hands and knees, his fingers sinking into the blood-soaked soil as the chill fluid seeped through the legs of his trousers. He reached out for Dr. Cruttenden's flailing left hand, but she wouldn't, or couldn't, keep it still.

"Try and grab my hand!"

Her response was a barrage of beleaguered coughing. And then, "I am trying, you know! But I can't!"

Chambers leaned out further. He could feel the slippery soil beneath him starting to encourage him over the edge.

"Try harder!"

Karen reached out with her free hand. Just as she did so, the soil she was resting on gave way and she, too, tumbled over the edge.

Just as Chambers managed to grab Dr. Cruttenden's hand.

Now the two women were swinging in space, their only attachment to land being Dr. Cruttenden's left hand that was grasped by Chambers's right, and their combined weight was quickly pulling him over the edge.

"Try and dig your feet in!" he cried as they swung back and forth. "The soil should be soft enough for you to climb up!"

He felt their combined weight swing beneath him once more as his body continued to slide toward the edge. Then they stopped, and he heard Karen's voice coming from what sounded like far below.

"It's so soft I can barely get a hold!"

She was obviously trying, and she obviously failed as Chambers felt himself pulled further over the edge. Now half his own body was hanging in the air as he held on desperately with his left hand and did his best to anchor his pelvis with his hip muscles.

"Climb up over Dr. Cruttenden, then!"

"But that could pull you over too!"

Chambers licked his lips. The situation looked hopeless either way. "If you don't hurry that will happen anyway," he cried. "You may as well try, while I've still got a hold up here."

There was silence as he presumed Karen to be contemplating his words. Then he felt a pull and braced himself again. A protesting "Ow!" from Dr. Cruttenden suggested Karen was following his advice.

But she had to hurry. Despite all his effort, he could feel himself sliding, inch by inch, over the edge. He took a deep breath to tell her to hurry up, but at the same moment he slid forward and the wind was knocked from him.

"Nearly there!" came Karen's voice from below. It was true. He could see her now, clambering over the distressed lecturer.

"Be careful!" he cried as she reached for his arm. "I'm nearly over!"

Rather than go slowly, Karen took that as her cue to climb faster. She grabbed his arm and pushed herself up and onto the ledge just as Chambers slid over.

Almost.

Karen had hold of his right leg, and somehow her grasp felt firm enough that he was able to encourage Dr. Cruttenden to do what Karen had just done.

"I can't possibly," she said. "I simply haven't the strength."

"You're going to have to!" he shouted. "If you don't, we'll all go!"

It seemed like an age, but eventually Dr. Cruttenden pulled herself up a little, which in turn allowed Chambers to get a better hold on her.

God only knew how Karen was managing to prevent herself from falling, but everything stayed steady as Dr. Cruttenden levered herself up over Chambers and back onto the step. Then between them, the two women pulled Chambers up.

"How the hell did you not slip?" he said, once he had regained his breath.

"With a little help from one of our friends here." Karen was pointing to the writhing figure behind her, then she pointed to a large tear in her sleeve that had been put there by the thing's teeth. "Mind you, I was worried the cotton was going to give out."

"I think I'll just say I owe you one, and leave it at that." Chambers smiled. It broadened as he realized he felt no anger at all. The emotion had left him like a cloud lifting.

"Yes," said Dr. Cruttenden, wiping the worst of the mud from her clothes. "I feel it too. I suspect our little act of cooperation has proved we're not meant for this circle, and consequently the forces that have been trying to keep us here have given up."

The crucified dead hadn't given up, though. They continued in their efforts to snap at the three of them as Karen, Chambers, and Dr. Cruttenden made their way to the bottom of the pit. The ground there was much firmer, and they paused for a rest before making their way across.

Karen eyed the line of the dead that stretched across the base of the pit. They seemed to acquire their crucifixes somewhere in the center, but it was difficult to see exactly where.

"I'm guessing it's best if we just keep well away from them?" she said.

Chambers shrugged. "I suppose so. We'll have to deal with them when we go up the other side anyway."

"What if the way out is in the center?" Dr. Cruttenden's breathing problems seemed to have rectified themselves at the same time as their anger had faded. "If we miss it, we'll just end up going all the way around again until we find it."

Karen looked back the way they had come. "I don't fancy having to come down those steps again."

"Me neither." Now Chambers's eyes were following the line of the dead as they found themselves bound to their crucifixes and had to hobble to the first step up to the next stage of their torment. "I suppose as long as we keep our distance, we should be okay."

Once they had rested, they set off. The dead seemed less interested in them now, and far more concerned with each other and their own predicament. The ground, so wet and slippery when they had started, became increasingly dry as they made their way to the center of the pit.

Where a door was waiting.

Chambers hoped it was a door. Unlike the others they had encountered, this one was merely a patch of powder-dry earth about three feet across. When Chambers put his foot on it, he sank in up to his knee.

"Do you think this might be it?"

"It could be." Dr. Cruttenden was scratching her head. "If it's not, then I don't suppose you'll live very long to find out."

"Perhaps we should go up the steps on the other side, just to make sure?"

"I don't think so, Karen." Chambers pointed. From here it was possible to see the blood oozing down the walls from the sodden staircase. And the angry dead, free from their bonds, who were now glowering at them. "If we don't try this, I think we're going to be here forever anyway."

Karen chewed her lip. "Well, you go first, then."

Chambers grinned. "I rather thought you'd say that." He took six steps back, drew a deep breath, and then ran forward, jumping the last couple of feet so that he would land dead center in the dry area. At the last minute he closed his eyes.

And felt himself falling.

TWENTY-NINE

THE GROUND WAS HARD and cold. And, Chambers discovered as he stretched out an exploratory hand, as smooth as polished glass.

He was yet to open his eyes as he had only just landed, if that was what the sensation he had just experienced could be described as. His left leg had twisted under him and felt bruised but not broken. The rest of him felt uninjured.

Time to see where he was.

His first impression was that he was in the corridor of some great building. He was lying on his right side on pale gray floor tiles. If he turned his head to the left, he could see, high above him, an ornate ceiling decorated with ornamental plasterwork. He couldn't quite make out what these decorations were meant to be as the light was too poor, but at least it was bright enough for him to see where he was.

Where were Karen and Dr. Cruttenden?

He heaved himself to his feet, noting that he had been quite right about his left leg and he would probably be limping a bit as a result of it.

How had he gotten here?

The ceiling looked intact, but of course that could be an optical illusion. Any second now Karen and Dr. Cruttenden might come tumbling through it. With that in mind, he shuffled over to the right-hand wall and leaned against a pillar. Now that he could inspect it more closely, he could see it was a column of Corinthian design. There was an identical one across the way. Wherever he was, it was quite extravagantly decorated, which made for a pleasing change. The walls on either side were of red marble, through which ran veins of gold and white. They were surprisingly warm to the touch.

Well-decorated and warm, Chambers thought. Could this be the Comfortable Circle of Hell?

Suddenly reminded of where he was, he looked about him for any trace of those damned to imprisonment here, but there was no one. He waited for Karen and Dr. Cruttenden to turn up. Nothing.

Perhaps they had already arrived, but were elsewhere? Chambers tried his weight on his left leg and was rewarded with searing pain shooting up from his ankle to his knee.

I need a crutch.

Doing his best to ignore the discomfort, Chambers hobbled forward a few steps to find himself confronted by a robed figure. He almost fell backward with fright as he stifled a cry.

Then he saw the figure wasn't real.

It was remarkably lifelike, though, as his probing fingers revealed both the face and fingers to be made of wax. The scarlet robes were real enough, and had been fixed to the torso sufficiently well that they could not be removed.

The scepter that the figure was holding in its right hand, however, came away easily. Chambers examined it carefully. It appeared to be made of a heavy dark wood, possibly ebony, and the tip had been carved into a point. Two spirals of tiny dancing figures made loops down the shaft to the brass ferrule fitted over the bottom end. Most important of all, it was sturdy enough to take his weight.

Grasping the engraved shaft of his new walking aid, Chambers began to make his way down the corridor, the brass ferrule clicking on the floor tiles as he moved.

It wasn't long before the walls parted, and he found himself in a vast, high-ceilinged chamber filled with statues like the one he had borrowed the staff from. Some were in glass display cases, others stood free. All were different—dressed in different clothes, arranged in different positions—but all seemed to represent some religious office. Some weren't even human.

Chambers came to a crossroads, where an eight-foot-tall statue of the Egyptian god Anubis stared at him, its face half in shadow. He resisted the urge to stare back.

Which way?

He debated calling out, but figured that might only attract whatever cursed creatures were probably wandering the corridors. There was still no sign of Karen or Dr. Cruttenden, and he was starting to get worried.

He looked up at Anubis.

"Which way do you think I should go?" he said before he could stop himself.

The figure remained silent. Was it his imagination, or was more of its face in the light than had been before?

He took a step back. The eyes of the figure seemed to follow him. After all he had been through, he could not bring himself to dismiss the thought as ridiculous.

Chambers took a step to the left. Now he was standing at the center of the crossroads. He was also out of the eye-line of the statue.

Until it turned its head toward him.

Chambers didn't wait to see if he had been mistaken. Instead he set off down one of the aisles, hobbling faster now. Almost immediately he regretted his choice. The exhibits here seemed to be a collection of the worst creatures from an Aztec's nightmare. A group of huge, bird-like creatures with jutting, blood-streaked fangs had been poised over a monstrous ape with tusks, frozen in the moment of tearing its heart out. Was he hearing things, or was that the rustle of feathers behind him as he passed by?

He tried to ignore the distant sound of slow, heavy footsteps as he rounded another corner. Here the exhibits seemed to be marine-based, but were no less terrifying for it. A barracuda with bat-like wings atop a pedestal was being worshiped by tiny human figures, while further on something that seemed to consist of nothing but a mass of tentacles and teeth hung over an altar of polished granite.

The footsteps behind him were getting louder.

There were other noises now as well, and Chambers suddenly found himself loath to look behind him in case each of the displays had somehow come to life with his passing.

"Karen?" If the exhibits were alive it wouldn't matter if they heard his cries, and it was far more important now that he find his friends. His voice caused a flurry of activity behind him and he began to move faster, his ankle protesting with a grumbling ache that he was just going to have to put up with.

"Karen? Anyone?" He rounded another corner and barely looked at the primitive creatures displayed there. One seemed to be devouring the sun, while another held the moon in arachnodactylic fingers. The noise behind him was louder still and, though he had been trying hard not to, Chambers finally gave in and risked a glance over his shoulder.

The scene behind him was terrifying.

It was what a painting might look like, he thought, a painting designed to show all the horrors of Hell bursting forth from it in one huge, heady onslaught. Pig-creatures, squid-like monstrosities, wolf-men, hyena-things and much, much worse, all hindering each other in their mad scramble to reach their quarry.

His attention was on the mass of creatures pursuing him, and so Chambers failed to notice the hand reaching out to grab him and drag him into a shadowy alcove. He gave a cry, but stopped the moment he saw who it was.

"Karen! How long have you been here?"

"About half an hour," Dr. Cruttenden whispered from behind her. "Waiting quietly here and deciding what to do next."

"What are those things?"

Karen clamped a hand over his mouth as the hideous, otherworldly entourage passed them by.

"We are in the Circle of Heresy," Dr. Cruttenden explained once the creatures were gone. "Therefore it follows that everything you have seen is the product of some religion that has existed in the past. You were being pursued by false gods."

"But that makes no sense," Chambers hissed back. "Where are the souls who are meant to have been banished to this level?"

"You haven't worked it out, then?" Even in the darkness Chambers could see Karen wasn't impressed. "Those are the dead, the heretical dead, cursed to a never-ending torment as the very idols they worshipped in life. Now we've come down here and upset everything because, like on every other circle we've been to, we're the ones who could offer them a potential way out."

"Did you work all that out yourself?" Chambers nodded at Dr. Cruttenden. "Or did you have help?"

"Don't be childish, Professor Chambers." Dr. Cruttenden was admonishing him, and he deserved it. "We have survived here for a good thirty minutes without making a sound, and consequently without disturbing a single of the exhibits out there. You, on the other hand, seem to have caused quite a rumpus. You've even stolen something that belongs to them."

Chambers looked at his staff. "I couldn't walk without this."

Karen sniffed. "Then perhaps you should have stayed where you were."

Chambers wasn't going to let that pass. "That wouldn't have helped us get out of here, would it?"

"Stop it, both of you. We know there must be a way out, but what we don't know is how big this place is. We also now have the added difficulty of having a pantheon of undead deities looking for us." Dr. Cruttenden looked at Chambers. "Or rather, they are looking for you."

"Well, I'd love to act as bait and draw them off while you two hunt for the way out"—Chambers was gripping his staff defensively—"but in case you hadn't noticed I can't actually walk terribly quickly, much less run from those things out there."

"Nobody's suggesting it should be you who distracts them." Dr. Cruttenden licked her lips and looked at Karen, who visibly flinched.

"I'm not going out there," she said.

"I was merely suggesting that we will have to watch out for Professor Chambers as we all go together to try to find the way out."

Dr. Cruttenden's explanation helped Chambers pull himself together. "I should be okay," he said, pressing on his ankle and doing a fine job of keeping a straight face as the sprained joint did its best to cause him all kinds of agony.

Karen peered out from their hiding place. "They seem to have gone."

"I imagine it won't be long before they're back." Dr. Cruttenden gave Chambers a prod. "You go first so we can keep an eye on you."

It was sensible, of course, although Chambers hated the idea of being watched, doing his best to hobble along and pretend nothing was wrong. He also wished the ferrule on the end of his staff was a bit quieter, but his attempts to remove it while they had been talking had met with little success.

The staff clicked on the polished floor as he levered his way out.

"Can't you—?"

"No, I've already tried," he hissed, cutting off Karen before she could say any more.

Dr. Cruttenden followed, with Karen bringing up the rear.

"Which way?" Chambers asked.

"Well, we came from down there." The lecturer pointed straight ahead.

"And I came from there." Chambers pointed to the left.

"Right it is, then," said Karen, urging them on.

They came to another crossroads, each length of corridor lined with display cases alternating with religious tableaux. It was difficult to tell what many of the specimens were meant to depict in the semi-darkness, but Chambers saw creatures covered in hair and wielding tapering claws, and harpy-like monstrosities tearing the flesh from human bodies that looked uncomfortably lifelike.

Straight ahead of them, at the very end of the corridor they were following, was a painting on the wall. If Chambers squinted, he could just make out the segmented body arching up over its tiny worshippers, and the strange, tripod-like arrangement of its hind limbs. Above and beneath it were words in a foreign language.

It was the painting from the wall in All Hallows Church.

Chambers recognized it just as the things in the tableaux around them began to move.

"Keep going," he said as Karen and Dr. Cruttenden shrank back from the creatures advancing on them from four directions. "Keep going until you get to that picture."

"But it's a dead end!" Karen looked around her, but there was nowhere else for them to go.

"A dead end that's guarded by the Anarch!" Dr. Cruttenden grabbed Karen's hand and urged her to follow Chambers. "If there was a secret way out of here, I would have expected it to be guarded by Him."

The corridor was filling with creatures now, moving slowly but gaining strength as they awoke from their deep sleep. A long, drawn out wolf-howl from far behind them signified that Chambers's pursuers from earlier knew where they were now as well.

"Come on!" Dr. Cruttenden placed a hand on his shoulder to help Chambers forward. He was having to lean more heavily on the staff now, and as the things from either side plucked at his sleeves he found himself slowing down and almost overbalancing.

"Not far!" That was Karen, as she put his left arm around her shoulders so now he could lean on her as well as the staff.

But it seemed hopeless. As tentacles and claws brushed his face, and he sensed barbed insectoid limbs digging into his clothes, he felt both of them being dragged to a standstill.

"We can't give up now!" A hearty thrust from Dr. Cruttenden shoved them both forward as she bellowed above the noise of the things that were pursuing them, that were either side of them, that seemed to be all around them, clutching and pawing and scratching.

Suddenly, they were there.

Chambers did not so much see the wall as collide with it, his staff clattering to the floor as he put out both hands to stop himself from dashing his face against the surface. He almost expected his outstretched palms to pass straight through the painting, but they didn't. Instead they came up against cold, damp-feeling plaster.

"There's no way through!" he said. His searching hands felt their way around as much of the image as his reach would allow.

"There has to be." Dr. Cruttenden was at his side now, while Karen had picked up the staff and begun to beat at the creatures that surrounded them. "Perhaps if we say the words?"

"You'll have to," Chambers gasped. He couldn't move away from the wall without suffering appalling pain. "I can't get back far enough to see what they say."

Karen thrust the staff at a hawk-beaked monstrosity with arms thick with copper-colored feathers and the dead eyes of a psychopath, as Dr. Cruttenden took a step back and hesitantly read aloud the legend that had been painted on the wall in thready black ink. It was the same as the words that Dr. Chesney had uttered back in the church what seemed a lifetime ago now.

"*Ph'nglui mglw'nafh Cthulhu R'lyeh wgah'nagl fhtagn.*"

Nothing.

"Perhaps you have to read it more than once?" Chambers didn't know what else to suggest, but he knew the power that the ancient chant possessed.

Dr. Cruttenden tried again and again, but still nothing.

"How many churches were there?"

"I beg your pardon?"

Karen swiped at a green-skinned thing low to the ground, its only facial feature a round hole lined with suckers. "I asked how many models of churches were there, back in the crypt?"

"Seven." Chambers remembered counting them as each one was encountered.

"Then try saying it seven times."

Three down, four to go. Dr. Cruttenden mouthed the words as rapidly as possible. As the last twisted syllable left her lips, the outline of the flea god became a blinding white light and Chambers suddenly felt the wall give beneath his touch.

"It's working!" he said, feeling himself start to pass through. "What's waiting for us in the next circle?"

He could feel Karen beside him as the world turned white, but Dr. Cruttenden's voice seemed very far away as she uttered a single word that filled him with dread.

"Violence."

THIRTY

SCREAMS.

That was what Chambers's senses encountered first on his arrival in the new realm. Tortured, agonized screams. And they were coming from close by.

He opened his eyes to discover he was standing on a rough wooden balcony, or viewing platform, that ran the entire circumference of the chamber in which he found himself. A dim, smoky glow was provided by flaming torches set high into the damp stone walls at regular intervals. The light was too poor for him to see how high the ceiling was, but he guessed it must be low as the smoke was refusing to rise very far.

There were other people on the balcony with him. Too many.

Crowded against him to his right were Karen and Dr. Cruttenden, and he acknowledged their presence with relief. He was about to look at those buffeting him to his left and behind him when his attention was distracted by another scream from below. He looked down on a spectacle straight out of the Middle Ages, or perhaps something the Spanish Inquisition might have devised.

The balcony looked onto a torture chamber.

It had to be at least twenty feet below where he was standing, but there was no doubting what was taking place there. He could see five different devices, each bearing a helpless victim. He only caught the briefest glimpse of what was being done to them before he tried to close his eyes tightly.

And found he couldn't.

"I think that's meant to be part of it," Dr. Cruttenden shouted to him over the noise. "You have to endure the violence as part of your damnation."

"But we're not damned!" he shouted back, before a terrifying thought struck him. What if they were? What if this was the place they were destined to end up? And now that they had arrived, passing through the other circles of Hell, was this the place from which they would be unable to escape?

"Let's hope not," he thought he heard her say as another scream tore through the hot, smoky air and he felt his neck being turned against his will so that he was forced to look down again at the spectacle being presented before him.

Furthest away, a young man pinned in a semi-recumbent position was having each of his teeth pulled out with an instrument that looked more suited for chipping wood. Next to him, an elderly woman who had been lain flat on a stone table was in the process of having the skin removed from her right leg.

And still that was not the worst.

Directly beneath where he was standing were two more victims. It was impossible to determine whether they were male or female. Their faces had not so much been removed as reconstructed to create monstrous, blood-streaked caricatures of their former selves. Displaced flesh was held in place by crude stitches of blackened cord that hung in long, untrimmed strands and had become plastered to their skin in the welter of blood that had pooled around their necks. These two made no sounds, as they no longer had mouths with which to scream.

Chambers tried again to close his eyes. When his lids remained stubbornly open, he knew that if they didn't get out of there soon he would go insane. The Seventh Circle of Hell, the circle of Violence, was by far the most terrible they had encountered so far, and if things got worse from here on in, he would rather take his chances with the heretics, or that pit of anger, or any of the other places they had passed through on their way here.

He was wondering how much longer he would be able to maintain a grip on his sanity, when he felt someone to his left nudge him. Suddenly allowed movement, he found himself able to turn to see the woman who was trying to gain his attention. It was difficult because she, too, had obviously been a victim of the practices in the pit, and the twisted malformation that was the right side of her face meant that any attempt at speech was accompanied by a noisy exhalation. Eventually, Chambers was able to make out what she was trying to tell him.

"A . . . competition . . ."

"What?" He tried his best to make himself heard above the screams that were still emanating from down below. "You mean this is? What's going on down there?"

The woman nodded. "Longest . . . wins."

Presumably she meant whoever could withstand the greatest degree of mutilation.

"Wins what?"

This time she said nothing, but merely pointed upward.

"Do you mean death?"

She shrugged at that, and he could see her face had not been the only thing to receive the torturers' attentions.

"Or escape?"

That was met with a more urgent nod.

Chambers's insides turned to liquid. This was the first time any of them had been able to communicate with one of the damned souls in any of the circles, and now it was obvious why. The only way out was to be the one who could withstand the most pain.

"What did she say to you?" Karen had been allowed to move as well, now, and she shouted her question across in a desperate, trembling voice that suggested she had little distance to go in terms of losing sanity herself.

How could he answer? He wasn't going to lie. After all, according to Dr. Cruttenden, Fraud was the next circle after this one. The corner of his mouth threatened to crease with the trace of a tired smile at that, but something kept his muscles frozen as they were.

"I think I know a way out," he called back. "But it's not going to be pleasant."

With that he glanced down into the pit.

Karen said nothing, while Dr. Cruttenden started to squeeze past him. "May as well get on with it," she said through bloodstained lips. "The longer we stay up here, the less we're going to feel like going down there. Can you see where we're supposed to go?"

Chambers couldn't until she asked. Now an alcove in the wall behind them had opened up, revealing a narrow passageway and worn stone steps leading down. Dr. Cruttenden pushed her way through the mutilated individuals crowding her way, grabbing Chambers by the hand in case he was having second thoughts. He in turn made sure he was gripping Karen's arm.

Karen refused to move.

He knew what she must be thinking, and he hated to have to put her through this but, if there was no other way, then the alternative would be for them to be trapped there forever.

"We have to go!" Once again he had to shout over the sound of screaming. "We have to, or we'll never escape!"

Karen was silent for a moment, but it looked as if she was battling to speak. Eventually, the words came.

"Escape to where? To worse than this? To much worse than this? Have I got to go down there and be tortured just so I can go to another one of these circles and have something else terrible happen?"

"We're nearly there!" Chambers didn't know if that was true or not, or what they would find when they came to the end, but he knew they had to keep going or Hell would be welcoming three new residents. Perhaps it already had, but if he started thinking like that he would give up, just like Karen seemed about to. "Do you really want to stay here and try and bear . . . this?"

"Can't we go back?"

"There is no going back." That was Dr. Cruttenden, pulling at Chambers. "We have to see this through to the end now. Not just for us. You do understand that, don't you?"

It didn't look as if Karen did, or perhaps she was unwilling to. Chambers tried again.

"Karen, if you stay here, then we'll have to stay here too. We can't make it without you."

It wasn't much, but it was enough. Karen took one step forward, and then another.

"I don't want to do this." She was talking through teeth clenched so tight he could barely understand her.

"None of us do." He held her hand and squeezed it tightly. "Come on."

Still she held back. "Will it hurt?"

What could he say? "Not as much as staying here. Not as much as giving up."

She followed him down the steps. Chambers was impressed with Dr. Cruttenden's resolve as she led the way at a steady pace. The light dimmed as they reached the arena, just as another wave of louder, much closer screams, assaulted their ears.

Dr. Cruttenden passed through the stone archway first, stepping boldly into the space beyond. Chambers didn't think he could do it, and he knew he would have to pull Karen though as well. She was already beginning to resist.

But there was nothing else to do. He tightened his grip on Karen's hand and dragged both himself and her into the arena.

It was empty.

The screams that had until that moment filled them with terror had vanished, along with those who had been making them. The torturers, too, were no longer there, having disappeared along with their victims.

All that remained were the torture instruments.

"Are we supposed to torture each other?" The prospect of momentary respite seemed to have allowed Karen to find her voice again.

Chambers followed Dr. Cruttenden to the center of the circle, avoiding the bloodstained straw as best he could.

"I don't know," he breathed, surprised to realize he could hear himself. He had expected the crowd on the balcony to be making noise now that they were down here, jeering at the strangers to their realm, egging on the torturers who were going to submit them to the ultimate test. Instead, they were oddly quiet. When Chambers looked up he could see why.

The spectators, too, had vanished.

As had the archway through which they had entered.

Dr. Cruttenden looked down at the tray of rusted instruments beside her and picked up a tarnished-looking meat cleaver. When Chambers and Karen both took a step back, she responded with a mirthless laugh.

"Don't worry," she said, giving the cleaver an experimental swing. "I'm not going to harm either of you. The problem is, I don't believe I am capable of torturing myself either." She offered the cleaver to Chambers. "You're the medic," she said. "I don't suppose you would care to . . . ?"

Chambers shook his head.

"I didn't think so." Dr. Cruttenden dragged the instrument table over to the dentist's chair they had watched the young man being tortured in. She sat down, rested her left arm on the bench, and raised the cleaver high.

It was thirty seconds before she put it back down again.

"It's no good," she said. "There's no way I'm going to be able to do this."

"I can't either." Karen was eyeing the other tables of instruments. "I just . . . can't."

Chambers swallowed and shook his head. "We haven't had to do anything like this before. Perhaps it's not the way out."

The shuffling sounds above them resumed. Chambers looked up to see their audience had returned. "Why do I get the feeling we've just failed some sort of test?" he said, as the archway reappeared.

Karen looked around her. "What's that noise?"

"I believe our audience is coming to join us," he replied. "We've proven we can't escape from here, so I have a horrible feeling they're coming to welcome us into the fold."

The sound of limping footsteps was growing louder now, and it was being overshadowed by something much worse. The gargling, groaning howls of those damned to the Circle of Violence.

"What will they do to us?"

It was Dr. Cruttenden who answered Karen's question. "Nothing more nor less than what they have been cursed to do forever to each other, I should imagine."

"Then we have to get out of here!" Karen's eyes were blazing with fear, but there was something else there now as well—a determination borne of utter terror.

She picked up the cleaver Dr. Cruttenden had put down and looked at both of them. "If you won't go first," she said, "then I will."

Eyes still bright with approaching madness, Karen raised the cleaver high above her head. She was about to bring it down on her outstretched arm when a cry from Dr. Cruttenden stopped her.

"Wait!"

The shuffling sounds were getting closer now.

Karen blinked tears from her eyes as she looked at the older woman. "Why?"

Chambers was wondering the same thing.

"There may be another way." Dr. Cruttenden was raising her arms above her head.

The violent dead were beginning to enter the chamber now. Whatever her idea was, Chambers thought, she'd better do it quickly.

"*Ph'nglui mglw'nafh Cthulhu R'lyeh wgah'nagl fhtagn.*"

They were the ancient words that had effected their escape from the Circle of Heresy. But would they work again here?

At first Chambers thought all hope was lost, and from their expressions both Karen and Dr. Cruttenden shared his despondency. But then Dr. Cruttenden moved slightly, and Chambers realized he could see one of the dead approaching from behind her.

And that he could actually see the damned soul approaching *through* her.

A little of Dr. Cruttenden's substance had vanished.

"Say the words again!" he cried. "And keep saying them!"

Dr. Cruttenden looked confused, but she didn't argue. She recited the unearthly phrase a further three times and, on completing each guttural chant, she became more wraith-like. There was little more than a shade of her left when Chambers turned to Karen.

"You have to say them too."

Karen looked close to panic. "I can't!"

"Yes, you can!" He took her hand. "Say each part after me."

Dr. Cruttenden had now completely vanished. The dead shambled over the area of floor where she had recently been standing. Karen stared at the approaching creatures, numb with horror.

Chambers squeezed her clawed fingers tightly to get her attention.

"*Ph'nglui mglw'nafh...*" he said.

Karen shook her head.

"You can say it! Now come on! *Ph'nglui mglw'nafh...*"

Sounds only vaguely approximating what Chambers had said issued from her lips.

"No!" He hated shouting like this, but he was starting to panic as well. "Again! *Ph'nglui mglw'nafh...*"

"*Ph'nglui mglw'nafh...*"

"*... Cthulhu R'lyeh...*"

"*... Cthulhu R'lyeh...*"

"*... wgah'nagl fhtagn.*"

"Say that one again."

Chambers repeated the phrase more slowly. *How had Dr. Cruttenden managed to master the alien language so quickly?* he wondered. Karen repeated it to make sure she had it. Then they began to move away from the shuffling horde to the back of the chamber.

"Now say it again. *Ph'nglui mglw'nafh Cthulhu R'lyeh wgah'nagl fhtagn.*"

Karen repeated the phrase. The words came out without the polish of a practiced scholar or member of the Human Protection League, but they seemed to be working.

"Again!" Chambers shouted. They were up against the wall now, and there was nowhere left for them to go. "Again and again and again!"

The dead were reaching for them both as he felt Karen slip from his side and into nothingness. Chambers babbled the eldritch phrase, mouthing the words as fast as he could without allowing them to lose their clarity. He could feel splintered bone scraping at his skin, the stink of corruption in his nostrils. As he slid down to the floor, preparing himself for an eternity in violent darkness, he hoped that the others would be all right without him.

THIRTY-ONE

CHAMBERS OPENED HIS EYES expecting blackness, which just made the glaring white light all the more shocking.

Where was he?

His eyes were still adjusting, and all he could see was a brightly lit blur. He was lying on another floor. This one was smooth, but more slippery than any surface he had found himself on so far. So frictionless was it, that he tried to get up twice and succeeded in little more than having his heels skid.

He put both palms flat on the ground behind him. It felt like glass. Chambers turned himself over so he was face down and peered at the surface through narrowed eyelids.

It *was* glass, and he felt a moment of sudden vertiginous horror as it dawned on him that the ground beneath the platform on which he was lying had to be several hundred feet below him. At least, that was what he was able to judge from the size of the myriad tiny human forms he could see scattered on the earth far beneath him.

Had they fallen from here?

He tried hard not to panic as he turned carefully onto his back again. How wide was the platform he was on? And how stable? He sat up and, using his right hand to shield his eyes, allowed the world to come into focus.

Under any other circumstances, he would probably have been delighted to be beneath a cornflower blue sky, and it was wonderful to feel sunlight on his face again. It only took him seconds to be reminded of his situation, though, and with a deep breath of the chill but fresh air, he looked around him.

It was a very good thing he hadn't moved too far when he had turned over. He was lying on a sheet of glass approximately ten feet square. There were no barriers or safety guards of any kind, each edge merely meeting with open air.

And the glass itself was almost frictionless.

Chambers took two deep breaths, holding each for as long as possible before exhaling. He had never liked heights, could feel his fear mounting, and was determined not to hyperventilate. If he did, he just might end up dizzy enough to . . .

Don't think about it.

Where were Karen and Dr. Cruttenden? He had no idea how far he could see, but there was no sign of them in the vast blue expanse that seemed to go on forever. Except down.

Perhaps that's where they are? Perhaps Dr. Cruttenden was on here before you, and she fell. Now it's your turn. Once you're gone, Karen will appear and the same thing will happen to her.

You're not helping yourself.

Chambers was tempted to give himself a slap, but the danger of slipping meant he decided against it.

How was he going to get down?

Much as he didn't want to, he turned himself back over and stared at the ground far beneath him. The longer he stared, the more he began to realize that the platform on which he was lying was not suspended in space by some supernatural means. Rather, it stood at the top of an immensely long, narrow staircase, which switched back and forth beneath him. The narrowness of the switchback was the reason he hadn't noticed it before, but if he moved his head from side to side he could just make it out. The steps appeared to be composed of the same glass as the platform, and were almost invisible. Each step was about four feet wide. There was no handrail.

Even if I could get onto that, I'd never be able to reach the ground.

But what was the alternative? Stay up here forever until his muscles seized? The breeze was cool and not uncomfortable, but if he stayed here for hours his muscles would soon begin to stiffen. He could already feel them beginning to ache.

You've got to get going soon, or you'll never get going at all.

Chambers pressed his face against the glass platform and cupped his hands around his eyes. There was the glass staircase, zig-zagging its way up to him, the glass platform sitting on top of it like a birdhouse on an immensely long pole.

But from which side of the platform did the steps lead down?

He gazed hard at the staircase. As far as he could tell it just came straight up—there was no deviation to any particular edge of the glass once it neared the top. Which could only mean one thing.

The way out was directly beneath him.

Chambers moved his right hand from his face to his side, and then slid exploratory fingers beneath his abdomen. It wasn't long before they found a ridge approximately four feet square. The discovery filled him both with hope and with horror. There was a way off this platform, but to open the trapdoor he was going to have to balance on the very edge of the glass.

As he was thinking this, he was eyeing the bodies on the ground far below him. He now had no doubt that they must have been subjected to the same test, and failed.

Either that or, of course, they had been put there to discourage him.

The thought hadn't occurred to him before, but now he remembered that Dr. Cruttenden had said that this would be the Circle of Fraud. Maybe that meant that nothing here was as it seemed. But which was real, and which was fake?

He reached out with his left hand and pulled himself two feet closer to the left side of the platform. The glass felt real enough, and a quick exploration with his fingers confirmed that the edge ended exactly where it appeared to. But was the drop real? Or the bodies? Or the staircase? Should he just get to his feet and step off the glass? Was that how to pass the test and escape this particular realm? Or would that just add his corpse to the ones below who, for all he knew, were the banished dead of this circle, the ones who had not been able to tell the difference between what was false and what was true and had paid the price for it?

The wind picked up, as if to remind him that his time was running out.

Slowly, carefully, and with all the patience he could manage under the circumstances, Chambers used his right arm to push himself farther to the left, all the while feeling for the edge of the glass. The surface was so smooth very little pressure was needed to get him to move. When he was almost at the edge, he stopped and felt the rim of the trapdoor again.

He still wasn't far enough over to open it.

He was close enough to the edge that he only had to crane his neck to be able to see over. With infinite care he moved a little closer.

A little closer still.

A sudden gust of wind caused him to cry out as he gripped the edge of the platform, his fingers white with the exertion. He waited for it to die down and, eventually, it did.

All part of the test.

Those gusts of wind would probably come more frequently the longer he delayed. Something was determined for him to descend, by one means or another.

Chambers pushed himself as close to the edge as he was able, and then felt for a means of opening the exit.

Nothing. Not a switch, or a handle, or a button. Apart from the rim suggesting a door was there, the exit may as well have been invisible.

Holding onto the platform edge with his left hand, he began to press the outlined square, hoping that at some point it would give, or tip, or spring open.

Still nothing.

Another gust of wind, harder and stronger and coming this time from the opposite direction, tore loose his grip and sent him skidding across to the other side of the platform. Scrabbling at the glass, the fingers of

Chambers's left hand dug into the groove of the trapdoor while his right hand gripped the opposite edge of the platform.

And felt a switch.

He doubted that last gust of wind had been intended to help him, but on the other hand it would not surprise him to learn he was being toyed with. Which led to a new question.

If he pressed the switch would it open the door, or cause something worse to happen? Perhaps the entire platform would tilt, causing him to slide to his death. Or flip up, catapulting him into the void.

Stop thinking like that.

Besides, he thought, it was the only thing he had found that could open the door.

Press the button.

Chambers reached beneath the platform, his index finger hovering over the switch. Far below he could see the tiny bodies of those who had failed. Had the same thing happened to them? Had they found this switch and pressed it?

This place is making you indecisive. Get on with it.

It was true. Normally he wouldn't be dithering like this. His life, possibly his soul, hung in the balance, but he had been in worse situations than this.

He pushed the button.

There was a click as the trapdoor swung downward. Chambers peered over the rim of the open doorway to see the top of the glass staircase six feet below him. Because it was almost perfectly transparent, he could see that pushing the button had caused something else to happen below him as well.

Far beneath him, the previously prostrate bodies of the fallen were beginning to rise.

Chambers cupped his hands around his face to cut out the glare once more. It was still difficult to see exactly what was happening way down there, but the figures were definitely moving now. Slowly, sluggishly, once they were on their feet they moved aimlessly for a short while. Then, as if they had suddenly managed to get their bearings, they all began to stagger toward the same place.

The staircase.

All of his horror and panic now turned to dread. That switch hadn't been intended to give him access to freedom, it had been intended to give the dead access to *him*.

He could see them clustered at the bottom of the staircase, like flies around a rotting carcass. It was difficult to tell if they were coming up, or if a similar barrier to the trapdoor existed at the bottom and was yet to be opened by his blundering.

He was wondering what to do when another savage gust of wind caused him to lose his grip and blew him toward the opened trapdoor. His flailing fingers failed to save him and, before he knew it, he was through and on the top step of the staircase. It was farther away from the platform than he had estimated, and now, standing with his arms raised, he knew there was no way he was going to be able to get back up there.

Which only left him one option.

Of course he could stay where he was, but he reasoned that the nearer he got to the ground, the less his chances would be of being killed when he finally jumped to avoid the creatures that were coming for him. He looked down, banishing his vertigo to a part of his brain where it could scream all it wanted—he couldn't afford to let it take control of him now. The cluster of shapes seemed to have narrowed, and he knew that could only mean one thing.

They were coming up the staircase.

Time to get moving.

The steps were farther from the platform, and they were also narrower. Therefore, Chambers's first act was to sit down. He hadn't descended steps like this since he was a child, but it would be much safer, especially if the wind picked up again.

Which it did just then.

He held onto the sides of the top step as the gust buffeted him, gritting his teeth and wondering what else this realm had waiting for him.

The wind lasted longer this time, and he was sure it was more ferocious. When it finally died down, he slid himself onto the next step down, then the next, and then the next.

So far, so good.

He was five steps down when they turned to ice.

At first Chambers thought it was an effect of the wind, which had become more chill with every blast. When he next lifted his left hand, however, he found the palm was stuck to the frosty surface and he had to force it. When he looked at it again, the skin was wet.

The seat of his trousers was wet through too.

He slid down two more steps, and looked back to see that the step he had been on had almost melted to nothing. A dripping hole in its center gaped into nothingness.

Someone's very keen for me to keep moving.

The figures below him were closer now. Chambers wondered how they were coping with the ice and wind before realizing there were probably no such problems down there. In fact, every attempt was probably being made to speed up their ascent.

Are you sure this isn't the Circle of Paranoia?

He still couldn't be sure what was fake and what was real. Perhaps the steps melting was a sign that they didn't really exist. For a moment he was tempted to launch himself into space, but somehow he knew that was the kind of action that would keep him here forever.

There was nothing to do but to keep on going down.

The faster Chambers moved, the faster the steps dissolved behind him. Soon he had no option but to get to his feet and start running. Even then he could feel the water forming beneath his feet. The figures were much closer now, and he could begin to make out details. Each one looked the same—dressed in rags and limping. But the most shocking and obvious thing about them was their blackened appearance, as if they had just emerged from a coal mine or stoking a ship's boiler.

Or as if they had been horribly burned.

As he got closer, Chambers could see the discoloration of their skin was not because of fire, but because of age. The creatures making their way up the steps were immeasurably old, and their skin had mummified to the point of becoming charcoal.

He was twenty feet from the ground when he decided to jump.

The creatures were much closer, of course, which was the reason he felt it was time to take his chances. It was impossible to make out how soft the ground was, but he figured breaking every bone in his body would be preferable to the bony embrace of the things that were coming for him.

That were now ten steps away from him.

He took a deep breath. Behind him, the last of the ice steps melted and crumpled in on itself. It wouldn't be long before the step he was on would go the same way.

Time to fly.

Chambers was well aware of documented examples of people suddenly finding themselves able to do the impossible. Feats of strength, or courage, of which they would never have thought themselves capable. Leaping a wall to escape danger, running faster than they ever had done to save someone from an oncoming car, withstanding pain that would usually render them helpless.

He also knew that there are the times when minds and bodies fail, when it is suddenly impossible to do what has to be done. When one freezes in panic, unable to do anything but look on helplessly when the few seconds of opportunity available should be snatched and acted upon.

Chambers couldn't move.

The cursed souls of the Circle of Fraud were almost upon him and he needed to jump, but he couldn't. His legs refused to do what his brain was telling them. He could feel the step he was on melting beneath his feet, and still his limbs refused to move.

The creatures were five steps away.

Jump.

Four steps away.

For God's sake what's wrong with you?

Three steps.

Jump!

Two steps.

Now!

One.

Chambers closed his eyes and waited for his flesh to be eaten, his soul to be drained from his body, his eyes plucked from his skull to be used as playthings.

Instead, he felt a gentle hand shaking his left shoulder. He opened his eyes to see a familiar face.

"Karen?" He could scarcely believe the eyes that by now ought to have been torn from his head by the creatures that had been approaching him. Creatures that he could no longer see.

He was no longer sitting on a melting staircase either. Instead he was in a cave, sitting on a hard-packed earthen floor. He couldn't make out the source of the orange glow that lit the place. But that didn't matter. The creatures were gone, the steps were gone, the dizzy height was gone. It was possible that this was the ground that he had been so afraid of hitting with force but, even if it was, that didn't matter now. He went with his instincts and gave Karen the biggest hug he could.

"Am I dreaming?"

"No." The voice came from behind the woman crouching before him, and it was instantly recognizable. "Unless, of course, you'd like to consider everything we have experienced so far as a dream."

Chambers gave Karen a relieved smile and then looked over her shoulder at Dr. Cruttenden. "Was I dreaming before, then?"

"No, you were being tested, just as Karen and I have been tested."

"You have?" He looked at Karen, who shook her head in a way that told him she didn't want him to ask.

"We are in the Circle of Fraud," the lecturer continued. "I presume you were encouraged to do something that would endanger your life? Something reckless that, if the circumstances were real, would have led to your death?"

Chambers nodded.

"Well done for resisting. I don't know what it was you had to do, and to be honest I don't want to. Just know that if you had failed, we wouldn't be here talking to you now."

Chambers looked around him. "Where exactly is *here*?"

"We're hoping it's the way out," Karen said as she got to her feet and extended Chambers a helping hand.

He dusted himself down and gave her a curious look.

"Is something the matter?"

No, he thought, *not exactly*. He looked her up and down. "The words." He was still trying to work out what exactly he was thinking of. "You got them right."

Karen looked bewildered. "I don't remember saying any words. Should I?"

Yes, he thought, *and there was something else I wanted to ask*, but he couldn't quite recall what it was.

"Memories of the circle before this one." Dr. Cruttenden still seemed to have all the answers. "And best not thought about. I'd suggest you forget all about it and concentrate on going forward. We only have one more circle to go, and the exit is that way."

She was pointing into the darkness of a narrow passageway ahead.

"What happens then?" Karen asked.

It was obvious from Dr. Cruttenden's face that she didn't know.

"Perhaps that's when we get a reprieve and are sent back to All Hallows," said Chambers. "I never thought I'd say it, but I'm starting to miss the place."

"Even with the things we left behind there?"

Karen had a point.

"Somehow they don't seem quite as scary after everything we've faced here," he replied.

"We haven't faced everything yet," said Dr. Cruttenden. "I very much suspect the worst is yet to come."

She began to lead the way, as Karen called after her. "What is the Ninth Circle again?"

Dr. Cruttenden's answer echoed around the chamber as they made their way toward the glowing portal that had appeared.

"Treachery."

THIRTY-TWO

AFTER EVERYTHING HE HAD already been through, Chambers dreaded to imagine what the Circle of Treachery might look like. Perhaps a room filled with people talking behind each others' backs, he thought, or (God forbid!) another torture chamber, one where you had to deceive your way out of being a victim only to end up as one of the torturers.

What he wasn't expecting was a narrow corridor.

The floor was tiled with linoleum that was scratched and gray, and the walls paneled in a dusty, scabrous oak that reached as high as Chambers could see. Ahead of him, the corridor seemed to end abruptly.

"Where are we supposed to go after that, I wonder?"

"I very much suspect all will be made clear," said Dr. Cruttenden from behind both him and Karen.

She was right. Instead of ending, the corridor took an abrupt right-hand turn, ending in a heavy oak door. It was reinforced with rusting iron rails, and the wood itself bore the weary traumas of what looked like kicks and scratches to its stoical frame.

"Seems as if people were eager to get through this." Karen was looking over Chambers's shoulder.

His face was grim. "Perhaps they were being chased by something that hasn't caught up with us, yet." He gave the door an experimental push. It refused to yield. "There's no handle," he noted. "Do you think we have to say the password?"

"Well, if we do, you'd better hurry up and work out what it is." Karen was looking behind her.

"Why?" Chambers was banging on the door now, despite the evidence that this was unlikely to prove successful.

"Because the corridor walls are closing together." Dr. Cruttenden pushed her way to the front. "If there's a password it's probably here somewhere, just not in plain sight."

While she searched, Chambers looked behind him. The paneled walls had taken on an elastic, almost fluid consistency, and were now coming together toward them. It would only be a matter of minutes before they were crushed.

"You'd better hurry, doctor."

"I am aware of that." Dr. Cruttenden was crouched down low, passing her fingers over something carved into the wood. "No, that's not it," she mumbled to herself. Then, to the others, "I think I'm going to need some help here."

"What kind of help?" The corridor was barely four feet long now, and both Karen and Chambers were in danger of crushing Dr. Cruttenden before the walls did.

"If you could both place your palms flat on the door as I'm doing. It may be that one is only admitted if one is worthy."

Worthy of treachery? It didn't make any sense to Chambers, but at this point he wasn't going to argue. He reached over Dr. Cruttenden's head and put both hands flat on the damp-feeling wood. To his right, Karen did the same.

Nothing.

"It's not working." Karen pressed harder, as if that would help.

"We have to give it time."

"That's the one thing we don't have," said Chambers as, with a creak, he felt the wall on the left begin to crush his shoulder. Although the wood had become elastic, the pressure it was exerting was enormous, and it was all he could do to keep his hands firmly on the door. As the walls came together and they began to struggle for breath, the door also began to take on the same elastic qualities.

"That's it." Dr. Cruttenden's voice was more of a strangled croak. "Push now! As hard as you can!"

It was nearly impossible in such a confined space, but they did their best. Chambers could feel the now-spongy consistency of the door giving way beneath his fingers at the same time as he was being squeezed by the vast, heaving bulk of the corridor either side of him. He took a deep breath, knowing that it would probably be his last, and thrust himself forward.

For a split second, he felt crushing, stifling agony. Then there was the sudden blessed feeling of release as he fell forward onto a rough wooden floor, palms stinging as they came down hard on the unyielding surface. Once he had regained his breath, he was somehow unsurprised to discover, when he pushed himself away, that the part of the floor on which he and his companions were now lying was the door they had been pushing against.

Looking around him, Chambers could see that the door was just a single tile in the floor of what had to be the Circle of Treachery. It was only when he got to his feet that he realized the floor was not endless. In fact, there were very well defined boundaries on all four sides, boundaries fashioned from the same scratched wood as the floor. The room was poorly lit, and Chambers got a sense of weariness from this huge chamber, paneled in ancient oak and tired of absorbing the pitiful cries of those who had been condemned within its walls; sentenced to ensure they would never again commit the sordid atrocities for which they were being punished.

Because Chambers, Karen, and Dr. Cruttenden appeared to be standing in the center of an enormous and ancient courtroom.

To their left, in a crumbling jury box, sat twelve blackened and mummified corpses, lifeless now but no doubt once a verdict was required they would become charged with chattering life. In front of them sat a wizened stenographer, curly black hair framing a face that was little more than a skull over which parchment-like skin had been stretched. A few teeth still remained in the sockets of the grinning jaw, and the thing clicked them together with obvious glee at the arrival of the new defendants. The stenographer's bony fingertips were welded to the keys of the machine in front of it. As if to emphasize the permanence of the stenographer's position, heavy, ribbed wires from either side of the stenotype's casing extended to the creature's skull, where they appeared to be fused to the bone. Every time it turned its neck, the mechanism creaked with the sound of something that had lasted for centuries without lubrication.

The stenographer, however, was nowhere near as terrifying as the judge.

The immense and ancient creature that presided over this courtroom of the damned had sat in its sagging leather chair for so long it had become one with it, its cynical, world-weary flesh presumably having fused with the dead animal skin with which it had remained in contact for so long. Its heavy, scarlet robes were faded and worn with use, and the head that emerged from the fraying neckpiece was so large, and the eyes so small, that for a moment Chambers was unsure if it actually possessed any at all. The mouth, on the other hand, was so wide that when the blackened lips parted a set of uneven peg-like teeth were revealed, each as rotten and riddled with infection as its neighbor. Huge, fleshy jowls the color of beetroot hung from the tiny eye sockets, and ears the color of old newspaper bracketed a monstrous skull crowned with wisps of black, greasy hair among which crawled beetles and other invertebrates.

The judge spoke with a voice that sounded like a worn-out foghorn on a windy night. "The condemned shall step forward."

The condemned bloody well isn't going to, Chambers thought, knowing full well to whom the judge was referring. However, it soon became apparent that he didn't have a choice, as he felt his legs move of their own accord, and his feet each take one involuntary step toward the bench. He was unable to resist, and unable to move either. He couldn't even turn his neck, but he was sure he could sense Karen to his left and Dr. Cruttenden behind him.

"How do you plead?"

It was unlikely to make any difference what he said, and so Chambers opened his mouth with the intention of launching into a vitriolic rant. To his surprise, all that emerged from his lips were two words.

"Not guilty."

"And you?" The judge-thing was looking at Karen now. She seemed to be experiencing the same paralysis, if the croaking words that emerged from her dry-sounding throat were anything to go by.

"Not . . . guilty."

The stenographer clicked its teeth as if in acknowledgement of their pleas and began to type.

"And you?"

The judge was looking over their heads now, presumably asking for Dr. Cruttenden's plea. Chambers expected similar forced words from the woman behind him, and so he was surprised when a voice quite unlike her own gave its reply.

"Guilty."

Chambers watched, helpless and rooted to the spot, as Dr. Cruttenden brushed his right shoulder as she walked around to face them. What was happening here?

"But you two should have realized that by now. At least, I should hope you would have, otherwise I've seriously underestimated you."

Underestimated us? Chambers wanted to say it, but couldn't get the words out.

"These are the ones?" Spittle sprayed from the judge's lips and landed perilously close to them.

Dr. Cruttenden nodded. "They are."

"And you intend to take them below?"

Another nod. "I do."

The judge-thing raised its right arm, allowing Chambers to see that it ended not in pudgy, rotting fingers, but an iron gavel. When it hit the sounding block, the resonance of the deep booming sound produced was deafening.

"I therefore proclaim that you be taken from this place to another place, where you will face the Sea of Darkness, and all therein that may be explored."

There was a rumble from beneath their feet. As suddenly as it had arrived, the paralysis lifted and they were free to move. But there was nowhere to go.

Chambers rubbed his throat and looked at the lecturer. "What on earth are you talking about, Dr. Cruttenden? You're with us. You always have been."

The old woman shook her head. "No," she said, her voice normal once more. "I'm afraid I haven't. I was offered a glimpse of the ultimate, and at my age you just can't say no to such an opportunity."

Karen was shaking her head. "It must be something in this circle possessing her," she hissed to Chambers.

"That's closer to the truth." Dr. Cruttenden's voice had resumed its unnatural, over-confident tone. "But the process has been going on for far longer than you realize, and I'm sorry. There was nothing I could do."

"I still can't believe it." Karen had tears in her eyes. "You've been so nice, so helpful."

"Of course I have," came the reply. "I dared not give you any reason to suspect me, and I had to get you here safely, didn't I? Otherwise the entire exercise would have been pointless."

Silence descended on the courtroom. Eventually Chambers pointed at the woman whom he had thought was their colleague.

"What about her?" he asked the judge. "You haven't sentenced her."

The chortling that came from deep within the judge-thing's flaccid throat was reminiscent of an especially self-satisfied and very ancient toad. "Oh I have," the thing said. "Many, many times, and many years ago."

"And now you're coming with me." Dr. Cruttenden's normal voice had returned once more, and she seemed more like her old self again. But something of the person who had given the plea still remained in the eyes, which were like ice, and the posture, which was far more confident now, like someone who knows they have won the prize even though the result has yet to be announced.

"But . . . you said you were guilty." Karen was getting used to being able to speak again. "Don't you have to stay here?"

Dr. Cruttenden looked around her, and then smiled in a way that wasn't like the woman they knew at all. "I *have* stayed here, my dear. Here, and every other circle we've visited on our little trip. I just thought it would be most appropriate for you to find out here. Besides, I could hardly lie considering where we are, could I?"

"The Circle of Treachery." The rumbling was getting louder now, and the room was beginning to shake. Chambers was having trouble keeping steady. "But you still haven't told us *why*."

"And I'm not going to," came the reply as cracks began to appear in the wooden walls of the chamber. "Not just yet. However, I do think it's time I cast off this rather uncomfortable appearance."

With that, the woman before them began to change. The transformation was at once fluid and yet jarring, sinuous and yet utterly awkward. Both flesh and clothing metamorphosed simultaneously as the figure both Chambers and Karen had thought they knew so well increased in height. Chambers was beginning to feel dizzy watching it, and closed his eyes to combat the nausea.

By the time he opened them again, someone new was standing before them, someone entirely different. A robust-looking man, whose silver-gray hair and lived-in face suggested him to be in his early sixties. The faded period costume he wore indicated either fancy dress or that he had been plucked from the eighteenth century.

"Thomas Moreby," he said, with an unpleasant grin and a small bow. His voice sounded strong, and yet the way he spoke suggested the world-weary experience of centuries. "I would add at 'your service,' but that is not the case. Not the case at all."

Chambers found himself lost for words. Karen, also speechless, was blinking away her disbelief as the figure before them spoke again.

"Time for us all to be going, I think."

The stenographer was still typing as dust began to rain down from the ceiling. The jury, motionless until now, was finally starting to rouse. Clad in tattered rags, parts of their faces crumbling to reveal bare bone beneath as they struggled to stand, the twelve members of the jury began to make their tottering way toward the center of the courtroom, where a black circle had appeared and was now expanding as the chamber around them began to fall. It was ten feet across by the time the first of the treachery undead reached it and began to descend by means of the spiral staircase that had appeared within its depths.

"After you," said Thomas Moreby.

"I'm guessing it's not the way out." Chambers knew they had no choice—it was take that exit, or be crushed and end up staying in the Circle of Treachery forever.

"It is most certainly the way out for me," came the sardonic reply. "And possibly for you, too, although probably not in the way that you might imagine." A chunk of masonry fell from somewhere high above and scoured the floor. "Come along," he continued jovially, "time for all good boys and girls to do as they are told."

"Where are we going?" Karen said, as she dodged a crack that had appeared in the floor while she looked out for more falling masonry.

"Did you not hear the judge?" They looked at the bench, but the creature that had been presiding over them had vanished. "We are descending to the final level, the very bottom of this magnificent construct that has been fashioned over the centuries by theory, and belief, and devotion. The very Pit of Hell itself, if you like."

Moreby gestured toward the staircase. The very last of the undead were now making their way down. "Now it is your turn," he said pleasantly. "And please do not worry, I shall be right behind you, as I have been all the way. And you will have all your answers once we are there— all the answers you could ever wish for, and much more besides. Come. It is time for you to face the Sea of Darkness."

THIRTY-THREE

THERE WAS A BREEZE blowing.

It brought nothing pleasant with it, however. No sense of refreshment, no cleansing of the senses. No, the fetid air that plucked at clothes and wormed its way through hair carried only the scent of death and decay; a grim, musty odor that dried the back of the throat and clogged the nostrils with gray dust. So thick was it that Chambers found himself repeatedly coughing to try and clear his throat.

The dusty plain on which the three of them were standing undulated gently, like the sand dunes of a desert, or the lifeless landscape of a barren planet too far from a star for it to receive sufficient sunshine, but not so distant that it was forced to exist in complete darkness. Like the land and the wind, the light, too, seemed to be constantly at the point of death. The sky was bruised with a kind of lifeless maroon hue that appeared to be aching inexorably for darkness, but which had been forced to continue existing as perpetual dusk.

Above the far distant horizon, where purple twilight met lifeless land, something blurred and obscured by the dust seemed to be hanging in the air, Lord of all it surveyed. Chambers tried not to look, but he couldn't help himself.

It had been difficult to see how many stone steps had led down away from the courtroom and, as they had descended, so they had been enveloped with a soft blackness, their feet guided from step to step by forces beyond their volunteering. Karen had gone first, followed by Chambers, with Moreby close behind.

As soon as they had entered the Sea of Darkness, the steps had vanished. Chambers was still looking around him, wondering where they had gone, when Karen asked, "What have you done to Dr. Cruttenden?"

Moreby gave her a vulpine grin, but said nothing.

"Well?"

It was a while before he answered her, and when he did his voice was almost charming.

"That all depends, my dear."

"Depends?" Karen was looking around her now as well. "Depends on what?"

"On whether you truly believe Dr. Cruttenden ever existed. Or any of them, for that matter."

"Any of whom?"

Moreby pretended to look shocked. "Why, the colleagues with whom you entered All Hallows Church, of course, Miss Shepworth. That motley collection of experts, ne'er-do-wells, and dabblers put together by your charming self and your less-than-charming gazette for the purpose of investigating the strange occurrences within the building in question."

Karen opened her mouth.

"Before you utter anything else," he held up his palm, "please do not for one moment consider that you, yourself, are actually the reason why you are here. Your coming to this place—and yours, too, Professor Chambers—has been long in the planning, and it would be unfair of me to allow you to apportion any of the blame to either of yourselves for what is about to happen."

Chambers narrowed his eyes. "And what *is* about to happen, Mr. Moreby? And who, in actual fact, are you?"

The figure took a step back, and spread his arms wide. "You do not recognize me then? After all your research? All your reading up about All Hallows and the events that took place upon that site before the building was but a few scratches of charcoal from the fevered imagination of a beleaguered architect?" The figure tapped his temple with an index finger, the nail of which was chipped and engrained with dirt. "Ah, but then Dr. Cruttenden was the historian, was she not? Or at least, so you were led to believe. Why should you have worried about the history of that place, when you had her to do all the thinking for you?"

"You talk a lot about our lost colleague, but you seem reluctant to reveal anything about yourself." Chambers knew he was taking a risk by baiting the man standing in front of them.

"Myself?" Chambers certainly seemed to have ruffled his feathers. The man drew himself up to his full height and took a deep breath. "My name, my dear sir, madam, is Thomas Moreby. Records state that I was born in the year of your Lord seventeen hundred and two. I say 'your Lord,' because that deity that so many seem to profess faith in and a loyalty to never did anything for me, and most certainly is not mine. But more of that in a moment. I died in . . ." There was little humor in his smile. He spread his hands. "The date of my so-called death is not important. As you can surmise for yourselves, I am still here to conduct myself in a manner appropriate to my breeding and standing as a gentleman."

"Oh, you mean *the* Thomas Moreby?"

The figure glared at Chambers. "Be careful what you say, sir. I have been a long time down here, and poor attempts at wit are the thing I am apt to tire of the quickest."

Chambers pressed on regardless. "I mean Thomas Moreby, the man who was an apprentice of Nicholas Hawksmoor, who oversaw the construction of the crypt and undercroft for All Hallows?"

"And so much more, allow me to assure you." Moreby seemed to appreciate being recognized. "During my existence, I have been the architect not just of buildings, but of plans to conquer death itself, plans of which both you and the lovely Miss Shepworth here are an important part."

Karen flinched at that.

"Ah, but pray forgive me—where are my manners?" Moreby bent down and gathered a handful of dust. Straightening, he held the powder out before him on a flattened palm and blew on it, creating a whirlwind of gray between himself and the two of them. "Before we do anything else, perhaps I should reacquaint you with your friends. You remember the good Father Michael Traynor?"

We hardly had time to get to know each other, thought Chambers, as the figure of the priest emerged from the depths of what Moreby had created.

"Father Traynor was assigned the task of disposing of any evidence within All Hallows that might incriminate the Holy Mother Church, were it to be discovered by any of you. Of course, no such items existed, at least not anymore, but it amuses me to think they were still worried enough to send him—someone whom they did not mind sacrificing, should the powers they believed to exist within the building turn out to reside there still."

Father Traynor had remained motionless throughout Moreby's speech, a gray-faced automaton unaffected by the procession of mummified and rotting figures that had begun to pass him on either side, walking away from where they were standing and heading in two columns toward the horizon. Chambers hadn't noticed them before but now, as the creatures shuffled by, he realized he recognized them.

They were the residents of each of the Circles of Hell.

They had become mixed in with one another, it was true, but nevertheless it was easy to make out those who had belonged to the Circles of Violence, and Heresy, and Greed, and Lust, and all the others—all those who had been damned, cursed to their fate, imprisoned in the corner of Hell that had been especially reserved for them.

But imprisoned no longer.

"He does not notice them." Moreby's voice cut through the noise of the swirling dust storms. "And neither does your other colleague, the False Scientist."

Now it was Peter Chesney's turn to emerge from the dust. As expressionless as Traynor, he stood beside him, staring silently at the lifeless ground before him.

"He came to All Hallows expecting vindication for his life of deceit—both of others and himself. He was even easier to attract into this realm than Traynor which, of course, is why I took him once I had acquired the inexperienced little priest. The world above is full of both of them—the one who feels he can do good because he has no real knowledge of the evil that man is capable of, and the other who believes he can pull the wool over the eyes of all, to the extent that in time even he will begin to believe his own lies. Suffice to say, both represent the very things that this realm thrives on."

The stream of figures passing them was now becoming a river of the dead and the damned, ever-increasing, all marching toward the horizon with the same purposeful intent.

"Where do we fit into all this?" It was a reasonable question, even if Chambers didn't imagine he was going to like the answer.

Moreby's smile held little humor in it. "You two are perhaps the most important element of all. To pass through the Nine Gates of Hell is a remarkable feat indeed, and one that could only be achieved by individuals such as yourselves."

That wasn't an answer.

"What do you mean?"

"I needed you. Both of you. Two interconnected, yet uncorrupted souls who could pass through the Nine Circles, thus opening the Nine Gates so that the undead of each circle might pass freely between them." Moreby's gaze became more intense. "You do understand that, do you not? This was the secret that Verney finally imparted to me upon his deathbed in the madhouse. Your passing has released all those damned souls who were trapped in their individual corners of Hell. Now they are free to roam between the levels, and enter this Sea of Darkness. And from here to return. Return to *your* world . . ."

The significance of this last remark was not lost on Chambers. He was about to speak, but Karen interrupted him.

"Where's Paul Hale?"

Moreby's smile broadened. "As every religion must have its figurehead, so too it must have its sacrifice. Mr. Hale, an innocent destined for a glory even greater than yours, was chosen by the Almighty to take on His aspect and give Him form in this realm."

"You mean . . ." Chambers could barely bring himself to say it, as Moreby nodded savagely.

"Behold . . . the Anarch!"

The dust was clearing now, and the thing that hovered over the horizon became terrifyingly, overwhelmingly clear. It was the image of the creature they had seen on the wall of the church. A huge, flea-like monstrosity, with a segmented body whose myriad bristles shone with an unearthly light. From its lower end, an awkward tripod-like arrangement of jointed limbs emerged, although they did not make contact with the ground. Two huge compound eyes gazed over the realm that belonged to it, while vicious-looking mandibles clacked together in glee and frond-like antennae waved as if beckoning to the ragged hordes that swarmed toward it.

Karen stared at the thing in horror, open-mouthed.

"And that . . . that was Paul?" She could barely croak the words.

"Only at the very beginning," Moreby explained. "Once the essence of the Anarch had filled his body, there was nothing left of the individual you knew, only the supreme might of the God that you see before you now."

"Your God." He had been slow on the uptake, but Chambers understood that now. He tried to keep the tremor out of his voice as he beheld the monstrous leviathan. "Your Almighty. But not ours."

"*No!*" Moreby spat the word at him. "Not yours. A secret and ancient god, one of a mighty pantheon known only to those few who have sought the sacred knowledge; have journeyed far to places where only the bravest and the most foolhardy would dare to ever venture; have lived and died and lived again so that they might continue their studies, and enter into that most vital of pacts with the Ancient Ones capable of bestowing upon them that which they most desired."

Chambers shielded his eyes from the insect god. "You talk as if you yourself have lived many lives."

"Indeed I have!" Moreby seemed more than happy to discuss the matter with them. "Tell me, why was it that you both decided to embark upon an investigation of All Hallows Church?"

Karen and Chambers looked at each other.

"Because of the scrolls," Karen said eventually.

"What scrolls do you speak of?"

"The ones that were found, sealed in the clay pots."

"Ones that just happened to tell a story, by any perchance? A story that foretold of things to come?"

Chambers shook his head. This was just too incredible. Then he checked himself. No, after everything they had been through, nothing was too incredible anymore.

"You're not trying to tell us that . . ."

Moreby nodded. "It took many centuries of work to achieve the goal of lifetimes. Naturally, I had to assume the persona of many different individuals to achieve it. 'Geoffrey Chaucer' was but one of these, and in thus guise I was able to lay the foundations of a plan that is soon to bear fruition."

"Remember what Dr. Cruttenden told us about Chaucer?" Karen was squeezing Chambers's arm. "About how he went on a mysterious sea voyage in 1377? And then disappeared from the historical register altogether in 1400?" She glared at Moreby. "Where's Dr. Cruttenden now? What have you done with her?"

Moreby shook his head. "Through her I have guided you to this place. The exertion of one will over another is not without its consequences. I am afraid that by the time we reached the Ninth Circle, there was very little of Dr. Cruttenden left to manipulate." He gave a tiny shrug. "And now there is nothing left at all. She knew it might end like this, but she was willing to give herself up for the knowledge I allowed her, for the insights into aspects of history that none but the dead are party to."

"She died for knowledge?" Even as he said the words, Chambers believed them. Academics wanted for nothing else, and if it came at the cost of their own lives, he knew more than a couple who would be willing to pay that ultimate price.

"But of course." Moreby seemed to find this unremarkable. "I visited her once in Oxford—in fact, I believe you both were there—and then again, later in the church. After that it was an easy matter to both guide her mind and take her soul. You never guessed though, did you?" He smiled at that. "I must admit that she did do a marvelous job of getting you here without either of you suspecting a thing. I would offer her my heartfelt congratulations . . . if there was anything left of her to congratulate."

Suddenly Chambers remembered the question he had wanted to ask Dr. Cruttenden back in the Circle of Fraud. But now he knew the answer. Of course it was Moreby who had been able to speak the alien incantation so perfectly and effect their escape from the Circle of Violence.

"What is this plan? The one that's taken hundreds of years and cost the lives of the people we knew?" The glow from the flea god was increasing now, and Karen was shielding her eyes.

"Not just people you knew." Moreby glanced at the thing hovering on the horizon for a moment. "So many souls over the ages have been sacrificed for this one cause, and the Anarch is only a small part of it."

Chambers licked his lips. "Well, seeing as we're also part of it, and seeing as we're most likely going to die too, you might as well tell us what it is."

"Very well then. You should know what fate has brought you to this place. I followed the directions in the *Liber de Nigra Peregrinatione*." Moreby almost had to shout to be heard over the noise of the mass movement around them now. "I found the legendary city of Chorazin, and its whispered Black Cathedral. And I made a deal with what I found within."

"The Anarch?"

Moreby nodded. "That is not its true name. But no human tongue could pronounce it. An ancient and forgotten god, trapped on a plane beneath Hell and yearning with the desire of eons to return to the world."

"Trapped?" Chambers pointed at the vast insectoid creature. "How could something like that become trapped?"

"It was imprisoned in the Sea of Darkness by the changing beliefs of men and women throughout the ages, as they created layer upon layer of ideas of what it meant to be eternally damned, ideas that were eventually summarized and given form by Dante Alighieri in his *Divina Commedia*."

"There are other belief systems, and many other visions of Hell." Chambers was partly stalling for time, but he also wanted to know. "Was Dante the one who somehow miraculously got it right, then?"

"There are many ways to descend to the Sea of Darkness, but all have Nine Gates to keep those banished here from returning back into the world. In return for opening them, my God has granted me immortality—His gift for a job well done. The distance from the pit of Hell to the civilized world has always been impossibly vast. Now, thanks in part to you two, it is considerably shorter. And it can be bridged."

The first of the denizens of Hell had reached the horizon now, and the air was sparking with blue lightning as energy passed from the image of the Anarch to the tiny figures. As each one was struck, it turned away from the fallen god, and began to return to where they were standing.

"Behold!" Moreby's eyes glinted with the zeal of madness. "The Anarch who is the Servant of God and I who am to be His representative on Earth! With His army of Hell I will bring his gift of chaos to a world that has been too long without it!"

"What do you mean?" Karen's eyes were still fixed on the horizon, at the myriad blue flashes that were now crackling from the immense figure and momentarily encasing the creatures beneath it in the same, blinding light.

"He is imbuing them with His power, the power of the Old Gods." Moreby seemed almost too overwhelmed by what they were witnessing to speak.

"Then what?"

"Then He is sending them back. They will pass through the circles, through the Gates which you have opened, so that they shall ascend through each one until finally . . ."

". . . they reach our world." Chambers's face was grim.

"And chaos shall once more reign over all!"

The returning dead were closer now, moving much faster since they had been filled with the Anarch's power.

Karen gripped Chambers's arm. "We have to stop this!"

"No one can stop it!" Moreby was triumphant. "You opened the gates, now they can pass through! No one can stop the might, the will of the Anarch!"

There was a rumbling behind them. Chambers and Karen turned to see, in the distance, that a broad staircase of spiraling black stone had emerged from the pallid landscape. Puffs of dust fell from it as it rose, higher and higher, until it penetrated the purple sky high above them.

"They are coming!" Moreby pointed at the closest ranks of the dead, then at the staircase. "And soon they will rise again!"

"Not if we stop them first." Chambers grabbed Karen and began to run toward the steps.

Karen pulled him to a halt. "How can we? Dr. Cruttenden said all along that we can't go back."

Chambers shook his head and urged her on. "I don't think Dr. Cruttenden told the truth as often as we thought."

"But how can we close the gates?" Karen asked as she followed him.

"If we opened them, it stands to reason we're the only ones with any chance of being able to close them too. Perhaps passing back through the circles will have the reverse effect."

"It is too late!"

From far behind them, the sounds of Moreby's voice urged them both on. They reached the first step when he shouted again. "You have broken things that cannot be repaired! Not even Verney's constructs will be able to save you now, should you even get that far!"

Karen was following Chambers up the stairs. "What does he mean?"

"I've no idea." Chambers was starting to get dizzy. The higher they went, the more blustery the fetid wind became. "Just keep going."

When they were a hundred feet above the plane of the Sea of Darkness, they both looked down, and both wished they hadn't.

The dead were coming.

Crawling, stumbling, clawing, the denizens of Hell were making their sure and certain way up the staircase, crowding the broad steps to the extent that many fell from the sides. Those who landed in the gray dust below merely dragged themselves back to their feet and began climbing again, no matter how great the distance they had fallen. Chambers was reminded of soldier ants piling over and on top of one another in their single-minded efforts to reach their destination. On the horizon, the unchanged dead were still pouring toward the Anarch to receive their unholy blessing. The god was so immense that even at this height and distance it towered over them.

"Hurry!"

Chambers had begun to slow, but Karen's cry spurred him on. On and on they went, higher and higher, until the ground below them seemed miles away, the Anarch ever-present, dominating the horizon and delivering blue flash after blue flash of energy to the dead still arriving to receive their obscene communion. It was only when the black stone beneath his feet began to blur, and the air through which he was walking began to thicken in a haze of purple cloud, that Chambers knew they were reaching the exit. Before he had time to think anything else, they were out of the Sea of Darkness, and back in the Ninth Circle of Hell.

THIRTY-FOUR

THE COURTROOM WAS DESERTED.

Chambers was not surprised. The jury that had presided over their "hearing" had been the first to descend into the Sea of Darkness. Even the judge-thing had vanished, leaving behind it a vast impression in the worn leather of the chair in which it had been sitting, and marks on the bench where moldering fingers must have gripped the wood in ages past.

"Where is everyone?"

Chambers answered Karen as he searched for the way out. "They went before us, remember? They were the first ones down into that hellish plain of Moreby's."

"I don't mean those. I mean the others, from all the other circles. Surely they have to come through here on their way down to the Sea of Darkness?"

Chambers hadn't thought of that. "There must be other courtrooms like this," he replied. "Perhaps an infinite number of them." He began tapping on the wood paneling of the walls. "One thing's for certain, though," he said with a grimace, "the undead who are coming away from the Anarch, the ones who have received their 'gift,' will likely be coming through here soon, so help me find a way out of here."

Karen joined him in tapping and kicking at the walls and floor. Every now and then she glanced over at the corner of the room near the judge's bench, where the staircase yawned.

"Still no sign of them," she said as Chambers began to give serious consideration to trying to lever the oak boards off whatever wall they must be attached to. "Just a minute. Yes, I think I can hear them coming now."

Chambers searched around for something he could use to tear the wood free, but there was nothing that even remotely resembled a useful tool. Perhaps there was some sort of steel light fixture hanging from the ceiling? He looked up.

And saw the way out.

"Give me a hand with this!" Chambers rushed over to the jury stand and wrenched at the wooden enclosure. It came free easily. With Karen's help, they positioned it under the glowing purple circle that had appeared dead center in the ceiling.

"Hold it steady," Chambers said. "Let me get up there, and then I'll pull you through."

A low moaning was now coming from the staircase.

"Hurry up!" Karen held the enclosure steady as Chambers climbed onto it. He stretched, but still couldn't quite reach the exit.

"I'm going to have to jump," he said.

"Well go on, then!"

Chambers took a deep breath and launched himself at the exit just as the head of the first zombie appeared above the rim of the steps. Arms outstretched, but with his angle misjudged, Chambers missed by inches and fell back. He yelped as the foot of his injured leg landed on the thin rim of scarred wood.

Two zombies had entered the Ninth Circle now, and were shuffling toward them.

"They're almost here!" Karen screamed.

"I know!" Chambers crouched as best he could, and then launched himself into the air once more. This time his fingers met with the lip of the exit. It felt curiously soft, like plunging his fingers into a velvet cushion. He thought he was somehow summoning superhuman strength to pull himself up, until he felt Karen pushing from below. Then he was through and leaning back downward into the Ninth Circle, arms outstretched to grab Karen.

Five of the undead had surrounded her, and she was climbing onto the wooden enclosure just as they began to reach for her.

"Grab my hands!"

She jumped.

She missed his hands by a whisker and fell back to the floor.

There were now more zombies in the room.

Somehow Karen managed to dodge between them and get back to the wooden frame. It was slowly being pushed across the room by the movement of the creatures. She tried to push it back, but the combined force of the undead was too much for her. She climbed on anyway, launching herself at an angle in an attempt to grab at Chambers's flailing hands.

He caught her right wrist just as the enclosure collapsed beneath her.

"Pull me up!"

Chambers was too busy doing just that to reply. As he dragged her through the exit, they could both hear the howls of anguish as the Anarch's undead were deprived of their first human victims. For now, anyway.

They were back in the Circle of Fraud, halfway up Chambers's ice staircase. Karen skidded a little and clung onto him. She looked over the edge to the land far below.

"It'll take them a while to climb that," she said.

"Except that none of this is what it seems. We're in Fraud, remember?" Chambers looked up, then down, then over the side.

"We're going to jump," he said.

"Are you insane? We'll break our necks if we fall that far!"

"We won't fall. To escape from Fraud it's important that you don't go along with it . . . that you don't go the way it wants you to. So the way out of here is neither up nor down, but straight across."

Without another word Chambers grabbed her and pushed them both off the steps. He closed his eyes, expecting to plummet. Instead they toppled over and landed in moist earth.

Bloodstained earth.

The Circle of Violence.

"How do we get out of here?" Karen looked around the arena, now bereft of the violent dead because they, too, were making their way to the

Anarch for their blessing. She looked around at the rusted, bloody instruments. "Do we have to recite that incantation again?"

"We won't need to." Chambers was already making his way toward the exit. "We opened all the gates, remember? Hopefully all we have to do is go back to where we arrived, up on that balcony."

They made their way up the narrow staircase and onto the viewing gallery. There was no one up there either, although the floor was littered with evidence of its previous inhabitants. Scraps of clothing, pieces of gauze, and much, much worse.

"Don't touch any of it." Chambers was stepping gingerly between the debris. "Just in case."

The exit was ten feet away, a ragged hole that had opened up in the dripping stone wall, when the discarded pieces began to move.

"Run!"

Karen jumped and dodged between the fragments as they twitched and writhed their way toward them.

"What are they?"

"Parts large enough to still maintain a fragment of their cursed life, all just as eager to get their blessing, but happy if they can just delay us until the creatures they belong to get here. Now jump to me."

Karen shook a leech-shaped piece of plum-colored flesh from her shoe and leapt toward him. Together they passed through the portal and found themselves in one of the corridors of Heresy.

Chambers pressed a warning finger to his lips.

Karen looked around her. "I can't see anything."

"They might not have gone to the Sea of Darkness like the others. I find it hard to believe false gods would want to pay homage to the Anarch. They could still be in here."

"This place is a maze," Karen hissed. "How are we supposed to find the way out of here?"

"I'm rather counting on us being drawn to it." Chambers knew that was tantamount to crossing his fingers and hoping. He wondered if he should do that as well.

There was a noise from behind them.

"Is that the exit opening or . . ." Karen's eyes widened as the shape rose to its full ten feet in height. There were others behind it.

"Come on," Chambers grabbed her hand. "It has to be around here somewhere."

They moved more quickly now, not bothering to keep quiet. They turned left, only to be confronted by yet more of the creatures.

"Straight on." Chambers wondered how far they would get before all their exits were cut off. They tried turning right at the next crossroads, but a collection of gods and monsters herded them back. There were more creatures straight ahead, and even more back the way they came, which only left one option.

Straight ahead the corridor ended in a wall.

"Isn't this what happened last time we were here?"

Chambers nodded.

"Does that mean we're going to end up back in the Circle of Violence?"

"Possibly." An idea had occurred to him. "Or possibly those things behind us aren't trying to harm us at all. Perhaps they've been showing us the right way to go in the only way they know how."

It was a gamble, but there was nowhere else they could try. As they approached the wall the surface began to shimmer, the paint began to peel and the plaster to fall away. A faint purplish tinge outlined the crumbling brickwork.

"The way out or the way back to Hell?"

Chambers looked at Karen. "Only one way to find out."

She nodded. "And only one way to go anyway. If it's the wrong one, it's been nice knowing you."

Another leap into the unknown brought them out in the Circle of Anger, right where they had left it.

"We have to . . ."

"I know." Karen gave him a wry smile and began to lead the way. "We have to get back to the place where we arrived. I'm getting used to this now."

It wasn't long before they were back on the grassy plain dotted with crosses. There were still a few unfortunates who were either too weak or too decayed to be able to wrench themselves free and make their way to the Sea of Darkness.

"It makes you almost want to help them," Karen said as they watched the pathetic creatures try to pull withered hands free from spikes that had been driven through their mummified skin.

"If we do, it'll just add to the number of the undead who are already after us." Chambers looked behind him. "Still no sign of them, for now."

"Perhaps they couldn't get out of the Circle of Treachery. We found it difficult enough, and we had that jury box to stand on."

"I'm sure they found a way." Chambers was remembering how the undead had piled onto the stone staircase in the Sea of Darkness, climbing over one another like ants. "We're just managing to keep ahead of them, that's all. But we've got to keep going."

They staggered on, the forest of crucifixes thinning until just one or two dotted the landscape, propped in the earth at awkward angles as if they were leering at the man and the woman who stumbled through their domain. Ahead of them, where drifting clouds met anemic grass, stood the portal, a perfect oval of endless night. But getting to it was more difficult than they had at first thought. The faster they ran, the farther away it seemed to drift. Eventually Karen had to stop, coughing and gasping for breath.

"It's no good," she said. "That gate must be miles away, or it keeps moving to ensure we can't reach it. Perhaps this is the place where we were always meant to end up."

Chambers was grateful for the brief rest, but couldn't wait to get going again. "Nonsense," he cried. "We'll get to it. This place hasn't exhausted us yet."

The wind picked up, blustering from behind them and carrying with it such a howl as might come from the creatures that were pursuing them. Karen looked over her shoulder and Chambers followed her gaze. He wished he hadn't.

From the opposite direction, pouring over the hill and breaking down the crucifixes as their relentless mass shambled forward, came thousands of the living dead.

"There's some encouragement for us." Chambers grabbed Karen's hand once more and dragged her forward. "Come on, or it won't just be the end for us, but the entire world as well."

They ran, hearts hammering, temples pounding, throats so dry they felt like sandpaper, until the portal seemed a little larger, and then a little larger still. Every now and then Chambers risked a glance behind, only to see that the passage through Hell's circles seemed to have lent the dead an urgency they had not possessed before. Instead of shambling, they were now moving quickly. A few out in front were actually running.

"Let's hope they can't get through this all at once." Chambers made sure Karen went through the exit and then he followed her.

They both landed at the same time on a familiar street in the Circle of Greed.

"It was a building that was the way out on this level, wasn't it?" Karen was already trying door handles and hammering on the plate glass of windows. "One of the buildings led us in and out of here."

"That's right." It was odd to run down these city streets now they were bereft of their occupants, all gone to receive the Anarch's blessing and then join the living-dead army that was making its way after them. For a moment Chambers thought he could hear the distant rumble of thunder. Then he realized, with horror, that it was the footfalls of a thousand and more undead, all making their way to the place they were standing now, the sound so loud it could be heard through the gates of Hell.

"Found it!" Karen was standing by an open door. Chambers followed her through, only to find himself standing beside her in a dark and narrow corridor.

"Maybe it's higher up." He pointed to the staircase to their left.

"I seem to be spending most of my life climbing stairs." Karen gave him a rueful smile. "So you're probably right."

They began to climb. Time passed, but for once they did not tire, even though the steps seemed to go on for far longer than they should have.

"It would be nice to think someone was looking after us for a change," Karen called to Chambers behind her. "You know, like a God or something."

"It would," Chambers agreed. "But my hopes for that rather got dashed when I saw Father Traynor. I had hoped he might have been fighting on our side, instead of just being another of Moreby's puppets."

"I know what you mean." Karen slowed slightly, but Chambers kept her moving. "I could understand it of Dr. Chesney—I never liked him— but it was as if Father Traynor was lost from the beginning."

"Perhaps he needed to be possessed first for that very reason. Can you see anything yet?"

"It's so dark here, it's all I can do to feel the steps, but yes—I think there's a tiny point of light up ahead."

Five minutes later the point had increased in size to the outline of a closed door. Chambers fully expected it to be locked, but the handle yielded and they found themselves walking out onto the roof of the tallest skyscraper either of them had ever seen.

"Let's hope the way to the next level is around here somewhere." Chambers was already searching, while Karen went to peer over the edge.

"We've got company below," she said.

Chambers joined her and looked over to see, far, far below, streets swarming with the undead.

"They don't seem to know which building to enter, though."

"They will if they see us." He pulled her back from the edge. "Now help me look for the portal."

They both stared at the broad, flat graveled expanse of gray roof.

"If it's here, it's not exactly obvious," Karen observed.

They both looked up, but there was no purple-rimmed oval of jet in the slate-gray sky.

"Maybe we've come up the wrong building?"

God, he hoped not. "That can't be right. Why have a street of fake buildings and then have the only real one lead nowhere?"

Karen shrugged. "Because it would be the punch-line to an especially shitty cosmic joke?"

There was a crash from far below. Chambers glanced over the edge to see the creatures coalescing around the building on which they were currently standing.

"Well, it looks as if we're not the only ones who think this is the way out," he said.

"Perhaps it's invisible?"

Chambers took a step forward, his foot crunching on the gravel as he did so. It was worth a try. He picked up a handful of chippings and flung them straight ahead of him. They landed with a clatter. He flung another handful to his left. The same.

Karen picked up two handfuls and flung them to the right.

The ones that flew over the far corner of the building disappeared.

"You were right!" Chambers clapped her on the shoulder.

There was only one problem.

The gravel chips had flown through the air and off the edge of the building before disappearing. Which meant the exit wasn't on the roof of the building at all.

It was floating in mid-air, just off the corner of it.

"Come on," said Chambers. "We're going to have to . . ."

"Jump?" Karen looked to where he was pointing with weary resignation. "And if we fall?"

"We won't fall. I'll go first if you like."

"And fail to see me plummet to my death?" She pushed him out of the way. "Not bloody likely." With that she ran to the corner of the building and leapt. For a fraction of a second she hovered in mid-air, then her body began to fall. Chambers's heart was in his mouth as, suddenly, she vanished.

Must remember it's a bit lower than I'd expect, he thought as the door to the roof burst open and the first zombies spilled onto the concrete.

Must also remember these things can move much faster now.

In fact, they were almost upon him as Chambers jumped. He felt the dizzying, sickening sensation of falling that continued as he crashed to the floor and landed in a mess of sticky fluids and semi-digested matter.

At first he was struck by the horrifying thought that this was all that was left of Karen after her passage through. Then he remembered he was in the Circle of Gluttony. He tried to get up, but his hands skidded in front of him, causing his elbow to jar against the surface.

"Do you need helping up?"

"They're right behind us," he said as she pulled him to his feet.

An ominous rumble added weight to his words.

"I think the way out's through there."

Chambers followed Karen, passing the broken table and the high window they had used as their way of getting out of here before. But now they needed to go up, not down. They passed through rooms filled with the remnants of huge meals, the constituents of which were already reforming so the meals could be gorged upon once more.

"Through there!" Karen pointed to an arched doorway, beyond which lay another grand banquet hall.

With a portal at the far end.

They entered the hall just as the first of the undead emerged from the Circle of Greed. Then another came, and another.

"What are you doing?"

They were right by the portal when Karen ran to the banquet table. It was recharged and replete, and a full meal stood waiting for the damned of this level who would now never eat it. Karen selected the largest cake and, hefting it expertly, flung it at the first zombie that came through the doorway.

"I've just always wanted to do that," she said as she followed Chambers through the exit. "I saw it in a movie once."

The portal changed as they passed through it, constricting and squeezing them with its newly fleshy and muscular walls.

"What the hell's going on?" Karen gasped.

"It's the Circle of Lust next, remember? I'd be surprised if the things that live here have managed to leave."

They hadn't.

Karen and Chambers picked their way across the flesh-strewn land-scape. As they did, the creatures that had pursued them before began to be aroused, melding and shaping themselves into things capable of chasing them.

"Why haven't these gone to the Sea of Darkness?" Karen jumped and skipped to avoid the creatures plucking at her heels.

Chambers had no idea. "Perhaps they're not as aware as the residents of the other circles. I mean, have you seen anything around here with a brain?"

"True." Karen pulled her calf free from a grasping hand attached to a thrusting leg that was propelling itself along by bending at the knee. "I suppose it's the part of the body lust would discard first." She kicked at the thing, which kept grabbing at her with dogged persistence. "Do you think they'll do this to what we're being chased by?"

Chambers stamped on the thing's arm to pin it down, then pulled the fingers free one by one. He picked the arm up and flung it into the mass of flesh behind them. "Let's hope so," he said. "It might buy us some time."

The portal was up ahead, a welcoming patch of darkness amid all the urgent flesh-colored writhing.

"Why is it so easy now for us to find these?" Karen was voicing what Chambers had been wondering for some time.

"I'm beginning to wonder if it's us," he said as they approached the exit. "We opened the gates, perhaps we have some sort of affinity for them. This place isn't exactly logical. The landscape is elastic and reality is fluid—if you can call it reality. These doors could occur anywhere—ten feet or a million miles away. I think the reason we're finding them is because we're meant to."

"You mean something's helping us leave?"

Chambers nodded. "But not in the way you think. I don't imagine it's our best interests that are being indulged here. What matters is not that we get back to All Hallows Church; what matters is that we lead all those things back there."

Karen's eyes widened. "Should we stop?"

No, that wasn't the answer. "For all we know, the gates will be just as easy for the undead to find with or without us. We have to keep going, not because we opened them, but because we may be the only people who can close them again."

"We don't seem to have been doing a very good job so far." Karen pointed over Chambers's shoulder. "Here they come!"

The damned of nine Circles of Hell came pouring through the portal at the opposite end of the chamber they were in. As Chambers had predicted, the lust zombies, already aroused by the passing of him and Karen, immediately latched onto their new guests. However, as soon as they sensed that the flesh they were touching was dead, that the limbs they were stroking were home only to necrotic tissue, the lusting flesh zombies fell away, uninterested. Instead, they joined with the forward-moving mass, adding yet another misshapen element to the army of darkness.

"Thank God we're nearly there." Chambers levered himself over a final mound of pulsing flesh and into the portal, noting with relief how the texture of the tunnel he found himself crawling through quickly changed from taut muscle to cold, lifeless rock. Before long he was able to get to his feet, and soon he and Karen were ascending another spiral stone staircase, with the suggestion of light above them.

Chambers's first impression was that Limbo had not changed. Then he turned to look at the sky behind him, and saw the faint but definite impression of the Anarch hovering high above them both.

"His influence is spreading." Chambers pushed Karen toward the nearest opening in the sheer cliff ahead of them. As they passed by, creatures began to emerge from the stone floor, ossified monsters more rock than human. However, they moved as if they were weighed down by little more than bags of sand.

"How do you know this is the way out?" Karen said as she stumbled into the corridor ahead of Chambers, and avoided the things that were emerging from the stone walls.

"I don't," came the reply. "But I figured we wouldn't have a chance if we tried anywhere else."

An arm emerged from the wall in front of him. As Chambers watched, the fingers fused into a point and the forearm streamlined itself into a spike. Before any more of the figure could emerge, he grabbed the arm and pulled on it with all his force. The limb came away at the elbow with a sickening crack.

"My God, what did you do that for?" Karen was looking at him in horror.

"I didn't fancy it swiping at us with this," he said, brandishing it before him. "Besides, for the first time since we arrived here, we now have a weapon."

Fortunately, they didn't seem to need it. Despite the sounds from behind, the way ahead remained clear, and soon they were ascending a short, steep staircase.

When they reached the top, they were back in the crypt.

"I never thought we'd see this place again." Karen looked nervously over her shoulder at the open portal. "Is there any way we can close that thing?"

"Any suggestions would be appreciated." Chambers blinked as he tried to see in the dim light. "For now, I think we'd better just keep going."

He took two steps forward and collided with something.

The church of glass.

"Maybe this will stop a few of them." Karen was beside him now as Chambers nursed a bruised finger. "Hopefully they'll bump into it like you did."

"Perhaps." Chambers was staring at it.

"What's the matter?"

"Something Moreby said, as we were leaving the Sea of Darkness. 'Not even Verney's constructs will be able to save you now.' Do you think he meant this?"

"Well he said 'constructs,' plural, so perhaps he meant all of them."

That was a good point. "Maybe he did. But what? What might there be about these things that could save us?"

There was a grating sound from behind them.

"Well, whatever it is, you'd better think of it quickly." Karen was looking back toward the portal again. "They're nearly here."

"What?" Chambers almost screamed the word as he raked his scalp in frustration. "What the hell am I supposed to do with them?"

A gray claw appeared around the edge of the portal.

"I don't know! We know Verney was some sort of servant of Moreby's. Perhaps he put these models here because, without them, you can't get down into Hell. Who knows? Maybe he sacrificed children and buried their hearts in the middle of these things so they'd cause the portal to appear all these years later? Who cares what he did?" She clenched her fists as the first of the undead shambled into the crypt. "Smash the fucking thing."

"My pleasure." Chambers raised the heavy stone spike high, and brought it down with all his might on the exquisite sculpture.

The sound it made as it shattered was deafening.

Chambers brought the stone bludgeon down twice more for good measure. It was only after the third blow that he registered how loudly Karen was screaming, and what she was screaming at.

She had been almost right. It wasn't a child's heart that had been set at the center of the glass sculpture. It was a monstrous flea, the size of a Rottweiler and almost as black. Of course, that might have been an effect of the preserving fluid that had been used to prevent decay. The stink of ancient and fetid alcohol was almost overpowering.

"Watch out!"

Chambers ducked as a stone zombie lunged at him. It missed, but its momentum carried it forward, causing it to fall into the remains of the glass cathedral and sending shards skittering across the flagstones.

"Come on!"

Chambers was grabbing at Karen's hand again, but she shook it off. "Don't worry about me, worry more about finding all the other models!"

The crypt was bathed in the eerie blue glow that was now emanating from the portal to Limbo, making it easier for them to find the other models, as well as avoid the living dead. The second of Verney's constructs they came to was the church of glazed clay. It took two hammer-blows to destroy it, and this time they had to dodge out of the way of its preserved flea-creature as it slid from its earthenware prison.

"Did it move?" Karen's voice was almost a whisper.

Chambers resisted the urge to kick the monstrosity. "I don't think so," he said. "But let's not hang around to find out."

Next was the church of coal. The black rock splintered and crumbled as Chambers dealt it a series of savage blows with the spiked end of his weapon. Once again, he had to step aside as the fluid-soaked body of a misshapen monster slid from where it must have been carefully placed within.

The church of steel posed more of a problem.

"You're going to have to leave it." Karen was looking around her nervously, and Chambers could understand why. The flickering shadows in the corners of the crypt were moving a little too purposefully to be mere plays of light on stone.

He had delivered five heavy blows to the smooth structure, and succeeded only in breaking several chips of stone from his weapon. He ran his finger over the spire he had been trying to dislodge. There was not even a scratch. He hated to leave it, but the shadows were drawing closer.

"Let's hope six out of seven will be enough," he said, as they came upon the cathedral of black marble. It was harder to smash than the model made of coal, but fortunately the marble used was fragile and the model itself very fine. Another creature in the Anarch's own image flopped to the floor.

The church of wood splintered easily, which just left the church of granite.

Which didn't want to break at all.

"We'll have to leave this one too." The undead were emerging from the shadows now, and it was obvious the crypt was filled with them. Karen pulled at Chambers's sleeve. "Come on, we've got to leave it!"

"We can't!" Surely she knew that as well as he did? Chambers hit the granite model again. "We've smashed five of these things, and nothing has changed." He dealt it another blow. "If we don't destroy this, then we may as well not have bothered." He struck it again, and again. "Don't just stand there, help me!"

Karen didn't know what to do. Chambers watched as she reached into her pocket and eventually produced her apartment keys. She held them in a fist with the longest and heaviest pointing downward, and hit the interlocking granite blocks as hard as she could.

A crack opened up where she had struck it.

Chambers looked at her in astonishment. "My God, what did you hit it with?"

Karen hit it again. "Just these," she said, holding the keys up as the crack widened, allowing Chambers to force the end of his stone weapon into the rent. He levered with all his might as, with a deep cracking sound, half of the cathedral of granite was prized away. The flea was there, still embedded in the other half.

Chambers crouched down on one knee. "Do you think we have to remove it?"

Karen looked up to see the undead nearly upon them. "If you're going to, you'd better hurry up," she said.

He didn't want to. Oh God, he didn't want to touch it, but the cracking of the cathedral of granite still hadn't effected any change, or none that he could see at any rate.

He reached in, and, with both hands, took hold of the creature.

The sensation was like nothing he had ever experienced. His fingers touched a gritty carapace matted with hairs that presumably would have bristled stiffly outward when the thing was alive, but which now lay flat against its bulbous body. The fluid it had been preserved in burned his fingers, his nostrils, and his eyes as he drew the creature toward him. It was still firmly lodged within the granite, and Chambers had to pull hard before it finally moved. Then it came free with a jerk, sliding onto the floor amid a pool of preserving fluid and its own body juices.

"Let's hope that's done it." Chambers got to his feet, shaking his hands dry.

"Not a moment too soon," said Karen. "Here they come!"

There was a deep, ominous rumble from below, dislodging the pile of rubble that was blocking the exit to the undercroft.

"Let's go," said Chambers. "While there's still time."

THIRTY-FIVE

Friday, December 23, 1994. 7:02 A.M.

THE UNDERCROFT WAS EMPTY.

Chambers breathed a sigh of relief. Presumably Traynor and Chesney were still behind them somewhere, part of the undead army that was pouring into the crypt. He looked around him. After everything they had been through, it was strange to see normal everyday things like a kettle and a fridge.

The fridge.

"Give me a hand." As Chambers unplugged it, the ground shook again.

"To do what?"

"Block up that hole in the wall. It won't take them long to get through, but it's better than nothing."

Together they heaved the heavy white refrigerator across to the rent in the wall that led to the crypt. There was another rumble, and dust trickled from the ceiling.

"It doesn't look as if it's going to need to stay there long," said Karen. "It feels as if things are building to an earthquake."

"You've been in one before?" Chambers was heading for the stairs.

"Just the once," she replied. "And the enemy chasing me was alive rather than . . . than like those things back there."

The steps shook as they ascended. As had happened in the undercroft, Chambers felt a curious sweep of nostalgia as they entered All Hallows Church once more. It had markedly changed, however. The image of the Anarch on the wall of the north aisle was now depicted in such bright and vivid colors that it looked almost like the real thing. Something even larger and more monstrous was rising up behind it, while the tiny figures beneath it had changed as well. Now there were many more, swarming beneath the creature, a constant flow both toward and away from it. And it would be impossible to mistake those hairline streaks of white striking the figures for cracks in the masonry.

"There must be millions of them," Chambers breathed.

"What?" Karen was still looking around her, on the alert.

"There must be millions of them," he repeated. "All wanting to walk the Earth. We've got to stop it."

The rumbling was getting louder now.

"Well, let's hope we already have," she said. "I don't know what else we can do." She looked over to the door. "By the way, how are we going to get out?"

Chambers had to shout over the noise. "We can't leave, not until we know we've stopped them." He pointed to the church exit. "Otherwise that door will be the only barrier between the world and the Apocalypse!"

"So we just wait and see?"

Chambers didn't know what else to do, so he nodded.

The entire building was beginning to shake. To the left of them, a pillar collapsed. From downstairs there was the sound of metal scraping against stone.

"Sounds as if they've gotten through." Chambers looked around for a weapon, and remembered he was still holding the stone spear.

Muffled scraping sounds were coming from the direction of the undercroft steps.

"You know, I didn't think anything else could possibly scare me," Karen was backing against the wall. "But I've never been so terrified in my life as I am right now."

There was a horrible grating noise, and a crack appeared in the wall of the south aisle opposite. It quickly spread from the ground up, creating a rent that snaked its way to the ceiling.

"We may not live long enough to have to worry about them." Chambers backed away to the north transept, where Paul Hale's cot was still lying.

And where what was left of Ronnie was waiting for him.

There was so little of her she was easy to miss, crouching in a corner, her graying flesh almost one with the stone. Withered fingers clutched the wall as the rotted face turned to hiss at him. Chambers kept his distance, until he saw her lower limbs were gone, along with her left arm. It was all she could do to remain upright.

"I'm so sorry," was all he could whisper.

The floor was shaking as the first of the undead appeared from the undercroft. A shambling thing with a skull of wrinkled purplish skin that resembled a beetroot left too long out in the sun, it staggered forward to make way for those that followed it.

"What do we do now?"

Chambers had no idea what to tell Karen. They could run for one of the apsidals, or the vestry, but it would make no difference. The dead would catch up with them eventually.

"I don't think there's much else we can do," he said, as he pulled her to him and the undead of the Nine Circles of Hell began to fill the church.

The zombies were almost upon them when the floor exploded.

The rumbling had become thunder which, accompanied by a loud series of cracks, had heralded the lifting up of the floor of the nave. Pews flew into the air and a shower of flagstones followed, falling back to earth with a loud crash. The shock threw the walking corpses to the floor with such force that some of them broke limbs, and others shattered completely. Karen and Chambers merely stared in horror.

Out of the debris, something was rising.

Two things.

Two enormously long, bristling, powerful-looking things.

Two tree-trunk-thick, segmented, insectoid front limbs of the thing they had left behind in the Sea of Darkness.

The Anarch.

And between the gnarled and pointed tips of those two front limbs, clasped with infinite delicateness so as not to crush it, was lifted high above them the tiny figure of a human being.

Thomas Moreby.

The limbs held him close to the ceiling as his eyes scanned the scene of desolation beneath him. When he spotted the two humans whom he had last seen many levels beneath the earth, he glowered.

"You may think that you have defeated me," he said. "You may think that you have put an end to all my plans, but you have not. This is only the beginning. The steel church was always intended to remain, its secret left undisturbed for now, just as the others were meant to be destroyed. You have merely done exactly as I wished."

The dead that were able to were rising to their feet now, and still more piled into the church.

"Why?" Chambers shouted. "Why such a complex plan? And to what end?"

"Would you really expect the attainment of eternal life to be easy?" Moreby sneered from on high. "Do you really think that you just sign your name in a book, agree to sell your soul, or promise to sacrifice a few virgins, and that is all? Such a complex and precious gift comes at a great price. But now that you have released my pets, that price has very nearly been paid."

"The undead, you mean?" Chambers was sweating, despite the deathly chill that had descended.

"No, my dear sir, I do *not* mean these poor reanimated souls." Moreby gave him a horrible smile. "The arrival of the walking dead on this plane of reality was merely the first part of my goal. The second is about to come through that door."

Chambers turned to see the dead that were still clamoring to enter the church from the undercroft being pushed aside by heavy dark shapes, close to the ground and covered in bristling hairs. They did not so much walk as hop horribly, and with a chill realization he understood what he had released.

"The Servants of the Anarch!" Moreby screamed with glee as the huge flea creatures leapt into the church. Almost immediately they began to feed, consuming the pieces of fallen undead that lay scattered among the rubble, before turning their jaws to those that were walking.

"What the hell is going on?" Karen asked.

Chambers had no idea. "We should take cover," he said.

But it was impossible. The flea-things were bounding around the church, chewing and then sucking up anything they could find. One came down with a thud close to Chambers and Karen. It ignored them both, but sprayed what remained of Ronnie with a corrosive fluid, sucking up the resultant fleshy broth with a curled proboscis that retracted when it had finished. Chambers fought the urge to vomit, and kept his arms tight around Karen. He waited for the creature's digestive acid to hit him, for his body to burn and melt, but the sensation never came. The flea-thing continued to ignore them, and moved on.

With six of the ravenous creatures moving so quickly, the church was soon emptied of the undead that had strayed into it, as well as the creatures gathered at the doorway to the undercroft, climbing on top of each other in their desperate urge to eat the zombies that came up from down below.

The noise that came from the doorway, the terrible groans of the undead, the crunching and slurping of the flea-beasts, seemed to last forever. Then, eventually, one of the creatures broke away from the group.

It seemed to have tripled in size, its heaving bulk now bloated like that of an overfed leech. Gone was the skittish movement of its fellows. This one was moving heavily now, still light on its feet but obviously weighed down by the meal it had consumed.

It turned to its left, hopped with some difficulty onto the outstretched limb of the Anarch, still holding Moreby aloft where he was surveying the scene of horror. Then it ran up the limb toward the architect himself.

Rather than look horrified, Moreby seemed to welcome the bloated creature.

"The first," he cackled as the flea-thing scuttled up to him. For an instant they were face to face, the human monster opposite the inhuman one.

Then the creature extended its tube-like proboscis.

Moreby responded by opening his mouth.

The monster's body juddering with the force that it put into the effort, the flea-beast squirted what looked like an endless stream of tiny red particles straight down Moreby's throat.

No, thought Chambers, *not particles*.

Fleas.

Actual, normal-sized fleas. Just like the ones that had caused the outbreaks of the Black Death in the 1300s and the Great Plague of 1665.

Hundreds of them, thousands, being poured down the eager throat of a man believed dead for nearly two hundred years.

Finally, exhausted and empty, its body now nothing more than a deflated empty black sack, its job done, the flea-beast fell from its lofty perch and landed with a wet thud on the broken floor tiles of the church.

There was another waiting behind it to take its place.

And another.

Chambers and Karen watched horrified, as the six creatures emptied their burden of digested souls, now transformed by the Anarch's power into crimson-colored fleas, into the body of Thomas Moreby. Then, one by one they fell, landing in a heap far beneath his feet. When the last emptied carapace had fallen, he turned to address Chambers and Karen once more.

"The time is not yet upon us," he said. "But soon it will be, when the stars come right again. Thanks to you, the Gla'aki Rituals have been completed, the Anarch has been satiated for now, and the gift of eternal life which was bestowed upon me long ago has been consecrated. In time to come, my army of the dead will bring chaos to a world already steeped in chaos, but that time is not with us yet. The world of man is not yet ready to benefit from what I, and from what my God, have to offer it. You may think upon that if you wish. It may help to distract your petty minds when the men from the bedlam come for you."

Chambers opened his mouth to reply, but Moreby was already descending, the monstrous limbs dragging him down, deep into the earth and leaving a gaping hole behind. Flattened against the wall of the north aisle, Chambers and Karen found themselves standing on a tiny remaining ledge of what had once been the stone floor, peering into an abyss, a deep rent in the ground beneath All Hallows Church. They could see, far below, hundreds if not thousands of feet down, something glowing redly.

"How are we going to get out of here?" Karen asked, eyeing the distance from where they were standing to the door. Chambers shrugged as he dug his fingernails deeper into the wall behind him.

But the rent was already closing, the flagstones of the floor falling back into place and reconstructing like a giant jigsaw puzzle. Each time one floor slab met another, there was a sound like a hundred heavy doors being slammed shut, and their ears were ringing by the time it was over.

"Has he really gone?" Karen whispered.

The interior of the building looked as if a bomb had hit it, but otherwise there was nothing to suggest the place was anything other than an old church that had been allowed to fall into ruin.

Chambers nodded. "I think so."

"Have *they* gone?"

"If you mean the bodies of those flea things, they were dragged down with Moreby. If you mean the undead, I suppose we should go and look."

Together they stumbled over the debris. The grayish tinge lent it by the light outside gave it an uncomfortable resemblance to the Sea of Darkness. But rather than the dust of fathomless ages, here was just stone and ceramic, wood and iron. There was not a trace of a body, undead or otherwise.

The door to the undercroft stairway was hanging off its hinges. The stairway itself was empty too. Downstairs it looked as if the kitchen that had been constructed for them had not been used in years. The fridge they had moved to bar the entrance to the crypt was ancient and rusting, and the entrance itself had vanished completely.

"We didn't dream all of this." Karen picked through the remains of food boxes, their contents long since moldered and turned to dust. "I know we didn't."

"There's nothing left to prove our story, though." Chambers examined a couple more items, still expecting the wall to burst open and the undead to come flooding through at any moment. "If we were to tell it."

"But we have to!" Karen gave him a look of disbelief. "We have to warn people! We have to tell them . . ."

"Tell them what?" Chambers was shaking his head. "That we met the architect of this place, that he was at least three hundred years old and he was living in the Sea of Darkness that exists at the bottom of Hell? That he has a plan to bring chaos to the world, but just not yet? And no, we don't have any proof that any of it happened?"

He began to make his way back up. "Moreby was right. The men from the bedlam would enjoy the bedtime stories we'd have to tell them."

"But we can't just do nothing!" Karen was chasing after him.

Chambers knew that, just as he knew that the truth would be too much. The events of the past twenty-four hours were already beginning to feel unreal to him. By tomorrow he would probably be wondering if he needed to be committed himself. And though his colleagues in Washington, D.C. might believe him, he knew even they would have trouble taking in everything he would eventually have to tell them.

He looked around the remains of the church. The sun was rising, bathing the rubble with a golden hue, the freshness and purity of which made him want to cry. What actually made a tear fall from his eye was the sight of the church doors, hanging open.

"We've been given permission to go," he said.

"Permission?" Karen frowned. "You mean our time is up?"

"I have no idea, and I don't care." He was looking around now, trying to find something. Eventually his eyes alighted on Dr. Chesney's machine, the one he had never had the chance to use. He tore off a long strip of squared paper.

"Have you a pen?"

Karen gave him an exhausted look. "I'm a journalist, remember? I'm never without one." She passed it over.

It was Chambers's turn to frown. "I thought you'd have something a bit fancier than a crappy ballpoint," he said with a faint smile.

"I'm also someone who's used to lending people pens and never getting them back," she said. "What are you writing?"

"I'm just leaving a message," he said. "For when the television and newspaper people get here. It's still early, and looks pretty quiet out there now. I'm guessing they'll be along later for the great opening. By which time you and I need to be long gone."

"But the story!" Karen looked over to where her apsidal was, where her tapes would be stored.

"I'll bet those tapes will have nothing on them." Chambers was following her train of thought as he scribbled. "Rather than tell the story, the best thing you and I can do is be part of it."

He left the note pinned to Dr. Chesney's machine. He had written it in big enough letters and weighed it down with the heaviest of Chesney's self-published books, and so he hoped no one would miss it. Whether or not they would heed the warning was another matter entirely, but there was little either of them could do about that.

"What do you think he meant?"

"Who?" asked Chambers.

"Moreby," Karen replied. "Back in the Sea of Darkness, when he said that our souls were interconnected?"

Chambers smiled. "I have no idea," he said, "but maybe it's time we found out." He took her hand and walked with her through the doors and out into the fresh sunrise of a beautiful December morning.

"It's time for this particular story to end."

Memo

From: The Office of the Secretary to His Holiness Pope
John Paul II, and subsidiary members of The Vatican
Advisory Committee on The Incidents at Blackheath

To: His Eminence Cardinal William Thomas, Archbishop of
Westminster Cathedral

William,

The events at All Hallows have been noted.

We still await your report.

Signed on behalf of the Vatican Advisory Committee

Saturday, December 24, 1994. 6:34 A.M.

Memo:

From: His Eminence Cardinal William Thomas, Archbishop
of Westminster Cathedral

To: The Office of the Secretary to His Holiness Pope John
Paul II, and subsidiary members of The Vatican Advisory
Committee on The Incidents at Blackheath

Be assured that our Holy Mother Church has been
seen to have little or no involvement in the matter.
Father Traynor has been appropriately discredited and
his current whereabouts stated as unknown. British
government assures us that matter is in hand. Suggest
no further action that would draw attention to the site
or the family members of those who are considered to
be missing as a consequence of the disaster.
William

Memo

From: The Prime Minister, 10 Downing Street

To: Michael Howard, Home Secretary

Dear Michael,

Re: the message found at All Hallows Church

Is this something we need to be worried about?

Best wishes,

J

Sunday, December 25, 1994. 9:05 A.M.

Memo

From: The Office of Michael Howard, Home Secretary

To: John Major, Prime Minister

Dear John,

Sorry you were bothered with this. Situation has been contained. Nothing to worry about.

Happy Christmas to you and Norma.

Best wishes,

Michael

[Note: The listed program was never broadcast, being pulled from the BBC schedule at short notice and a rerun of the popular entertainment show *Morecambe and Wise* substituted in its place.]

1 BBC 1

8.00 Panorama
All Hallows Church: Disaster, Publicity Stunt, or Both?
The BBC's current affairs programme presents a special edition in which recent events at All Hallows Church are investigated in the wake of the disappearances and the subsequent media frenzy. Are newspaper corporations and commercial television channels becoming increasingly irresponsible in their search for ratings? How long will it be before the individuals who formed the "ghost hunting" team are allowed to come out of exile? Or do newspapers now have sufficient financial resources to maintain such a hoax indefinitely?
We present a profile of those involved, and investigate reasons for the continued silence from the *News of Britain*, the British Museum, the Catholic Church, and the British Government regarding the matter.
See page 29.
Director/Producer Stephen Volk
Repeated 12 midnight

Acknowledgements

Thanks to John Llewellyn Probert for his patience and understanding while this book was put together at a very difficult time for me, personally. He superbly rose to the challenge of combining two different series into the kind of crossover story that I used to love reading as a kid, while at the same time paying homage to both the H. P. Lovecraft Mythos and those sleazy Italian zombie movies of the 1980s that we both love so much.

Thanks also to artist Douglas Klauba for listening to my cover brief and turning it into, literally, a work of art, and to Claiborne Hancock, for his trust and support in publishing the ongoing exploits of the Human Protection League.

—SJ

First and foremost, I would like to thank Stephen Jones for giving me the challenge of linking the exploits of *The Lovecraft Squad* to his bestselling *Zombie Apocalypse!* series of books in a novel set before the actual zombie apocalypse of the latter series takes place. It turned out to be the most enjoyable novel writing experience of my career so far. Thanks, Steve, for letting me play such a large part in such an ambitious project—I had a blast. Special thanks also have to go to my friend and writing colleague Reggie Oliver, whose expertly sown seeds in the second *Zombie Apocalypse!* anthology—*Zombie Apocalypse! Fightback*—I was able to use as a springboard to create the extraordinary events you have just read about. I always intended this book to be in part a tribute to Lucio Fulci, the master of the Italian zombie movie, and there are a few in-jokes that refer to his exemplary work in the genre peppered throughout the text. So if you thought you spotted references to *City of the Living Dead* or *The Beyond*, you were absolutely correct. Similarly I have to thank Nigel Kneale and Clark Ashton Smith, both writers I have always greatly admired, and both hugely influential in the writing of this particular novel, even though it may not be that obvious.

Finally, and most important of all, my thanks to my wife Kate, aka Thana Niveau. My First Reader and everlasting love, if I'm ever trapped in a church filled with flesh-eating monsters, as long as you're with me I know we'll both be fine.

—JLP

JOHN LLEWELLYN PROBERT won the British Fantasy Award for his novella *The Nine Deaths of Dr. Valentine* from Spectral Press, and the Children of the Night Award for his collection *The Faculty of Terror* from Gray Friar Press. He is the author of more than a hundred published short stories, seven novellas (including his latest, *Dead Shift*, from Horrific Tales Publishing) and a horror novel, *The House That Death Built*, from Atomic Fez. Endeavour Press has published *Ward 19*, *Bloody Angels*, and *The Pact*, three crime books featuring his pathologist heroine Parva Corcoran. His stories have appeared in all three volumes of the *Zombie Apocalypse!* series edited by Stephen Jones, and his latest tales can be found in such anthologies as *The Spectral Book of Horror* and *Horror Uncut*. He is currently trying to review every cult movie in existence at his House of Mortal Cinema (www.johnlprobert.blogspot.co.uk) and everything he is up to writing-wise can be found at www.johnlprobert.com. Future projects include two new short story collections, a lot more nonfiction writing, and a couple of novels. He never sleeps.

STEPHEN JONES lives in London, England. A Hugo Award nominee, he is the winner of three World Fantasy Awards, three International Horror Guild Awards, five Bram Stoker Awards, twenty-one British Fantasy Awards, and a Lifetime Achievement Award from the Horror Writers Association. One of Britain's most acclaimed horror and dark fantasy writers and editors, he has more than 140 books to his credit, including *The Art of Horror: An Illustrated History*; the film books of Neil Gaiman's *Coraline* and *Stardust*, *The Illustrated Monster Movie Guide* and *The Hellraiser Chronicles*; the nonfiction studies *Horror: 100 Best Books* and *Horror: Another 100 Best Books* (both with Kim Newman); the single-author collections *Necronomicon* and *Eldritch Tales* by H. P. Lovecraft, *The Complete Chronicles of Conan* and *Conan's Brethren* by Robert E. Howard, and *Curious Warnings: The Great Ghost Stories of M. R. James*; plus such anthologies as *Horrorology: The Lexicon of Fear*, *Fearie Tales: Stories of the Grimm and Gruesome*, *A Book of Horrors*, *In the Shadow of Frankenstein*, *The Lovecraft Squad*, and the *Zombie Apocalypse!* series, and twenty-seven volumes of *Best New Horror*. You can visit his website at www.stephenjoneseditor.com or follow him on Facebook at Stephen Jones-Editor.